ONE MORE LAST DANCE

A NOVEL

Jerome Mark Antil

LITTLE YORK
BOOKS
New York · NY · Dallas · TX

To Leah Chase
January 6 – 1923 – June 1, 2019

A Southern Louisiana Bayou

CHAPTER 1

HE KNEW IF HE DIDN'T RUN FROM BAYOU CHENE, he would die. Cajun French and—best guess—he was nine years old when he waited for the right moment to shimmy up and grab the splintered branch crotch of a bald cypress. It held him long enough to lower himself into a hollow in the trunk. In the dark he stepped on fresh Wood Duck eggs and live ants with his bare feet. Beyond fright he stood motionless for the better part of two days. When he heard cussing and what he assumed an empty whiskey bottle smashing against a rock below and a pickup driving off, he waited until dark, and then chanced the coast was clear. He climbed down and ran along the bayou shoreline and then a mile or so through grassy shoulders of a highway until he saw a flatbed truck with a tarp over its load at a rest area. He climbed on and hid under the tarp for several hours until the truck came to a full stop. He jumped off and tended a bleeding ankle with moist leaves and he crawled in a trash bin at a slaughterhouse to hide. His stomach was too empty to vomit from the smells, but he took shallow breaths and managed to sleep. Before dawn a creaking of hinges awakened him. The lid lifted under a blinding alley lamp and a foreman with torn white rubber boots in his fist growled.

"Scat, boy!" and "On your way, Peckerwood!"— before tossing the boots into the bin. Looking older than his age, the boy convinced the foreman to give him chores in trade for the boots and something to eat. Impressed with his work, the man handed him bandages for his ankle, two sandwiches and a Saran-wrapped dill, along with the boots and mending tape.

"Check back with me. If we're short, I'll give you day work."

Feeling freedom on his face for the first time, and hoping he had run to a new life he walked about, sack in hand, exploring

1

the town of Carencro and wound up on Bab Road in his patched rubber boots when the sharp, slithering sounds of saw blades ripping dried lumber caused him to pause and look about. Nibbling on his dill like it was a dessert from Antoine's he couldn't help noticing through an opened doorway of a small shed large circular saw blades hanging like Christmas ornaments. A man holding a clipboard stepped out and paused. To Peck he looked honest. The boy could see a wood and canvas sleeping cot standing on its end, leaning up against the inside wall behind the blades. The wooden shed was the blade shed for the mill of the boat builder, and he handed the man his hunting knife.

"It's my Dundee, Mister."

"Nice knife, son, but I'm not in the market," the man said.

"Touch the blade, Mister, jes touch it," the boy said.

The man felt the blade.

"I'm impressed son, but I'm not—"

"It ain't for sale, Mister. I keep it sharp is all. You got axes, knives and blades about. I see 'em in the shed."

The boy tried to barter his blade-sharpening skills for the use of the cot and asked about the broken lawn mower on its porch.

"That old mower?" the man asked.

"*Oui*." ("Yes.")

"Only worth the metal, I reckon."

"It don' go summore?" the boy asked.

"Not in years."

"If I can spear-a-ment and fix it, can I use it?"

"You know motors too, do ya?"

"I t'ink I can did dat one. Dass for true."

"What's your name, young man?"

The boy knew his given name— Boudreaux Clemont Finch, but as a runaway he was guarded about making it known to strangers.

"Most I knowed call me Peck."

"How do you keep your blade that sharp, Peck?"

"I rub it with eggshell."

"Broken eggshell?"

"Whole egg, afore it's boiled."

"I thought only my grand-mere knew that one," the man said. "That's how she sharpened her sewing scissors. How old are you?"

"Old enough to do you a good job, mister."

"You got any family, son?"

"Ain't nobody but me."

The man extended his hand.

"The name's LeFleur. Marcel LeFleur."

Mr. LeFleur shook Peck's hand, said yes to his sleeping in the shed in barter for blade sharpening. He gave Peck the broken-down mower and threw in a pair of pliers, two sparkplugs, and a hotplate he had in his pickup.

"Unplug this when you're not using it, Peck. Wood dust sets off easy enough. Let's not help it with sparks."

"I'll make sure I did that, Mr. LeFleur."

"Look in the cabinet. There should be a blanket, a coffee pot, maybe a skillet."

"Yes sir."

"That light bulb stays on at all times."

"Yes sir."

"And no gas cans in the shed."

"Never sir."

That was years ago and Peck's been full grown for some time now but not certain how old he was and when the boat builder one day said he looked to be in his twenties, he was good with that. Unable to read, write or cipher, he creates multiple-syllable words and converts their meanings. He knows French. When telling stories of his past he references age as—"I could swim," meaning he was eight or nine or "I couldn't swim," meaning he might have been as young as three or four—or as he would say in a Cajun patois, "I was four maybe t'ree." When not mowing the lawn at the hospice, he'd be seen at bayou shores casting trotlines or at town markets trading his catches—snapping turtles, mashwarohn, and frogs to fish-and-egg buyers for a few dollars on good days—for a few brown eggs if his catch was poor. He trades with a grocer his washing the store windows for a twelve-ounce can of French Market chicory and a shaker of ground cinnamon from India. On the hot plate burner in the mill's blade-sharpening shed where he sleeps, he boils four eggs in his morning pot of chicory coffee. He'll eat two and save two for lunch. Thursday is his one day to mow.

Every Thursday morning, he'd walk in darkness to this quiet hospice overlooking the calm of Bayou Carencro—it was once the stately Hildebrandt mansion. From the day he took the job nearly ten years ago, up until a week ago he never missed a Thursday mow. At first sparkle of sun on the bayou he'd be at water's edge casting his baited trotline into the bayou behind the hospice for an end of day retrieval before fueling and starting his mower.

But today is Wednesday, and a private detective just handcuffed Peck to one of the park benches on the hospice's rear lawn. He warned him not to try to escape, that he'd likely be shot and he wished him good luck with the law before walking away. Now alone at dawn, Peck waits an unknown fate, and he watches a snapper slowly climb the root of a bald cypress for the morning sun beginning to break through a layer of fog. A crawfish snake swimming across a shallow to where smaller frogs and crawfish were plentiful catches his eye. A keen sense of observation isn't a game to Peck, it is how he survives.

"Gators still sleepin'," he muttered. *"Vous gagnez cette fois, serpent."* ("You win this time, snake.")

CHAPTER 2

PECK'S PROBLEM BEGAN THE DAY he hitched a ride in Carencro for him and his friend, Gabe. Gabe was a patient at the hospice where Peck mowed the lawn. He was a pleasant spirited black man, a retired, army officer who had served valiantly in Korea and Viet Nam. He was a fairly hefty old man now, half a century later and he and Peck were sitting in the front cab of a forty-foot long cattle hauler rig and going to where they thought would be I-90. Peck's plan was to follow that interstate to Newport, Rhode Island. Turns out, this was the day Gabe got a taste of how unreliable Peck might be in strategic thinking away from a bayou. The old man wasn't taking an inch of his gratitude for the boy's big heart and heroic cunning in getting him out of hospice with his pills. He was genuinely grateful. While planning the road trip walking down Guilbeaux Street they shook on it that the goal was a simple one, to get to Newport, Rhode Island for the August jazz festival so the old man could get in a zone one last time listening to live jazz before he dies. Gabe learned in the army, to lead, follow, or get the hell out of the way, so on the subject of getting to Newport he stepped back and had confidence in Peck's initiative. Gabe was happy and it made him no never mind which way they went as all he was thinking was stretching out on a lawn with a Chivas, some salami or a brick of cheese, and listening to jazz and watching life and sunsets mill around for a week.

"Gentlemen," the truck driver said. "That was some good coffee and morning conversation. I've enjoyed your company."

"T'anks for the coffee, frien'," Peck said.

"I'll be letting you out about a mile or so up."

"Hanh?" Peck asked, as though he'd just awakened.

"We're coming into Kenner. It's just up ahead," the driver said.

"What do you mean let us out?" Peck asked.

"That's where I make my turnaround. I drop this load and pick up a load of pine logs so I don't deadhead back to Carencro."

"But you say you was going to I-95," Peck said.

"Naw, it was you telling me you were going to I-95, Peck."

"We ain't even took out of Lewisana."

"We did a long haul from Carencro. You're closer than you were this morning."

"But you say you were going—"

"Naw, I didn't, Peck," the driver said.

"You say—"

"You're mixin' my words."

"I'd swear to it," Peck said.

"Peck, ain' no need to be swearing. I asked you where you were headin' off to—I was watching you buy bottles of water at 7-Eleven."

"You did dat, now dass for true," Peck said. "I remember xactly. But then I remember you saying back we could hitch wit you far as you go."

"Well, 'er you go, Peck."

"I remember him saying that, Peck," Gabe said.

"Hanh?"

"This here is as far as I go."

Peck looked at Gabe.

"Seems I might'a ax him where 'far as I go' was."

As they both appeared to think back from the fix they were in—of where they started in Carencro a few hours before, they would have been better off if they had headed straight on up to Memphis and kept going north from there. It was too late for all that, and the cattle hauler-driver pulled into a truck stop in Kenner and braked the rig short of a pothole full of muddy rainwater. Peck had known the driver from drinking beers and shooting quarter-a-piece, eight-ball pool with him at a saloon down the road from the slaughterhouse where Peck worked one summer, killing calves. He liked him.

"This is it for me, boys," the driver said. "Good luck to ya both."

Peck and the driver gave each other a blank stare. Peck reached out with his good hand and they shook hands.

"What happened to your hand, Peck? Why the blood?" the driver asked.

"Tore it with some fishhooks," Peck said."

"Ya'll might have you a better shot to 95 by starting on the interstate up at I-12," the driver said. "I take it on my way back, if you want a ride."

Gabe and Peck looked at each other, considered the proposition and shrugged their shoulders. Gabe pulled a large, canvas, army duffel over the back of the seat and handed it to Peck, who threw it out the open door to the ground.

"Wait up a sec, Peck," the driver said.

The driver leaned and reached for a first aid kit from behind the seat. He took a tube of Neosporin disinfectant and a box of bandages.

"Here, take these, Peck," he said, holding his hand out. "Wash that hand you hooked, keep it clean and bandaged tight until it heals. Don't let it get infected."

"T'anks frien'," Peck said.

Peck crawled from the truck cab first then helped Gabe climb down. They stepped out of the way and turned as the truck's airbrakes farted their tweets, lurching the rig forward, right front tire splashing in a pothole and bouncing the diesel's stack, belching black billows. The driver tugged the leather airhorn strap, sending two friendly goodbye blasts.

When the truck was out of sight, Peck turned with a sheepish look. There was something on his mind.

"Gabe, I know what you must be t'inking about now, but I swear as I'm standing here—I sure enough thought that there rig was our ride to I-95, all the way. Now here we is put out in middle of someplace I ain't hardly heard of in one of them cities they build and I already got us lost before we get out of Lewisana."

"Don't be tough on yourself, friend," Gabe said. "It could have..."

Peck interrupted. "Might could be I'm jus' not your guy."

"Listen to you," Gabe said.

"Hanh?"

"Here we are on an adventure of a lifetime—well my lifetime, for damn sure—and so what if we took a wrong fork? That's what life is, son. I'm telling you—so what? The fork in that road we took sure enough is all the proof we'll need to be certain we're going to have some fun. That's what an adventure is all about, Peck—having fun along the way."

"I don't see no fun, Gabe."

"Here we are in Kenner, son. Rejoice, my brother, cause because of this here fork in a road, we're just a short way from New Orleans and the Quarters and some fun."

"The Quarters, Gabe? You mean the French Quarter?" Peck asked.

"Not exactly, my brother. Frenchmen Street—it's near the French Quarter," Gabe said. "It's all a difference for those of us in the know, knowing where to go if we're on a budget and those traveling men or ladies in town overnight on expense accounts looking for beignets and seafood, or maybe a night of some out-of-town boy-toy or poonani."

"Now there you go, Gabe. You're thinking fool's gold, and me I'm just a lawn man. I can't afford no Quarter or no Frenchmen Street ain't no way. Oysters there are near a buck apiece and they ain't no better dan ones from Lafayette. Ain't no better t'all. Plenty shrimpers tole me and dass a fact."

"This adventure is on me, son. You be keeping your word by looking after your old friend here, and I'll see to it you get treated proper and maybe we'll have some fun along the way." He reached his hand to Peck. "Do we have an understanding, son?"

"We have us a deal, Captain," Peck said, shaking Gabe's hand.

Gabe smirked a satisfying grin, swiping the air with a right cross.

"Now that's what I'm talking about," he announced.

"I'll go in de truck stop yonder and ax around," Peck said.

"What for?"

"I'll see who might be goin' into de Quarter and can give us a lift," Peck said.

"It's early, my brother, and the sun's warm," Gabe said.

Peck turned slowly toward Gabe again, head down, looking at the ground in a don't-distract-me sort of way, like he was about to kick a pebble.

"Gabe, I been meaning to ax you something."

"Anything, my brother."

"Now don't go taking it to any offense or unkindliness, but I t'ink you has to stop calling me your son or your brother. It just don't seem natural coming off the tongue like dat and it ain't right your making people have to t'ink more than they ought—like they tend to without help—with you a black man and me being a boney white Cajun and all."

"Boney, you're not, my brother. I've watched the nurses stare out the windows at you with your shirt off. Ain't nothing boney about those shoulders. Why those ladies were maybe laying odds on who'd get to your Johnson first."

"Boney is my way of saying it is all, Gabe. I meant bein' white, not about my build or nothing like dat. They did? Which ones?"

"Son and my brother are figures of speech for me too," Gabe said. "I'll cut them out if it's how you feel."

"Oh it ain't me, Gabe. I'm proud to have your acquaintance and friendship, but it's other more ignorant folks, you know. It'd be hokay if it weren't for ignorant folks. They's a lot of us around, dass for true."

Gabe pointed east.

"That there's the way into New Orleans," Gabe said.

"So we can catch us a ride to I-95 all the way," Peck said.

"Let's start walking. Frenchmen Street won't be far behind."

"Hanh? Walk?"

"We'll walk steady and be there by dark or right after sure enough. I saw a mileage sign back a way. Eleven miles."

Peck balked. "Just hold on. I plumb forgot what I wanted to say. Here I go sneaking you out of hospice and there's no telling what kind of trouble I'm going to get into for dat, and Gabe, you can lie to your own self all you want but you can't lie to me—you know you ain't well or you wouldn't had been in there in de first place. Now what did you t'ink they're going to say when

I let a sick old man walk from Kenner clear into New Or–lee–anhs?"

"I'll never tell," Gabe grinned.

"What will they say when you drop dead, Mr. Captain Jordan, army veteran? They'd get me for murder, sure as I'm standing here."

"I'm dying, Peck. I'm not sick," Gabe said. "Let's go."

Peck dropped the canvas bag and stomped a foot for emphasis.

"Just hold on a dang minute, Captain. I may be ignorant, but I ain't *coo-yon. (stupid)* If you was in hospice, you is sick, right?"

"My heart and legs are fine," Gabe said. "I'm rusting out from the innards is all. I got termites in my belly. I can walk—it keeps the pain away. Now I'd appreciate you not reminding me of it every two minutes, and I would enjoy it if you'd have a mind to join me and for once stopped bellyaching."

Peck relented, and the two started a healthy pace east out of Kenner, canvas duffel over Peck's shoulder.

"Gabe, now t'ink this one good," Peck said.

"What's on your mind, son?"

"Was she the blonde with nice *tétines* who was a looking at me with my shirt off? T'ink more better, old man."

"It was her and that day nurse, the sister with a green Afro," Gabe said.

"Both of em? For true?"

"Playing you with their eyes like you were a porterhouse."

"Ain' t the blonde one married or going with a dude in a Ram truck dass been dropping her off?" Peck asked.

CHAPTER 3

IT WAS JUST AFTER A RED SUNSET when the old man and his young friend first stepped onto St. Charles Avenue pausing under a streetlamp to catch their breath and watch a streetcar pass them by.

"Smell that air, Peck," Gabe said. "Take it all in, son. Inhale it big. This is what living is about. We can surely smell for a reason, my brother. Breathing is God's doing—is what it is."

"Hanh?"

"Smells and smelling, my brother. Powder sugar, beignets, shucked oyster shells, charcoal smoke, chicory, a lady's perfume. My, my...if this ain't what heaven smells like, nothing is. I can smell termites gnawing on the roots of the dogwoods."

"Where we going to did it, Gabe? We restin' here or goin' in more?"

"Let me have a look," Gabe said.

Gabe felt for the proper pocket and took out a worn, sun-cracked, tan leather wallet. In it was his driver's license, twenty-eight dollars in bills, and two receipts from Dunkin' Donuts he kept because one had the name of the drink he liked and the other had the name of a breakfast sandwich he liked. In currency, there were two tens, a five, and three ones.

"Twenty-eight dollars," Gabe said. "By the looks of it, we can afford a drink or two each, a beer, not Chivas, maybe some crawfish gumbo with rice. Listening to music is free most places. At least here in New Orleans it is. Let's walk to Frenchmen Street for some smooth jazz. It's down this track a few blocks."

Peck took a stand.

"You mean to tell me we going to dat Newfalls place—"

"It's Newport," Gabe interrupted.

"Hanh?"

"Newport, Rhode Island, my brother."

"Hokay, Newport. You tellin' me we heading clear across U-S-of-A and we only got us twenty-eight dollars in our kitty?"

"In fairness, son," Gabe said, "you might at least remember the name of the place we're going—it's Newport. Newport, Rhode Island. We've already come three hours southeast when we might have been heading north. Let's try to remember the city where we're going."

"I'm trying to be serious here, Gabe. What we going to did with twenty-eight dollars?"

"That'll be enough for—" Gabe started.

"I can't took you downtown with no twenty-eight dollars."

"I got my driver's license too," Gabe said.

"It ain't funny," Peck said.

"I thought we needed a little levity."

"I like blues like anybody, Gabe, but you ain't t'inking right."

"Blues?" Gabe asked.

"You heard me, Gabe."

"Did you say blues?"

"You know I did."

"I wouldn't say that too loud, Peck—not here in N'Orleans."

"Hanh?" Peck asked.

"N'Orleans is jazz, my brother. It's merchants, sailors, whiskey, and whorehouses—that's what made jazz. Blues is Beale Street. Cotton-picking slaves and a back's whip-strapping gave birth to the blues. Blues is Memphis. Cotton. Get it together, son."

"Why now I don' for sure know what's more stupider," Peck said. "Me hitchin' a ride I didn't know would end us in Kenner or smuggling you out of hospice. Me quitting a job, leaving a good trotline laying on the bank of the bayou, and heading off to this here Newport, wherever, with a whole whoop-de-do twenty-eight dollars to our name. Don't dat beat all for stupid?"

"Peck, how much cash have you got on you?"

"Pocket change is all, and you know dat. Now don' you go..."

Peck paused and inhaled.

"You know we didn't wait for my pay when we run off."

"Stay calm, my friend," Gabe said, "it'll all work out. You'll see."

"With twenty-eight dollars?"

"You need to be listening to some easy jazz to calm your nerves. Jazz was born from wanderers like us with no place to go and from sweaty bodies dancing and lying together with a window open for night air and street sounds. Listening to jazz won't cost us one thin dime, and it'll heal our souls, and that's a promise. Jazz is crazy gentle on purpose. Jazz is my people talking loud at night before being quiet at church in the morning. It's freedom to fit in, fly away without goin' no place, but not talked about in the daylight. It'll show us a way, baby. Be cool, my friend. Be easy."

"It may be easy for you, ole man, you're dying. Me, they'll catch me sure enough and hang me."

Blocks from the Quarter, in a side alley off Frenchmen Street, from an old shotgun house's living room, a saxophone solo wailed out into the street.

Vaaaa vaaaa da veeeeeeee...Vaaaa ve voooo vaa vaa vava ve voooooon, the sax jammed as though it was saying, "Come in, brothers, supper's on and you don't live here but come in anyway. Rest your feet and feed your soul away from the night."

It wailed from the house between the colorful bookends of a sleazy one-room stripper saloon with a second-floor balcony rail inside above for gawking. Its door open, and a barker in front handing out leaflets promising young men walking by every imaginable personal pleasure inside. Two worn, red lacquer-painted chain-links with an empty wooden swing seat hung motionless over an emptier bar. The bookend on the other side was a room for rent walkup with a sign on the ground floor door, that read *No Vacancies*, and another in a second-floor window read *Astrology & Massage* with an email address.

The music was coming from the whitewashed shotgun house in the middle. Soft velvet sounds of a sax rode a warm breeze into the night as if to get some air and to look for souls needing a lift. In the doorway, you could hear brushes on a snare drum's stretched skin, and a sensual slapping of a palm on strings of a base fiddle that were steady rhythm, like voodoo incantations—magnets for an old army captain's ear.

Not taking his eyes off a red neon beer sign glowing on the inside back wall, Gabe grabbed Peck's arm for balance and stepped up the two steps into the room. A four-piece quartet was playing. Bright, big white eyes of a blue-black-faced brother blowing on sax, opened wide, looked over at Gabe and closed again with a low wail, welcoming him in. The band was in the left corner on a foot-high stage. Small tables with an unlit candle each surrounded a center dance area. By the clock it was too early in the day for a crowd or to light the candles. A wooden floor that might have survived two world wars, maybe the Civil War, and more floods than termites, was shaker waxed for dancing or for sitting around and drinking if there was a show put on.

Along the right wall was a bar with eight chrome bar stools in front. A row of whiskeys and blends lined a bookshelf attached to a long mirror behind the barkeep. Looking over at the bar, their eyes were drawn to the milky white back of a lady in a red satin dress with bare shoulders, and a more than agreeable figure. Her right elbow rested gently on the bar, and her hand, with bright red nail polish, held a martini glass with lipstick marks on its rim. Next to this lovely was another, slightly shorter girl, in black shiny tights, her hair tied back. If the reflection in the mirror was true, she was as comely and curvy as the one in red. The one in shiny black tights was leaning toward a man to her right; she was holding a cigar about the size of a big thumb for him to light.

Seeing her cigar, Peck elbowed Gabe in the ribs.

"Did'ya ever, Gabe?" he asked.

"I saw that a lot in Nam," Gabe said.

"I'll be waggled."

"She probably drinks cognac," Gabe said. "A good cigar is best with cognac."

The man holding the cigarette lighter wore a white linen suit, had a blue sapphire pinky ring on his little finger, blue shirt with white collar and French cuffs, and tarnished gold cuff links. His straw dress hat was on the bar between them. Three other men were seated at the bar. One in overalls, with a cap with a stevedore button on it, looked like a dock worker. He was reading a racing form. One was sipping coffee. The jigger next to his coffee cup Gabe guessed was kalua. The one on the end, a black man, was writing on a small spiral pad with a pencil in his right hand. A glass of sloe gin was in his left hand.

Gabe pointed toward the band.

"Let's sit over there."

"Hokay," Peck said.

"I'm going to go splash my face, freshen up. Grab us a table by the band, Peck. I'll be out in two shakes."

CHAPTER 4

BACK WHEN GABE WAS A YOUNG TURK, in the days of the Vietnam war and the violent war protests, sit ins, race riots, flag and bra burning, he would sport young women about like arm candy, boasting his army medals and always knowing where the keys were hidden to any American inner city's night life. A young black man back then had to go on his wits pretty much, go his own way, but with agility, proper finesse and street smarts, he could have a good time making do.

Young men today of any color out and about in New Orleans pretty much all look the same in the eyes—the same blank stares. They live at home with parents and plan their future by the hour, between texts. If one had money in his jeans or a working debit card, he'd get through the next hour or two. If he didn't have means, his imagination would lock up and he'd conclude he couldn't do much. If he was straight, he'd likely try to hook up with a lady of most any age with sympathy in her eyes or one his age or younger with a similar depth of vision. He'd sweet-talk and convince his catch into letting him lie with her, at least tonight, usually underperforming her imagination's desire in between his nature's calls to a fridge for a beer in the raw and basic hope she would have the womanly instincts of his mother to see he was properly fed in the morning. Bacon is his definition of the joy of sex. A morning after meal is Millennium man's best climax.

But Gabe was not a young man of today. He was an old man from the fifties. A very old man. He was about to bring nigh on eight decades of wisdom of what celebrating freedom had been for him—a black man—back in the time when he was poorer than an alley cat.

The two settled at a table, taking it all in. They didn't talk while their eyes glanced at the band and then shifted over to the bar. The red satin rounded buttocks were firm and an hourglass waist was not unnoticed by either of them. Especially not by Gabe.

"I've always had a fondness for a fine ass," Gabe said.

"Ahh *oui*," Peck mumbled.

"Now that's some fine ass."

"You ever bedded with a genuine prostitute, Gabe?" Peck asked.

Gabe looked at him.

"I don't mean no floozy whore what'll take a couple dollars for a quick something. Nah, nah, I'm meaning how you call classy, full-fledged beautiful high-end call girl prostitute."

"Takes me back," Gabe said.

"Have you ever did, Gabe?"

"There was a time back in my Fort Campbell training days we'd catch a bus from the base to Newport."

"Where we're going off to, Gabe—Newport?"

"No, not that Newport, son. We're going to Newport, Rhode Island. This Newport we'd catch a Greyhound to is in Kentucky, on the river."

"Mississippi?"

"Ohio River."

"Hokay."

"It was back in the late fifties, son. My kind couldn't sit and eat with white folks at Woolworth's counters in Cincinnati—"

"Why not, Gabe?"

"Jim Crow. It was still dark times in America, son."

"I heard some of it, Gabe. Sorry, my frien'."

"But across the river in Kentucky, Peck—if it was after dark and we came alone, we could flash them twelve dollars at the door for a roll on a clean sheet."

"With white women?"

"White and lovely, each and every one of them, son."

"You old houn' dog," Peck said.

"I remember I'd always carry twelve singles in each of my pants pockets so the girl could take care of whoever she needed to sneak me in. With two pockets of cash I could go back for another go at it."

"A black man. I heard stories about back then, Gabe."

"It wasn't any secret the ladies in those second-story whorehouses had jungle fever after wasting days with virgins only working them up—those quick-draw white college boys from across the river in Cincinnati. They'd check me out at the door, give me a smile, look about and let me in. They could climb a black man for the full ride—they just couldn't talk about it to the wrong people."

"You horny old man. Tell me true Gabe, when you was a captain, was it different?"

"Different?"

"When you paid for it—was it different when you was a captain?"

"Only difference maybe was I could ask for my favorite girl, maybe stay a few hours if it were near closing for them," Gabe said.

"That must have been something ol' man."

"It was."

"But, you know, Peck says you deserved it, Gabe, all you had to go through. I mean being black and all, back then. I heard stories, let's don't forgot dat."

"I can tell you stories, son."

"Gabe, when you was a captain, being a real somebody and all, was it like heaven waking up with somet'ing soft laying beside you?"

"That would depend."

"Depend?"

"It would depend if I went to bed sober or drunk," Gabe said.

"Hanh?" Peck asked.

"Bedding down sober, I was where I wanted to be—with a woman I sugar-talked, got to know. That was always a pleasant morning waking up all funky-like. It was different bedding down drunk."

"Why's dat?"

"At closing time with the last woman sitting at the bar—if she'd have me we'd bed blind drunk and wake up with noses in armpits, afraid to open our eyes."

Drum brushes snapped to attention, scratched and snapped a solo on snare. Gabe flattened his hands on the table, fingers spread to feel the vibes of the bass and closed his eyes, rolling his head gently throughout the shuffle. When the bass came back in with slaps on wire, he opened his eyes again and smiled.

"Peck, my brother, our journey is going to be a long one. I'm an old man, and it is that distinction alone from which I will teach you things you will be able to use your entire life. And my grave, when I'm in it, will bloom a flower if you'll give me a smile and a thought from time to time remembering it came from me."

"Gabe, we have us twenty-eight dollars in your cheap ass wallet and a thousand miles to go. I don't get no wisdom in that arithmetic, way I see it, but please go on, professor."

"See here, my friend, if there ain't music inside a place, and you're looking for music and low on capital, one doesn't bother going into the place. There's nothing to benefit."

"Sounds like low on 'crapital,'" Peck barked with a goofy, snorting guffaw.

"In an establishment like this one—okay a joint—music of soul at its heart and a table of our own and our being low on ready cash, all we have to do is sit here and enjoy the music for as long as we can at absolutely no cost until someone decides it's time for us to buy a drink or libation. If they do, we have the option of ordering something or leaving. Now that's economy."

"Dat what they teached in the army, Captain?"

"It's called getting by within the rules, my brother. Survival."

"It's more like chummin' with no bait," Peck said.

Gabe looked at Peck as if he was wondering if it would be worth his time to talk more.

"My brother, I could, over a Chivas or two, explain my life as it was in uniform in a career in the army. But there isn't enough time in this lifetime or in the next, not enough gin at the bar—nor would you be interested if there were—to describe what it's like being a black man all your life in America. End of lesson."

Gabe grabbed his chair seat with both hands and shuffled it around until it faced toward the band.

Peck's eyes furrowed. He had a look on his face like he wasn't certain if he had offended his new friend, but decided silence was best. It was then that the lady in red looked over her shoulder, turned on her barstool and began stepping down. Her high heel led a long, captivating leg, bare over a red garter strap that dripped down a warm, white thigh and snapped to black, sheer French designer stockings. With her eyes not leaving Gabe as he watched the band, she stood, straightened her dress, and walked over to their table. Her dress looked designer expensive, as did her shoes, and she had a cleavage some men could lose their sanity for. Slutty wasn't the right word for the look in her beautiful eyes, but she did have a sensuality to go along with what appeared to be perfectly shaped breasts. Her smile was genuine and that of a woman who liked jazz and the blues.

"*Bienvenue messieurs,*" she said.

Gabe turned and looked up.

"I'm afraid my French—" he started.

"The bar is self-service," she said.

"We were just getting settled, I hadn't noticed," Gabe said.

"Charlie needs to put up a sign or something."

"That'd help. Thank you for telling us."

"As long as I'm here, what can I get you gentlemen?"

Gabe extended his hand.

"My name is Gabe."

"Hello, Gabe, my name is Sasha, nice to meet you."

"Momma named me Gabriel, hoping I'd be an angel."

"Why, aren't you a sweet one, you little angel?" Sasha asked.

"My momma was Creole—"

"Creole? You don't say? I'm Cajun French."

"— from Cameron Parish she was. I was born there. Momma always said I was her angel."

"Well that certainly makes you Creole, angel Gabriel."

"Actually, my momma was quadroon—"

"You're bronzy gold, Gabriel, like Louis Armstrong's horn—such a beautiful hue—"

"More like rust. I have some years on me."

"Was it your grandma or your grandpa, you know—a slave?"

"My papaw was the slave. Mamaw was Acadian from France down through Canada. Bought and freed him and asked him to marry her."

"Way to go, Grandma—I'd have loved to have met that woman."

"Momma said Mamaw was something else."

"Most us Louisianans are a mix breed, honey," Sasha said.

"My daddy was a hard-working piano maker, mover and tuner from Joliet. Black as the sharps and flats on the keyboard," Gabe said.

"Joliet?"

"Illinois—Chicago."

"So, you're a mix—with music in your soul."

"More like a mutt."

"Your momma was right—you are an angel."

She extended her hand. "Pleased to meet you, Gabriel. My friend sitting over there is Lily Cup. She would have come with me, but she's tied up at the moment."

"Honey, we can't afford no fun with ladies tonight, sorry," Peck said.

"Excuse me?" Sasha asked.

"The lad didn't mean anyth—" Gabe started.

"Lady, we come in for a beer maybe and some jazz, dass for true, not ladies, if you catch my drift," Peck said.

Sasha smirked and looked down at Gabe.

"Is your friend for real?" she asked.

"Please excuse—" Gabe started.

"What can I get you to drink, darlin'?"

"If we haven't offended you, beautiful Sasha, I'd like a Chivas on the rocks and a long neck for my friend."

"Chivas and a beer, coming up," Sasha said.

"Do they have a gumbo?"

"No gumbo, honey, but the best beans and rice on Frenchman Street, for four dollars a bowl. It's a big bowl and especially good. Charlie's mother makes it in the back room."

"Then forget the Chivas and make it two beers and two bowls of red beans. Thank you kindly, Miss Sasha."

Sasha smiled and turned away.

"They have a hot sauce?" Gabe asked.

"Tabasco for sure, and I think maybe Louisiana. I'll check."

"Louisiana, if they have it, sweetheart. I love it on chicken. Tabasco if they don't. Thank you."

By then the band members were walking past Sasha toward the bar, beginning their break. She stopped as though she had forgotten something, turned on her heel and strutted back in a march to the table, leaned down on it with one hand and looked Peck in the eye.

"I just got it," she said.

"Hanh?" Peck grunted.

"You implying we're hookers?" Sasha asked.

Peck sat up straight, speechless.

"I'm right aren't I, cowboy? You think we're goddamned hookers."

Peck looked at Gabe for an assist. No help was proffered.

"Don't be looking at him. What's your name?" Sasha asked.

"Peck."

"Nobody's name is Peck," Sasha declared.

"Hanh?"

"What's your name?"

"Boudreaux Clemont Finch," Peck said.

"I knew it. Nobody is named Peck unless they've earned that distinction being an asshole. Who was inspired to name you Peck, Mr. Boudreaux Clemont Finch? Don't fuck with me or I'll have Charlie throw you out. Who was it?"

"Mrs. Feller at school. It was her what did it," Peck said.

Peck's hands were restless, fidgety, but he found a calm staring into Sasha's cleavage, fighting for air between two breasts as she leaned.

"Mrs. Feller didn't name you Peck, did she?"

"Mrs. Feller sure—"

"Don't lie to me."

"Well..."

"She called you a peckerwood for shooting off your mouth with no thought whatsoever, am I right?"

"Something like dat," Peck said.

"And you quit school and stopped learning manners, I'll bet."

By this time, Peck's confidence was building as he figured she wasn't about to hit him with a heel of her shoe. The more he could egg her on, the more he could watch that cavern to heaven that was her chest. For maybe the first time in his life he kept his mouth shut and nodded his head in agreement, with pleasure.

"Peckerwood, listen good. Last year I put over ninety thousand in my 401K, I drive a Bentley convertible, own a caddy SUV, my three homes are paid for and I have nine full-time real estate ladies on my payroll."

Sasha paused.

She caught Peck's eyes staring down her bosom. She smiled and watched him a bit more, finding pleasure in his dancing eyes. She returned the impropriety, looked at his chest, his thighs in tight jeans and his shapely flexed arms, and raised her eyebrows with approval.

She stood up.

"Boudreaux, would you like your beer in a bottle or a glass?"

"Bottle would be good, ma'am."

Sasha extended her hand. "We going to get along easy, are we?"

"Like eatin' lettuce—easy," Peck said, shaking her hand.

She turned toward Gabe and winked.

"Angel Gabriel, maybe you can train peckerwood here what an apology is by the time I come back with y'all's drinks and beans—"

"I'll certainly give it a try," Gabe said.

"—and save a dance for me," Sasha said.

She turned, looked over her shoulder at Peck with a smile in her eyes and walked away, certain this time to do a proper sashay of hips for four eyes she was certain were glued to them.

CHAPTER 5

THE BAND WAS BACK and playing Louis Armstrong sounds when Sasha returned with a tray of drinks and two bowls of red beans and rice.

"Oh my, doesn't this smell good?" Gabe asked.

"The best on Frenchman Street," Sasha said.

"Won't you join us?"

"Well, that depends," Sasha said.

"Come sit and talk?"

"I don't sit with just any man who comes in. And I don't sit to talk."

"Depends on what, pretty lady?"

"Are you a dancer?" Sasha asked.

"New Orleans jazz and a beautiful woman—it doesn't get any better than that. This Creole mutt is a dancer, honey. I surely am."

She smiled, gave a wink, went back to the bar, retrieved her martini and purse and returned, swaying her hips to the rhythm of music as she walked. Gabe stood and pulled a chair out.

"Why thank you, Gabe. Such a gentleman."

She leaned and kissed him on the cheek.

"Are martinis your drink of choice?" Gabe asked.

"I find them most efficient," Sasha said. "And I like the way they look in my hand."

"I went through that," Gabe said. "There was a period when I thought I looked best with a tumbler of Chivas on rocks in my fist."

"Did you want a Chivas, Gabe?"

"Not tonight, darlin'—just enjoying the music and my red beans."

"You'd still look good with a tumbler in your hand."

"When I'm dressed, holding a tumbler shows off my French cuffs and links."

"Isn't it funny what people do?" Sasha asked.

"Excuse me, darlin' but these beans and rice are best I've ever had," Gabe said. "I wonder what her secret is, do you know?"

"She won't say, but I think she melts her butter in chicken broth, maybe dusts it first with flour and boils rice in that," Sasha said.

"Definitely the Holy Trinity," Gabe said.

"Hanh?" Peck asked.

"Nothing is cooked in New Orleans without onions, bell peppers, and celery, Boudreaux—Gabe here knows his stuff," Sasha said. "That's the Holy Trinity."

Gabe held a spoon of rice to his nose.

"I think you're spot on about the flour," Gabe said. "Maybe a roux with flour and chicken skin fat strained into her butter melted in chicken broth secret. This is a master blend of flavors—good eating."

"How about you, Peck?" Sasha asked. "Are you enjoying the rice and beans?"

"Yes'm."

"You're in real estate?" Gabe asked.

"I am."

"I'll bet Katrina turned your world upside down in New Orleans."

"You betcha it did, and BP's oil spill didn't help, either," Sasha said. "Then Harvey, Nate, they just keep coming, we just keep surviving."

"I'm delighted to know you seem to be thriving," Gabe said.

"Why thank you."

"Nothing more satisfying than a woman on top of her game."

"Gabriel, are we going to talk all night or are we going to dance?"

She glanced at Peck.

"Don't look at me," Peck said.

"I wasn't," Sasha said. "I was thinking you ought to go sit with Lily Cup at the bar or maybe get her to come over here with us."

Peck looked at Gabe with anxiety, knowing he didn't have a nickel in his pocket. He was waiting for some sign from Gabe.

"You'll like her, Peck. A bowl of beans and rice are good at room temperature. It'll hold," Sasha said. "It'll outlast the night."

"We're finding ourselves a little short tonight," Gabe said.

"How's that?" Sasha asked.

"We stepped in for a drink and maybe a bowl of gumbo and to listen to jazz. The place looked befitting our budget."

"There's nothing short about you, Gabriel," Sasha said.

"What a pleasant surprise to meet someone who dances, as lovely as you," Gabe said.

"Gabriel, you bring style into this place that it hasn't seen in a long time. I could tell you were a jazz man when you came in."

"Be still, my heart," Gabe said, tapping his fingers on his chest.

"You're both on my tab tonight, sweetie," Sasha said.

"You're too kind," Gabe said. "But you don't..."

"I'm thinking you'd rather have a Chivas."

Gabe smiled.

"I'll go get one, now taste your beans. When I get back, let's dance."

When Sasha returned with a Chivas for Gabe, she looked at Peck. "Boudreaux, go inform Lily Cup that her presence is required."

"Hanh?"

"Grab a chair for her when you do."

"You mean ax her to come over here?" Peck asked.

Sasha winced.

"Peck, say asked."

"Hanh?"

"Say the word *ask*."

"Ax."

"My lord," Sasha said. "Yes—go ax her to get her ass over here."

"R'at now?"

"Right now."

"What I'm gonna did?"

"Help her walk. She's getting shit-faced."

Peck stood, thinking of approaches.

"And make her leave her cigars at the bar," Sasha said.

Gabe pushed his bowl away, placed his napkin over the top, stood and extended his hand to Sasha.

"They're playing Joe Williams, my darling. Shall we have a go?" Gabe asked.

Sounds were deep and slow, a vibrating mellow with notes flowing out like they were paying their own rent just for coming into the room. To Gabe the sax was Joe Williams in song. Early on the two modestly held each other, as strangers politely do when they first dance. It was a second set for a sax solo when Gabe's arms reached around her waist, pulling her tightly to his body. Sasha's face gently nuzzled into Gabe's neck. She could smell sweat on his collar and the dispenser soap on his neck. She put one hand on the old man's shoulder, rested the other on the back of his neck.

"You smell good," she whispered to herself.

Gabe closed his eyes and respected the musical notes with short, deliberate steps and body sways. They became one in a room beginning to fill with local patrons. The room was also coming alive with smells of butter in red beans and rice, and respectful laughter politely subdued for an easier listening to sounds of bass and drums. It was five slow dances in a row before the two of them opened their eyes.

"What am I going to do with you?" Sasha asked.

"It's like we belong on the dancefloor," Gabe said.

"Oh my," she sighed.

They turned and walked to the table.

"Ish about time you two," Lily Cup slurred. "Sit down and join the party."

"Gabriel, meet my friend, Lily Cup," Sasha said. "Lily Cup, meet Gabe."

Lily Cup raised an unsteady hand—it swirled in small circles.

"Hello Gabe," Lily Cup said. "You'll have to pardon my—well, I may be a little..." Lily Cup hiccupped, "Oh fuck it, I'm drunk."

Gabe shook her hand, lifted his Chivas in toast. "It is distinctly my pleasure, Miss Lily Cup. Good to meet you."

Lily Cup jerked her head, blinking her eyes like wiper blades, giving Gabe a belchy grin for his courtly gesture. She weaved an index finger around her bodice and pointed it at Peck with her eyes still on Gabe.

"Have you met Peck, Mr. Gabriel?" Lily Cup asked, pushing her finger into Peck's ribs. "This is Peck. Hee'sh vera nice."

"Do call me Gabe, Lily Cup, and yes, I have. In fact I had the pleasure of coming in with Peck earlier. We've met."

"Huh?" Lily Cup asked. She hiccupped.

"Ready for another beer, Peck?" Gabe asked.

"I can did that," Peck said. "One of doze be good."

Lily Cup broke her stare of confusion as her lips blew a bubbled, lip-snorting laugh.

"Don't you just love the way he—ya know— talks?" she asked.

"Peck's part coonass, Lily Cup. A bona fide, genuine French Cajun," Gabe said. "He gets his thoughts across in his own artful way. It takes a good ear at times, but we get along quite well, don't we my brother?"

Peck wrinkled a grin.

"You speak Cajun French?" Sasha asked. "*Vous parlez le français, Cadien?*"

"I know some," Peck replied. "*Je sais que certains.*"

"Interesting," Sasha said.

"Want to know what?" Lily Cup asked, spilling some of her drink on the table.

"What?" Gabe asked.

"At first I thought he said his name was Pecker," Lily Cup said. She snorted into her fist. "Pecker—get it? Pecker?"

"Peck, what say you go ask Charlie for a strong black coffee for Lily Cup here—lots of sugar?" Sasha asked.

Peck pushed away, stood and started toward the bar.

"Wait," Lily Cup slurred. "Lemme go with you. Charlie's my friend."

She stood, tipping the back of her chair over. Peck caught it, put his arm around her waist, propped her tightly to his side and they ambled away.

"Wanna dance, honey?" Lily Cup slurred.

"Peck!" Sasha said.

Peck turned.

"Hahn?"

"No more rye—"

"Hokay."

"Black coffee—sugar," Sasha whispered.

Peck and Lily Cup made it to the barstools.

"I have a sense that young lady has something big weighing on her," Gabe said.

"She's in the middle of a murder case," Sasha said. "Trial starts tomorrow."

"Oh my," Gabe said.

"She believes he's innocent and the responsibility has her frightened she may lose."

"Is she the lead attorney?" Gabe asked.

"Yes, and she's damned good," Sasha said.

"That's why then," Gabe said. "No wonder she's feeling her liquor."

"This always happens when her trials start. She pretends rye clears her brain cells."

"That's one way of putting it, I suppose," Gabe chided.

"She needs a Peck tonight," Sasha said. "Let's hope he can sober her and can get her to forget her court case for a while."

"Sounds like a plan, but I wouldn't go telling Peck about her case or what she does," Gabe said.

"If you say so. You may have a reason, but may I ask why?"

"Let me put it this way...you can *ax* me...how'd that be?"

"Oh, I get you."

"This is the same peckerwood that all but called you a hooker before you were introduced."

"Gotcha," Sasha said. "You're a smart man."

"I've got some years on me, princess, and you and the music have awakened my inner spirit," Gabe said.

"Well let's dance before it goes to sleep again," Sasha said.

They stood, assumed positions like they had danced together for years. Gabe held his arms out for her.

"Jazz is mostly swing—some blue notes here and there," Gabe said. "This is free jazz—straight old school from as far back as in the fifties. These guys are good."

Sasha leaned in and kissed his neck.

"Shut up and hold me, Count Basie," she whispered. "Hold me tight."

Gabe slid his right hand down over her buttocks, giving a friendly pat, and moved it back to her waist.

"I want to take you home," Sasha mumbled. "But my boyfriend might be there."

"That does paint this scene in a new light, doesn't it?" Gabe asked.

"Oh, nothing like that, Gabe. I just want to keep you around—for dancing."

He lifted his head and kissed her ear as they turned with a dip.

"What brings beautiful women like you and your friend here to an alley off Frenchmen Street, when you could be somewhere fancy in the French Quarter?"

"Because you're here," Sasha said.

"You're here tonight because you knew we were coming? "

"It was a metaphor, sweetie."

"I knew that."

"It's alive in here. The booze is straight, the people are sweaty from honest day jobs, and there's the live music, the reason they come."

"Touché," Gabe said. "I wasn't thinking."

"You smell good," Sasha said.

Gabe turned them through a sax riff back with a trombone slide.

"Better than your boyfriend?"

"Just dance."

"Can we be expecting him and there bein' a scene?"

"James is not like that."

"All men are like that, darlin'."

"James is a wimp—probably over at Commander's Palace right now, impressing his friends. He's a surgeon in Baton Rouge."

"The man lives in Baton Rouge and he dines in New Orleans?" Gabe asked.

"He's here three days a week," Sasha said.

"Interesting."

"We both have busy careers."

"I'm an old man, darlin'."

"You don't dance old."

"I know about love."

"I'll bet you do, my Creole friend."

"Doesn't sound like love to me—not that it's my business."

"Just dance."

"Do you love him?"

"I love how you smell," Sasha said.

"If smells gave us a road, beautiful lady, we'd be on the moon now," Gabe said. "You waft of powders and scented oils, of a lazy morning with sheer curtains flowing from the open window, a horse carriage clip-clopping by below, and yellow rose petals resting on gentle curves of your smooth, firm stomach."

Sasha gripped Gabe closer, as in climax.

"Damn," she whimpered. "You are good."

"I'm an old black man raised on the South Side of Chicago," Gabe said. "Momma made me read every day, play nice and to always tell girls how pretty they were. When they drafted me into the army, she told me to stay put there and learn a trade."

"What a nice momma," Sasha said.

Sasha kissed Gabe on the neck.

"You do your momma proud," she said.

"Momma would love to hear you saying that."

"What am I going to do with you? I want you to hold me like this forever."

"I'm flattered, young lady, but after the dance I'll still be an old man, and you'll still be beautiful and your surgeon man is having his dessert at Commander's Palace, waiting to bed you tonight."

"Gabe, do you know who Satchel Paige was?"

"Famous pitcher, a brother. Of course, I know Satchel Paige."

"Do you know what he said when they asked how old he was?"

"They think he was near a hundred when they asked him. Yes, I know," Gabe said. "He said— 'How old would you be if'n you didn't know'd how old you were?'"

"Where do you and Peck live? I'll give you a ride home," Sasha said.

"We don't live in New Orleans."

"Oh? Where are you staying?"

"We aren't."

"What do you mean, you aren't?"

"We have to hit the road," Gabe said.

Sasha lifted her head. "What?"

"We're going to Rhode Island."

"When's your flight?"

"We're not flying."

"You're going to Rhode Island?"

"Yes."

"Tonight?"

"We'll catch a ride somewhere."

Sasha stopped dancing and pulled away.

"Gabe, you have no money."

Gabe didn't speak but pulled her to him and into a turn.

"I know Peck has no money," she added.

"Gabe turned her again with the music."

"What's in Rhode Island?"

"Newport. It's a long story. Let's not get into it now," Gabe said.

She stopped dancing and pulled away.

"You're damned straight we're getting into it now, Gabe."

Gabe looked away.

"I don't dance with a man all night and not get attached— I'm attached. Now why Newport? Why tonight?"

Gabe pursed his lips.

"That does it," Sasha barked. "I don't care why you're going. I'm driving you as far as Memphis, you stubborn old man."

"We'll be fine," Gabe said. "Thank you for the offer, but—"

Sasha reached for her purse.

"You're not a serial killer or anything like that are you?"

Gabe looked her in the eye with exasperated lowered lids.

"Where's Peck?" Sasha asked. "Their barstools are empty."

Peck and Lily Cup were nowhere in sight.

"I wonder where they ran off to," Gabe said.

Sasha pulled her dress down, adjusted her bodice and walked toward the bar, looking for their drinks at the empty stools and then into a back room where the toilets were. In a few minutes, she came out, walking towards Gabe muffling a smile.

"They'll be out in a minute."

"Uh oh," Gabe said.

"I think she's sober now," Sasha said.

"If my imagination serves me—the look on your face, woman, I'd say your attorney friend has treed a young Cajun raccoon."

"Put it this way," Sasha said. "She's not thinking of her murder trial at the moment. I'm certain of it."

Gabe pulled his Chivas and his rice and bean bowl toward him.

"I'm going to go get my car," Sasha said.

Gabe looked at his watch and pushed his Chivas away.

"Meet you both in front—fifteen, twenty minutes, tops," Sasha said.

"Honey," Gabe said. "This is wrong. You don't have to…"

"I had to go to Memphis anyway. There's a building developer there looking to buy a hotel in the Quarter or Garden District to take condo. I'll call on him when we get there," Sasha said.

"This has been a beautiful evening…" Gabe started.

"Not another word," Sasha said. "I'm driving you to Memphis and by the time we reach Jackson, I want to know the story, understand, sir? *Comprenez-vous, Monsieur*?"

Gabe looked up from his beans and rice.

"I do, my dear. Hurry back."

Sasha took his cheeks in her hands, leaned and kissed his nose.

"Tell Peck not to go anywhere and tell Lily Cup I'll call her later, not to worry," Sasha said. "Finish your beans. I'll see you out front. We have a six-hour drive."

Gabe and Peck walked a smiling and sober Lily Cup outside and put her in a taxi. Gabe didn't ask Peck questions. He let the lad alone in whatever afterthoughts he had from his backroom encounter. When their ride drove into the alley, it was a light blue Bentley convertible with the top up.

"My goodness," Gabe said, admiring the lines of the elegant car. He swept a gentle hand across its hood. "It's blue and magnificent."

"Light blue," Peck said, "*Bleu clair.*"

Sasha stepped out, walked around behind it and clicked the trunk open with her electronic key.

"Is Lily Cup still here?" she asked.

"We cabbed her home," Gabe said.

"Damn. She has my house keys."

"Should we go get them?" Gabe asked.

"No."

"I don't mind," Gabe said.

"I can make do."

"You're not driving us to Memphis in a satin dress, Sasha."

"Put your bag in the trunk, Peck honey, it'll fit—you sit in the back," she said.

"Let me have the honor of driving this beautiful machine, darlin'?" Gabe asked. "I want to see what it feels like. I have a valid license and I only nursed one Chivas all evening."

"Good idea," Sasha said. "Let my vodka wear off."

Gabe's face grinned like a schoolboy as he stepped around to the driver's side and got in. Still in high heels and Chanel satin, Sasha pulled the passenger door open for Peck.

"Watch the upholstery, Peck," Gabe said. "Be careful. It's a classic."

Sasha leaned from the sidewalk and through the opened door.

"Do you know where we're going, Gabe?"

"To Memphis?" Gabe asked.

"You take a right at St. Charles, left at Calliope, and head to 90. We're looking for I-10 then I-55 north."

She pulled the passenger seatback forward.

"I'll find it. I know the city," Gabe said. "Sasha, do you want to look in my duffel to see if there's something you can put on?"

Peck crawled into the back seat.

Sasha leaned down again.

"Peck, is there a gym bag behind the seat?" Sasha asked.

Peck lifted it and held it by the door. Bending in she took it and set it on the front seat and unzipped it.

"No peeking, guys," Sasha said, lifting garments from the bag.

"You can go to Charlie's ladies' room, Gabe said.

"In my modeling days, I had to change outfits in the middle of streets and crowds of onlookers. This'll be quick."

Standing in her red Chanel satin sleeveless dress, she took black tights and a sweatshirt from the bag, flinging each over a bare shoulder. Her hand rested on the opened car door to help her keep balance as she stepped out of Dior spiked heels. To take her stockings off, she reached down between her legs, grabbed and pulled the bottom of her dress up, exposing black thigh-high French stockings on beautiful, slender legs and linen white thighs; then further up to a pantyless crotch draped with a delicate saddle—a black, satin laced garter belt clinging to her hips like a café curtain above a sensual firm stomach. She caught the eyes in the car focusing on her bare lower belly.

"Heavens boys, don't gape," Sasha said. "Can't a lady get a little privacy?" she asked with a grin.

"Sorry." Gabe chuckled.

"Certainly, you've seen a girl's clamando. *L'entrejambe d'une fille?*"

There were sheepish grins but no response.

With an unsnap the garter belt fell loose from her thighs and now hung from two buttoned hooks on the top of each stocking. Draping her hips with the dress she pushed her stockings down and off a leg at a time, tossing hose and garter belt into a shopping bag. Taking black tights from her shoulder, she slipped each foot into a leg of them and swayed in jerks, her thighs and hips from one side to the other, maneuvering them up and under her dress, to her waist. She asked for an unzip. A girl on the sidewalk obliged and the red satin dress dropped to her ankles, leaving her standing in tights and a black, strapless bra. She stepped one foot out of the dress, carefully lifting it with the other foot and placing it on the car seat. Still facing the car's opened door, she took the sweatshirt from her shoulder and handed it to the girl behind her to hold. She stood there in black tights and her black strapless bra showcasing a cleavage of milky white breasts. She reached behind her back, unhooked the bra, letting her supple breasts push the bra off. Both Gabe and Peck, three bystanders at the corner, and a couple waiting to walk around the opened car door that was blocking the alley's sidewalk, gave full attention with mouths open, staring as the bra fell from her breasts. Sasha ignored the couple waiting to get by, leaned down to pick up the bra, looked at Peck and grinned. She looked over at Gabe and winked.

"We're near the French Quarter, *mes amis.*"

The girl handed Sasha the sweatshirt. She pulled it over her head and down, covering her breasts before kissing the girl on the cheek a "thank you."

"There's nothing with our natural bodies that can't be seen about in N'Orleans, especially during Carnival—Mardi Gras and beads, am I right?" Sasha asked.

"Nothing," the girl said.

"Apparently during summer too," Gabe quipped, feeling the steering wheel with both hands. "I'm not complaining, mind you."

"It's how we do it here, honey," the girl said.

"Pick your chins from the floor, both of you," Sasha said. "Pull your eyes back in and let's get going. We've got a six-hour drive to Memphis."

Sasha rolled her dress, shoes, and bra into a very expensive ball and stuffed them in the shopping bag and handed it to Peck.

"Thank you honey," she said to the girl standing by her.

She then turned to the onlookers.

"Mardi Gras is over, folks." There was light applause as she climbed into the car.

"Peck, put the bag in the cubbyhole behind you, sweetie."

Eventually Gabe learned a Bentley started itself with a touch of a button, and they rolled, slowly down the alley onto Frenchman Street. Two men having a night they wouldn't soon forget and their woman accomplice along for the ride on an impulse, determined to learn the mysteries of her new dancing friend and of the Newport she's only heard of and read about— and of the man who danced warmer than anyone had ever danced with her.

CHAPTER 6

NO ONE SPOKE. They let Gabe embrace his moment inspecting the finer details of a dazzling, state-of-the-art dashboard glowing in the night like a jet pilot's instrument panel. The car seemed to float from street sign to street sign as thoughtfully as the old man's feet moved on a dance floor. Gabe's smile was as though he were young again, back in his army days, on leave.

It wasn't until Ponchatoula when Sasha lifted her head from a nod off. She looked behind her to see Peck, his head back, sound asleep. She looked at the side of the old man's face, his eye, wide awake and gleaming with a pride of driving a dream car, concentrating on the road. She reached over the console and lightly scratched Gabe's inner thigh with her nails.

"You okay?" she asked.

"I'm enjoying this piece of machinery," Gabe said, not taking his eyes off the road.

"Wanna talk?" Sasha asked.

"Talk to me, baby," Gabe said.

"Wanna tell me about Newport?"

"Did you say Newport?"

"Newport, yes."

"Nothing to tell."

"Nothing?'

"Newport. Rhode Island."

"Gabe, I thought we had something back there."

"On Frenchman Street?"

"On the dance floor," Sasha said.

"Oh, that we did," Gabe said.

"If we did, don't do me like this."

"We're headed to Newport is all," Gabe said. "What more can I say?"

"If I was wrong, then okay—I was wrong."

Gabe didn't respond.

"Vieil homme têtu!" she whispered. "Stubborn old man."

"We're going to the Newport Jazz Festival," Gabe said.

"Okay. All right, I can see that, jazz man, especially after dancing with you for five hours," Sasha said. "Now that wasn't hard, was it?"

"We're going there."

They watched the road in silence for a mile, maybe two.

"But what's with the secrets, baby?" Sasha asked.

"What secrets?"

"Why no money, why the hitching? Make it all make sense."

Gabe kept his mind on the road.

"If you don't know you can talk to me by now—"

"I have money," Gabe said.

"It seems to be eluding you tonight, darling," Sasha said.

"I have money."

"I'm not after your money, honey—I love how you dance."

"My money is what you might say tied up at the moment," Gabe said.

"Are you married?"

"It's nothing like that," Gabe said.

"Then what?"

"It's a temporary glitch, a momentary setback, and Peck and I enjoy walking, so we didn't give it much thought and started hitching rides."

"You we're doing a bad job of it, sweetie."

"Bad job of what?"

"Of hitching rides."

"How so?"

"You might consider another approach," Sasha said.

"Your point being?"

"I don't understand your story about hitching rides," Sasha said. "You started with beans and rice on Frenchman Street and didn't want to accept your first hitch—my offer of a ride to Memphis. Care to explain if there's something I'm missing?"

"We started this morning."

"From New Orleans?"

"From Carencro," Gabe said.

"From Carencro?"

"Carencro."

"Carencro, like in Louisiana? Our Carencro?" Sasha asked.

"One and the same," Gabe said.

"You two might avail yourselves of a compass—"

"I know how it looks," Gabe said.

"—or a good road map."

"It's our first day on the road."

"No offense, Gabe. Carencro is west of Frenchman Street maybe two, three hours, and Newport is north, least it was last I looked," Sasha said.

"My compass is sleeping in the back," Gabe said.

"Him?"

"Him."

"Peck is your compass?"

"We've since had a shakeup of management responsibilities."

"Let me get this straight. You counted on boy wonder back there to find the way—thousands of miles?" Sasha asked.

"I'll admit if he headed a space program, young Peckerwood Finch might have landed the Apollo moon mission near Raleigh, be my guess."

Sasha looked at a console light glowing on Peck's faded, blue-jeaned thigh.

"He does have a nice bod," Sasha said.

"Lily Cup didn't want to let go of his leg when we put her in a cab tonight, seems she agrees," Gabe said.

"She needed that," Sasha said.

"So'd the boy, truth be told. It's first time since I've known him when he's stopped blabbing his mouth with blurts the way only he can."

"How long have you known him?"

"I've known him for some weeks now—only met him this morning."

Sasha rested back, watching the road ahead.

"If you get tired, I'll drive."

"I'm good," Gabe said. "If I wasn't driving this fine car, I'd be sitting up all night watching out a window."

Another mile went by in silence.

"What's the story, Gabe—you and Peck?"

"Ask me no questions, honey—I'll tell you no lies."

"Talk like that frightens me," Sasha said.

She turned and lifted herself, her elbow on the console. She leaned and kissed Gabe on the shoulder.

"You smell so good." Sasha whispered. "Tu sens si bon."

"You're in good hands, beautiful lady. No worries."

"I take my friendships seriously," Sasha said. "I'm Cajun French, sue me."

"Baby, you make this old Creole feel like I'm in high school. You are truly blessed with a spirit all your own, like a fine wine," Gabe said.

"Then be my friend, Gabe. Don't make me a fool begging you to open up."

"Honey, I—" Gabe started.

"That's not what friends do," Sasha said.

Gabe's face tightened. He wanted the dance to go on forever, but he knew the band always had to go home eventually. A Conway truck passed their light blue Bentley. He gathered his thoughts, looking at the speedometer.

"They have everything. My social security card, my Visa card, my discharge papers, my birth certificate— everything I own is in their safe in Carencro," Gabe said. "Under doctor's orders they stripped me down like a recalcitrant child, took it all away when they checked me in."

"Why?"

"They said it was for safe-keeping."

"I don't understand, who—the police?"

"They even tried to take my fucking watch, but I wouldn't let them. They said I could keep an empty wallet and my driver's license in case I wandered off and someone found me."

Sasha sat back. She felt it best to let him ramble.

Still in the dark it was another mile of silence when Sasha prodded again.

"So, who is Peck to you?"

"Peck is the yardman and caretaker—"

"Caretaker?"

"And yardman."

"He mows lawns?"

"Iif they don't fire his ass for this—he mows at the hospice in Carencro where I was dropped off and left to die while they tested me."

Gabe gripped the wheel, disappointed the truth came out before he wanted it to. He tightened his lips.

Sasha's body fell limp in her seat.

"*L'Hospice*," she whispered.

"Hospice," Gabe mumbled.

She turned her head and looked forward into the night. She turned back, sat quietly watching Gabe's eyes. Quiet miles helped her think.

"You and Peck are running to Newport to listen to the music, aren't you?" Sasha asked.

"Jazz," Gabe said.

"One more last time," Sasha whispered to herself.

Gabe overheard her.

"Just one more last dance," he said.

She reached, gently squeezing his forearm. Neither talking for the longest time.

"It is beautiful," Sasha whispered. "*C'est beau.*"

"I'll say one thing," Gabe said.

"You don't have to, Gabe. I didn't mean—"

"That boy back there may not be a rocket scientist, but he had the heart to see an old man not wanting to die on the banks of a Louisiana bayou—he walked away from every possession he owned—his trotline rig, his mower and rakes, his job—he made a decision, kept his dignity and snuck an old man the hell out of there. The boy volunteered on his own to grant a wish and help an old man go die where he wanted to die."

"Peck did all that?" Sasha asked.

"That young man gave up everything for me. I do love him for it, so I'm tolerant of his ways."

A tear rolled from Sasha's eye as she stared at the fleeting stripes in the road rolling under the car, truck taillights ahead. She placed her palm on Gabe's thigh, scratched an x and o "kiss and hug" with her nails, patted his leg and left her hand on his thigh.

"Promise you'll wake me if you need me to drive?"

Gabe nodded. His lips pursed. "I promise, baby. Get some sleep."

It was three miles south of the Hazlehurst exit when hail started to come down. At first a crackling of it on the hood and trunk sounded like a snare drum in a march. The cloth roof rumbled from the pelting ice storm. It then came in blistering sheets—as though the ice pellets were thrown at the car from snow shovels.

"What in the hell?" Gabe blurted.

"Wha...what's happenin'?" Peck shouted from the back seat.

Sasha's head jerked, she sat up, taking it in.

"Damn," she said.

"Storm," Peck said.

"A hailstorm—and at this time of night," Gabe said.

"The worst kind," Sasha said.

"I'm slowed to thirteen miles-per-hour," Gabe said. "I can't see a damn thing—afraid to stop—afraid to pull over and park—we could get hit either way or we could go off into a swamp and all drown."

A fifty-foot trailer truck crept by on the driver's side.

Sasha pointed at it. "Those taillights," she said.

"What about them?" Gabe asked.

"That truck. Follow its taillights."

"Will do."

"Keep your eyes on them."

"Makes sense, but first overpass we're pulling over," Gabe said.

"Don't take your eyes off those taillights," Sasha said. "And try to keep up with the truck."

Sasha leaned forward and adjusted the GPS on the dashboard.

The rocks of hail got larger and bolder as they pounded on the car, drowning out interior sounds.

"Hazlehurst," she shouted.

"What about it?" Gabe shouted.

"It's up ahead. There'll be an overpass or a bridge or something there that we can park under."

"Hazlehurst—got it," Gabe shouted. "Will that GPS thing tell us when we're close to it?"

"It should. I'll watch the GPS, you watch the taillights."

Three claps of lightning turned the sky white, showing at least two inches of hail gathering on the road.

"I thought hailstorms were a spring thing," Gabe said.

"Hail knows no season in the south," Sasha said. "Auto insurance in Louisiana is half if you park in a garage away from the hail and sun."

"It looks like hell's freezing over tonight," Gabe shouted. "Lord, don't let me die in an ice storm."

"Gabe," Sasha shouted, sitting up. "Get ready to slow down and pull over."

"Tell me when, baby."

"The GPS will tell when we're about to go under the overpass. You have to be ready to pull over and stop."

"Hazlehurst," Gabe repeated.

"Hazlehurst," Sasha confirmed.

"I'll be ready," Gabe said. "Say the word."

A truck passed on the left, slush splashing on the side of the car. It brazenly drove on, passing the truck Gabe was following.

"Get ready, it's coming up," Sasha said.

Gabe leaned into the steering wheel, alert and ready.

"Almost," Sasha said.

She repeated, "Not yet...not yet...not yet...get ready, Gabe...slow down...now!"

The ravaging rattling sounds of hail hitting the car stopped.

The overpass was held up by enormous concrete trusses, easily eight feet in width each, reaching twenty or more feet to the highway they supported above. Gabe brought the car to a crawl with his eyes peeled for a space to park.

Three cars, an RV camper, a pickup hauling a boat trailer, and a motorcycle were under the overpass, parked on its roadside. Gabe pulled to the right of one of the cars and maneuvered up the concrete embankment that sloped under the bridge.

Sasha turned in her seat, getting on her knees. She leaned over the console and took Gabe's head in her hands and kissed him soundly once on the lips, leaned back and said, "Thank you, my darling. You are our hero tonight."

They sat quietly to settle their nerves from a harrowing twenty-mile drive through sheets of rock-hard hail stones. Occasionally a car would drive out from under the overpass and go on its way, and another would pull in. Gabe lowered his window and took a fistful of hail and held it for Sasha and Peck to look at.

"Let's pray this fine car isn't damaged," he said.

"To hell with the car," Sasha said. "We're safe is all that matters."

Gabe opened his door and put his foot out on the ground.

"Where're you going?" Sasha asked.

"I have some business to attend to," Gabe said.

Sasha smiled.

"I'll be behind one of those concrete pylons, if you need me."

"Leave it running, for the heat, sweetie," she said.

Gabe crawled out and closed the door behind him.

Sasha turned and got on her knees to look at Peck in the back seat. She pulled the driver's seatback forward.

"Peck?"

"*Oui?*"

"Gabe told me what you did."

"Hanh?"

"You are a good friend," she said. "Quitting your job an all."

"What's he been say'n'?" Peck asked.

"That you're about the best friend a man could ever have."

"Gabe say dat, for true?"

"He said you gave up everything you had so you could help make his dying wish come true."

"If'n your talking about me getting him the hell out of there, dass all I did, cher. I don't know about any wish, lest you're talking going to hear jazz up at Newport," Peck said.

"All that jazz," Sasha said. "Just like the song."

"You'd a did the same t'ing seeing his eyes, him sitting on dat park bench," Peck said.

"You're a good man, Peck, God will reward you."

"Is dat for true?"

"You're helping a dying man," she added. "*Vous avez aidé un ami mourant.*"

"I help a frien' is all," Peck said.

"What goes around comes around. You'll be rewarded."

"You plenty rewarded me on Frenchman Street, you surely did," Peck said.

"You mean introducing you to Lily Cup?"

"Well, dat too." Peck guffawed. "I was meaning beans and rice and maybe I was t'inking your dressing on the sidewalk like dat. Whew, boy, I tell ya."

"I am so embarrassed," Sasha quipped, feigning to put her hand over her eyes. "*Oh, mon dieu, je suis tellement gêné.*"

She raised her eyebrows inquisitively and pointed index fingers at her breasts.

Peck grinned, conjuring his memory of her changing outfits.

"What is it about boobies', Peck?"

"Hanh?"

"Can you tell me?" Sasha toyed. "They're just breasts."

"I see'd more than dat, cher, but if you're axin', all I can say is guys pay money to gets a look close-up, like at clubs around," Peck said. "Lots of money."

"A close look? You mean a close look at breasts?"

Peck didn't answer.

"You go to those clubs, Peck?"

"Nah, nah, I never," Peck said.

"Why not?"

"Ain' been to no club like dat."

"Don't you like to see girls naked?"

"Ain' dat—no money to go," Peck said.

"You got to see Lily Cup's titties. Did you like them?"

"Naw, I didn't."

"You didn't like seeing her—"

"We didn't got her shirt off."

"Can you see me in this light?" Sasha asked.

"Not like a giggin' lantern, cher."

Sasha flipped the map light above her head on and turned her torso enough, so the GPS and console spotlighted her front.

"Now I can," Peck said.

She pulled her sweatshirt up over her breasts.

"Me to you, Peck. Here's your Valentine."

"Ma dang," Peck yelped.

"This peek is a thank you, big guy, for helping Gabriel," Sasha said. "These are my girls?"

"Me oh my, they shore is purdy."

Peck took them in with a memorizing stare. To help, Sasha leaned forward with a smile, watching Peck's eyes to maybe a count of ten, sat up, and pulled the sweatshirt down again and turned around.

About then the driver door opened, and Gabe leaned in.

"Peck, can I see you for a minute?" Gabe asked.

"Hanh?" Peck asked.

"Need to see you out here, son," Gabe said.

Peck's first thought was that Gabe saw the two of them—was upset and wanted words.

"Ya t'ink he seen us?" Peck whispered to Sasha.

"Peck, I have to talk to you," Gabe said.

"I think he needs help," Sasha said. "Better go see."

As Peck climbed out, Gabe took him by the arm, closed the door and forcibly walked him around back of the car. He stood Peck between him and the trunk.

"Don't be looking now, but behind me, the skinny one on the black motorcycle—he's wearing black leather, over my shoulder—"

"I see him," Peck said.

"He's the one on the bike behind the boat trailer back there."

"I see him. What about him?"

"He's the motherfucker that stole my pills."

"Your pill bottle, Gabe? Whole t'ing?"

"My Contin, my pain medicine," Gabe said.

"He taked your pill or the whole bottle, Gabe?"

"The whole bottle. It's morphine, son. Without it I'll be doubled over wanting to die with the pain it'll give me by this time tomorrow."

"He just come up and—?" Peck started.

"I was back there peeing and then taking my pill—right behind that pylon, that one over there. The bastard slapped me on the back of the head with a fist and grabbed the bottle out of my hand and ran."

"Did you take you a pill?"

"I took my pill, swallowed it without water but I no more got the cap on, and the sonofabitch whacked the back of my head and grabbed the bottle. I fell to my knees, so I don't think he knows I got a look at him. I could see him run to his motorbike."

"Git in the car," Peck growled.

"What?" Gabe asked, confused. "Help me—"

Peck grabbed Gabe's arm firmly. "Go git bag in the car, close the door and pop the trunk."

"What are you thinking?"

Peck grabbed the front of Gabe's shirt and pulled him close.

"Now, goddammit, Gabe, 'afore he takes off. Git in the car, old man. Git in now."

Gabe stepped around the side, pulled the door and started to climb in.

"Pop the trunk," Peck yelled.

CHAPTER 7

THE BENTLEY ROCKED with the trunk being slammed shut. Peck yanked the passenger door open, saw the seat empty, Sasha behind the wheel and Gabe in the back seat. He got in and pulled the door closed.

"Take off," he barked.

Sensing tension, Sasha nodded, brought her window down enough to look out to her left.

"Let's go," Peck grunted.

There was an opening between a small car and a large RV camper, and she edged her way through the gap. Watching for approaching headlights, she pulled onto the interstate and nervously picked up speed. The more confidence she felt behind a tractor-trailer she was following the faster she would drive to keep up. When they passed a mile north of Crystal Springs, they saw no signs of any hail or rain. The road was completely dry. It was as if they had left one room and entered another.

In the new quiet Peck reached his arm back between seatbacks, his knuckles touching Gabe's thigh. Gabe's fingers grasped Peck's hand, realizing his pill bottle was in it. He took the bottle, and with both hands he squeezed Peck's hand a *thank you, my brother...thank you.* Gabe smiled, and could finally lean his head back and wait for sleep to come.

Sasha got the speed up to seventy and set the cruise control.

She knew not to ask, but she saw in the reflection from the dash that Peck had retrieved Gabe's medicine. She was moved, watching him hand the pills to Gabe. She looked at Peck and smiled. He was a simple man. And his passion was a simple one, letting his trotline feed him at night, and earning enough mowing and sharpening blades to pay room rent somewhere; and he cared about people, risking giving up what he owned to help an old man he didn't know.

"Why if you keep this up...your helping my dancing man—Captain Jordan back there—way you do, why bless me I'm going to owe you a basketful of thank-you roses, Mr. Boudreaux Clemont Finch," Sasha said. "Whatever's a girl to do?"

Sasha looked into the rearview mirror and caught Gabe's smile, with eyes closed, appreciating her caring, encouraging her fun. This simple young man acted to help his friend immediately—without thinking—and in his world an immediate response was appropriate.

Peck grinned at the compliment, raised his right hand, letting his fingers welcome a sense of importance as he brushed his sun-bleached front hair to the side. Impulsively Sasha reached and took his right hand and guided it to her side of the console—Peck having to turn his body.

"Whatever am I going to do with you, Boudreaux?"

She raised his hand and kissed it. She kissed it again.

"What's your cell number, Peck?"

"Hanh?"

"Your cell number. Text me so I have it," Sasha said.

"I don't have a phone, cher."

"It was a brave thing you did back there," Sasha said. "You're our hero."

She kissed his hand once more and held it to her breast.

"When I get home," Sasha said. "I'm going to get you a phone. You ever had a cellphone before, Peck?"

"No ma'am."

"Why not?"

"I ain't had money, sides I wouldn't know who to call."

"You'd have to take care of it," Sasha said.

"I taked good care of my t'ings," Peck said.

"Peck, don't answer this if you don't want," Sasha said.

"Hanh?"

"Can you read and write?"

"No, ma'am. I didn't stay with it—school," Peck said.

"Come to New Orleans when you're ready. and I'm going to see to it you learn to read and write."

"Dass for true, cher?"

"Would you like to learn?"

"T'ird grade was about all I could take and it was firs' week," Peck said. "I run away from dat and my foster nanna. I only need my trotline to get by."

"Will you let me try?" Sasha asked.

"Nah, nah."

"I know a good tutor."

"Could I read with nobody laughing at me?" Peck asked.

"Nobody there but you."

"I surely would."

"You'll have your own private tutor," Sasha said. "You'll pick it up fast."

"Wouldn't dat be something now? If I could read, you know contracts and things, I'd might could get me a pirogue and run crab traps and sell to fancy restaurants."

"Big money in soft-shelled crabs," Gabe said.

"I can did fifty traps without a license," Peck said. "If I could read and get me a license I could have t'ree, maybe two hundred traps."

"You'll need a bigger boat than a pirogue, Peck," Sasha said. "Maybe we could be partners."

Sasha lifted his hand from her chest, extended hers for a shake.

"We got a deal?" she asked. "*Nous avons une affaire?*"

"We got a deal," Peck said, shaking her hand.

He leaned back, rested his head with eyes closed and a smile on his face. Gabe too. They were both asleep by the time three Mississippi state trooper cars approached from ahead and whooshed by, one as fast as the next, with white and blue lights flashing like a summer electrical storm, racing south at breathtaking speeds. Sasha watched them pass by and kept an eye on their flashing lights in the side and rearview mirror until they were out of sight. The sleeping Peck and Gabe were none the wiser.

Now Sasha had her ways, this was certain. She was first a woman—and she celebrated every moment of her femininity—

but she was also an equal—a diligent, confident woman running her own successful real estate firm. She was chamber president two years running; she enjoyed the company of a younger surgeon from Baton Rouge, who hadn't made his mind up if he was ready to grow up enough to be married; and she enjoyed the independence of her occasional masquerade for men and boys, so long as they were good jazz dancers. She enjoyed playing dress-up with her best friend Lily Cup and prancing around in low-cut, expensive Chanel and Givenchy satins and their Prada's, gathering stares while listening to jazz and dancing to slow dances at Charlie's Blue Note a few nights a month, where they were safe and celebrated as graceful New Orleans belles. Charlie always walked them home. Sasha was a good citizen who obeyed the law—and now, after seeing those trooper cars, a concern came over her face.

She watched the road ahead, preoccupied about what she should do. She patted and squeezed Peck's thigh.

"Peck?"

"Hanh?"

"Wake up, honey," she said.

Peck bolted, sat up and wrinkled his eyes, rubbing his knuckles on them.

"Yeah?" Peck asked.

"I have to ask you something," Sasha said.

"I'm awake," Peck said. "Ax me."

In the back seat, Gabe sat up, rubbing his eyes.

"Peck, back there in the hailstorm..."

"Hokay?"

"Back under the bridge, did you do anything we might be in trouble for?" Sasha asked.

Peck sat in silence.

"We need to know, Peck."

Peck sat in silence, looking ahead.

"Did you do anything that would have the police looking for us?" Sasha asked.

"Better tell her, son," Gabe said.

Peck was silent, as though he were thinking what to say.

"She knows what you did for me, my brother. We love what you did, but answer her, son."

"He told me first off to go fuck myself," Peck said.

"Talk to us," Gabe said, leaning his head over the seatback.

"So I told him if he needed an old man's medicine so bad maybe he didn't need his motorcycle key. I took the keys from his bike so he couldn't start it and run off," Peck said.

Sasha and Gabe waited.

"Dass when he pulled a knife."

"Oh, God," Sasha said.

"Two guys driven the pickup haulin' the boat come around from pissing back of the post and ax what was happening and I tole them and they offered to help me. I grabbed the robber's knife-hand quick and he wrestled me down, but I got him on the ground and edged his hand and the knife to his bike tire and pushed the blade into his tire and cut it too big to fix."

"What then?" Gabe asked.

"Then I took my elbow and whomped it back on him, whomp, whomp, but I didn't kill him."

"Talk to us, my brother," Gabe said.

"I just elbow whomped him."

"With your elbow? His neck or face?" Gabe asked.

"I know difference between a killing hit and a whomp, Gabe. Dass when one of the other guys found your medicine in knife man's coat pocket and gived it to me. They tole me t'anks and said he'd prolly gone through their truck and the RV camper too. Tole me to go on and git and they'd see to the biker."

"Is this true?" Sasha asked.

"Yes'm," Peck said.

"Every word?" Gabe asked.

"Well, nah, nah," Peck said. "Not ever word."

"Talk to me, my brother," Gabe said.

"I wanted to kill him, Gabe—"

"Oh my God," Sasha said.

"—just like he did you by taking your pills. He could of killed ya, boss. I wanted to shore enough kill him, but I swear I didn't."

Gabe sat back. Both fear and tears grew in Sasha's eyes.

"But I didn't, Gabe. I swear it."

"I believe you Peck," Gabe said.

"I know how to kill plenty good. A whomp is just a setback, not a kill. It ain't a bonk. Sides, he was setting there holding his bloody nose and his ear was bleeding when I gived his bike key to the fellers."

"I believe every word," Gabe said.

"Me too, but if those troopers were going to that bridge, something happened since we left."

"Might be an accident in the hail back there," Gabe said.

"We can't take chances. They may look for this car," Sasha said.

"A Bentley in Mississippi," Gabe said. "Spot us in a heartbeat."

"I only whomped him," Peck said.

"We believe you, Peck. Go back to sleep," Sasha said.

"He was settin' there when I walked away with Gabe's pills, I swear."

"I'm getting off the interstate in Jackson. We'll go to Vicksburg and then north to Memphis," Sasha said. "It'll keep us out of sight but add an hour or so. We'll be in Memphis by morning."

Sasha made it to Vicksburg, headed north and turned the radio on low to a blues sound. Each town she drove through seemed to pass by with a welcome and a smile and an ease of a slow dance—Yazoo City, Cleveland, Clarksdale, Helena. It was just at dawn when she turned into the Peabody Hotel and came to a stop at the outside concierge station. She lowered her window for a man approaching.

"Welcome to Peabody. May I be of service?" a bell captain asked.

"Can you give me two, three minutes, honey?" she asked.

"Of course, Ma'am, take your time."

"I'll wave you over."

The bell captain tipped his cap and backed away. She raised the window and put her cellphone to her ear.

"Welcome to the Peabody, how may I direct your call?"

"Yes, hi—room reservations, please," Sasha said.

"Certainly. One moment please."

"This is Peabody reservations, for what date of arrival?"

"Yes, hello, I need two connecting rooms. With an early morning check-in. One night only. Do you have rooms today?"

"Let me check to see if we have two connecting rooms."

"Thank you."

"Certainly, ma'am. Yes we do. When will you be arriving?"

"We're here now," Sasha said. "We just arrived."

"Name, please?"

"Michelle Lissette," Sasha said.

"Can you spell Lissette?"

"Two s's and two t's," Sasha said.

Sasha read off her credit card number, said a "thank you," and with the phone still to her ear, she motioned the concierge over.

"I have you registered, Ms. Lissette. Two connecting rooms for an immediate check in."

"Thank you."

"My pleasure, and welcome to Peabody."

"Could you send room keys out here to the concierge valet stand while we gather things from the car?"

"I'll send them right out with a bellman."

"I'll come in and sign in a few," Sasha said, hanging up.

Gabe and Peck sat in wonder. Sasha looked in Gabe's direction.

"Best there's little or no talking," Sasha said. "Don't offer anything. We're tired. We've been driving all night from a conference in Chicago."

"Michelle?" Gabe asked. "Michelle Lissette?"

She handed Gabe a twenty. "Give this to the bellman when you get to the rooms."

"Michelle Lissette?" Gabe asked.

"I'm Sasha, Gabriel," Sasha said.

Peck and Gabe climbed out of the car and stood as though they were waiting for further instructions.

"Car's no worse for wear," Gabe said. "I don't see a scratch on it."

As the bellman came out of the hotel with room keys, Sasha popped the trunk and asked Peck to lift the duffel out. She closed the trunk. The bellman followed them with a cart carrying the army duffel, and they walked down the inner ramp leading into one of the more celebrated hotel lobbies in Memphis.

Gabe had been in the hotel before. It still impressed him.

"Peck, you may not know about Elvis Presley," Gabe said.

"I knowed Elvis," Peck said.

"He signed his RCA contract in this lobby."

"Who don' know Elvis?"

Peck stopped in his tracks with eyes wide open. The lobby was a world of its own, as large as a city block. A bouquet of hundreds of red flowers sprayed over a dripping water fountain in the middle, and a lone Steinway grand piano sat beneath a crystal chandelier high above the tables and leather chairs arranged on fine oriental carpets. Shops' entrances and a bar at one end of the lobby were of matching dark mahogany. The ceiling was seventy feet high, decorated with hand-carved beams, painted murals, gold trim, and framed by a wrought-iron, second-floor balcony.

"They built this place right after the Civil War," Gabe said. "It's historic, Peck. Take it all in, son."

"Bye, guys," Sasha said. "I'll call your room later."

She pointed her hand to the left at a large bank of elevators as their destination, and with a bellman following the two men, she turned right and toward the front desk to sign paperwork and check in.

It was a few minutes after noon before anyone was awake enough to think of making contact.

CHAPTER 8

SASHA RAPPED HER KNUCKLES ON THE DOOR between their rooms.

"Gabe?" she asked. "You in there?"

"One minute," Gabe said.

A bolt lock clicked, and the door pulled open.

"Come in, come in," Gabe said. "Have a seat. We woke a few minutes ago. I was just heading down to get some coffee."

"You going to go watch the ducks?" Sasha asked.

Sasha wrapped her arms around Gabe and gave him a hug and a kiss on the neck.

"By golly, that's right," Gabe said. "I forgot about the famous duck march, Peabody at noon."

He looked at the clock on the desk.

"It's too late, but I'll run down and get us some coffee."

"Gabe?" Sasha asked.

"What, darlin'," Gabe said.

"Sweetie, knowing what you told me, I just can't up and leave you right now," Sasha said.

"Sasha darlin', if I thought it could change anything, I wouldn't have told you."

Sasha watched his eyes now knowing about his hospice stay.

"Peck and ole Gabe here will be just fine. Don't you worry."

"I called my office and was able to switch appointments and open houses around. It'll give us some time to figure this whole thing out."

"Where were you, when I was half my age?" Gabe asked.

"At least one day," Sasha said. "I'll call on that hotel buyer prospect while I'm here."

She kissed him on the neck.

"You can call room service for coffee," Sasha said.

"I just want to go down and look around, walk. I want to take it all in and jog memories of when I was here in the service. I'll get a pot of coffee on a tray, maybe some Danish. I need the walk."

"Charge it to the room," Sasha said.

"I have enough money to at least treat us to a pot of coffee. I want to stroll that grand lobby again. It's been years since I've stayed at this lovely old lady," Gabe said.

"What do you know, a dancer and a romantic," Sasha said.

"You wait here," Gabe said. "Make yourself comfortable, there's a newspaper on that side table. I won't be long."

"Where's Peck?" Sasha asked.

She stepped over to the easy chair and sat down.

"In the tub," Gabe said.

"Sounds pretty quiet in there," Sasha said.

"He said," Gabe started, "—and this is a direct quote: he told me he 'didn't want no shower what needed a secret combination just to get it to run hot or cold.' Ha! He's in there soaking in a tub and looking at his map like Magellan."

"That's Peck, all right," Sasha said.

"I'll be right back," Gabe said.

"I'll be here. Enjoy your stroll. Ask when the ducks march again."

Sasha pulled a desk drawer beside her. She lifted out the WHERE visitor's guide and one from the Memphis chamber. She looked at her phone for messages. She slipped her shoes off and began paging through the magazines. It was fifteen minutes when the bathroom door opened and out walked Peck as bare-ass naked as a newborn baby with both hands gripping a towel over his head rubbing his hair dry like he was in a day spa. It was Sasha's turn to sit with her jaw open, savoring its waggle—a moment for a future memory. The lad's arms and legs were a sun-burned red, his midsection and buttocks were as white as a cotton sheet.

"Lily Cup, you lucky girl," Sasha mumbled to herself.

Peck pulled the towel from the top of his head and started rubbing his ears when he first saw Sasha sitting there, staring.

He jumped back like he had stepped on a rattlesnake and lowered the towel to cover his groin.

"Commando too," Sasha said.

"How long you been here?" Peck asked.

"Long enough," Sasha smirked.

"A body needs to be tole they's a lady in the place."

"Now, who went and told you I was a lady, Peck?" Sasha asked.

"You know what I mean," Peck said.

"Remember what I told you when I showed you my girls?"

"Better tell me again," Peck said.

"What goes around comes around," Sasha said. "You got a good look at my girls and kitty, it's only fair I get a good look at—tell me, Peck, have you named your friend?"

"Funny," Peck said. "No, I ain't named it."

"How about Willy?" Sasha asked.

There was a gentle repeating kick on the door. It was Gabe, wanting to be let in.

Peck stood behind the door, with the towel over his groin and Sasha not missing the opportunity to memorize his flexing bare buttocks. Gabe walked in with a tray, balancing a pot of coffee on it, three cups, a silver milk pitcher, sugars, and an assortment of breakfast rolls.

Peck edged back into the bathroom.

"Gabe, get me my pants off the bed," Peck said.

Gabe smirked at Sasha, imagining she's had sport eyeballing a young man's personals. He set the tray on the desk and tossed Peck his jeans.

"And it ain't no Willy," Peck barked.

"I think you're right, moon pie," Sasha said.

"Hanh?" Peck queried.

"Willy is a little boy's name."

"How do you take your coffee?" Gabe asked.

"Have you seen it, Gabe?"

"Darlin' I know the boy and I are friends, but hell no I haven't—"

"Hmmm. I'd say he's such a big boy, maybe a Willard, or perhaps a William."

The bathroom door closed behind Peck with a slam.

"Two sugars and spot of cream."

"You're going to give him a nervous breakdown," Gabe said, pouring the coffee.

"Him a breakdown?" Sasha asked.

"The lad's not even housebroke," Gabe mused.

"How about me? He walked out here towel drying his hair with it swinging about, loose and looking happy. My blood pressure went up just sitting here."

"Did you say cream?" Gabe asked.

"Just a drop."

Gabe handed her a saucer and cup of coffee, took his and sat on the edge of the bed.

"Gabe, we need to talk."

"So, let's talk."

"If you still want to get to Newport."

"And I do."

"Think about it a minute," Sasha said.

"I've been thinking about it for months," Gabe said.

"You wanted to go there when you didn't think there was anything else for you, right?"

"I'll admit that was a factor, yes."

"Now there is—"

"Is what?"

"You have friends now. You've got Peck...You've got me. We'll stick by you, sweetie, through it all. No matter what."

Gabe smiled. "Where were you all those years ago?"

"You're going to need money."

"I'm becoming aware of that. Everything being so final, the thought of needing money never came to me."

Tell me again, Gabe. How is yours tied up, exactly?"

"They kept whatever valuables I had in Carencro," Gabe said. "They pay any expenses with my insurance or my credit card. It's like I have no control over the card or what they charge to it."

"Who's your bank?"

"Bank of America."

"For us to do anything, a bank will need two forms of ID."

"I only have one."

"What do you have?"

"They kept my Social Security card, so I wouldn't have two forms. I only have my driver's license."

"I think you're being paranoid, Gabe. They really do care about you."

"If I'm so paranoid why wouldn't they allow me to leave with my medicine?"

"Your medicine is a narcotic, Gabe—they were only protecting you from getting hurt."

"Or robbed," Gabe added. "Like I was."

"Yeppers...or robbed," Sasha added.

"Hard to think straight at a place like that."

Sasha checked her phone for an address of a Social Security office close by.

"There's a Social Security place on Monroe Avenue," Sasha said.

"What about it?"

"We'll walk there, get a temporary card and then we'll go to a bank and get you another bank card."

"Can't Carencro folks trace a debit card?" Gabe asked.

"What do you mean?"

"I saw somewhere where all the ATMs take video pictures now of any transactions."

"Good thinking," Sasha said.

"Those cameras see everything," Gabe said.

"So, here's what we'll do," Sasha said. "Today we get your temporary Social Security card. We go to a bank and get a debit card. They can print one out while we wait. Then we'll go to Walgreens where you buy some prepaid credit cards with it all in one transaction and put four or five hundred dollars on each. They'll only be able to trace the one Walgreen's transaction on your card here in Memphis, but not for a few days with this going into a weekend."

"And if I buy the cards at Walgreens there won't be an ATM camera."

"I'll put you both on a plane to Rhode Island, and your trail will go cold here in Memphis."

"Smart woman," Gabe said.

"We go to Beale Street and party tonight—my treat," Sasha said.

"Let's find us some blues," Gabe said.

"We have the rooms all night," Sasha said.

"Woman, if I were younger my front hooves would be pawing like a young bull about now," Gabe said.

"Old bulls are better Gabe, don't you know that?"

"They are? Well you could have fooled me," Gabe said.

"Slow and easy—better," Sasha said.

"You are some woman."

"I bet you tell that to all the ladies, ya big ox," Sasha said, sipping her coffee.

Peck stepped out of the bathroom in jeans and no shirt.

"Well, hello Peck. Would you and William like some coffee?" Sasha asked.

Peck ignored her and sat next to Gabe on the bed.

"Look at you. You're red as Tabasco," Sasha said.

"Walkin' from Kenner to the Quarter," Peck said.

"I can't believe you two walked from Kenner to Charlie's Blue Note."

"Afternoon sun is the hottest."

"When we go out, I'll get aloe vera and rub your back and arms," Sasha said.

She proceeded to peruse the room service menu, reading aloud the options for lunch fare. Peck made his several selections of favorites with a flashing of his eyes.

"Where ya going?" Peck asked.

"Gabe and I have some errands," Sasha said. "They could take a couple of hours."

"Hokay."

"Will you be okay staying here and watching television until we get back?"

"Yes'm," Peck said.

"I'll order food up."

"I'm hungry...most we et since we run off was beans last night."

"I'll sign for it downstairs," Sasha said. "Just listen for them to knock and let them in."

"Yes'm," Peck said.

"I'll put a twenty on a bedside table," Sasha said. "Give it to whoever delivers the food."

"Yes'm," Peck said. "But a whole twenty dollars?"

"Peck, there're two kinds of people—those who won't work without a wage—and those who work on trust," Sasha said. "Wait people work on a trust that we'll say thanks with a tip if we like the service. Give the whole twenty."

Peck appeared to understand.

Several hours later, Gabe's room door opened, and they walked in carrying an envelope from a bank. Peck jumped up to welcome them.

"Peck, honey," Sasha said, "you go over to my room— turn on the television. "Gabe needs a nap before we go to Beale Street later."

As Peck started to step in the doorway Gabe stopped him.

"Before you go, Peck. Hang on a minute, my brother," Gabe said.

He took five prepaid debit cards from the Walgreen's bag, tore the packaging off each and held them out in his hand.

"Here, you take care of the money," Gabe said.

"Hanh?" Peck asked.

"I'm an old man, my brother. Somebody will roll me and take

everything we've got—like my medicine."

"Mais pourquoi moi?" Peck asked. ("But me? Why me?")

"You're my best friend, Peck," Gabe said. "See nobody gets it."

Peck felt his back pocket, then his front.

"Gabe," Peck said. "Could I borrow your wallet?"

Gabe handed his wallet to Peck. "You mean this cheap-assed old thing?"

Peck carefully placed five pre-paid credit cards into Gabe's wallet, folded it, and put it in his front right pocket for safekeeping. He looked at Gabe as a son might, indicating with his eyes he wouldn't let him down. He backed into Sasha's room and pulled the door to a near close. Gabe sat down and then stretched out on his bed. Sasha unlaced his shoes and pulled them off. She lay down beside the old man, putting her arm over his chest, her nails dancing on his shirt, lightly scratching his upper chest.

"That was a sweet thing you did," Sasha said.

"What?" Gabe asked.

"Think your friend is up to all that responsibility?"

Gabe turned his head, looking into her eyes.

"I'm sorry, I didn't mean—" she started.

"Honey, if I could figure out the words—if I could even figure how to write what it's like being a black man—being born black in America doesn't come with any set of instructions, you know. If I could, then I'd be able to express what it's like being an old black man so people like you could understand."

"You can say it, Gabe. White people, like me."

"One thing I do know after all these years is people. A black man, if he's smart, learns early on who to trust and who to just walk away from. The young man in that room over there walked up to me on his own steam yesterday morning and without thinking twice about what color I was, he said, 'Old man, you want to get out of here, don' ya? I can see it in your eyes.'"

"Peck said that?" Sasha whispered.

"You know something, pretty lady? If Peck left the hotel right now, and disappeared for good, he's already given me more honor and respect this old black soul of mine has seen from one man in this lifetime—and that's a long time."

Sasha smiled, leaned over and pecked a sweet kiss on Gabe's lips, gently touching one cheek in her hand.

"I'm sorry," Sasha said.

"You're fine," Gabe said.

There was a moment of silence.

"Gabe?"

"What, darlin'?"

"Do you want to talk about it?"

"Can you talk about Michelle Lissette?" Gabe asked.

"Michelle Lissette has a boyfriend, James. She loves him, and he says he loves her," Sasha said.

"Michelle Lissette should be with her man, darlin'."

"But he doesn't dance."

"Not a step?" Gabe asked.

"Only if I make him and never like you, Gabe. Sasha loves to dance, and she and Lily Cup dress up and go out and play a few times a month, to dance. I become Sasha."

"Girl's night out," Gabe said. "So, who is Lily Cup in real life?"

"Lily Cup is Lily Cup, the one and only."

"So, it's only you incognito at Charlie's Blue Note?"

"Uh-huh."

"And you dress to the nines to attract the dancers?"

"A girl can tell a lot about a man on a dance floor."

"Does Michelle Lissette love her man?" Gabe asked.

"Michelle Lissette loves James, but he doesn't, like, turn Sasha on like—well, you know."

"I don't know," Gabe said.

"Let's leave it at she's comfortable with him. Yeah, Michelle loves him...and the sex is good."

"But—" Gabe started.

"But I'm not certain Michelle would go out of her way to drive him to Memphis all hours of the night."

"The surgeon seems respectable enough by sound of it," Gabe said.

"He is."

"That goes a long way in picking a man for life."

"I know."

"I hope Michelle Lissette isn't risking a future with this young man by being up here in Memphis with us two vagabonds. Ain't much future with me, you know."

"I'm not here because I've fallen in love with you," Sasha said.

"Our bond goes beyond all that," Gabe said.

"I'm here because I've fallen in love with the person you happen to be, and what you've taught me in a matter of hours."

"I'm just an old man, not wanting to wait around to die," Gabe said.

"You're more than that, old man," Sasha said.

Gabe gave a curious nod.

"You're the most sensitive man—and the best dancer that ever held me on a dance floor," Sasha said.

"That's thoughtful, darling, but not quite..." Gabe started.

"You're a teacher of life—you stubborn old man. I thought I knew music and you go and teach me the difference between jazz and blues last night—"

"I did tell you Memphis was the home of blues, didn't I?" Gabe asked.

"—and I refuse to go back home until we've danced the blues."

"Now I remember."

"Certains hommes peuvent être si épais!"

"And just what in the hell does that mean?"

"Men can be so thick!" Sasha said.

"Well now you have a bedtime story for your grandchildren," Gabe said. "Your midnight ride to Memphis with two complete strangers."

"For now, it's my story. It'll be a beautiful chapter in my book," Sasha said.

Gabe turned his head and looked at the ceiling.

"Stomach cancer," he whispered.

Sasha heard the words, kept her eyes occupied watching her nails moving on his chest.

"Three months back they only gave me two months to live—said if cancer didn't kill me peritonitis would...and that's just about all I want to say about it."

Sasha had heard the hospice reference on the drive to Memphis but was stunned at the frankness of the moment. She let a quiet moment or two pass by, and she tried humor.

"Would having sex be a bad thing for you?" Sasha asked.

"My having sex would be a Goddamned miracle," Gabe mused.

"You smell good, you sweet man," Sasha said.

"My darlin', your hugs, kisses, that smile, and your scratches are better than any sex I've ever had, let me tell you."

"You are such a lovely man."

They lay quietly looking for diversions like wall art and the ceiling molding in a silence that lingered.

"Of course," Gabe said, interrupting the silence, "you do have some handsome tatas—now that's a fact."

Sasha bellowed in laughter, bolted up on her knees, straddled Gabe while yanking her sweatshirt up over her head, flipping it to his face. She grabbed a breast in each hand.

"Tatas?" she barked.

"Oh, my lord," Gabe said.

"Tatas?"

"Hee hee," Gabe wheezed.

"Why Mr. Gabriel Jordan, sir," she proclaimed, caressing her breasts. "I don't think you've been properly introduced. I want you to formally meet my girls. I'm changing their names in honor of you, darling."

"Well I never," Gabe said. "Ain't this something?"

"Gabe, this girl here is now named Gabriella—after you. Gabriella is my bold one."

"She's the Democrat," Gabe said.

"She can be naughty," Sasha said. "Say hello to Gabriella."

Sasha leaned in, letting her nipple touch Gabe's face. He smiled and kissed it gently, respectfully. She straightened, displaying her other breast.

"And from now on and forever forward," Sasha said, "this girl here is Jordan. She's kind of shy. Talk to her softly."

Sasha leaned in for Jordan's kiss. She paused, lowered her head in thought and sat up, her smile turning into tears, then silent sobs.

"I don't want you to die, Gabe."

She covered her eyes with her hands.

"This is no time for tears," Gabe said.

"I feel like crying," Sasha whimpered. *"J'ai gros couer."*

"I'm a happy man. All I ask is that I get to live until I die. A man can't ask for anymore. Let's us live every minute we're together—and not waste a second on tears. It's been a long time since I've been happier in this old life than I am right this minute. I thank the girls, Gabriella and Jordan, but especially I thank you, my darlin'. I'm telling you your Baton Rouge surgeon is one lucky man."

"He is, isn't he?"

"Now wipe the tears."

"Is there anything in this world I can do for you, Gabe? Anything? Tell me."

"Now you mention it, there is one thing," Gabe said.

"Anything, Gabe."

"You can let me get some rest while you go down and get yourself something to wear on Beale Street tonight. We're dancing the blues and all you have is an expensive red satin dress rolled up in a ball in the trunk of the car—"

"That's right, I almost forgot."

"—and we'll be enjoying the best blues and ribs in the country, and that's a promise."

Sasha stood from the bed, walked towards the door when she gasped a guttural guffaw, stooping and laughing in gasps of breath.

'You okay, darlin?" Gabe asked.

"I just got it..." she stammered.

She turned and pointed to her left breast.

"Gabriella—she's the Democrat..."

CHAPTER 9

SASHA REDISCOVERED THE SHOPS in downtown
Memphis before finding her way back to their rooms.

She juggled shopping bags while managing to get into
her handbag. She fumbled for her room key card, trying it first
on Gabe's room door, and then successfully on her room door.
Inside, she set packages on the floor. Peck in his jeans and no
shirt was sprawled on his back. He was sleeping soundly with
a pillow pulled over his face and the television tuned in on the
hotel guide channel. She pushed on the connecting room door
and peeked in. Curtains were drawn, and in darkness she could
see Gabe asleep. He breathed heavily in his sleep. Sasha went
to his bed, lifted a comforter from under his legs, and covered
him. His hand pawed, clutching the comforter, tucking it under
his chin with a sleepy smile of appreciation. Sasha watched the
old man for a moment and then stepped back into her room.
She pulled the door to lessen any glare of light going into
Gabe's room. She picked up a Walgreen's bag and sat down on
the bed next to Peck. She lifted a jar of aloe vera, read the label,
unscrewed its lid, and scooped some in her fingers.

"This might be cold," Sasha whispered to the now half
sleeping Peck. She swabbed his white abdomen, that had no
burn, with a flat palm of her hand. He sat straight up with a
bolt.

"What...?"

"It's aloe, for your burn, honey. Relax."

Peck looked about, rested back, stuffed a pillow behind his
head and neck, his eyes following her hand, and feeling it slide
from one side of his waist, over his stomach to the other side
and return. He made no mention that it wasn't his stomach that
was burned. Sasha's watched the motion of his skin rippling
below her hand, of his muscles as her hand met his flesh. She

scooped more aloe vera in her hand and started at his navel pushing the gel like a sensuous snowplow up the middle of his chest as far as his neck. Her hand would push the gel up and then by cupping her hand she would pull it back down the middle of his chest to his navel which gently heaved from pleasure and cold, and then slowly with her fingertips to just below the inside top of his jeans. She picked the jar up, filled a palm with gel and with the base of her palms lowered the jar to the floor.

"You going to run out," Peck said softly.

Sasha looked at his eyes without distraction, stretching and reaching both hands, targeting his chest and nipples, flattening her hands on each, holding still enough to perhaps gather her thoughts.

"I have more," Sasha said, smiling coyly, her eyes rolling at the feel of his muscles, of pouted nipples on her palms and outstretched fingers. Her hand movement walked a thin line between the application of aloe vera on sunburn and an erotic massage. Peck was good with either distinction. His eyes studied her hands. It was as though he could feel the sensations she felt.

"I'll get a towel," Sasha said.

"Hokay."

"Unzip your fly."

"Hanh?" Peck asked, sitting up and resting back on his elbows as Sasha stood up.

"We need a towel for when you turn over, you goose," Sasha teased. "We don't want to get this messy stuff on their bed linen, do we?"

"But..." Peck started.

"Unzip and turn over," Sasha said.

Hearing "turn over" lessened his vulnerability of cheating on his new best friend, Gabe, so Peck obliged.

They met less than twenty-four hours ago, and he hadn't had time to learn that both Sasha and Lily Cup were, in their own right, fisherwomen of sorts, listening to jazz at Charlie's Blue Note in the alley just off Frenchman Street. They understood lures and the simple patience of when and where to cast their trotlines.

Peck sat up and let Sasha spread a bath towel on the bed cover. He unbuttoned his jeans, unzipped two inches down and rolled over onto his chest.

Sasha smiled, an unopened jar in her hand. She climbed on Peck and straddled him at his knees.

"Lift your butt," she said.

"Hanh?" Peck asked.

"Lift your ass a second," Sasha said.

He did, and she grabbed each side of his waistline and gave his jeans a yank, lowering his front zipper to its base.

"Oh," Peck said.

Sasha pulled the back of his jeans down to his crack and straddled the buttocks she had admired earlier that afternoon getting out of a tub. With the same care as his front, Sasha covered Peck's back and upper butt, emptying a jar of gel.

"Feel better?" Sasha asked.

"Yep," Peck muffled into a pillow.

Sasha crawled off wiping her hands with a towel.

"Want to see what I bought for tonight?" she asked.

"Hokay," Peck said. He reached under himself and zipped his fly. He pulled a pillow to his crotch and rolled on his side to see what more Sasha might have in store.

"I got three outfits," Sasha said. "I can't decide which to wear."

"Hokay," Peck said.

"A lady at this shop said we should go to BB King's place for the best blues and dancing. You like ribs, Peck?"

"Ah *oui*," Peck said.

Standing by the shopping bags, Sasha lifted her sweatshirt over her head and off. She pulled her tights down a leg at a time, standing completely nude, looking at Peck as if she was looking through him in a thoughtful moment, thinking what to try on first. It was as if there wasn't a soul in the room with her. As a young man who lived most of his life in a blade-sharpening shed, Peck was mesmerized by this whole experience. As a fisherman, he was curious.

"Where'd you get raised up?" Peck asked.

"Excuse me?"

"Where'd you growed up, cher?"

"Why are you asking that?"

"Where?"

"Where was I born or where did I grow up?"

"Growed."

"Down near Pecan Island."

"Ah *oui.*"

"But I went to school in N'Orleans with Lily Cup since we were six."

"Hokay."

"Why'd you ask that?" Sasha asked.

"I knowed it be someplace like dat, you growed."

"Someplace like what?"

"An island, near the water, cher," Peck said.

"You did? How?"

"You sure get nekked a lot."

Sasha smirked, placed hands on her hips, twisting her torso.

"Are you complaining?"

"Nah, nah, oh no, ma'am."

"The salesgirl suggested we get there early to get a table on the dance floor," Sasha said. She slipped a black jumper over her head and pulled it down over her naked body.

"I always leave tags on, until I'm sure I like them, in case I want to return them," Sasha said.

The jumper had long sleeves, did not require a bra and her cleavage and upper chest were delightfully packaged and presented in a frame of fabric. The dress went down to midthigh. She turned about once, and then again, leaning back, looking over her shoulder and down. "What do you think, Peck? Do you like this one?"

"I like it a lot."

"I wish it didn't have sleeves—it's so warm out," Sasha said.

"I like it," Peck said.

"Good," Sasha said. "But it's too short for clamando, so I got some panties, just in case. Check these out, Peck."

Sasha lifted three pairs of panties, shuffled them and dropped two to the edge of the bed, stepped into a chosen black pair and pulled them over her hips, then adjusted her skirt. She raised her eyebrows toward Peck, seeking approval.

"You look nice. Mighty nice."

"Good—you're dancing tonight, so you look nice too," Sasha said.

All Peck had was what he had on. He was sitting on the bed as if he were gathering his thoughts about what had just happened in front of him. Today was another world for him.

"I took a pic of you earlier and showed it to a man in a store and he guessed you had a thirty-two waist."

"Hanh?"

"Here're new jeans, a sexy belt I picked out and a T-shirt you can wear tonight. If the jeans don't fit we can take them back."

"You taked a picture of me?" Peck asked. "When?"

Sasha took off her dress and hung it in the closet. She pulled her panties down and set them on the bureau. She walked over to the bed, picked another new pair, red, stepped into them, pulled them up and stepped to the door between the rooms. Peck was distracted.

"I took it earlier," Sasha said, picking up her sweatshirt. "I'm going in to talk with Gabe. We'll let you know when we're going to Beale Street so you can get ready."

Sasha may have thought it best for the safety of her phone camera that she not show Peck a picture of him toweling his head dry, swinging free in his altogether, or to tell him she had texted it to Lily Cup and got a text in return of a smiley emoticon with a tongue hanging out and a *"Where are you?"*

While Gabe slept, Sasha went through his army duffel and pulled out dress slacks and a shirt. She unfolded a hotel's ironing board and pressed both with the hotel iron and hung them in his closet. She pulled the drapes and with her phone took pictures of the setting sun.

"Time to get up, sleepyhead," she said.

She sat on his bed, leaned in, and ran her nails gently around his back and over his shoulders. Gabe rolled on his side, awake.

"Is there anything you can't eat, sweetie?" she asked.

"Pretty much everything is okay so long as I take my medicine."

"Ribs tonight?" Sasha asked.

"I love the ribs in this town, honey, but I might have to tone it down. I'll do shrimp and rice," Gabe said.

A concierge met the three at the lobby elevators and escorted them outside to a horse-drawn carriage Sasha had asked for. The night was warm and still, the sunset a blazing red and with the last few honks of afternoon traffic the carriage clip-clopped its way to historic Beale Street.

As the three walked arm-in-arm into BB King's the band was playing Beale Street Blues. Sasha wasted no time gesturing to a hostess about a table near the dance floor. A trombone was doing a riff with a tuba backing it up—banjo and drum as rhythm. Sasha motioned to Peck to follow the hostess and save a table, took Gabe's hand and led him to the dance floor, circling him around as if he was her prize for the evening. Well rested, he was up to the task, extending his hand, embracing her waist, and pulling her close to him. With feet not moving, but bodies swaying they'd begin and pause, begin and pause, rocking forms like football or basketball players, with head-motions and fakes back and forth. They'd hang on and jerk and sway to blues, with a dash of Dixie—and they'd pause and rock to and fro once, twice, three times, then still again, syncopated jerking and swaying some more back and forth to the piano, the trumpet, and the clarinet.

It was as though a curtain had opened and they were at center stage of a new play, rocking back and forth with sensuous thrusts and pulls. The night was about a trombone, clarinet, banjo, tuba, and drums—it wasn't about hailstorms, highway medicine bandits, and bad times. Gabe was feeling good and wanted to live in the moment, and he was moving well tonight. The band would end a jam, applause would fill the room and music would begin again, Gabe's thighs leading Sasha's hips as though they were both on top of a wind-up music box. Sasha's dress crawling up enough to warm the evening's curious, but still ladylike tight on her beautiful thighs, letting eyes concentrate on her motion but their souls on the rhythms of the band.

It was five sets before the band stopped for a break, and they ended with a deep dip. Sasha wrapped her arms over Gabe's shoulders and kissed him on his neck, first on the left then on the right. It was as though she were marking her territory for a crowd that had gathered to watch them dance. They joined Peck at the table.

"Whew," Sasha said.

"I'm telling you, honey," Gabe said, "there ain't nothing like the blues...it's sad and it's happy. Both at once—that's the thing about it. It's being in a cotton field all day from sunup telling yourself, oo yi yi! I'm so sad now, oh, my day is so sad but there'll be music later. Lord, just get me through these rows of cotton, just get me through this one day—there'll be music tonight."

"Food," Sasha said. "Peck, have you looked at a menu?"

"Ribs and beer," Peck said, pointing at a picture of it.

"Shrimp and rice, maybe a Chivas for me, darlin'," Gabe said.

"I nibbled some today while I was shopping," Sasha said. "I'll have a martini and just pick off your plates, if you boys don't mind."

Gabe flattened a folded handkerchief to his forehead, dabbing it, his cheeks and neck.

"Will you be okay driving back to New Orleans after you drop us at the airport tomorrow?" Gabe asked.

"You sure you want to talk about that now?" Sasha asked.

"We're waiting for food, let's talk," Gabe said.

"Can it wait?" Sasha asked, trying to drop a hint that they should talk alone.

"While we eat baby, before we dance again," Gabe said.

Sasha pointed at Peck. "And you're dancing tonight," she said.

Sasha leaned back and checked out Peck's outfit.

"Doesn't Peck look nice in his new jeans and T-shirt, Gabe?"

"He's a new man," Gabe said. "My brother."

"You owe me a dance," Sasha said to Peck.

After picking on food, enjoying the moment and Memphis sounds, Gabe and Sasha went to the floor and embraced through five more songs, moving as one. She would end a dance with a kiss on Gabe's neck.

"You smell good," she'd whisper.

"Hotel bar soap," he'd say.

At the table, sipping her martini and picking at food, Sasha told Peck he'd better be ready, because the next slow dance was his.

"Gabe, something I need to tell you, so you don't get mad if I hadn't told you," Sasha said.

"Say what?" Gabe asked.

"I only learned today."

"What's wrong, baby?"

"You can't fly to Rhode Island tomorrow," Sasha said.

"What? Why not?"

"At least with Peck, you can't."

Gabe leaned in over the table to listen.

"I didn't want to talk about it here," Sasha said, "but I don't want you angry for me not telling you."

"Talk to me, baby. What's up?" Gabe asked.

"Peck doesn't have any ID," Sasha said.

"What's your point, darlin'?"

"No ID nowadays, and you can't buy an airline ticket. While I was meeting with the man looking for a hotel in New Orleans, I asked his travel agent for your tickets. She told me."

"Peck, is this true?" Gabe asked.

"Hanh?"

"Don't you have an ID, son?"

"Nah, nah," Peck said.

"No driver's license?"

"Nah, nah," Peck said.

"You don't drive?"

"Can't have no license in Lewisana lest you can read and write. Can't have no ID lest you have a birth certificate."

"You been walking all these years, son?"

"Walkin' or bus," Peck said.

"How about you both come back to New Orleans?" Sasha asked. "We'll have fun dancing at Charlie's. I'll look after you guys—I'll get Peck a job."

"Honey," Gabe said, "I know you mean well and you have a heart as big as the sun, but ole Gabe here is going from this place to the Newport Jazz Festival, where, God willing, I'll get to sip some Chivas before I die."

He turned about in his chair facing the wall. The reality of the moment came over each of them. It wasn't an adventure they were on; it wasn't a joy ride; it was the final passage of a man who shared his dying wish with his new friend, a friend who came forth and wanted more than anything to help him make it come true. Sasha stood, leaned and kissed pouting Gabe on top of his head.

"We'll work it out, honey," she whispered. "No worries. I'll figure a way to get you both to Newport."

She extended her hand to Peck. He looked up when she snapped her thumb and finger and pointed her finger at him.

"C'mon, muffins," she said. "We're dancing."

She motioned to a waitress to bring Gabe a glass of port.

The band was playing a soft, slow, and painful "I believe to my soul."

Before they embraced, Sasha looked at Peck with different eyes. She was jarred by Gabe's wakeup, calling them back into the reality of the moment. She yanked Peck to her, pressing on his back with her hand so her breasts warmed his heart.

"Follow my lead," she said.

It was several minutes of dancing close before Peck got the hang of it, and Sasha worked up the nerve to try to make sense of the truth of the moment.

"He's dying, Peck."

"I know, cher."

"What should we do?" Sasha asked.

She tipped her head back to watch his telling eyes.

"I want to go with the old man," Peck said. "I promised."

Sasha smiled, leaned in and kissed his neck, a thank-you kiss.

"I promised the old man," Peck murmured. "*J'ai promis le vieil homme.*"

Sasha squeezed Peck.

"You holding out, Peck?"

"Hanh?"

"You speak French?"

"Very little," Peck said "*Très peu.*" My foster nanna teached me some, gator man teached me mostly cussin'."

They circled the floor.

"You're a good man," Sasha said. "Gabe is lucky to have you."

They turned in a sway, moving slowly to an electric guitar, wailing in tears.

"You have no driver's license, so you can't drive, or I'd rent ya'all a car," Sasha said.

"Gabe can drive, cher."

"It's too far for Gabe to drive it alone."

Peck leaned back enough to see Sasha's front pressed against his chest then he'd pulled her close again.

"You could take a train or a bus," Sasha said.

Peck lifted his head. "Can you come, cher? We all go in your car?"

"I have to work," Sasha said. "I have open houses all week."

Their hips locked in a turn, his thigh nudging between her legs.

"Peck, honey?" Sasha asked.

"Uh huh?"

"Is that William?"

Peck didn't answer. He kept dancing.

"I do believe it is," Sasha said. "Oh my."

"I ain't doing that on purpose, cher."

"I'm not complaining."

"Nah, nah."

"He's certainly proud, isn't he?"

"You can't tell Gabe."

"Our secret," Sasha said.

"Hokay, t'anks."

"Just tell me you'll get Gabe up to Newport like you promised."

"I will, cher."

"You'll take care of him and protect him."

"I keep my promises."

Sasha paused and flexed her thighs against Peck's friend.

"I ain't trying to did dat, cher, I swear."

"William has a mind of his own."

"Won't tell?" Peck asked.

"Nothing to tell."

She kissed Peck's ear. "Does your sunburn feel better after my aloe rub?"

"Mighty good, dass for true," Peck said. "I ain't peeling."

"I should do it once more, to be safe," she whispered. "Later."

Peck gave her a look, not certain it was a proposition or a medical opportunity.

The music ended. Sasha stopped motion and held Peck.

"Thanks for the dance," she said. She lowered a hand and gave his buttocks a squeeze.

"Walk close behind me, honey, no one will notice your friend."

They sat with Gabe, toasted the evening, finished the food and talked of jazz trumpeters, blues guitarists, and which ones influenced Elvis most.

"Elvis learned from listening to the poor black street musicians around Beale Street during Jim Crow and the gospel singers in churches around Memphis," Gabe mused. "Roy Orbison inspired his vocal range."

"Gabe, you know more about music than anyone I know, and I grew up in New Orleans," Sasha said.

"Study people, you'll know their music," Gabe said.

"You're a Chicago boy and you've had a busy career, Captain Jordan. When did you have time to study people?"

"My army training was mostly in the south, darlin'. Rode in the back of a lot of buses down here—a person gets to study people sitting in the back of the bus."

Gabe enjoyed a gentle balance of a glass of Port and a bowl of shrimp and rice, and he was still good as late as midnight on the dance floor. At their table he would demonstrate how big band leaders, Count Basie and Glenn Miller, would use a strumming guitar beat for rhythm.

Peck got the last dance while Gabe stepped out for fresh Memphis night air, and to watch the festival called Beale Street, and wait for their horse-and-carriage ride back to Peabody just after midnight.

They agreed the spirits had the better of them, and they would crash tonight and plan over coffee and breakfast in the morning. Sasha brought a glass of water to the bedside and handed it and his pill to Gabe, who was stretched out and looking up at her with a smile.

"Why do I have this feeling?"

"What feeling?" Sasha asked.

"The feeling you're not quite ready to sleep?" Gabe mused.

"You can tell that looking at me?"

"You have a look in your eye."

"How many martinis did I have, Gabe?"

"I didn't count, honey, but too many to lie down without first getting your bearings," Gabe offered.

"I'm not tired," she said.

"Maybe Peck'll volunteer to stay up and give some points of view on the merits of vodka and vermouth."

"Ya think?"

"Well, you did teach the boy how to dance," Gabe said. "It's the least he could do."

Gabe smiled and rested his head on a pillow.

Sasha tucked him in and told him she was thinking of maybe whiling away a bit of time attending to Peck's sunburn again.

Gabe chuckled. "I want to feel your arms around me one last time."

"I'll be back."

"Honey, that would make my day. You both do your whiling and attending, just let this old man wake up with you in the morning."

Sasha knelt on the floor, staring into Gabe's tired eyes. She didn't want to spoil his evening by tearing up. She pulled the blanket under his chin, leaned in and kissed his hand.

"Sleep well, you beautiful old man," she said. "*Bien dormir, tu beau vieil homme.*"

She rose up.

"I'll be back, darlin'," she said. "I promise."

Gabe reached for her hand and gave it a squeeze.

"Just don't give our boy a heart attack. He and I've got a road ahead."

CHAPTER 10

DRAPES WERE DRAWN in Gabe's room, blocking a Mississippi River sunrise, muffling morning sounds in this late-night blues capital. Sasha's curves nestled under the blanket, motionless. Gabe, in his reading glasses, in a lounge chair with desk lamp pulled close, quietly turned pages of the Memphis newspaper. He had already made his first trek to the lobby for a walk around and to retrieve a pot of coffee with cinnamon, a cream pitcher and three cups and saucers. The captain's first cup gave him time to scour the music and arts pages, combing for the big-name talents he had known throughout his heyday. He especially liked finding pictures of them and remembering the times they conjured up. It was his second cup when he turned and folded the paper to the local news page.

"Uh-oh," he murmured to himself. He lifted and rested his reading glasses on his forehead as he folded the page down again into a more manageable size. He held it close to his face, letting his glasses drop from his forehead to over his eyes.

"I'll be," he said quietly.

He read on.

"Why that sonofabitch," Gabe said.

Sasha awakened, lifted her head, pulled a sheet and comforter from her face, eyes squinting in the reflection of the lamp's light.

"What?" Sasha asked.

"Good morning, darlin'," Gabe said.

"What's going on?" she whispered.

"Would you like a coffee and cinnamon?"

"You said, 'That SOB,' Gabe. Who are you talking about?"

Gabe poured, added a bit of cream and walked it over to her. She sat up and lodged pillows behind her, taking the saucer from Gabe. He sat back down and picked up the folded newspaper.

"What time is it?" she asked.

"Have a listen," he said.

"To what?"

"It's got a whole column. Listen to this."

"*Two men were attacked and robbed of their pickup in Hazelton, Mississippi late Thursday evening. Brock Singleton and Winton Makaylah had parked under the Hazelton overpass during a hailstorm that blanketed one-inch hailstones over a twenty-eight-mile area that evening. The two had stepped from their vehicle, leaving it unattended, to ask a trailer-truck driver about road conditions ahead when they reportedly saw the suspect rummaging through the cab of their pickup. A scuffle ensued. The suspect allegedly pulled a knife and stabbed Singleton twice, once in the chest and once in the face. While they were distracted with the wounds and trying to stop the bleeding the thief drove off in their pickup, leaving his own motorcycle behind. The motorcycle's tag had been removed, making it more difficult to trace. Mississippi State Police are asking witnesses to come forward. Singleton has since been moved to an emergency eye clinic in a hospital in Knoxville, where his parents live. Tennessee authorities are cooperating with the Mississippi State Police, permitting access to Singleton for informal questioning in hopes of uncovering clues. The family is offering a reward for information leading to the conviction of this highway bandit fugitive, who is considered armed and dangerous.*'"

"Those were the state trooper cars that passed us," Sasha said.

"Rightly so," Gabe said. "The SOB knocked me on my head and then stabbed this fellow twice."

"Gabe, do you think they're the same two who saved Peck from being hurt?"

"There's something funny about this report," Gabe said.

"Like what?"

"They're leaving a lot of the story out."

"What are they leaving out? It sounds right to me."

"Must be a reason," Gabe said.

"You've lost me, Gabe. What am I missing?"

"Like what about the knife hole in his motorcycle's tire? It wasn't mentioned," Gabe said. "Like what about the scuffle with the bandit after Peck whomped him with his elbows. That wasn't mentioned."

"You're right," Sasha said. "Didn't Peck say they told him they would take care of the guy and for him to go on."

"That all would have come out in questioning," Gabe said.

"So, what are you thinking?"

"Six years in army internal affairs. I'm trained to know when facts are left out."

"You mean left out on purpose?"

"There's a reason."

"Like what – give me a clue?"

"They're fishing for something."

"Hope it's not my Bentley."

"I wouldn't think so," Gabe said.

"Wait. Are they looking for Peck?"

"Probably some unfinished drug or motorcycle gang thing."

"What about what the newspaper says has you thinking?"

"Two men who tell Peck they'd take care of the bum wouldn't be calling 911 in the first place," Gabe said. "And a man who wasn't on the run already—"

"You mean the motorcycle guy?"

"Exactly, if he wasn't on the run, he would stay and fix his tire and not have to steal a truck and take off. I don't care how much he got beat up, he'd lick his wounds, but stay and fix his tire."

"So, you think he was on the run all along?"

"I think so, and I think the law knows it and is fishing for clues," Gabe said.

"What time is it?"

"Eight oh two."

"I have to get up," Sasha said.

"Finish your coffee," Gabe said.

"Our plane is at one. I'll jump in a shower and you order breakfast up."

"Hold on there."

"What?"

"Just a moment, pretty one. Aren't you going to share?"

"Share what?"

"Just when did you crawl in with me last night?"

"Not long after you were fast asleep."

"I'll be," Gabe said. "Last I remember you were on a prowl."

"I was not."

"You were howling at the moon, darlin'."

"You can't ever let me have more than two, well, three martinis," Sasha said.

"You weren't eating anything. Vodka has a way of not wanting to say good night on an empty stomach."

"Oh my God, what a head," Sasha said, standing up.

"What plane? I thought you said Peck can't fly."

"He can't," Sasha said.

"So, what's with the plane?"

"You and I are flying to Providence at one."

"Would you mind filling me in?"

"I'll find you a place to stay. I have a return flight with a nine o'clock landing. Tomorrow I'll put Peck on a Greyhound, with instructions on how and where to find you, and I'll get back to work. He'll be with you in two days, tops. I've got it all worked out."

"What's Providence have to do with it?"

"That's where we're flying to, Providence."

"But I'm heading to Newport," Gabe said.

"Newport is full up, hotel-room wise," Sasha said.

"I never thought of that," Gabe said.

"I'm getting you into a nice place in Providence. You'll have to cab it down to Newport. The long-term stay may even have a shuttle to the festival. It all starts tomorrow. You were in no mood to talk about any of this last night."

"We did do some fine rhythm and blues moves, didn't we?" Gabe asked.

"Best ever for me. You're one incredible dancer."

"So how did our boy take it—your walking in on him last night?"

"Peck?"

"Did he think he'd died and gone to heaven?"

"He enjoyed my stripping down to my panties to put my sweatshirt on, he loved my rubbing aloe on his back, but I think his watching me hold my head over a toilet bowl for an hour, puking—I don't believe it was his idea of a conquest. I splashed my face, brushed my teeth, gargled, came over and crawled in with you," Sasha said.

"So close, yet so far," Gabe mused. "Poor kid."

"I wouldn't have done him."

"You have your surgeon waiting on you back home."

"Least I don't think I would have," Sasha said. "I don't know—never say never."

"It's funny how the older we get the more we stop to think about consequences," Gabe said.

"I suppose we have too many miles on us together in these—can you believe—thirty-six hours?" Sasha asked.

"It's been a wonderful journey, it surely has," Gabe said. "I feel like I've known you both for years."

"Call room service," Sasha said. "I'm going to my room and shower. I'll send Peck over here where he belongs for appearances sake. I'll be fast. Pull the door closed between our rooms."

Gabe picked up the receiver and pointed it at Sasha. "Anything special?"

"Very large V8, Tabasco, but don't add it—send up a bottle, I'll add it—two light scrambled with chopped onion, and side of burned-to-a-crisp bacon," Sasha said. "Toasted English muffin, dry."

Gabe was on the phone with room service when Peck walked into the room, pulling its door to Sasha's room closed behind him.

"Three scrambled, sausage, biscuits, and grits?" Gabe asked.

Peck smiled his approval.

Gabe watched Peck fold his new jeans and T-shirts, setting them on the bureau. He placed the food order, gave his room number and set the phone down. Noticing the newspaper containing the article he had just read to Sasha, he picked it up.

"Peck, there's something I want to show you."

"Yep," Peck said.

"No," Gabe said. "On second thought, I better wait for Sasha. We'll talk over breakfast."

"You hokay, Gabe?"

"I'm fine, my brother. It can wait," Gabe said.

Peck poured a cup of coffee and sat on the bed.

"You were doing some mighty nice turns on that dance floor, young man. I'm here to tell you."

"For true?" Peck asked.

"Why, you were keeping up with the best of them, you truly were. You picked it up fast, son. Isn't it heaven holding on to that woman while they play the blues?"

Peck didn't answer. He nodded and seemed to stare at his memory.

"How's your sunburn doing, son?" Gabe asked with a grin.

Peck's eyes looked at Gabe's and darted away.

"No peeling. Dat stuff works," he said.

Gabe was a gentleman, a respected retired army officer, and a loyal friend. He wouldn't belabor the tease. A knock on the door signaled breakfast had arrived. Gabe opened it and held it for the bellman to roll in and set up the fold-out table.

"I'm setting this for three?" the bellman asked.

"Yes, that's right," Gabe said. "We have a guest coming."

"How far have you traveled to be here?" the bellman asked.

"New Orleans," Gabe said. We came early yesterday."

"Two cities of great music," the bellman said. "Where do you go from here?"

"Heading to Newport for the jazz festival. It's in Rhode Island," Gabe said.

The bellman finished, handed a check folder to Gabe and a pen. Gabe signed it and put a twenty-dollar tip on it.

"Thank you, good sir," the bellman said. "Safe journeys. I hope you've enjoyed your stay at the Peabody. Call us if we can be of service." He nodded his head, first to Peck and then to Gabe, and left.

"Gabe, I thought we ain't supposed to tell nothing," Peck said. "Like weren't we from Chicago or something?"

Gabe put his hand to his mouth thinking, looking over at Peck.

"Fuck it," he grunted. "I'm an old man, I can't be expected to remember everything. We'll be fine."

"I ain't trying to..." Peck started.

"Peck, if they put you on a stage under a spotlight and a hundred people were standing three feet away to guess where you were from, believe me, my brother, it wouldn't be Chicago."

Sasha rapped on the door and Gabe pulled it open. She was dressed like a million bucks in a conservative gray pantsuit, creased pant legs with a white, heavily starched blouse, and crossed ribbon tie. She wore low black heels, and her hair was tied back in a businesslike bun.

"Well, I'll be..." Gabe started.

"Morning gentlemen," she said. "Whatcha' looking at?"

"Why..." Gabe started.

"Us Quarter girls clean up good, now, don't we, hon?"

"I'll say," Gabe said.

"It's an outfit I got yesterday, knowing we had to travel today. I wanted to look nice," Sasha said.

"You outdid yourself, darlin'," Gabe said.

"I have some things for you," Sasha said. She reached in a shopping bag and handed him a pair of aviator sunglasses.

"Put these on."

She pulled out a Bermuda islander straw hat and handed it to Gabe. Following that she pulled out a classic golf shirt with the famous Peabody duck embroidered on the front.

"Now you're ready for a jazz festival, honey," Sasha said.

Gabe celebrated his dashing new image in front of a mirror. He set the hat, sunglasses, and shirt on his bed, pulled up a chair for Sasha to sit and gestured to another for Peck.

As they ate, businesswoman Michelle Lissette picked up her alter ego Sasha's cellphone and brought herself up to date, checking her appointment schedules and flight tickets. A moment or two later, she was reading an incoming text. She looked up at Peck.

"Peck, where were you born?"

"I don't know," Peck said.

"We have to find a birth certificate for you."

"Hanh?"

"We need one so we can get you an ID."

"Peck, in that cattle hauler rig just before we got to Kenner you were talking about a foster nanny, my brother. Do you remember where she was and her name?" Gabe asked.

"Prudhomme," Peck said. "Alayna Prudhomme, 'tween Bayou Sorrel and Choctaw."

"Lily Cup is going to help," Sasha said. "You remember Lily Cup, don't you, Peck?"

Peck grinned.

"She's an attorney."

Sasha winked at him and texted the information to Lily Cup.

"Boudreaux Clemont Finch, right?" Sasha asked.

"*Oui*," Peck said.

"And she's already met William."

Peck put his head down sheepishly with a grin.

"I'll pay any cost," Gabe said.

"It's handled," Sasha said. "Helping a friend. *Aider un ami.*"

"Cho! Co!" Peck said.

He leaned and thank-you kissed Sasha on a cheek.

Sasha held his head to hers and took a selfie, texting it to Lily Cup. She waited for a response, set her phone down and picked up her fork.

"Peck, you're going to have another boring day at the hotel," Sasha said. "I'm taking Gabe to Rhode Island, but I'll be back tonight, and tomorrow I'm putting you on a bus."

"Why can't I go today?"

"Because you won't know how to find him until I find a place for him to stay and come back and tell you," Sasha said. "Tomorrow we put you on a bus and you'll be there overnight, in two days, tops."

Peck looked at Gabe.

"You be good with dat, Grandpa?"

"I'm good with it, my brother," Gabe said. He raised his fist, and Peck raised his, and they fist bumped.

"Peck, give Gabe his wallet. He'll need his license and charge cards. I'll see you have pocket money today and tomorrow on your trip."

"You're a sainted woman," Gabe said. "God will bless you for this."

"He already has," Sasha said. "He put me here to get you two to Newport. Peck, there's something you need to know."

"What I need to know, cher?"

"The man you fought with in Mississippi stabbed another man and stole his pickup truck."

"Dass for true, cher?"

"He's on the loose."

"I only whomped him."

"Point is we know he was heading north," Sasha said.

"Hokay?"

"So he could be coming through here. And they may be looking for witnesses," Gabe said.

"Did he kill a man?" Peck asked.

"Stabbed him in the chest and face," Gabe said. "The man is in the hospital."

"Witness like me?" Peck asked.

"We just have to be careful," Sasha said.

"Not so much the law," Gabe said. "The biker. If he sees you he may remember you can be a witness. He's already stabbed one man."

"So I stay?" Peck asked.

"I'll be back tonight," Sasha said. "Maybe we'll dance before you get on a bus tomorrow."

"Now, remember you two," grunted Gabe with a sly grin.

"What?" Peck asked.

"No more than three martinis," Gabe said.

"Ain't dat a true?" Peck asked.

"No worries there," Sasha said.

"How so?" Gabe asked.

"I have to get back to work tomorrow. I'm dropping Peck on an early bus, and I have a six-hour drive to Vieux Carre."

"Be careful, darlin'," Gabe said. "You're precious cargo."

"What if the stabber sees her Bentley?" Peck asked.

"He's pointed north. Sasha is heading south," Gabe said.

After breakfast Peck moved his clothes into Sasha's room. Sasha tried unsuccessfully to buy Gabe a proper suitcase. He preferred his army duffel with *Cpt. Jordan* stenciled on it. Sasha checked out of the room Gabe was in and extended her room for one more night. Peck settled in for a long day of watching television and eating in the hotel.

CHAPTER 11

"FASTEN YOUR SEATBELT, HANDSOME," Sasha said.

"It's going to be a bumpy night," Gabe chuckled.

"Buckle up," Sasha said.

"I took my butterfly to that movie," Gabe said.

"What movie?"

"All About Eve, 1950. Maybe it was '51. I was at Fort Benning. You're too young for that one."

"I like classics," Sasha said. "I'm here with you, aren't I? Buckle up."

"I got it," Gabe said.

"Want me to put your hat in an overhead?"

"Oh no, ma'am," Gabe said. "I'm enjoying my new sporty look. It's been a while. And first class too—can you just imagine?"

"Gabe, were you ever married?"

"I've been a widower for thirty-six years come September. Woman was the love of my life."

"Was she that butterfly you took to the movie?"

"She was."

"That's so sweet," Sasha said.

"We had a son, Harold. Strapping image of me. He made us proud."

"Had? Is he gone?"

Gabe squeezed her hand. "He's still in my heart. Lost him in Iraq. He was career army, like me. Would have made captain too."

Gabe turned his head, staring out the window. Sasha motioned to a flight attendant for two coffees.

"His platoon was at chow in a big tent, nowhere near any action."

Sasha held his hand.

"They say a mortar hit an ammo truck parked outside. Took them all out."

"I'm so sorry," Sasha said.

"They think it was friendly fire."

An attendant interrupted, handing each a coffee.

"Was your wife a dancer?"

"My, but how she could move," Gabe said.

He rested his head back and stared up at the ceiling of the plane.

"There wasn't a dance we wouldn't try, and believe me, we tried them all. That woman taught this Chicago know-it-all some moves."

"If she was a dancer, I know she had your heart."

"That woman was my everything, from the first day I saw her eyes. She was putting a nickel in the Coca Cola machine."

"A nickel?"

"That's what a Coke cost in those days. We met while I was on a transfer leave back to the states from Korea. First thing we did when we looked in each other's eyes was put a quarter in a jukebox at the non comm Officers Club and dance."

"Non comm? You were a Captain, weren't you?"

"Not then I wasn't. My, but how my butterfly could dance."

He turned his head and looked at Sasha.

"Without saying a word to each other, we danced."

"You can say her name, Gabe."

"Fort Dix, it was."

"You said Fort Benning."

"I did?"

"It doesn't matter, Gabe. Try to rest."

"I'm losing it. The more time that passes, the more I lose," Gabe whispered to himself.

"She'll always be with you if you say her name, Gabe."

"It was Fort Dix. We danced and caught a train into Harlem."

Gabe's eyes glazed in thought.

"I mean it," Sasha said. "It's good luck to mention a loved one's name, Gabe. She'll always be with you, and she'll be with you when...well, you know."

"Beverly," Gabe said.

"Beverly, a sweet name."

"I called her Butterfly."

He turned his head and looked out the window.

"Beverly sounds perfect for you," Sasha said, handing Gabe a napkin.

Gabe looked back at Sasha.

"How about you, Michelle Lissette? Any past you want to share?"

"I've never been married. Been engaged twice, but something in me won't let a man rule my roost. I like making my own money and feeling independent. I always seem to run them off somehow."

"You and Lily Cup go to Charlie's a lot, do ya?"

"I wouldn't say a lot. Maybe when the moon is full, or we just get in a mood to be held. We'll doll up as sexy as we can and check them out as they walk in the door. Sometimes we get lucky."

"Does your surgeon man condone this extracurricular— sometimes lucky?"

"Well, there's partying, and there's cheating. By lucky I meant that we find a good jazz dancer. I don't cheat."

"The red gown you wore when we met was striking. It left little to the imagination but certainly stirred my libido."

"Wearing Chanel and Givenchy is half the fun. A sensual dance in them to the best jazz on Frenchman Street is the other half. Our fun may get risqué on a dance floor, but mostly we go home alone. Charlie walks us home."

"So, you two had an eye on us when we walked in?" Gabe asked.

"Oh yes," Sasha said. "Sized you up the second you came in."

"And me an old man, pray tell how?"

"As soon as you stepped in, I knew it just watching you through the mirror behind the bar."

"How'd you know I was a dancer?" Gabe asked.

"When you sat by the band. That's how. I saw you point at a table and tell Peck to go save it while you went to the bathroom."

"How about Peck? Any first impressions of him?"

"Lily Cup poked me with an elbow when Peck walked in with you. She was speculating if Peck was, well, as, shall we say, 'packaged' as he was sunburned and good looking, like boys his age."

An attendant retrieved their coffee cups, and the plane landed in Charlotte, giving them time to walk the terminal to a gate for the connecting flight to Providence. This time Gabe let Sasha put his hat in an overhead and leaned back in his seat and snoozed. Sasha read magazines. In Providence, Sasha found the Courtyard Hotel and computed their long stay rate per week. Gabe left his card number to guarantee it and put his duffel in his room before taking an elevator down to the lobby, where Sasha was gathering information leaflets about the city and the festival.

"You hungry?' she asked.

"I am."

"Let's get something to eat," Sasha said. "We can talk while we eat."

Sasha held Gabe's arm as he led her from the hotel two blocks to the Woonasquatucket River. The river was narrow and had iron baskets resting on concrete pilings lined maybe thirty yards apart down the center of the river.

"Have you ever been here?" Gabe asked.

"I haven't."

"At night, they'll stack those iron baskets with firewood and light them. They call them *WaterFire.* It's quite a sight," Gabe said.

"I bet it's beautiful," Sasha said. "Romantic."

"Let's go to Canal Walk." He pointed. "It's just over there. We'll get a hot dog or something from one of the vendors."

They walked to the Canal Walk crossing.

"Which way are we headed?" Sasha asked.

"Let's see," Gabe said. "If that's Point Street Bridge—it should be over there. Yes, there it is, this way. It's not far."

The two walked, taking in the sights of a city's downtown. They bought food from two carts and carried it to the Point Street River overpass before sitting down on a bench.

"He's still here, I can tell," Gabe said.

"Who's still here?"

"See across the river, up there under the bridge?"

"Yes, but I don't see anyone."

"You can tell where he stands and leans on the wall to play," Gabe said. "The wall's worn smooth where he leans back on it."

"Who?" Sasha asked.

She squeezed a mustard packet onto her hotdog.

"He wails the prettiest alto sax—prettiest I've heard north of Memphis," Gabe said.

"Point Street Bridge," Sasha said. "Learn something new every day."

"Great sax," Gabe said.

"How can one man make a smooth mark on the wall?"

"His leather jacket," Gabe said. "He leans back in his leather jacket, I don't know. Over the years— he's still here, I can tell."

"I believe you."

"It'll be after dark."

"Be careful walking alone after dark," Sasha said.

"I promise, darlin'," Gabe said.

"Maybe leave your valuables in your room and put on the *Do Not Disturb*," Sasha said. "Always keep your driver's license with you. Maybe a color copy of it and leave the original in your room."

"Seems as the time floats by, the more vulnerable an ole man gets," Gabe said.

Sasha finished her food and scanned her touchscreen phone while Gabe ate some fries.

"Okay, Gabe, according to this, preliminary entertainment and some sideshows for the Jazz Festival start tomorrow. I'll get you a pass that'll cover everything."

Gabe fumbled in his pocket and pulled out a charge card. "Use this." He handed it to Sasha.

"Weather's good," Gabe said. "Lucky—let's hope it holds the week."

Sasha concluded a ticket purchase transaction in her phone.

"Okay, you're set. We have festival passes for you and Peck," Sasha said. "We'll print them out at the hotel. Newport is thirty miles away."

"There'll be buses, I'm sure," Gabe said.

"Gabe, instead of the hassle of trying to find shuttles, take Uber. We'll open an account on one of your cards. You call a special number and order a car and tell them where you're going. They pick you up and it's all paid when you arrive. You don't have to sign. It'll have fare and tip already included, and you don't have to carry cards or a lot of cash."

"You've thought of everything, baby," Gabe said. "I can't thank you enough."

Sasha looked deeply into Gabe's eyes.

"That's just it," she said. "I'm trying *not* to think of everything."

"Live every day until we die," Gabe said. "It's the best we can hope for, darlin'."

As they walked to the hotel listening to city sounds, Sasha held back tears and fumbled through her purse. She lifted out a fifty, folded it and pressed it into Gabe's palm.

"Give this to your friend," Sasha said.

"My friend?"

"Your alto sax friend under the bridge," Sasha said. "Have him play 'When Sunny Gets Blue' for me."

Gabe clutched her hand and the fifty, wrapped an arm around her shoulders. They stopped in front of his hotel. She kissed his cheek, first on one side, then the other. She flagged a waiting cab. She held Gabe, head resting on his chest, neither saying a word. She took his hand and goodbye kissed it twice.

"I've got to go," she said. "I'll call your room tomorrow and tell you when Peck's coming in on the bus. If you don't answer the phone, I'll leave a message or keep calling until you do. Maybe you could meet him at the bus station. Don't forget to call Uber."

Sasha handed Gabe business cards with her contact information.

"Best I meet him," Gabe said. "The city could overwhelm the boy."

"I'll get him a couple of shirts at an airport here or in Memphis when I land," Sasha said. "See he looks nice when you take him to the festival. Don't let him wear a T-shirt."

Gabe smiled. "You're such a momma hen."

"Have you got enough medicine?"

Gabe looked at her eyes. He kissed her hand and let it go.

"Until we meet again, my love," Sasha said. *"Jusqu'au revoir, mon amour."*

"I'll wait while the music plays," Gabe said.

Sasha landed in Memphis at 8:45. A ride to the Peabody gave her time to answer emails, buy Peck's bus ticket to Providence, and text Lily Cup she would be on her way to New Orleans early in the morning as Peck's bus departed at 4:30 a.m. She thanked the driver, stepped out and tipped a bellman for pulling a hotel door for her, welcoming her back.

"What did you do all day?" Sasha asked.

"I walked and learned some of Memphis purdy good," Peck said.

"I thought you were going to stay in and not risk being seen by that motorcycle creep."

"Nah, nah."

"You promised."

"Sides, I had to get me a bag to hold stuff."

Peck held up a new canvas sport duffel.

"That's a nice bag for your things."

Peck picked up a large spool of black fishing line.

"Got me this too," Peck said.

"What on earth for?"

"Two-hundred-pound line, dass what for."

"Why did you buy that?"

"Man gave it to me free for buying a duffel bag."

Having slept on her flight Sasha was alert, but muscle weary from sitting. She handed Peck a shopping bag with two new shirts, set her purse on a bed table and stretched her arms, suppressing a yawn.

"Put these in your bag, Peck."

"Is Gabe hokay?" Peck asked.

"He's fine. He's in a nice hotel, he knows how to get to the festival, and he has a ticket for you."

"A ticket?"

"A pass to the jazz festival and the side shows. You need one to get in."

"I miss ole captain already," Peck said.

"Your bus is at 4:30 in the morning."

"Ah...hokay."

"You feel like dancing tonight?"

Peck looked at her eyes, remembering last night.

"Ribs," he said, rolling his eyes from her into the bag with shirts.

Sasha removed her jacket, her blouse, her shoes and slacks, and laid them on the bed. She unsnapped her flesh-colored bra and tossed it on the pile. She walked toward the bathroom. Peck looked up from the bag she had handed him. She caught his eye and turned.

"I'm jumping in the shower."

"I'll sit here, cher."

"We'll go in half an hour or so. Look nice," she said.

Peck held up one of his new shirts.

"Perfect, sweetie. Be a dear and hang up my suit and blouse?"

Peck picked up garments as the bathroom door closed behind her.

In time, Sasha came out in the black jumper she had worn the night before. She stepped into her shoes next to the bed.

"Toss me the panties on the bureau, baby," she said. "The red ones."

Peck obliged and watched her bend to step into the panties and pull them up to her waist.

BB King's was crowded with a blend of locals and tourists. Blues wailed slow from an inviting electric guitar solo. Sasha handed the maître'd a twenty to find seats. Two opened, if they didn't mind sharing a table on the dance floor. Sasha took Peck by the hand and led him to their table, pulling out a chair for him. The couple sharing were young, early twenty-something newlyweds, enjoying ribs. Holding a neck of a beer bottle in one hand and a rib in another, the groom was in cargo shorts and a golf shirt and a hand-molded straw hat he bought from a street vendor on his way in; she was holding his arm with her arm wrapped through his and holding a rib in her hands like an ear of corn. She was wearing jean cutoffs and a T-shirt.

Sasha said "hey" to both and then leaned toward Peck.

"I'm not drinking tonight. I have a long drive tomorrow."

"Me too, then," Peck said.

"How about a Virgin Mary?"

"What's dat?"

"V8 with Tabasco and a stalk of celery," Sasha said. "It's hot."

"Hokay," Peck said.

Sasha ordered the drinks and a rack of ribs to share. As the waitress walked away, she leaned, gave Peck a kiss on the ear.

"Let's dance."

She held Peck tight, her arms over his shoulders, face resting on his neck; his arms around her waist, hand spread and holding her close. Peck could feel her tears on his neck and back as they moved slowly from one blues guitar solo to the next. Her breasts heaved, her stomach contracted as she sobbed quietly to herself, thinking no doubt of Gabriel, a friend she was about to lose forever. They danced four sets and returned to the table. The groom's stare at Sasha from across the table was met with a deadly stare from his bride and a knuckle into his ribs. He picked up his long neck, put it to his lips and gave Sasha a come-on smile.

Peck picked a rib and gnawed. Sasha looked away, lifted her drink with her left hand and sipped. With her right hand, she took a cloth napkin and reached under the table to rest it on Peck's lap. She slid her palm over Peck's thigh, unintentionally nudging a waking William. Peck's neck bolted. Sasha smiled and leaned into his ear.

"Thanks for being Gabe's friend," she said.

"Ol' Gabe is my frien' now, cher," Peck said. "Proud to even knowed the man."

Sasha gave his thigh a quick nail scratch and pulled her hand away. She picked up a rib and waited for another set to start.

"Honey, if you can't read, how do you remember things you have to remember?"

"I just remember is all."

"So, if I told you Gabe was at a Courtyard hotel downtown, you could remember?"

"Can you write it for me?" Peck asked.

"I thought you couldn't read."

"I can't, but if you write it I show it to folks and find it dat-a-way."

Sasha leaned in, her eyes on the groom still copping looks at her chest. She kissed Peck on the ear as though she was appreciative of his simple, innate thought process.

"Let's dance," she said.

They moved to sad wails of the guitar. Peck held her close. Her sobbing stopped but her grip around his neck and head gave him a feeling she sensed a desperation of emptiness that comes over caring people at times.

"I have a phone for you in the hotel."

"Hanh?"

"It's prepaid. I put three hundred dollars on it. You'll have to get Gabe to show you how it works."

"Yes'm, but why, cher?" Peck asked.

"I want you to call me if anything happens."

"Ah, *oui.*"

"Understand?"

"Yes'm," Peck said.

"You be sure to call me right away, if anything at all happens," Sasha said.

Her face buried against Peck's neck and the contractions of her stomach against his body again signaled quiet sobs. It was after midnight when Sasha's awareness of Peck's William on her inner thigh distracted her as the electric guitar begged a high libretto, as if it were a tear falling into a wailing climax.

The set ended with them motionless in embrace. Thinking only of herself, this emotionally drained Sasha placed her hands around Peck's waist, lowered them to his butt cheeks, firmly pulling him to her flexed thighs. Her eyes opened as she woke from loneliness. She clung blindly to Peck's arm as he led them back to the table. The groom had gone to the men's room, and the bride was stirring her daiquiri with a straw. Sasha flagged a waitress for a check and leaned in over the table.

"Honey," she said, "all guys are lookers."

"He's always doing it," the bride said.

"When were you married?"

"Yesterday. We got married in Little Rock."

"He's a lucky man," Sasha said.

"It's so embarrassing. I know he loves me."

"How long have you known him?" Sasha asked.

"Since fourth grade," the bride said.

"Do you love him?"

"More than anything, I love that man."

"Then don't let it bother you, honey—"

"I know he loves me."

"Next time you catch him looking, just point at a dude in the room and whisper in hubby's ear you wonder how big the guy's dick is."

The bride snickered.

"Point at a real looker... and ask your guy how to tell a dick size."

The bride's eyes squinting as she lifted her hand and held delicate fingers over her mouth.

"He'd kill me."

"He won't kill you, honey. Tell him now he knows how it feels when he gawks. He'll learn to behave."

She paid the check, winked at the bride, now with a grin on her face, took Peck by the hand outside and flagged a carriage to Peabody.

Under the lamp glow Sasha set the alarm on her phone for 3:30 a.m. and set it on the bedside table. She stripped from her jump suit, pulled her panties down, leaving them on the floor next to the bed, and crawled under a comforter and top sheet as Peck came out of the bathroom in briefs and edged around the bed.

"What time did I got to be on my bus?"

"I'll get you there by four," Sasha said.

"T'anks, cher."

"I'll come back here and sleep before I check out and drive to New Orleans."

"Hokay, good."

On the other side of her bed he started to pull a blanket.

"Where do you think you're going?"

"Oh?" Peck asked. "Maybe on the floor then, maybe?"

Sasha smiled, reached and pulled the sheet up, inviting him in.

"If I'm naked, you have to be naked," Sasha said. *"Si je suis nu, tu dois être aussi."*

Peck snorted a nervous guffaw and started to crawl in.

"Mais non, mais non," Sasha said. Still with a raised sheet in her hand, she pointed at his underwear.

Peck crawled in, kneed the sheet up and bounced as he pulled his underwear down and threw it over to the bureau.

Sasha turned the light off. The room became still and quiet for the longest time. There was no motion on the bed, as neither had turned about, or so much as pulled on the sheets or comforter for positioning.

"Peck?"

"Oui?"

"You're a good dancer."

"Merci, cher."

"You'd look dashing in white tie, tails—and tuxedo."

Peck didn't respond.

"There's a Mid-Winter Cotillion in N'Orleans."

Peck didn't respond.

"Would you be Lily Cup's date to the Cotillion?"

"Hanh?"

"It's the grandest of balls in N'Orleans, Peck. I'm a chaperone. I'll be in Givenchy. Lily Cup is in my court and would look dazzling in her diamonds with you on her arm in white tie and tails."

"Maybe, cher."

Quiet uncertainty filled the darkness—like times when you feel like you're the only one awake.

"Peck?"

"Oui?"

"You have a girlfriend?"

Peck's head turning toward Sasha made sounds of rustled starched pillow linen.

"Nah, nah."

"No girlfriend?"

"Nobody special," Peck whispered.

"Have you ever had one?" Sasha asked.

"Hanh?"

"You know, a real love, have you ever—?"

"You sad for Gabe, cher?"

"I won't get to dance with him again," Sasha said.

"You dance good with him, cher."

"I'm so sad."

"Dreams can be good," Peck said.

"You mean memories?"

"*Oui.*"

"Memories are good."

"I bet he dreams of you."

"You do?"

"He dreams of you dancin' with him, cher."

"Do you dream of a girl?" Sasha asked.

"I know a girl, cher."

"You do? Where is she?"

"Down in Anse La Butte," Peck said.

"Does she love you?"

"She no boo, cher."

"Do you love her?"

There was a silent pause.

"Do you do it?" Sasha asked.

Peck leaned his head back and grinned into his pillow, like he had been caught with his hand in a cookie jar.

"Do you?"

"She ain't no boo, but we do it good, I'll say."

"Is she pretty?"

"Yes'm, surely, she is."

"Who's sexier? Me, Lily Cup, or your lady boo? Be honest."

Peck's warm hand gently touched Sasha's firm breast in the dark. It searched about slowly, found a nipple and gently played with it.

Sasha placed her hand on the back of Peck's hand and lightly followed it as it explored the curves of her breast, nipple, and soon the other breast and nipple.

"You like my girls, Peck?"

In the dark, his tongue found her breast, and his warm lips rested on her aroused nipple and suckled. Sasha placed the back of a hand over her mouth and closed her eyes. She was patient with his tenderness.

"We'd better not, Peck," Sasha whispered.

Peck licked her breast around her nipple.

"We're both sad and vulnerable," she said.

Pecked sucked.

"I wonder if Gabe is asleep."

Peck lifted his head slightly but kept his hand gently fondling and kneading her breast in a silence of not knowing what to say.

"Do you love her?"

"Her man is on a rig," Peck said.

"She's married?"

"Not married, but she have a man on a rig, though, t'ree weeks out, two weeks back," Peck said.

"So, William is there to lend a hand, is he?"

"Can I touch you down there, cher?" Peck asked.

"Why, Peck," Sasha said.

"Can I?"

"What are you up to?"

Peck's hand made its way down a warm, smooth stomach, cupping Sasha's own.

"You have gentle hands," Sasha said.

Peck didn't speak. As he found her pearl, he favored it gently with soft touches of his finger until her thighs lifted slightly to his hand, her head pressing her pillow. He slowly, patiently circled her pearl with his finger, rolling it between two as he would a small, wine-soaked raisin.

"We'd better stop, Peck," Sasha whimpered.

"*Faut-il aider vous oubliez, jolie dame?*" Peck asked. ("Does it help you forget, pretty lady?")

"It helps," Sasha said. "*Il aide.*"

Peck's fingers patiently circled her pearl in the silence, waiting for the sounds he would recognize. It was when Sasha's thighs lifted firmly, her buttocks flexing again and again in twerks, rising off the mattress into Peck's hand, her fingers gripping and pulling sides of the pillow around her face. She made no sound. She didn't have to. Her buttocks and thighs tightened, quivered a peak, then released, and sank deep and motionless into the warm mattress. Peck moved his hand and rolled on his back and looked off into the darkness.

It was quiet again.

"What's her name?"

"Elizabeth."

"She speaks French, doesn't she?"

"*Oui.*"

"I could tell."

"How, cher?"

"Your French is good."

"I knowed her a long time."

A quiet filled the room again. Perhaps anxiety, contemplating what next.

"Let's get some sleep," Sasha said.

"Yes'm," Peck said.

Sasha rolled toward Peck, lifting her leg over his thigh, pushing past William and saddling his hip, resting her leg on his stomach. She could feel a throbbing on the base of her thigh.

"Elizabeth is lucky to have you and William on lonely nights," Sasha whispered.

Peck didn't speak.

"Night," she said.

"Good night, cher."

Sasha leaned and softly kissed Peck's ear, resting her head on his pillow.

"Thank you," she whispered.

Peck didn't respond. When Sasha was asleep, he turned his head toward her face. He could feel cold teardrops on the pillow. He knew he owed it to her friendship and to Gabe's to just sleep.

CHAPTER 12

LIKE A ROBOT, THE BENTLEY'S GPS POINTED THE WAY on an early morning navigation from the Peabody to the Greyhound terminal. Between Sasha and Peck, no mention was made of the dalliance. Tears on a pillow told her story. Sasha parked, and they went inside a brightly lit bus terminal.

"You want a breakfast sandwich?" Sasha asked. "We have time before they board your bus."

"You don' have to wait," Peck said. "You be tired. Go get some sleep."

"Let's sit over there and have a coffee while we wait," Sasha said.

Sasha went to a counter and retrieved two coffees, a sausage and egg bagel for Peck, and a toasted everything bagel for herself.

"Your bus ride is thirty-six hours. It's a day and a half."

Peck looked up from his sandwich.

"You should be pulling into Providence sometime in the afternoon day after tomorrow."

"Hokay," Peck said.

Sasha lifted an envelope and package from her handbag.

"I bought you a Discovery pass for the bus."

"Cher, you don't have to be buying—"

"I didn't buy it. Gabe bought it with his card."

"Ah."

"It's good for thirty days, so hang on to it. And here are some twenties in this envelope—don't open it here. Put it in your pocket. It's enough to buy food along the way and pay cab fare or emergency money if you need it when you get there,"

Sasha said. "Gabe will meet your bus in Providence, but just in case."

"T'anks cher. What's a discovery pass?"

"It's a ticket that will get you on any Greyhound and take you anywhere for thirty days from today. You can use it to come back to New Orleans. It's a pass to get on any bus."

"Ga-lee," Peck said.

"Peck, this is your new phone. This is from me. It's prepaid. Have Gabe or someone teach you how to use it."

"Gabe don have no cellphone, cher."

"Then ask someone else. They'll show you. Or I'll show you back in New Orleans. Put it in your bag."

"T'anks, cher."

"I wrote down Gabe's hotel, phone number, and address in case you need it. And here's my business card. Put it in your pocket and don't lose it. If you ever need to find me no matter what, ask someone to help you use your phone to call or text me. Use a charger cord and plug it in on the bus so it keeps charged."

"Peck's gonna miss you," Peck said.

"Remember the motorcycle creep?" Sasha asked.

"*Oui*," Peck said.

"I'm worried he's still on the loose," Sasha said.

"I know."

"You be careful, Peck."

"I will."

Public-address announcements echoed as they called the bus gate for boarding. Sasha walked Peck to the bus. She gave him a long last hug and a kiss on his cheek.

"Think Peck can maybe read sometime?"

"Soon," Sasha said. "Bye, baby. Give Gabe a hug for me. Take good care of him. I'll set up a tutor when I get back to the Quarter."

Peck boarded, stepping up and in cautiously, studying faces on both sides of the aisle—some asleep, some reading, some looking on their iPad screens, some looking back at him. He took an empty seat toward the rear by a window behind two sleeping girls wearing torn jean cutoffs and the same T-shirts (Princeton University). He looked out and saw Sasha waving.

She couldn't see through the dark-tinted windows, but she waved lovingly at her new friend. As the bus's engine roared to a start, it backed into the night and drove away with a sweeping curve onto an empty city street. Sasha turned and walked to her car.

Peck had no sense of how long he had slept when he woke to motions of the bus comfortably making its way down the interstate. The sun was up and well off the ground. He raised his head and sat tall, looking over the rows of heads in front of him. He watched the road ahead with a Walmart truck far off in the distance.

"Good morning," a fellow sitting next to him said. He was a hefty, broad-shouldered young black man. He had a gentle smile and a conservative haircut. He sat tall, with earphones in both ears. His collar was starched and pressed, and a cellphone rested on his thigh.

Peck rubbed his eyes. "Where we are?" he asked.

"We'll be in Nashville soon," the young man said. "Where're you headed?"

"I'm going to Providence," Peck said. "A long way up a bayou. How 'bout you?"

"I'm headed to Parris Island," the young man said.

"Paris?"

"It's in South Carolina," the young man said.

"Ahh."

"I've joined up with the marines. Boot camp is in Parris Island."

"Coo-Wee, you're a marine?" Peck asked. "How long you in for?"

"I was supposed to go to San Diego, but I'm going to Parris Island."

"Hanh?"

"Parris Island is boot camp if you live east of the Mississippi," the marine said.

"Hokay."

"I live in West Memphis, and I was supposed to go to San Diego."

Peck looked at the young man, a bit confused.

"The recruiter in Memphis said they won't look close at the paperwork and think it being West Memphis I lived in— they'll think it's in Tennessee like Memphis is, so I'm going to Parris Island."

"West Memphis? I don't get—"

"West Memphis is in Arkansas."

"Hokay?"

"That's west of the Mississippi. If you live west of the Mississippi marines are supposed to be going to San Diego for basic, but I'm going to Parris Island."

He stopped trying to justify his traveling to Parris Island and picked up a portfolio from the floor filled with orders and printed materials regarding his marine training. He pulled a glossy picture of a marine in full formal dress uniform, holding a sword. He admired it and held it out for Peck to see.

"They don't give me this. They call them dress blues. I have to pay for my dress blues," the marine said.

"Nice uniform," Peck said.

"My daddy signed me in, and they're giving the checks to him to keep for me. They're paying for all my college if I keep staying in."

"When did you get on?" Peck asked.

"The bus?"

"Yeah."

"I got on the same time you did, in Memphis. I sat in front, but I had to go to the bathroom and came back and sat here. S'okay with you, I sit here?"

"Nah, nah. It's all good," Peck said.

"Girl next to me up front keeps reading a Bible. I don't have nothing against Bible reading, but it's a distraction with me trying to be online reading about Parris Island.

Peck pointed to the marine's phone.

"I got me one of them," Peck said.

"An iPhone?"

"A new one. My frien' going to teached me how to use it."

"How many megapixels does your camera have?" the marine asked.

Peck sat there stymied, as if he was wondering what the marine was asking and then he looked out the window, then back at the marine's iPhone resting on his knee.

"She goes to Baylor," the marine said.

"Bible girl?" Peck asked.

"She told me her father is a Baptist minister."

"Ah, poor *peeshwank*," Peck said.

"Her school let out two months ago. None of my business why she's only coming home now."

"Long time?" Peck asked.

The marine held up both hands, fingers outstretched.

"Ten weeks, that's a long time not to be coming home."

"Ah, *oui*. Dass for true," Peck said.

"I didn't ask," the marine said. "None of my business."

"Maybe dat be why she's reading a Bible," Peck snorted. "She's going home to papa."

They both watched the pine trees and a cliff through windows for a mile or so around a hillside curve.

"A marine life is a good life," the young man said. "Free room and board, cash bonuses, world travel."

"What's room and board, frien?"

"Bed and food is free."

"Good on you, man," Peck said.

"They pay for my uniforms too, but not the dress blues."

"Your family, they'd be proud in Memphis for you."

"West Memphis. It's in Arkansas."

"They'd be proud," Peck said.

"I wrestled in high school."

"You wrestle? Dass for true?"

"Won county," the marine said. "Hope I can wrestle in the marines. You ever wrestle?"

"Nah, nah, never did dat," Peck said. "I seed a man wrestle a gator one time—Bayou Cane, but jus' for show. He won him fifty dollar."

"You ever wrestled an alligator?"

"Nah, nah, I stay clear," Peck said. "I dive a turtle, jump a snake, but stay clear of gator shore t'ing."

"Where're you from?" the marine asked. "Mind me asking?"

"Raised up near Petit Anse Bayou," Peck said.

"I don't know that."

"I have a bed in Carencro."

"Is that near Memphis, where you got on?

"Lewisana."

"You really eat snake?" the marine asked.

"Bait, I catch 'em for bait—snakes," Peck said. "Trotline, I hook half a snake on my snood lines."

"Snakes make good bait for fish, do they?"

"They too small for gators to waste they time on—just right for turtles. Mostly want bluegill sunfish or bass. They fry best."

"My grandmother makes turtle soup," the marine said. "She lives in Forrest City."

"Ah, *soupe à la tortue*," Peck said.

"How old are you?" the marine asked.

"Twenty-five, I t'ink," Peck said.

"Nineteen," the young man said.

"You a big'un," Peck said.

"You like to fish?" the marine asked.

"I did it purdy good," Peck said. "I guess I like it."

"Some friends and I tried the Mississippi a few times. We didn't have any luck, so we gave up."

"Mississippi too fast," Peck said. "Bayou best—lake's good, if you have to eat."

The two stared over heads through the front window of the bus, the marine looking for road signs, Peck looking for the angle and pitch of the sun, so he could tell the time. They sat for nineteen miles without saying a word.

"Here's my stop."

"Hanh?"

"See the sign? Westel Road, eleven miles ahead."

"Dass where you going, marine?" Peck asked.

"No, it's where I board a marine bus with other recruits. It'll take us in."

"Ah," Peck said.

"I have some time before we stop, I can show you how to use your phone if you want. I'm good at teaching."

"T'ank ya, no, man," Peck said. "T'anks though."

The bus slowed down to exit on Westel Road. There were three chartered buses filled with marine recruits waiting. The marine stood and retrieved his suitcase and a paper sack from the overhead. He reached his hand out.

"I'm Eddie," he said.

Peck shook his hand.

"Peck," Peck said. "Good to meet ya, Eddie."

The marine handed Peck his paper sack.

"There're two sandwiches in this and a pear," he said. "Take it in case you get hungry. My mom made them. She's a good cook."

"T'anks frien'," Peck said, accepting the sack.

"I don't know what they are, but they'll be good. She's a good cook. She loads them up."

Peck smiled a thank you.

"Good luck on your trip, Peck," the marine said. "I hope you catch a lot of fish."

Peck smiled.

"I'll write your name down when I do my diary tonight," the marine said.

My name is Boudreaux Clemont Finch," Peck said.

The marine lifted his phone, spelled out Peck's formal name with his lips and texted it to himself.

"So, when I write my book, I'll remember your names— Peck—as the first person I met on the first day of my life's journey. I'll get the name right."

"How 'bout Bible lady?" Peck asked.

"Oh yeah, her," the marine said. "I don't know her name, so she doesn't count."

He offered a military salute to Peck, turned and made his way down to the front and off the bus. Peck watched his new friend walking over and being welcomed by a marine drill sergeant in uniform. The sergeant checked his name off on a clipboard list and motioned which bus he was to board. Peck's bus door closed, and its engine revved, moving back onto the pavement, rolling onto an entry to the interstate and back up to speed.

Peck looked in the sack, smelled it approvingly, rolled its top closed and set it on the seat next to him. He pulled his cellphone from his pocket to have a look when a young girl with shoulder-length cinnamon hair and freckles made her way from the front of the bus. She looked about for the bathroom door and stepped up to the last row of seats, grabbed a seatback for balance. The girl wore no makeup, conservative Bermuda shorts and Nike running shoes. She was pretty. There was an innocence about the sparkle in her eyes. She pointed at the empty seats across the aisle from him. Peck couldn't read her T-shirt. It said "Baylor Bears Sic 'Em."

She held her fingers over her mouth to mask her teeth braces.

"Sir, would you watch my bags if I put them over there?" she asked. "I have to use the bathroom."

"I'll watch 'em, cher—dey be good."

"Thank you."

"You pass a good time," Peck said.

Bemused by his Cajun patois, she raised her brows in wonder. "You don't mind?" she asked.

"*Pouponer*," Peck said, motioning her to the bathroom. ("Powder your nose.")

She offered Peck a grinning smile, her teeth lined with thin braces and wires. She studied his eyes, his arms, and the paper sack on the seat next to him as she moved toward the bathroom. She paused, stepped back and leaned her head over the seatback, pointing bashfully at the seat with his paper sack.

"Could you save me this seat, maybe?" she asked.

"The seat is yours," Peck said. "*Le siège est à vous.*"

The girl beamed. "I'll only be a sec," she said. "Thank you so much."

Peck was holding his lunch sack and contemplating opening it when the girl came back. She had taken time to apply makeup, lip rouge and powder. Her cinnamon hair brushed. She had delightful, twinkly eyes. Peck stood and moved to the window seat, offering her the aisle seat across from her bags. She smiled and sat next to Peck.

"Oh," Peck said, looking over at her. "Who is dis lovely woman they send out of the *pot d'chambre*? What they did with my frien' I saving dis seat for?"

"You silly," the girl said. "I just wanted to look nice."

"Oh, you look more than nice, cher. Ooo la la."

The girl extended her hand.

"My name is Millie," she said.

Peck wasn't certain what to do so he took her hand and shook it.

"This is where you tell me your name," Millie said.

"Ah, *oui*. People call me Peck." He shook her hand.

"Is Peck your real name or a nickname?" Millie asked.

"Name's Boudreaux Clemont Finch," Peck said. "They call me Peck for talking so much. You call me Peck, cher."

"I don't know. Boudreaux is such a forceful sounding name," Millie said. "But I like Peck. I'm good with Peck...So—hi, Peck."

Peck held up his paper sack.

"You hungry?" Peck asked.

Millie looked at Peck's eyes, decided she liked him and could be his guest for a snack.

"I'm starved," Millie said. "I slept through the break stops in Dallas and Memphis. I haven't eaten since Waco, and that was last night."

Peck pulled a sandwich in a Ziploc bag and held it for Millie to take.

"Hold on," Millie said. "I have water."

She stood and reached across the aisle for a cloth shopping bag next to her suitcase on the seat. She retrieved it and sat down with the shopping bag in her lap.

"I know, I know—I must look like a bag lady," Millie said. "But I have water in here somewhere, I promise."

She lifted another, smaller cloth bag from the outer bag, handing the straps to Peck.

"Can you put this on the floor between us, please?" Millie asked.

"Yes'm," Peck said, taking the bag and placing it on the floor.

"Be gentle, it's my Charlie," Millie said.

"Charlie?" Peck asked.

She lifted a black Bible from a bag and handed it to Peck.

"Hold this. It's in here somewhere," Millie said.

Peck held the Bible.

"Here we are," Millie said, uncovering her packet of water bottles. "Told'ja I had water."

She took the Bible back and handed two bottles for Peck to hold while she put the shopping bag back on the seat across the aisle.

"*Qui est* Charlie?" Peck asked.

"Oh, you'll only laugh," Millie said.

"Hanh?"

"My boyfriend always picked on me about Charlie. He isn't my boyfriend anymore. Anyway you'll only laugh and think I'm silly."

Millie pulled half of the tuna fish and tomato sandwich from the sandwich bag and bit into it, holding a hand up covering her mouth as she chewed.

"Peck won't laugh," Peck said.

Millie looked into Peck's eyes with a twinkle.

"I promise, cher. You can tell Peck."

"I get off at Kingston," Millie said. "Help me watch for signs. I can't get off with makeup on. Daddy would freak, so I need to watch for signs so I have time to take it off."

Peck spared her the fact that he couldn't read road signs.

"He strict, your papa?" Peck asked.

"He's a Baptist minister in Kingston," Millie said.

"Ah, *oui*. Is that—?"

"He would kill me. He thinks I'm still a virgin. Watch for the Kingston signs."

"Charlie?" Peck asked.

"Oh," Millie said.

"Charlie," Peck said.

"But only if you promise not to laugh or make fun of me."

"Oh, cher," Peck said. "Never would I—"

Millie turned toward Peck. She stared into his eyes for confirmation. She held her little finger out, hooked around.

"Pinky swear," she said. "Pinky swear on your life you won't laugh."

Peck locked little fingers with her.

"Charlie," he said.

Millie reached between their legs and pulled a doll from the bag on the floor. It was a doll of a baby boy, life size and weight and dressed in pajamas. Millie handed her sandwich to Peck to hold, and she cradled the baby in her arms.

"This is my Charlie," Millie said. "I've had him since I was three. He goes everywhere with me."

"Charlie's a fine looking boy," Peck said.

"I know you're just saying that," Millie said. "But it's all right."

"Nah, nah—he's a handsome boy, Charlie is," Peck said.

Millie smiled up at Peck, raised her eyebrows, lifting her doll in his direction, gesturing she would like him to hold her baby Charlie. Peck put sandwiches in the paper sack, rested it on his lap and held her baby. Two people making bathroom trips would see the doll in Peck's arms and give him a look.

"How old is Charlie?" Peck asked.

"Seventeen," Millie said.

"*Qu'est-ce qu* seventeen?" Peck asked. ("What is seventeen?")

Millie bit into her sandwich pretending she understood.

"Charlie's heavy," Peck said.

"Doesn't he feel real?"

"I like Charlie."

"You don't think I'm silly?"

"Nah, nah," Peck said. "I still have Dundee."

"Dundee?"

"My hunting knife. Dundee, *mon enfance, couteau de chasse.*"

"What does that mean?" Millie asked.

"My hunting knife all my life," Peck said. "I name it Dundee, all my life I have it. Under my pillow."

"That's so sweet," Millie said. "So, you understand."

"Ah, *oui.*"

While handing baby Charlie back to Millie she noticed fresh scars on his hand from the fishhooks. She took his hand in hers, balancing Charlie in her other arm.

"What happened?" Millie asked.

"Fishhooks," Peck said. "Wasn't paying attention."

Millie leaned down and gave his scars a kiss. She set Charlie in his cloth bag on the floor and covered him with a baby blanket.

"I can tell, Charlie is pleased to make your acquaintance," Millie said.

She picked up her iPhone and scrolled several messages with her thumb, shrugged, and put it back in her shoulder bag. Peck handed her the other half of her sandwich and they sat in silence, eating and drinking water.

"Why does a man tell a girl he loves her and then cheat on her with another woman?" Millie asked.

"He's a liar?" Peck queried.

"He probably had lots of girls," Millie said.

"And he lies to them all," Peck said.

"I know I'm not beautiful," Millie said. "But when a man tells you he loves you, it makes you feel beautiful. Shouldn't he try to mean it?"

Peck grasped her hand.

"You beautiful, cher. Dass for true."

"With all these freckles, my braces?"

He gave her hand a slight squeeze.

"You a bouquet of spring flowers."

Millie looked at his hand on hers, turned her head sideways, and with a blush looked up at his face. She grinned shyly and turned her head back down.

"How old are you?" Millie asked.

"*Vingt-cinq,*" Peck said.

"Is that old?" she asked.

Peck shrugged his shoulders.

"Not old, cher."

"Where do you live?"

"Carencro, down bayou," Peck said.

"Is that in Texas?"

"Lewisana."

"Oh."

"Saving for a pirogue and running crab traps and selling them to fancy restaurants."

"What's a pirogue?"

"A boat."

"Oh."

"A small boat."

"When grownups ask me what I'm going to be," Millie said, "I always tell them I want to become a doctor, so they'll leave me alone—"

"Ah."

"But I really want to be a teacher and have lots of babies and maybe live on a small farm and raise chickens."

"*Une bonne vie*," Peck said. ("A good life.")

Millie leaned her head over and touched it to Peck's shoulder.

"I love it when you do that," she said.

"What?" Peck asked.

"You know," Millie said, "talk French."

"Ma English not so good, but I hokay with the other, I say."

Suddenly Millie's head perked. She sat tall, pulling herself up by the back of a seat in front of her.

"Oh, no—oh my God!" she shouted.

"Hanh?"

"That was my sign."

"Where?"

"Kingston. We just passed the sign for Kingston."

She jumped up and bolted back to the bathroom, slamming its door and locking it behind her. Peck leaned toward a window to see if he could see towns or villages approaching. The driver pushed a button on his overhead microphone and announced a special stop in Kingston and for everyone to stay on board.

Peck could feel the bus slowing down—Millie still in the bathroom. As they came to a stop, the bus door opened. The driver stood and looked back for Millie, as he knew she would be getting off. The bathroom door burst open. She reached and grabbed her suitcase and her cloth shopping bag.

"Do I look all right," Millie asked, seeking approval.

"Ah *oui*," Peck said.

Millie reached, grabbed Peck's hand and squeezed.

"Goodbye, Peck," she said. "It was nice meeting you and thank you for the sandwich."

Her words followed her scampering down the aisle apologizing to everyone along the way for delaying the bus, and finally to a waiting driver. She jumped off, the door closed soon after, and the bus engine roared again.

As the bus rolled off the concrete curb shoulder and back onto the pavement Peck looked down and saw the bag on the floor with Charlie in it. He grabbed it and hurried to the front.

"Wait! Stop the bus, mister. She forgot a bag," he shouted.

"Can't stop," the driver snapped.

"You have to stop."

"It'll go into lost and found."

"Stop the bus. I'm getting off too, then," Peck blurted.

"We have a schedule, pal. I stop, you get off, you don't get back on."

"Stop the bus," Peck yelled. He dashed to the back to get his duffel. The bus pulled over and its door opened. Peck jumped off, gripping his duffel and the cloth bag holding Charlie. He turned and watched the driver giving him an annoyed look while pulling the door closed. The bus rolled away.

Peck started to trot back to the place where he saw Millie get off the bus to meet her ride home. Soon in the distance he could see Millie standing by an open door of a Suburban, speaking with a woman with a small dog on a leash.

He broke into a run. "Millie," he shouted.

No response.

"Millie," he shouted again.

This time both Millie and the woman looked his way.

Peck held the cloth bag high above his head.

"Charlie!" Peck shouted.

"Oh, my God, I forgot Charlie," Millie exclaimed.

Millie's mouth dropped open, her eyes burst wide, and she grinned with grateful delight, both hands nervously covering her braces. She sobbed in awe of learning she had forgotten her baby, and in a miracle of all miracles it had been found. Her eyes fastened on Peck's eyes and beamed with thankful tears.

"Charlie," she mouthed. "You saved my Charlie."

CHAPTER 13

MILLIE LIFTED BABY CHARLIE FROM THE BAG, bounced up and down, giving him a proper hug. Nestling the baby's head to her cheek, she put her hand on Peck's arm.

"Momma, this is Peck," Millie said. "His real name is Boudreaux but call him Peck."

"How do you do, young man?" the mother asked.

"We met on the bus, Momma, and he's going to..." She paused in midsentence and turned. "Exactly where is it you are going anyway?" Millie asked.

"Providence," Peck said. "Dat be in Rhode Island."

Millie gave pause with the patois and stared at his eyes.

"And you got off the bus just to bring me my Charlie?" Millie asked.

"*Oui.*"

"You mean you weren't getting off in Kingston?"

"*Vous avez oublié votre Charlie,*" Peck said. ("You have forgotten your Charlie.)

"Don't you love his French, Momma?" Millie asked.

"It's charming," Millie's momma said.

"So what is it you just said, Peck—just now."

"I say you forgot your Charlie, cher."

"Can we take him to a bus station, Momma?"

"What kind of ticket do you have, Peck?" the mother asked.

Peck pulled a Discover Pass from his pocket and held it up.

"Oh good," the mother said. "You can get on another bus with that."

"Are we going to take him to Knoxville, Momma?" Millie asked. "To the station?"

"Millie, let's take Peck home and feed him. I'm sure you both can eat something," the mother said.

"Momma, we had a sandwich on the—"

"We'll call from home and find when another bus goes through. We'll see to it he gets to the station in plenty of time."

"Take him home, Momma?" wide-eyed Millie asked, holding fingers over her mouth.

"I have stuffed bell peppers."

"*Delicieux*," Peck said.

"What about Daddy?" Millie asked.

The mother turned and raised her hand in prayer. "'Or what woman, if she has ten silver coins and loses one coin, does not light a lamp and sweep the house and search carefully until she finds it?'" her mother asked.

"Luke," Millie said. "It's from Luke."

Millie covered her mouth with an edge of her hand and leaned toward Peck. "It's from the Bible," she whispered.

The mother smiled at Peck, took Charlie from Millie's arms and cradling the baby doll, continued another verse.

"'When she has found it, she calls together her friends and neighbors, saying, 'Rejoice with me, for I have found the coin that I had lost!''"

Millie tweaked her shoulders up and down, grinning with squinty eyes. She took Charlie from her mother, placed him in his cloth bag, and stepped up and into the back seat of their Suburban, motioning for Peck to climb in.

"Does what you said—you know, the *delicieux* thing—does it mean you like stuffed peppers?"

"*Oui*," Peck said.

The Suburban soon pulled onto a driveway and rolled down a grade toward a large colonial house. Peck could see a lake in back at the base of a hill behind the house.

"*Grande bass, j'ai parié*," he said. ("Big bass, I bet.")

Millie giggled.

As an explorer would, Peck looked for flood lines and other tell signs of the lake's culture. As a fisherman, he was trying to get a feel for what could be caught in a lake like that.

On a desktop computer in a room just off the kitchen, Millie sat and went online to see when the next bus to Providence would come for Peck. She saw it wasn't until 1:00 p.m. the next day, and he had to catch it in Knoxville. She asked Peck his last name and went ahead making reservations for him.

"One o'clock tomorrow, Momma," Millie said.

"Knoxville is about forty minutes," the mother said. "You'll have to leave by eleven to be safe, Millie."

"Does it mean he can stay here tonight?" Millie asked.

"Your father would insist. Any young man who has sensitivity and caring to go out of his way to bring a friend happiness and joy is a man of God."

"Do you need to tell somebody you'll be late getting where you're going, Peck?" Millie asked.

Peck lifted Sasha's card from his pocket.

"Would you call Sasha at dis number, cher?" Peck asked. "Tell her when Peck gets to Providence?"

"You can use my phone," Millie said.

"Nah, nah, you talk better," Peck said. "Tell Sasha."

"This card says Michelle Lissette," Millie said. "Is this the wrong card?"

"Nah, nah. Ax for Sasha. She knows," Peck said.

Millie took the card, stepped out on a back patio and spoke with Sasha. She smiled several times throughout the conversation and grinned once.

"Sasha's so nice," Millie said, returning to the kitchen. "She's going to call the man you're meeting in Providence and tell him when you'll get in."

"Was she worried?" Peck asked.

"She wasn't worried at all," Millie said. "She told me to make sure you don't sunburn."

The two of them sat on barstools on either side of the kitchen's granite island and went through stuffed peppers and an assortment of leftovers from sausages to cheese. Millie watched Peck's eyes as he glanced with interest around the room at different wall coverings, bric-a-brac, family pictures, and art. If he turned his head out of her line of vision she would look at his arms and chest. She handed him a clean paper napkin and dabbed her lips with hers.

"It's early. What do you want to do?" Millie asked.

Peck looked out a window at the lake.

"You got tackle?" he asked.

"Tackle?" Millie mused.

"*Oui.*"

"You mean wrestle?"

She placed a hand over her braces and gave him a teasing grin as if she was amused, while a bit confused.

"Nah, nah," Peck said. "Fish poles, rods, fishin' tackle."

Millie blushed at her devilish misunderstanding. Peck smirked, apparently guessing what she had thought. She liked his smirk.

"In the garage," Millie said.

She stepped to the bedroom hallway. "Momma? Peck and I are off fishing, okay?"

"In the boat?" the mother asked.

"No, Momma. We'll be on the dock."

While Peck organized two sets of gear, Millie told him she knew nothing about fishing and would count on his patience to put bait on and to take fish off, if she was lucky enough to catch one. Peck listened to her patiently with nods of his head every so often, so she would feel connected. Before long they were sitting five feet apart on a long wooden dock her father had built.

"Is Sasha your girlfriend?" Millie asked.

"Nah, nah," Peck said. "A frien'."

"She told me to tell you she got back in New Orleans at four the same day she took you to the bus station," Millie said.

"Ah, good," Peck said.

"Peck, can I ask you something?"

"Sure," Peck said. "Ax."

Millie got up and walked over and sat next to Peck, hanging her legs off the side of the dock. "I didn't want to say anything in the house," she said.

"Ax," Peck said.

"Who's the bad man Sasha told me to tell you to look out for? Should you be worried?"

Peck cast several times out and reeled in while he was thinking how best to answer the girl's question. He handed his pole to Millie and asked her to hold it for him. He reached in his pocket and pulled the folded-up newspaper article Gabe gave him in Memphis. He handed it to Millie.

"Read dis," Peck said.

Millie read it carefully.

"My goodness. Is this about you?"

"Nah, nah," Peck said. "He's a bad guy, knife man."

"Is he after you?" Millie asked.

"Big hailstorm in Mississippi and we pull under a bridge," Peck said.

"Who pulled under a bridge?" Millie asked.

"Gabe, my frien', Sasha, my other frien', and Peck here, we stopped under a bridge in a hailstorm. The knife man stole my frien's medicine while he was peein'. He hit him on his head, knocked him down. Stomach medicine. I got it back."

"This man hit him?" Millie asked. "The same man who stabbed the man?"

"Same man," Peck said. "Man he stabbed and his frien' helped me get Gabe's medicine back. We left outta there and knife man did dat—all dat in dat paper there, after we gone."

"And he's still on the loose?" Millie asked.

"*Oui.*"

"No wonder Sasha is worried."

"I feel bad," Peck said. "Bad for the man he stabbed. He helped Peck."

"This says he's in Knoxville," Millie said.

"Who?"

"The man who got your friend's medicine back. He's in a hospital in Knoxville."

"Where we are to Knoxville?" Peck asked.

"We have to go there tomorrow, to Knoxville, for your bus," Millie said.

"Dat for true, cher?"

"You want to go see him at his hospital?"

"Oh, cher, dat be so good," Peck said.

"We can't tell Momma or Daddy about any of this, Peck," Millie said.

"Hanh?"

"They would freak and not let me drive you in—maybe not let you stay here."

"You hokay with me?" Peck asked.

Millie leaned her head on Peck's shoulder.

"I'm so okay with you," she said.

Peck folded his paper and pushed it deep into his jean pocket.

Millie placed both hands around Peck's arm, feeling his muscle.

"Did you really fight that man?"

"My frien's medicine keeps him alive. I had to," Peck said.

"You're so brave," Millie said.

"*Tu me faire sentir bien, cher,*" Peck said. ("You make me feel good, cher.")

Millie pulled close to his arm, resting her head.

"Is that good? What you just said?"

"*Oui,*" Peck said. "It is good. *C'est ci bon.*"

"Why Providence?" Millie asked.

"My frien' go there," Peck said. "Newport Jazz Festival. He need Peck to look after him."

"Look after him?"

"He's old," Peck said. "Very old. Not too long now."

"Not long?"

"You know hospice, Millie?"

"Yes," Millie said. "Sad place."

"Gabe from hospice I work at. He wanted to see jazz. I see he hokay and take care of him."

"You're going to be with him, your dying friend?" Millie asked.

"He be dyin' soon, maybe," Peck said. "Last wish for the ole man was to go see Jazz Festival."

Millie looked up and watched Peck's eyes staring off over their lake.

"You're such a nice man," Millie whispered, with a tear filling her eye.

Peck knew the setting for a good fishing time wouldn't work with more talking than patience going on. He did enjoy an outing and watching a new body of water, but he packed it in, and they walked with the tackle back up to their house and into the garage.

Reverend queried Peck at dinner. Peck told of the hospice where he worked and threw his trotline and how he was taking care of an old dying man from there—how he was going to meet him in Providence. Reverend opened dinner by calling Peck a good shepherd, leading by example, the way he was so thoughtful, sacrificing his own time to get off his bus and bring a doll back to his baby girl. Before they broke bread, he said a special prayer blessing Peck on his travels ahead and asked for God's guidance and safety.

Peck learned during dinner that the more he kept his mouth shut, the more recognition and second helpings he received. On into the evening the mother told Peck he'd be sleeping on a sofa in their den, so televisions in the bedrooms wouldn't keep him awake. She made a point of telling him he was welcome to raid the refrigerator. With every message of acceptance of her new friend, Millie would crunch her shoulders up in personal victory and down in tingly salute, and grin.

Reverend raised his glass of iced tea in toast.

"Tonight," the reverend said, "we celebrate our new friend, Peck. Tomorrow we'll celebrate the return of our college girl."

"Momma, I'm driving Peck to Knoxville early in the morning," Millie said. "I can show him downtown, and we don't have to rush."

"How thoughtful," the reverend said.

"Now Peck," the mother said, "if you come again, call or text Millie, and we'll be happy to pick you up at our Kingston stop, ya hear?"

"Yes'm," Peck said.

"I'll do the dishes tonight, Momma," Millie said.

The parents stood, walked down the hall calling their dog and went to bed, leaving Peck and Millie at the table.

"Momma put a sheet and pillow on the sofa," Millie said. "Will you be okay?"

"I be fine," Peck said.

"You get comfortable, Peck. I'll just put the dishes in the washer and give you some privacy."

Peck stood, stretched, and yawned. Millie glanced his way as she stacked the dishes. He went into the darkened den to make up his bed as she wiped the counters and gave the kitchen a final look. As if with a thought in mind, Millie stepped into the den.

"Peck, I want to go online..." she started, then bolted to a stop. In the distance by the sofa Peck was standing shirtless in tight white briefs with his jeans on the floor around his ankles. She lowered her head, put her hand over her braces and raised her eyes, staring at his briefs as if he couldn't see her look.

"Online?" Peck asked, paying no mind to her presence.

Millie composed herself, perhaps imagining being in a school dorm. She lowered her voice.

"Give me that newspaper you have," Millie said. "I'll go online in my room and see what I can find out—and if they caught him yet."

Peck stepped out of his jeans and bent to the floor to retrieve them, giving Millie ample ogle time, with the added benefit of Peck finding his folded newspaper clipping and walking over and handing it to her.

"Can I get you anything?" Millie asked.

"No, cher. I'm good," Peck said.

Millie nodded and mouthed "good night," turned the kitchen lights off and went to her bedroom. First thing she did was scan the newspaper article, saving it on her desktop. Then she folded it and put it deep in her purse. She left no chance her parents could find it laying around and maybe causing a scene. She put her pajamas on and brushed her teeth, staring into the bathroom mirror as though she were thinking of the boyfriend who had betrayed her, and was it her braces or her Charlie or some other flaw? And maybe it was kismet, her meeting Peck. The only thing she knew about him was his kindness and gentle nature, and that he was good-looking, muscular, and spoke French. Her mirror stare didn't seem to overlook her memory of his chest as he walked across the den in tight white briefs, to be certain. She spit into the sink bowl and returned to her computer desk.

It was two and a half hours after midnight when Millie found herself in her unbuttoned pajama top kneeling in the dark next to the sofa Peck was sleeping on, watching him sleep. An aquarium in a corner dimly lit the room. She leaned on the sofa's edge and kissed his bare shoulder. Peck startled, but settled, and waited without a word spoken. He turned his head toward hers, and she leaned even more forward and kissed his mouth, softly and gently with moist lips. She lifted her head to see his eyes.

"I've been wanting to do that all night," she whispered.

"*Très bien*, cher."

"Have you ever heard the scripture Song of Songs 7:6?" Millie whispered.

"Nah, nah," Peck whispered.

"How beautiful you are and how pleasing, my love, with your delights!" Millie whispered the verse.

Her warm left hand rested on his chest and traveled slowly down over his stomach and under his briefs, gently grasping the base of his erect William, now in full throb.

"Your stature is like that of the palm, and your breasts like clusters of fruit," Millie whispered.

Peck reached and with his thumbs pushed his briefs down over his thighs. Millie kissed his left nipple again and again, licked it once and crawled up and straddled Peck's stomach, her face kissing his chest.

Her scripture continued. "I will climb the palm tree; I will take hold of its fruit."

Millie reached down in between her legs, held Peck's William and directed it in between her wet lips, leaning back on it until it was deep inside, rubbing her G. Her pelvis rolled in steady motion, her buttocks lifting, squeezing and lowering, devouring every friction, savoring every throb from his William. As her buttocks rocked and heaved, she lifted his hands to her breasts, reciting more verse.

"May your breasts be like clusters of grapes on the vine, the fragrance of your breath like apples," she whimpered.

When it came, it was a long, silent, writhing mutual climax, his head lifting from his pillow, their bodies flexing with messages of ecstasy, filling one another as if their nerve ends embraced.

Millie squatted on Peck for the longest time, tasting his chest, savoring its memory, feeling secure. She lifted her head and slowly leaned forward toward Peck's face, causing William to come out from the warmth of her love and fall limp. She kissed his lips a soft, warm kiss.

"We have to leave early," she whispered. "We'll get breakfast in the city and then go to his hospital."

She kissed him again and crawled off.

"Night, cher," Peck said.

Millie didn't answer. She grinned, smelling her fingers, and hurried down a hall to her bedroom, quietly pulling the door.

CHAPTER 14

THEIR SUBURBAN PULLED OUT of the drive at dawn with Peck's duffel on the floor in front of him. Both had coffee thermoses in their hands as she drove east into a Tennessee sunrise.

"I went online. I found a lot of things about what happened under that bridge and about this man who got hurt," Millie said.

"You did?"

"First off, his name is Brock, but I can't tell if he and his friend are lovers or traveling companions, but they're close, I can tell."

"Maybe brothers?" Peck asked.

"No, I don't think so. One is Brock Singleton, and his friend is Winton Makaylah," Millie said.

"Ah...you so smart, cher," Peck said.

"I'm going to miss you, Peck," Millie said. "Do you think you'll miss me?"

"*Peck va manquer ta bonheur*," he said. ("Peck will miss your happiness.")

"Is that good?" Millie asked. "What you said?"

"Ah, *oui*, Peck will so miss beautiful Millie," Peck said.

"I'll write you and maybe when I get back to school, you can come see me, or I'll come over to Louisiana and see you," Millie said.

"Where you go to school?" Peck asked.

"Really?" Millie asked.

"*Oui*. If Peck knows I maybe come there."

Millie slowed her speed, pulled off onto a shoulder and brought the Suburban to a stop. She placed it in Park and turned to Peck.

"You can't read, can you?" Millie asked.

Peck looked at her as though she was disappointed.

"The newspaper article you have, you can't read it, can you?"

Peck turned his head and looked at the road ahead.

"You can tell me," Millie said. "It doesn't matter to me. You're perfect just the same."

"*Oui*," Peck admitted. "Sasha is teaching me when I get back to New Or–lee–anhs. You sad...with Peck?"

"Never, ever. Don't ever say that," Millie said. "You're my favorite friend so far."

"How you know, cher, I can't read?"

Millie pointed to her T-shirt.

"This," Millie said. "This says Baylor University. It's where I go to school."

"Ah," Peck said.

"I'm still writing to you," Millie said.

"*Je vais apprendre à lire un jour*," Peck said. ("I'll learn to read someday.")

"Show me your friend Sasha's card," Millie said. "The lady I called last night."

Peck reached in his pocket, retrieved it and held it up. Millie steadied his hand and took a picture of Sasha's card with her cell phone.

"I'll write you at this address," Millie said. "You'll figure it out."

Millie set her phone down, leaned over the console, took Peck's head in her hands, looked deep into his eyes and kissed him a long, warm, passionate kiss—a kiss they had matured into on the sofa earlier that morning. She sat back, buckled her seatbelt and drove off.

"Someday," Millie said, "you'll maybe even write me back."

"You honey sweet," Peck said. "You're a special frien'."

Neither spoke for several miles.

"When we get to hospital, I'll go in with you—as your girlfriend or your sister—or something," Millie said. "They may give you a form to fill out, or you may have to read signs. Who knows?"

"*Je te remercie*," Peck said.

"That's good, right?" Millie asked. "Is that good?"

He reached his hand over and gently squeezed her thigh.

"Very good," Peck said. *"Très bon."*

Millie turned in on Henley Street, crossed the Tennessee River and went to Main Street.

"You ever been to Knoxville Old City area?" Millie asked.

"Nah, nah," Peck said.

"It's historic," Millie said. "Close to the university campus, though, so they have neat food and places."

Carefully slowing the Suburban passing the US Courthouse, Millie let Peck take it all in. She turned left on Gay Street and pointed out a history center, the Tennessee Theatre. She found a parking spot on Union Avenue. They got out and walked into Market Square.

"I don't think anything is open yet," Millie said. "I just wanted you to see."

"It's a nice city," Peck said. "Old like New Or–lee–anhs."

They walked the Market Square, making their way back to where the Suburban was parked.

"When you can write, are you going to write me?" Millie asked.

"I don't know computers," Peck said.

"No computer," Millie said. "A real letter I can read and put under my pillow."

"Ah *oui*," Peck said. *"Je vais tu écrire ma toute première lettre."*

"Is that good?" Millie asked. "What you said?"

Peck took Millie by the hand, held it to his lips and smiled.

"My first letter is for you, cher," Peck said.

Millie beamed a blush, holding fingers over her braces. He lightly kissed her hand, and they turned and climbed the steps to find the Suburban.

"Let's go to the hospital, and we'll see if there's a place to eat," Millie said. "There's got to be something open."

The hospital towered in the background over Knoxville, a block from a McDonald's where they pulled in and parked, settling for coffee and breakfast sandwiches. They had worked up an appetite. Millie brought a complimentary copy of a Knoxville newspaper to the booth, while Peck picked up creamers and sugar packets from the condiment table. As Peck unwrapped the first of his two sausage, egg, and cheese biscuits, Millie found the hospital on her cellphone.

"Give me that newspaper article," she said.

"I don't have it," Peck said. "I gived it to you last night."

"Oh!" Millie said. "In my bag. Sorry."

She reached deep into her bag and retrieved his newspaper article, unfolded it and set it on the table. She picked up two French fries, bit them in half, and with an available finger, touch-dialed her phone and put it to her ear. The hospital answered.

"Hello?" Millie asked. "What are your visiting hours?"

"Maternity?" the operator asked.

"Oh no. Just a patient."

"Eleven to nine. No children under fourteen," the operator said.

"Thank you," Millie said. "Can you tell me if Brock Singleton is there?"

"One moment, please."

"Thank you."

"Mr. Singleton is here."

"Thank you."

"Are you family?"

"Why?" Millie asked.

Millie stuffed the rest of two fries into her mouth listening.

"He can only see family members."

"Really?" Millie asked.

"Are you family?"

"Can you tell me why, please?"

"I'm not at liberty, only family members permitted. Are you a family member?"

"No ma'am. Thank you."

Millie clicked her phone off. She opened her burrito and took a bite.

"Family only," Millie said.

"*Que?*" Peck asked.

"She said he can only be seen by family members," Millie said.

"Ah," Peck said. "You tried, cher. Merci."

Millie looked into Peck's eyes without saying a word. There was no telling what she was thinking. She sipped her coffee, lifted the breakfast burrito to her mouth and bit a third of it off and chewed.

"What's a pirogue?" she asked with a full mouth.

"Ah," Peck beamed. "A pirogue."

"What is it?"

"It's a flat boat carved from a tree, to find gators or lift crab traps."

"Alligators?"

"*Oui.*"

"How many traps does it take to catch your crabs?"

"Oh, maybe one hundred, maybe two hundred."

"A lot of traps," Millie said. "It must be a big tree for that pirogue."

"Nah, nah," Peck said. "Only some crabs in trap. Peck lift it from bottom, take 'em out, put shicken bone in and drop it to bottom again. No traps in boat. Jus' basket with crabs I catched."

"Interesting," Millie said, not taking her eyes from Peck's eyes.

"Crabs to all restaurants," Peck said. "Softshell to best restaurants. They pay good money."

"And you figured that out yourself?" Millie asked.

"*Oui,*" Peck said.

"And you won't give up until you get it to work?" Millie asked.

"*Mais oui,*" Peck said.

Millie bit into her burrito.

"My boyfriend gave up on me," Millie said.

"He not for you, cher."

"So, he's loser?"

"*Oui.*"

She chewed in thought, staring through Peck.

"Peck?"

"Hanh?"

"We aren't giving up. We're going to go see Mr. Brock Singleton."

"How?" Peck asked.

"I have an idea."

"Family only, cher, remember?"

"My Europe to 1600 history teacher—"

Peck placed his hand on Millie's hand to calm her.

"—Professor Thayer told us about how a bad man got his grandmother to send him five thousand dollars," Millie said. "He was a crook, and he just called her, and she sent him money, and she didn't even know him."

"She didn't knowed the man she sent money to?"

"No, she didn't know him. He pretended she did and she believed him."

"*Bâtard*," Peck said. ("Bastard.")

"Does that rhyme with what I think it means?" Millie asked.

"*Oui,* rhyme," Peck said.

"He called her and said, 'Gramma?'" Millie said.

"And *bâtard* didn't even know her?" Peck asked.

"No, that's just it," Millie said. "The second he said, 'Gramma,' my teacher's grandmother said, 'Baby Tim?' like she knew him. The crook then told her yes, he was Baby Tim, and he was in trouble and needed five thousand dollars and didn't want anyone to know. It was all too embarrassing."

"And?" Peck asked.

"And she wired him the money, five thousand dollars, every cent," Millie said.

"*Bâtard,*" Peck said.

"A total *bâtard*," Millie said.

Millie methodically picked up fry after fry, lifted them to her mouth and chewed, as her mind churned in thought. Her eyes would twinkle on occasion. She'd sip coffee. Then she paused, sat up straight, and pointed a finger up, as if she had a thought.

"Hold on," she said.

Millie picked up her phone and redialed the hospital.

"Wish me luck," she said.

"Hanh?"

"Let's see if they'll ring him."

Peck lifted her free hand, kissed it, and released it.

Millie squinted shyly and grinned. When the hospital answered, she straightened up again.

"Yes, patient Brock Singleton, please," Millie said. "That's Singleton."

Millie's eyes bulged, telegraphing they were about to ring his room.

"Hello?" the voice asked

"Brock?" Millie said into the phone.

"Yes, who—?"

"Brock, is that you?"

"This is Brock. Who's this?"

"Guess," Millie said.

"Tell me."

"You have to guess. One hint. I'm your favorite cousin."

Millie nervously put her fingers over her mouth, hoping, waiting.

"Kristen, is that you?"

"Yes!" Millie said.

"Are you really here in Knoxville?"

"Yes!" Millie said. "This is Kristen and I'm really here."

"Are you sure you want to see me? I look a mess."

"Can we come see you? We're only here for a while."

"Of course, of course," Brock said. I'll tell the nurse you're coming."

"With a friend," Millie said.

"I'll tell the nurse. I can't wait to see you, Kristen. Visiting hours aren't until eleven, though."

"That's okay," Millie said. "We'll come after eleven. Bye-bye."

Millie set her phone on the table, picked up one of Peck's breakfast sandwiches, took a huge bite, and then broke into a nervous giggle.

Peck could only stare at her, thinking what a good fisherman she would be—patient, cunning, knowing the right bait. Millie lifted her hand for Peck to shake.

"Hello," she said. "I'm Kristen, and how are you?"

They shared a laugh, refilled their coffee, and enjoyed each other, Millie's eyes going from wondrous, curious, thoughtful, to indifferent.

"He's such an asshole," Millie said, staring into Peck's chest.

"Who?"

"My boyfriend."

"He's not your boyfrien'," Peck said. "He betrayed Millie."

"Oh, right," Millie said. "*Bâtard.*"

"Ah, *oui, cher*," Peck said.

"He'll regret losing me," Millie said. "Someday he'll regret it."

"Nah, nah," Peck said. "He won regret anything."

Millie looked up at Peck, her mouth in a pout. "He won't?"

"*L'homme est trop stupide pour savoir ce qu'il est perdu,*" Peck said. ("He's too stupid to know what he loses.")

Millie tweaked her eyebrows at the thought of what Peck said, his using the word *stupide*. She smiled and sat back, enjoying the moment.

At the hospital, Millie walked to the nurse's station and asked someone to announce her—Brock's cousin, Kristen. They did and on the fourth floor Millie and Peck stepped by a uniformed policeman across a hall, walked into Brock's room, and let the door close behind them. Brock was sitting, resting his back on a pillow. Bandages covered half his face, including one eye and his jaw.

"Brock," Millie hurried, "I'm not Kristen. I had to say that or they wouldn't let us come see you."

Brock sat up in fear. "Who are you?" he stammered.

Millie pointed at Peck. "Remember him?" she asked. "You saved him under a bridge when he was fighting a knife man and you got his friend's pills back. Remember?"

"Hailstorm," Peck said.

Brock squinted an eye and looked keenly at his features.

"I remember," Brock said. "Now I remember. He knocked your friend down and stole his medicine."

"*Oui,*" Peck said. "*Oui.*"

Millie leaned in and looked at the damage to Brock's face.

"My name's Millie. Are you going to be all right, Brock?"

"They saved my eye," Brock said. "I need dental surgery on my upper jaw."

"It's so lucky they saved your eye."

"How did you find me?"

"The newspaper said you were here," Millie said. "Peck wanted to see if you were okay."

"He stabbed me twice in my face."

"Do they know who he is or have they caught him?" Millie asked.

"No," Brock said. "He got away. They're still looking for our truck, but they said he'd have changed my plates on it and there are a million white pickups."

"Do you live in Knoxville?" Millie asked.

"I teach in St. Louis," Brock said.

"All the way over in St. Louis?"

"We went to New Orleans for vacation and were driving back when this happened. My parents live in Knoxville. They brought me here."

"Is Winton, the man in this paper, here with you?" Millie asked.

"He had to get back to St. Louis—summer school," Brock said.

"I'm going to pray for you every day," Millie said.

"Thank you," Brock said.

"And my daddy is a minister," Millie said. "I'm going to ask him to say a special prayer for you."

"You're sweet," Brock said. "That's nice. Where do you know Kristen from?"

"What?" Millie asked.

"You used cousin Kristen's name to get in, where do you know her from?" Brock asked.

"Oh, I don't know her, I guessed—long story," Millie said. "We had to get in here to see you."

"I appreciate you coming," Brock said. "I'm glad you got away okay, Peck."

"T'anks to you, *mon ami*," Peck said.

"How's your friend—the one with the medicine?" Brock asked.

"He's good. You saved his life," Peck said.

"God bless you, Brock," Millie said. "You're going to do fine—I just know it."

"Thank you," Brock said.

"Let me get a picture of you two—a keepsake for you," Millie said.

She picked Brock's phone from the bedside table and stepped back.

"Peck, get close to Brock for a picture," Millie said, finding a camera button and holding the phone up in anticipation. She clicked.

"One more," she said.

Peck leaned in, shaking Brock's hand and smiling.

"Perfect," Millie said.

She opened the photo file of the phone to look at the results. Behind the two pictures she had just taken were four more—two of a black motorcycle, one with a white pickup in front of it, and another side view of a black motorcycle with Peck on the ground, fighting the knife man.

"Oh, these are good of the motorcycle," Millie said. "Did the police see these pictures?"

"Yes. I signed a release and they downloaded them, but they said he already removed the license plate from his motorcycle, so they can't trace him by using the pictures."

"What a rat that creep is," Millie said.

"I wonder if they looked at my video," Brock said.

"What video?"

"See if there isn't a video of him or his motorcycle on my phone."

"Hold on," Millie said. "There is."

She stood motionless for a second, her face without expression.

"Mind if I text this video to myself?"

"Be my guest," Brock said.

Millie texted to her phone the two pictures of Peck and Brock and the video taken under the bridge in the hailstorm. She deleted the outgoing texts from Brock's phone, turned his phone off and rested it on the bedside table. She held Brock's hand and smiled.

"We're all praying for you," Millie said. "And I can't thank you enough for saving this big lug here. Thank you and your friend."

"Thanks for coming in," Brock said. "And don't worry, I won't break your cover—Kristen."

He winked his one eye as they left his room. They didn't speak a word in the hall, walked past the policeman, stepped on an elevator, walked out through the lobby and climbed into her Suburban. That was when Millie burst.

"Wait 'til you see this," she said.

"See what?" Peck asked.

"Wait," Millie said.

Millie opened her cellphone and found her recent text to herself. She opened the video and leaned over the console.

"Look," she said.

She started the video. "Watch what happens."

The video showed knife man jumping into the pickup, but after he pulled the door closed, he threw a small license plate on the dashboard.

"What did he throw, cher. Was that his motorcycle plate?"

"I'm certain it was."

"Can you read it?" Peck asked.

Millie played it again and froze it with the plate in clear view.

"08N391," Millie said. "Underneath the number it says Motorcycle."

"Aye, yi, yi," Peck said.

Peck's fist clenched—his lips tightened as the memory returned to him. He didn't even wonder how Millie got the video. He only stared at an evening that was a nightmare. Millie lowered her hand holding her phone and turned toward Peck.

"If we could catch him, would you want to?" Millie asked.

"When you t'inking, cher?"

"Now."

"Oh, oui," Peck said.

"I'll have to come up with a lie to tell my parents, and you'll have to miss your bus and catch the next one."

"Hokay."

"You okay with all that?" Millie asked.

"To catch this man, *oui*," Peck said. "Gabe would say yes too."

"Do you know where he is, so you can call him?"

"Who, cher?"

"Your friend, Gabe."

Peck pulled out the papers Sasha had written the information on. In no time, Millie had the hotel in Providence on her cell and handed it to Peck.

"Hold this to your ear," Millie said.

"Courtyard, how may I direct your call?"

"Hello?" Peck asked. "Mr. Gabe Jordan."

"Hello?" Gabe asked.

"Gabe? How you are, my frien'?"

Millie stepped down from the Suburban, giving Peck some privacy.

"Gabe, your liking the jazz?" Peck asked.

"The jazz is phenomenal, my brother. The big show starts this weekend, but I've heard the best jazz since New Orleans."

Peck listened to Gabe as Gabe was dropping names from the world of jazz and of the sounds he'd been listening to.

"Gabe, I seed the man what helped us get your medicine under dat bridge," Peck said. "He purdy tore up, but he's hokay."

"How on earth did you find him? I hope you told him thank you for me."

"Ya, ya—the newspaper say his hospital, so I got off the bus. Gabe hokay with dat?"

"Totally okay with that. Take your time, son."

"You sure Gabe?" Peck asked. "More time, Peck be there?"

"See the sights, take it all in, my brother—it's a beautiful country."

"Bye Gabe," Peck said. "I see you soon."

"Goodbye, my brother. I love you."

Millie watched him take her phone from his ear, and she climbed into the Suburban.

"Gabe is fine," Peck said. "He say lots more days of jazz, so I be good another day."

"Perfect," Millie said. "I'll figure something to tell Daddy why I won't be home tonight. I know lots of girls in Knoxville. That will help."

"How we going to find knife man," Peck asked. "You dreamin' it?"

"Let me show you the video again, Peck. Take a good look at it."

Millie opened her albums and scrolled to the video of the black motorcycle and pickup truck.

"See?" Millie asked.

"His motorbike?" Peck asked. "*Oui.*"

"No," Millie said. "Look closer."

"*Que?*" Peck asked.

"His license number," Millie said. "We can find who he is from his license plate number."

"*Sainte merde,*" Peck said.

"That's good, right?" Millie asked. "What you said?"

Peck raised his left hand behind Millie's head, gently touched her cheek and directing her face to his.

"*Tu es si* special," he said.

"Mmm...I know that's good, right?" Millie asked. "What you said?"

Peck kissed her on one cheek, on her forehead, her nose and then the other cheek.

Millie turned forward in her seat, grinned, and buckled her seat belt, savoring the moment. She started the Suburban.

"We've got to find a computer," Millie said. "We have lots to do. Then we'll find this *bâtard.* He can't hide now."

"Gabe," Peck said, sitting back in his seat. "He sound happy. Much jazz there—dass good."

The Suburban backed out and rolled forward into a late morning.

CHAPTER 15

WHERE WE GOING, CHER?"

"We'll go to a public library and see if my Baylor card will get us in," Millie said. "If it does, we'll go online and check what buses you can get on later today or tomorrow. Then I'll call Momma with some excuse why I won't be home and we'll look up the knife man in the DMV."

"DMV?" Peck asked.

"The Department of Motor Vehicles knows who owns license plate numbers," Millie said.

The librarian was cordial. A woman at the desk knew of Millie's father and invited them in to use the facilities. Peck looked in awe at the number of books on shelves. He followed Millie to a computer desk where she sat down.

"Go ahead and walk around," Millie said. "Check it out. I'll be right here."

Peck made his way down one aisle and then the next. He would stop and touch a book cover on display. He would look between books on a shelf, watch someone sitting at a library table reading. He circled around approaching Millie, her face illuminated by a computer screen.

"Okay," Millie whispered. "There's a bus you can catch at midnight if we get lucky and find him. If not, another one tomorrow, same time as today, one o'clock."

"Hokay," Peck said.

"I cancelled your reservations for today. We'll make new ones when we know what we're doing."

Peck pulled a chair and sat beside Millie. Millie took the newspaper clipping from her bag, flattened it in front of her, reread it, whispering passages.

Two men were attacked and robbed of their pickup in Hazelton, Mississippi late Thursday evening.

"Okay, it happened in Mississippi, not Tennessee—"

"Ah, *oui*," Peck said.

"—so we need to check a DMV in Mississippi first," Sasha said.

She continued whispering as she read.

Brock Singleton and Winton Makaylah had parked under the Hazelton overpass during a hailstorm that blanketed one-inch hailstones over an thirty-eight-mile area that evening. The two had stepped from their vehicle, leaving it unattended, to ask a trailer-truck driver about road conditions ahead when they reportedly saw the suspect rummaging the cab of their pickup. A scuffle ensued, the suspect allegedly pulling a knife and stabbing Singleton twice, once in the chest and once in the face.

"That's wrong, Peck."

"Hanh?"

"Remember Brock telling us he was stabbed in the face two times?"

"*Oui*," Peck said.

"That poor man. Wasn't it awful how his face was wrapped?"

"Yes'm," Peck whispered.

Millie continued reading.

While they were distracted with wounds and trying to stop bleeding the thief drove off in their pickup, leaving his own motorcycle behind. The motorcycle's tag had been removed, making it more difficult to trace. Mississippi State Police are asking witnesses to come forward. Singleton has since been moved to an emergency eye clinic in a hospital in Knoxville where his parents live. Tennessee authorities are cooperating with Mississippi State Police, permitting access to Singleton for informal questioning in hopes of uncovering clues. The family is offering a reward for information leading to the conviction of this highway bandit fugitive who is considered armed and dangerous.

"Okay, here it mentions Tennessee," Millie said. "So, if we don't find him in Mississippi, then we have to try Tennessee."

"Why?" Peck asked. "Why Mississippi and how come Tennessee, cher?"

"Because we don't know which state to check first," Millie said.

"But, cher—"

"Peck, I know what I'm doing—I've been researching for papers three years now, sweetie."

"Don't a license plate tell you where a car or bike from, cher?" Peck asked.

"Yes, but…"

Millie paused. It had dawned on her what Peck was leading up to—the video she had of the pickup truck and the motorcycle license plate on her cellphone. She looked at Peck, covered her braces with her hand, grinned, and shrugged her shoulders. She had completely forgotten the video.

"And you're the one who can't read," Millie mused. "You're smarter than me, that's for sure."

She lifted her cellphone and opened to the video of the pickup truck with the license plate on the dashboard. She froze the screen and the license plate state was legible: Kentucky 08N391.

"What do you know about that?" Millie quipped rhetorically. "As easy as that. Our *bâtard* lives in Kentucky."

She reached her left hand over and patted Peck's leg.

"Good job, Sherlock," she whispered. "Just like fishing, eh?"

"*Tu es la magie, cher,*" Peck said.

Millie's fingers danced about the keyboard, her eyes focused on the screen and the occasional pop-up.

"I'm thinking that's good," Millie said. "What you said."

"*Oui,*" Peck said.

Millie combed the web, searching for a Kentucky DMV site.

"Every state does public information differently," Millie whispered. "I learned this doing research for characters in a book. My business law professor wanted us to voir dire an author's facts presented about characters in his book to see if he did good research, or if he was trying to pull the wool over our eyes."

"Pull wool?" Peck asked.

"It means to bullshit us," Millie said.

"Ahh."

"I had to find stuff in Minnesota and in Michigan, and that's when I figured out that every state does it differently."

Peck sat patiently, not having the faintest idea what she was talking about.

"Ah, here we go," Millie said. "Plate numbers by county. Kentucky."

She entered Kentucky's website and typed in DMV County. She then keyed in 08N391, pressed *enter* and waited.

"Laurel County," Millie said. "He lives in Laurel County. Now let's see if there's an address for him in Laurel County. Peck, reach in my bag and find my pen, will you please?"

The screen led her from one website to another until she found a complete DMV listing for London, Kentucky. There it was: his name, his address, and a registration and plate number for a black 2014 Harley Davidson.

"Mr. Eric Tandino, you are about to go to jail for a long, long time," Millie said.

Millie took the pen from Peck's hand and jotted down the street address. She handed it back to Peck. She looked at the screen.

"Let's see how far London, Kentucky is from here," Millie whispered.

"Why?" Peck asked.

"Drive time," Millie said.

"Can't we just tell somebod—"

Millie turned sharply, leaning to Peck with a determined look.

"I'm really good at this," she said softly. "Let me do my thing."

Peck nodded and sat back.

"*Oui.*"

"How far is London, Kentucky from Knoxville, Tennessee," she whispered to herself tapping the keyboard. She watched the screen.

"Hmmm," Millie said to herself. "One hour and twenty-nine-minutes driving with no traffic. There's no heavy traffic during the day. So, we don't have to worry."

Millie took the pen from Peck's hand and scribbled a note on the driving time and interstate routes.

"I'll set the GPS with this address."

She handed the pen to Peck and looked at her screen, striking keys as she spoke.

"Let's see if Greyhound goes to Providence from London, Kentucky, or if we'll have to come back here?" Millie asked herself.

Peck smiled at her confidence, her taking charge. A good fisher she was—she thought of every detail.

"Oh, good," Millie said. "Peck, there's a bus to Providence from Knoxville that goes to London, Kentucky, and then up that way to New England. So, the bus that leaves here at midnight, gets into London at one fifty-six in the morning and leaves London at two thirty. It's a break stop, or they're picking up mail or something."

"What are you saying, cher?" Peck asked.

"I made you bus reservations from London, Kentucky for two thirty tomorrow morning, so what I'm saying is we're going after this *bâtard*."

"Cher, don't we jest tell the cops?" Peck asked.

Millie folded Peck's newspaper article, put it in her shorts' pocket, stuffed written notes in her bag, and closed computer windows she had opened. She stood and motioned Peck out of the library, where they could talk. There was a new confidence in her stride—one Peck hadn't seen before. Outside she stepped down four steps to the first landing and waited for three people to pass by. She turned to Peck.

"This *bâtard*, this Tandino guy could have killed your friend, Peck."

"Dass for true," Peck said.

"Your friend could have died without his medicine."

Millie turned a full circle, thinking. "Look what he's done to poor Brock," she said. "Scarred his face for life."

"Ah, *oui*," Peck said.

"We've got to go to Kentucky and watch while they take him away to prison."

Peck saw in Millie's eyes a determination to make her life important, after a boyfriend had deflated her self-worth.

"Millie, will you call Sasha and tell her after my bus leaves so she can tell Gabe when I get there?" Peck asked.

"So, you'll do it?" Millie beamed. "You'll go with me?"

"Let's go," Peck said. "*Allons-y.*"

"Are you hungry?" Millie asked.

"*Oui,*" Peck said.

"We'll stop along the way," Millie said.

"Hokay."

"Wait a second. I have to call Momma."

Millie pointed to her Suburban and motioned Peck to go get in while she handled some personal business. She'd walk and pause—then she turned and walk the entire width of the library's step. She smiled, clicked her phone off and hopped down five steps to her Suburban and climbed in.

"I'm going straight to hell," Millie said.

"Hanh?" Peck asked.

"Straight to hell."

"Why, cher?"

"I just told Momma the biggest lie, and I'm going straight to hell for it," Millie said, starting the Suburban.

"What lie?" Peck asked.

"I told her I ran into a girl who goes to Baylor, and she was crying at McDonald's and told me she was pregnant, and her mother wouldn't let her get an abortion, and her boyfriend didn't want to marry her, and she may have to quit school," Millie rambled. "I told Momma I had to stay with her in Knoxville tonight and cheer her up and help her talk to her momma."

"*Whoo!* aye yi!" Peck blurted.

"Ya think?" Millie asked.

"Whoo! Whoo! Whoo!" Peck said.

"Straight to hell, right?" Millie asked.

"Hmm," Peck said sitting up in his seat. "Maybe not hell, cher."

"Hell and damnation," Millie said. "My daddy would skin me."

"Let me ax."

"Go ahead," Millie said.

"You know girls at dat"—Peck pointed to her T-shirt—"Baylor, what are pregnant?"

"Do I ever," Millie said.

"You know girls whose boyfrien's don't wanna marry 'em?"

Millie looked over at Peck, lowered her eyelids in a dull stare.

"Duh?" she grunted.

"Oh, *oui*, sorry," Peck said.

"What's your point?" Millie asked.

"So everything Millie say to your mamma is true, just backwards out of order," Peck said.

"And I won't go to hell?" Millie asked.

"Oh, you can go to hell, cher, but for something good, I'm t'inkin'. Not for a bad lie."

Millie dabbed a happy tear from a corner of her eye, grinned and drove off. She smiled at herself in her rearview mirror.

"But better read your Bible, cher," Peck said, leaning back. "Just in case."

As Millie found Interstate 75 to London, she soon saw an exit sign touting a Subway sandwich shop. She exited, found it, pulled in and parked. They ordered. Millie filled cups with iced tea, found a corner booth and sat down, waiting for Peck to bring sandwiches. He joined her, sliding her sandwich over the table. His was a meatball—a foot long and hers was a traditional salami, lettuce, tomatoes, and cheese with olives and jalapeño slices.

"I always carry a toothbrush in my bag," Millie said.

"What for?" Peck asked.

"Seeds," Millie said. "Tomato and jalapeño seeds stick in my braces." She opened wide and took a decisive bite from the end of her Subway sandwich.

"Ah," Peck said. "Good t'inkin'."

Millie looked over at Peck, mouth chewing and an afterthought twinkle in her eyes. Through a muffled mouthful she asked, "When you learn to read, Peck. What kind of books do you think you'll like?"

Peck paused reflectively, holding his sandwich like a saxophone right outside his waiting mouth.

"Panography," Peck said.

He bit into his sandwich.

Millie sat tall with a 'huh?' in her eyes.

"Yeah, dass for true, cher—panography," Peck muffled.

Millie's lips puffed a guffaw like a deep-sea blowfish, spitting parts of a tomato slice, a bite of chopped onion, and half a slice of jalapeño pepper onto the table. She gasped for air, red faced giggling near to tears. She lowered her face to the tabletop.

"Are you dying, cher?" Peck asked.

Face down, Millie nodded yes. In a few seconds, she lifted her head, hand over her mouth, her giggle calmed, and inhaled. Neither of the star struck lovers had to say another word. The dashing young man who couldn't read or write entertained a well-educated, sophisticated princess just as in a Disney fairy tale. To Millie, Peck was as charming as any prince. To Peck, Millie was a delight to listen to and to watch.

By late afternoon they were driving into London, Kentucky. Millie pulled into a gas station, handed Peck a credit card so he could pump gas while she located the address on her phone GPS.

"Regular," Millie said. "It's the button on the left."

They drove slowly through the streets, listening to the instructions voiced from her phone. It took them into several twists and turns.

"Maybe this wasn't such a hot idea, Peck," Millie said.

"Just keep moving, cher," Peck said.

"This is not a good area," Millie said. "Look at these places."

The small homes were not only poor, they seemed disheveled and cluttered. This was not just a poor neighborhood—it was a dangerous neighborhood. GPS brought them to the side of a two-story home that looked like an old farm home the city grew around. It looked vacant, with weeds crawling its exterior walls.

"Back up," Peck said.

"What?" Millie asked.

"Go back a way."

"We're getting out of here, right?"

"Nah, nah, just back up a way and stop."

Millie put the car in reverse and backed up slowly.

"Stop," Peck said.

Like a hunter he leaned his head around and looked. He pointed to a mobile home fifty yards behind the vacant house.

"Look," Peck said.

"Look where?"

Peck pointed.

"it's a motorcycle," Millie whispered.

"It's blue, not a black motorcycle," Millie said.

"Is this the address that thing say, cher?"

"My GPS? Yes. That's the address."

"That's him then, I can tell," Peck said.

"Wait, let's see if it's the same plate number as the black one under the bridge," Millie said.

She opened an album on her phone and scrolled two pictures with a motorcycle in them.

"It's not the same motorcycle," she said.

"Prolly he stole this one," Peck said.

"Same number," Millie said.

"Same number?" Peck mumbled, almost as though seeing it made him relive an evening's hailstorm and a bridge in Mississippi.

"What do we do, Peck."

Peck didn't respond. He was preoccupied with looking around at all the houses, looking for clues.

"So, do we call the police?" Millie asked.

"Nah, nah," Peck said. "Not this neighborhood, nah."

"Why not?"

"They not come—or they on the take from drug here in dis place."

"Now I'm frightened," Millie said.

"Let me t'ink," Peck said.

"Let's get out of here."

"Nah, nah. Let's wait," Peck said. "Let me t'ink."

Inch by inch, as though he were studying the telling ripples on a water's surface at a marshland bayou, estimating where best to throw his trotline, Peck studied with his eyes, inch by inch, every foot, every yard, every porch, every discarded, rusted-out junk, fallen bicycle, and appliance.

"Wait here," Peck said, reaching for the door handle.

"I'm going with you," Millie said.

"You should wait," Peck said.

"I'm scared, Peck."

"We don' know…"

"I'm going with you," Millie insisted. "He's hurt people. He could have killed your friend stealing his pills. He stabbed Brock, could have killed him. I'm going with you and that's settled."

Millie knotted her eyebrows into a serious expression, insisting Peck relent.

"Hokay, then," Peck said. He pointed to a house across the street. "But you wait here while I get something and I'll come get you before we go to his place."

"You promise?"

"I promise, cher."

"Okay," Millie said.

"Lock the doors," Peck said as he stepped out.

He walked at a quick, attentive pace, crossed the street and picked up an aluminum bat resting on a fifty-gallon barrel. He pulled a baseball glove from the bat and set it on a barrel lid. He hid the bat next to his side as he hurried back to the Suburban, where he asked Millie to unlock the door.

"You sure?" Peck asked.

He lifted the bat for her to get a sense of danger in what they were about to do.

"I'm going with you," Millie said.

"Get my duffel bag," Peck said.

"Besides, I'd be too scared alone here."

"Leave your bag inside and carry my duffel."

"I'll get it."

"Don't drop it."

Millie reached over the console, lifted Peck's duffel from the floor, and stepped out of the Suburban. She touched a button and locked the doors.

"Put the keys in your pocket," Millie said.

"Hokay."

"We can't afford to lose them."

"Stay with me no matter what, cher," Peck said as he moved around the front of the Suburban and picked up speed.

"I will," Millie said, determined to allay her fears and be brave.

Peck walked straight towards the blue motorcycle, first in a stroll, then in a hurried sprint, and when they were within thirty feet of the mobile home, the screen door was pushed open by the knife man, and as it slammed to an exterior wall of the mobile home a hundred plus-pound, teeth-baring, growling Rottweiler ran through the doorway at full speed and sprung from the porch, lunging at Peck and Millie. Peck swung the bat a full, deep sweeping circle from the ground, bringing it up over his head and with two hands down full-strength square on the charging dog's head with a hollow but decided *clonk*. The dog yelped once and instantly fell dead at their feet.

"Now you're a dead man, you motherfucker," the knife man screamed. "You killed my dog. You fucking killed my dog." He let go of the screen door and backed into his mobile home to grab a two-foot-long machete. He pushed the screen door open again. Peck lurched toward him, slamming knife man's wrist with his bat, jarring the machete loose. He kicked it away, dropped the bat to the ground and pushed him back inside the mobile home, and they struggled. Millie stood outside shaking with nervous tears, physically shuddering as she stared at the dead dog. Inside a window shattered from a fist smashing through it. A chair was turned over; another was tossed as a weapon.

"My duffel," Peck shouted.

"Peck?" Millie stammered.

"Bring my duffel."

"Me?" Millie shouted.

"Bring my duffel, cher," Peck said.

"Inside?"

"It's safe now. Come in."

Millie stared at the dead dog as she stepped around it and up on the stoop pulling the screen door open to see Peck straddling the knife man whose wrists were bound with Peck's belt. Peck had stuffed a dishrag into his mouth to shut him up. Peck had blood dripping from his forehead, and his knuckles were scraped and a bloody raw. She had never seen this outside of a movie theater. It moved her.

"My fish line," Peck said. "In my bag."

Millie shook as she looked at the knife man's eyes staring up at her. Not taking her eyes off him she unzipped the duffel and pushed her hand in and around and retrieved a large spool of black, two-hundred-pound tested fish line.

"This?" Millie asked.

"Oui," Peck said. "Open it up. Take the wrap off."

It stirred her. Millie's fears evolved to a feeling of confidence in Peck as her protector. Going about his business while bleeding, protecting her. She watched him use the fishing line to painstakingly tie the knife man's arms, hands, legs, and ankles, totally immobilizing him, her freckled cheeks turned a deep red flush with an excitement she hadn't known before. She looked around at the carnage, the broken window with blood on it, thrown chairs and the bleeding scars on Peck.

"Can he move?"

"He'll never move from here."

"Won't he die if we leave him?"

"We'll call the police, cher. He won't die here."

As Peck knelt back to see his handiwork in binding the knife man immobile—even tied to a refrigerator leg—to hold him until the law came, Millie grabbed his hair in her fist, pulled his head back snarled her mouth with unbridled passion kissing him upside down, causing him to turn toward her. Peck moved and sat on the floor, clutching her breasts and squeezing through her T-shirt, Millie straddling his lap, kissing him. Millie lifted to a squat, unbuttoned and pulled her shorts below her buttocks and sat down on his lap again. She kissed as she reached between her legs and managed to unzip his fly enough to grasp his fully erect, pulsating William. Her lips and tongue licking his sweat and kissing his face.

She lifted her pelvis and with her fingers guided William's head to the moist lips of her warmth in welcome and plunged slowly down its throbbing length, feeling the entire shaft stretch every centimeter of the walls of her lust. Fully engulfed, she lifted and lowered her squeezing, flexing, buttocks on his firmness, holding the back of his neck with her hands for balance and sucking his lips and kissing his closed eyes. In time Millie's eyes rolled back, and she began to writhe, her body shaking with Peck's as if they were in dance, his falling back onto his elbows.

Their climax was the perfect ending of an experience they would share in future memories.

Millie sat, engulfed with William, and pointed at a clean towel on the counter. Peck reached, grabbed it, and handed it to her. Millie watched his eyes as she lifted from his lap and stood over Peck, unconsciously letting the knife man stare at her. Catching his looks, she stared back with a sneer, wishing him a special spot in an eternal hell. He looked at her crotch. She smirked, wiping her inner thighs with the towel before pulling up her shorts. She tossed the towel on the counter and lifted the newspaper clipping she had stuffed into her back pocket. She placed it on the floor in front of the knife man for the police to see, but out of his reach.

Outside, Peck rubbed the bat free of fingerprints and dropped it on the ground next to the dog.

"I want to tip his bike over," Millie said.

"Nah, nah, cher, keep moving."

They hurried unseen and drove to downtown London before Millie, still shaking, pulled into a gas station and parked. They both gasped for breath, looking at each other, not a word spoken between them on the drive in, as if they were feeling a bond and realized they would have this moment all their lives, regardless of where life took either of them.

"That dog could have killed us," Millie said.

"Oui," Peck said.

"Would it have killed us, Peck?"

"I wouldn't let it," Peck said.

Millie looked at the blood dripping down Peck's forehead. It jarred her. It stirred her. She handed him a tissue.

"You were brave, cher," Peck said.

Millie smiled, took her phone and dialed 911.

"Laurel County Sheriff," the voice answered.

"Hello," Millie said.

"How can we help?"

"I want to report seeing a wanted murderer."

"You saw a murder? What's your name?"

"No, we saw a murderer. We know he's wanted, and we know he's at his home now."

"Do you have his name and address, ma'am?"

Millie gave the address. "His name is Eric Tandino, and he's wanted in Mississippi for stabbing a man in Hazleton."

"This murder happened in Mississippi?"

"Yes sir. He stabbed Brock Singleton, who's in the general hospital in Knoxville."

"And this Brock Singleton, he passed, did he?"

"I have to go."

"Your name, ma'am?"

"Can I be anonymous?"

"You can, but there may be a reward."

"I want to be anonymous."

"Thank you for the tip."

"You can give the reward to Brock Singleton's family. They may need it for medical bills."

"If that's allowed, we'll see that Brock Singleton's family get any reward, if this is the guilty party."

"Oh, he is, and if you need proof he's the man, look on Brock's cell phone. He has a video of the crime happening—his motorcycle and everything. It even shows him stealing the pickup."

"I'm sure we'll have that."

"No. The police took pictures off his phone but didn't look at his video."

"We'll check it out. Thank you."

"Okay then, goodbye."

Millie clicked her phone off.

"Murder?" Peck asked.

"I had to," Millie said.

"But murder?"

"You said it yourself, Peck. Cops won't come to a bad neighborhood jus' for a gang fight."

"*Oui*," Peck said.

"I learned the trick in my psych class," Millie said.

"Trick?"

"A master magician taught us sleight of hand. He said all magic is a matter of tricks, it was about getting an audience to look away at one of your hands—being distracted—while in the other hand you're preparing the trick, unnoticed. State troopers certainly will come in for a murderer. They even said so."

"*Ah, très intelligent,*" Peck said.

"I need the bathroom," Millie said.

"Inside, cher."

"To freshen up," Millie said. "Want anything?"

"Nah, nah. I'm good," Peck said.

Millie returned to the car, smiling, cinnamon hair brushed and with makeup.

"Let's find a place for coffee, where we can talk and then I'll drop you at the bus depot, and go back," Millie said.

"Where will you go?" Peck asked.

"I wish I could go with you," Millie said.

"Ah *oui,*" Peck said. "Ma frien' waits on Peck. He needs me."

"I know. I'm going home and tell Momma the truth," Millie said.

"The truth?"

"It's time she and I had our mother—daughter talk."

"Evert'ing?" Peck asked.

"Well, maybe not everything, like about all of this," Millie said. "She'd be hysterical."

"Dass for true."

"Just that I've grown up, and I like to wear makeup, and I like frozen daiquiris, and so what if I do? She'll have to get used to it."

"How 'bout Reverend?" Peck asked. "Your poppa?"

Millie reached in her bag and pulled out a wheel of birth control pills and held it up.

"Him too," Millie said. "I love my daddy more than anything, but it's time he knows his baby girl Millie could vote more than two years ago."

Peck reached and gently squeeze Millie's thigh. Millie grabbed his hand and held it.

"I know I'll probably wake up in the night a lot, screaming about all this, Peck."

"Ah *oui.*"

"Especially that dog, or his machete— everything," Millie said.

"*Oui*."

"But right now, I feel so good. Let's go get some coffee."

CHAPTER 16

GABE, DID I WAKE YOU?" Sasha asked.

"Sasha?"

"Hi honey."

"My baby," Gabe's voice smiled through the phone. "I've been up, already on my second cup. How grand it is to hear your voice."

"I have you on speaker, sweetie," Sasha said. "Do you mind?"

"I'll take you anyway I can get you, darlin'," Gabe said.

"I'm opening mail while we talk," Sasha said. "I have an easy foot tall pile I'm behind on."

"A big pile for the Big Easy," Gabe said.

"Spare me. It's too early. Haven't had my coffee, yet."

"His name is Donald," Gabe said. "He goes by Don."

"What on earth are you talking about?"

"Point Street Bridge," Gabe said. "Mister sax."

Sasha looked up from her letter opener and smiled.

"I gave him your fifty and he rolled into "When Sunny Gets Blue" so beautifully people gathered to listen," Gabe said.

"Oh my."

"When Sunny gets blue..." Gabe sang a verse into the phone. *"...her eyes get gray and cloudy..."*

"And then the rain begins to fall," Sasha sang. "Did he wail, sweetie...when he played it?"

"Pitter patter, pitter patter," Gabe sang.

"Could you feel us dancing to it?"

"He watched me the whole riff," Gabe said. "He knew it was special to me... important for you."

"Sweet man."

"I miss you, baby."

"So how is…you know…everything?" Sasha asked.

She pulled a tissue from the box behind her.

"Be honest."

"Early mornings are my worst time—early like around four or five."

"Do you still have your pills?"

"It used to go away with a pill. Now I break one in half and take one and a half. It helps."

"Are you worse than when you were here?" Sasha asked.

"We don't want to be talkin' about me, darlin'," Gabe said. "Let's talk about you, let's talk about jazz, about when we'll dance again."

Sasha put her letter opener down and lifted another tissue. She patted her eyes, no doubt thinking of Gabe dying alone in a hotel room in Providence.

"Peck will be there tomorrow at two a.m.," Sasha said. "I'm supposed to tell you not to pick him up. He'll catch a cab to you."

"I wrote it down, honey. I'll go get my friend. I miss him."

"Gabe, do you have your pot of coffee with you?"

"You know I do."

"Fill a cup, honey, I have a surprise."

"Hee hee, my baby," Gabe mused. "Hold on."

Sasha waited.

"Okay, full cup," Gabe said.

"You know that bastard who hit you and stole your pills?"

"Hailstorm, he stabbed a man, how could I forget?"

"That's him."

"How could I forget?"

"Well—"

"Don't tell me, they found him?"

"Better than that."

"They caught him?" Gabe asked.

"Take a sip," Sasha said, "and swallow."

"Hee hee. My baby."

"Peck caught him."

"What?"

"Our Peck caught the guy who stole your pills," Sasha said.

"How on earth?"

"It's true."

"Where? How?"

"Troopers are picking him up and hauling him into jail, holding him for extradition to Mississippi."

"Picking who up?"

"The pill thief."

"Wait, wait," Gabe said. "I want to hear the whole story, but nature's calling, can you hold?"

"Go, go," Sasha said. "Someone's at the door with a delivery. I'll be right back too."

Sasha went to the office door and signed for a courier envelope. She looked at its receipt. It was from Lily Cup's law offices. She walked back into her office, pulled her door closed and sat down as Gabe came on again.

"I'm here," Gabe said.

"Me too," Sasha said.

"So, tell me everything. Don't leave anything out," Gabe said.

Sasha placed the courier envelope on top of her pile.

"A girl helped him. You know about her already," Sasha said.

"Just a minute."

"What?"

"What girl?"

"Didn't Peck tell you about the girl?"

"All I know is Peck called me yesterday and told me he'd be another day. He didn't mention any girl."

"Oh?" Sasha asked.

"Better start at the beginning," Gabe said. "My Uber ride doesn't come for an hour."

"Seems our boy met a girl on a bus. Her name is Millie. In fact, they met on a Greyhound going through Tennessee."

"Good for him, but what's this—?"

"She got off the bus—"

"This Millie got off?"

"—and she forgot something, a bag or something on the bus. Seems our Peck made the driver stop to let him off so he could give the girl her bag."

"My brother."

"Seems the driver was pissed for making him stop."

"This was in Tennessee?"

"Tennessee, but the bus wouldn't wait and it took off and left him."

"Is that boy something or what? What a guy."

"He found the girl, gave her whatever it was she forgot, and she and her mother took him home for dinner."

"Well I'll be," Gabe said.

"Can you believe it, Gabe?"

"But what's this got to do..."

"So, he stays over, and she's a senior at Baylor University. "

"That's in Texas—Waco. I was stationed in Killeen, Texas not far from there.

"Texas, yes. So, I'm guessing red hair, freckles, maybe twenty, but she somehow sees a newspaper clipping about the stabbing under the bridge and looks things up on her iPhone, and one thing leads to another, and so he sleeps on their sofa."

Gabe mumbled a snicker into the phone. "How does your 'one thing leads to another' wind him up on a sofa?"

"I don't know, Gabe, the girl wasn't talking."

"Kids keep some secrets," Gabe said.

"I don't even know how they could, you know, do anything with her parents at home and her father a Baptist minister."

"So, what did he say?" Gabe asked.

"Who, the father?"

"No, Peck. What did he say?"

"Oh, I didn't talk to Peck. She called me. The girl Millie called."

"My man," Gabe said. "What a guy."

"Like I said, it seems one thing led to another, and then she drove him into a Knoxville hospital where they met the man who got stabbed. Apparently, his family lives in Knoxville, so that's where they put him in the hospital. The one who got your pills back for you. On his cellphone he had a video of a license plate from that motorcycle under the bridge, and that's how they traced this guy and the troopers arrested him."

"Arrested him in Mississippi or Tennessee?" Gabe asked. "I'm lost."

"That's just it," Sasha said. The motorcycle guy lived in London, Kentucky. That's where they found him and that's where Peck caught his bus last night after midnight—London, Kentucky."

"There has to be more to this," Gabe said. "Why would he be leaving out of London, Kentucky, and not from Knoxville? How did he even get to London?"

"I just told you. Maybe he'll tell it better," Sasha said. "The girl, Millie, was pretty tightlipped about it all. That's all I know."

"My brother, my Peck," Gabe said. "He has a way with the ladies, he surely does."

"He's a sensitive guy, if he filters his thoughts," Sasha said. "Girls like a sensitive guy."

"I hope the knife man goes away for a good ten years or more," Gabe said. "He needs to be off the streets."

"Are you enjoying your jazz festival, honey?" Sasha asked.

"It's heaven. Right here on earth, and it doesn't start for two days."

"So, what do you do all day?"

"The prelim shows are grand."

Sasha picked up another tissue, held it and listened to Gabe.

"Kamasi Washington played a rehearsal yesterday—saxophone. Oh, my God, how good was that? Sasha, when that man played I'm telling you, you could hear a pin drop. People swaying and in tears, in chills—every emotion. We all loved it."

"Good for dancing?" Sasha asked.

"If you were here baby, such good dancing. At the opening of the festival I'll get to see Chick Corea and Gregory Porter. They're what it's all about. Going to be fifty or more playing at different places around Newport, different venues."

"So much fun," Sasha said.

Gabe went on about the food in the area—how he preferred southern catfish to the flakier cod in New England; while corn on the cob in this neck of the woods was a delicacy it was so good with butter. He rambled as Sasha opened the courier envelope.

She interrupted.

"Gabe—Lily Cup just sent over Peck's birth certificate and his Social Security card."

"She found it?"

"She found it."

"Good for her," Gabe said. "Now he can be a somebody."

Sasha read the papers aloud.

"Boudreaux Clemont Finch—born 1996—"

"That makes him twenty-four, not twenty-five, like he thought."

"His parents are the state of Louisiana—it has him as a ward of the state somehow—and his race is unknown."

There was a moment of silence.

"What does that mean, Gabe—race unknown?"

"Slave states let slave owners mark the race of newborns – there was sex going on between owners and slaves. The color of the baby would determine if it was raised at the house or sent to the slave cabin, is my guess."

"So with it saying 'unknown' does that mean we don't know who the father is?" Sasha asked.

"We're all the boy's got," Gabe said.

"Seems so."

There was another moment of silence.

"Gabe, if I overnight these papers, can you check around and find out where you can get him a legal ID? Tell them it's an emergency so he can get an airline ticket."

"I'll call the VA office here in Providence. They'll tell me."

"Okay."

"But I wouldn't send it until he gets here."

"Oh?"

"He's missed two buses," Gabe said. "And me...well, let's wait until he's here, baby."

"Okay," Sasha said. "Maybe you're right."

While Gabe and Sasha, Providence and New Orleans, were chatting through her stack of unopened mail, the Greyhound driver made an announcement on Peck's bus that they were stopping in Charleston, West Virginia, for a thirty-minute break. Peck looked over at the portly back lady sitting next to him.

"Where'd he say?

"Charleston," the lady said.

"Wonder how food is in Charleston?" Peck asked.

"Should be good."

She began organizing her bags.

"Po folks eats good," she said.

"Charleston poor, is it?" Peck asked.

"Where they's a Greyhound station, it will be," the lady said. "Food should be good."

"You getting off?" Peck asked.

"My niece is havin' a baby," the lady said. "Here to hep."

"Dass nice," Peck said.

"How far you goin', hon?"

"Providence. Dass in Rhode Island...got me a way still."

Peck looked out through the window, watching people passing by on the streets of downtown.

"Can I ax you something, maybe?" Peck asked.

"What'cha need honey?"

"What makes po folk food better?"

"Fat. We leave the fat in."

He looked in store and restaurant windows going by. He watched a delivery boy riding a bike on a sidewalk. Their bus slowed and pulled into a station and eased itself into a slot at an angle. The bus driver said everyone could get out, eat, stretch their legs, walk about, but be certain to be back in half an hour or the bus would leave without them. Peck couldn't read a menu board, so he watched food preparers hand plates to customers until he saw a plate he wanted.

"What's dat?" Peck asked a man with a tray in his hand.

"Huh?" the man asked.

"Dat?" Peck asked, pointing to his bowl.

"Cheeseburger and bowl of chili," the man said, still walking. "Ask for a number two."

"T'anks, frien."

Peck turned, stood fourth in line and ordered a number two—a cheeseburger, a bowl of chili, with a Dr. Pepper.

After eating, he strolled by the rack of magazine cover pictures to take a walk an outside smelling of diesel fuel. Peck saw people gathering at his bus, so he boarded. He stepped to the back and got a seat by a window. As usual he kept his duffel underfoot, where he could see it. At two different break stops, Wheeling and Harrisburg, two different people sat with Peck. The first was an older man with a cane resting between his legs who kept his eyes on a *Wall Street Journal*. The second, a high school history teacher, who spent time reading on his laptop and searching the web for vacation, camping, and canoeing spots in Maine. When the teacher pulled his cellphone from his pocket it was the first time Peck spoke a word since Wheeling.

"I got me dat same phone," Peck said.

He reached down into his duffel bag and retrieved it, still in its wrapper.

"It's a nice phone. You'll like it," the teacher said. "It's not so loaded it needs a lot of battery. It'll do a good job for you."

"*Bon*," Peck said.

"It looks new, is it connected?" the teacher asked.

"I don' know," Peck said. "My frien' just gived it to me."

"Are you French?" the teacher asked.

"Cajun French," Peck said.

"Interesting," the teacher said. He folded his laptop. "I can set it up for you, if you'd like."

"Really?" Peck asked. "You know how?"

Peck handed his phone to the teacher, who removed its wrapping and protective adhesives from the sides and the screen.

"Do you have its charging cord?" the teacher asked.

Peck reached into his duffel, pulled out a cord. The teacher plugged it into Peck's phone and then into an outlet on the bus. A yellow light began flashing in the center of his screen, indicating a charge.

"Let's give it ten or fifteen minutes," the teacher said. He rested Peck's phone on the lid of his laptop.

"What's your email account?" the teacher asked.

"*Non, je prends des leçons de lecture*," Peck said. ("No, I'm taking reading lessons.")

"*Oh, si vous lisez le français, pas l'anglais?*" the teacher asked. ("Oh, so you read French, not English?")

"*Je n'ai pas lu, désolé. Si pas de mail, juste parler par téléphone*," Peck said. ("I don't read, sorry. So no mail. Just talk for phone.")

The teacher picked up Peck's phone and looked at its charge. He turned the phone on and waited for it to come awake. In a few seconds there was a *tink* sound on the phone. Then another *tink* and a third.

"What's that?" Peck asked.

"Those are texts," the teacher said. "You have three text messages already."

Peck looked at the teacher, not certain what a text was in the first place, and not certain if he had to do anything because of the messages.

"Can you read 'em?" the teacher asked.

"*Non*," Peck said.

The teacher looked at Peck, waiting for instruction. Peck motioned that perhaps the teacher could look at the messages and relay them to him.

The teacher nodded and scrolled down to the first text received.

"It says it's from a Michelle Lissette, and it says, 'Hello Peck, I hope you like your new phone. Call me.'"

"She gave me the phone," Peck said. "Dass Sasha."

The teacher waited for Peck to signal to open the next text. Peck nodded.

"This one says, 'Your Millie sounds sweet, happy they caught that bastard and locked him up. Call me.'"

The teacher furrowed his brow as though he was uncomfortable, as if he didn't know from the sounds of the last text how distant Peck was from his own culture. He appeared nervous after reading the second message. He was prepared to abandon the notion of setting up Peck's phone.

Peck could see one more line on his phone that read *Michelle Lissette,* He couldn't read it, but he was aware there was one more message. He motioned to the teacher to kindly open and read it. The teacher reluctantly obliged. He opened the text and read it to himself. He shut the text and held Peck's phone out for Peck to take.

"It was nothing," the teacher lied. "Just a repeat of the other one."

"Repeat?" Peck asked.

"It happens a lot," the teacher said.

Peck looked at his phone. He pulled his power cord from the outlet, wrapped it and put it in his duffel.

The teacher opened his laptop again and got busy working, sending messages and going online. Peck reclined his chair back and took a nap.

In Trenton, New Jersey their bus curiously pulled to a curb and stopped a block away from a Greyhound depot sign on the side of the terminal building. The door opened and three police officers boarded quickly and charged back up the aisle with their guns out and arms cocked, pointing them at the ceiling. They edged in quick shuffling steps to the last seat. The teacher pointed to Peck and edged himself out of the seat and stepped back by the bathroom door.

"Hands where I can see them and don't move a muscle, buddy," barked one officer, pointing his gun at Peck's head. "Not a muscle."

Peck sat, stunned. He furrowed his eyes and tried to look around at the teacher, but an officer touched the side of his head with his pistol and barked again.

"Do not move. Keep your hands where I can see them. I'll blow your head off."

All the passengers, except the teacher, were asked to leave the bus.

As the bus emptied an officer grabbed Peck's wrists and snapped cuffs on.

"Get him off and then we'll cuff him behind his back," the first officer said.

"Shackles?" the second officer asked.

"Oh, hell yes. This one's a runner."

They pulled Peck up by his cuffs, got him in the aisle, a gun still to his head.

"Is that his?" the officer asked the teacher. He was pointing at Peck's duffel bag.

"That's his," the teacher said. "He put his phone it that bag."

Peck didn't move a muscle. He watched, taking everything in and waiting, as if he were a gator surveying a still bayou. Peck wasn't one to overthink too much, but he suspected this was about the knife man he fought with in Kentucky, and maybe the knife man didn't make it. Maybe he pulled the refrigerator over on himself—or maybe a wild dog got him. Peck froze his emotions and followed instruction. Turning to be led down the aisle of the bus he caught the eye of the schoolteacher.

"Sorry, man," the teacher said. "I'm sorry."

Outside onlookers stood and stared as Peck's handcuffs were switched from his front to behind his back. Two officers knelt on either side of Peck and placed shackles on both ankles and fastened them. It was then they thoroughly frisked Peck. They grabbed under his crotch; they went through his bag, dumping its contents out on the ground and then picking everything up and putting it back.

"Well lookee here," an officer said. "Now what on earth would a man traveling a thousand miles on a bus be doing with a half-used spool of fishing line? What do you suppose?"

Two officers walked Peck to a squad car.

First officer looked Peck in his eye. "You have the right to remain silent and refuse to answer questions. Anything you say may be used against you in a court of law. You have the right to consult an attorney before speaking to the police, and to have an attorney present during questioning, now or in the future. If you cannot afford an attorney, one will be appointed for you before any questioning if you wish. If you decide to answer questions now without an attorney present, you will still have the right to stop answering at any time until you talk to an attorney. Knowing and understanding your rights as I have explained them to you, are you willing to answer my questions without an attorney present?"

Peck stared back with cold, gray eyes. It was a dark, distant stare. There was no telling what was going on in his mind. He was a gentle young man by nature, orphaned since birth, not knowing a mother or a father. He had nightmares of having been toughened by an abusive foster nanna who made him sleep in a drawer, then on a kitchen floor while keeping the state's bed and board money and slaving him out as soon as he was old enough to carry bait buckets for her drunkard of a boyfriend. He remembered being in grade school when he ran away, running trotlines and mowing lawns to survive. Peck understood about being alone and about the darkness in his life. He knew no one had friends in the bayou. You were a hunter or you were food.

The first officer brought his nose within inches of Peck's nose. "Can ya hear me, punk? Do you understand your rights, sir?"

Pecks eyes were a gray, cold stare, like a gator.

"Vous n'a pas d'importance pour moi—va te faire foutre," Peck said, turning his head away. ("You don't matter to me— fuck you.")

"Lock him up, fellas," the first officer said. I'll see to him in the morning."

"What do we book him on?" the second officer asked.

"Warrant says kidnapping, unlawful interstate trafficking," the first officer replied.

They pulled open a back door of a squad car, placed a hand on the top of Peck's head, shoved him into the seat, lifted his legs in, and slammed the door.

"IHOP or the diner?" the second officer asked.

"Doesn't kidnapping mean we leave the jewelry on," the first officer asked.

"The shackles and cuffs? You bet," the second officer said.

"Let's do the diner," the first officer said. "Roast beef and mashed potatoes tonight, all you can eat."

"The diner doesn't have mashed potatoes, they have whipped," the second officer said.

"What's the difference?" the first officer asked.

"Lumps, they're mashed. No lumps, they're whipped," the second officer said.

"Then they're whipped. Let's go."

"First we dump nature boy in the back seat off, lock him in the holding tank, and then we'll go eat," the second officer said.

CHAPTER 17

THE OFFICERS DIDN'T REMOVE his shackles. They lifted his feet from the car and pulled him out to a stand. They held his arms, helping him keep his balance as he climbed the stairs into a county lockup. A Trenton officer photographed his front and side profile and fingerprinted him. Two officers followed him, as he shuffled to the end of a long, dark, windowless corridor, where they slid a cell door open and motioned him in. Peck slid his feet through the cell's doorway, going in halfway, then he stopped and stood frozen, looking at a brick wall filled with graffiti and no window.

"I don't know if they're going to..." the second officer started.

He stopped abruptly, wanting Peck's attention.

"Hey," the second officer barked.

Peck didn't move.

"Hey," the officer shouted.

"Hey!" he repeated. "Fella, I'm talking to you."

Peck shuffled further to the back wall, turned around looking down at the floor, and sat on a thin mattress-lined steel shelf.

The officer stepped in and walked up to Peck.

"You goin' to teach him, Sarge?" queried one of the inmates in a next cell.

"Stand up," the officer said.

"Pretty boy needs to learn respect, don't he, Sarge," another voice asked from an adjoining cell.

"Stand up, nature boy," the officer barked.

Peck stood, gaining balance.

The officer looked over at the adjacent cell. "Turn around, fellas," he said.

Two of four in the cell complied. One was sleeping.

With his elbow cocked back, the officer slammed Peck in the gut with his closed fist, doubling him over. Peck gasped for air. The officer pulled Peck's head up by his hair and slugged him in his stomach again. Then he pushed him back on the cot. Peck fell over on his side, gasping and wheezing for breath.

"When an officer is talking to you, best you don't be rude, nature boy," the second officer said. "Is that understood?"

The officer backed away, stepped out of the cell and locked the door.

"Like I was saying, they might feed you tonight, or they might feed you in the morning, but I suggest you be polite when they do."

He turned and walked the dark corridor and slammed its door shut.

"What ya in for?" came a voice.

Peck lifted his shackled legs up on his cot and laid down on his side, his hands still cuffed behind his back.

"Ain't for shoplifting," came a voice. "Looks of him."

"The man don't hit a face, d'ja see that, Harry?" another voice asked. "The man always goes for the gut but not the face."

"What you mean?" another voice asked.

"If the man marks your face, judge don't like that," the voice said. "Slamming your guts out can't be seen. No evidence. The man don't hit the face."

"Fuck," a voice said.

"Too much paperwork, if a judge sees a busted lip or somethin', and he gets mad," a voice said.

"Damn," a voice said.

Peck's world was now little more than a dark five-by-seven holding tank. Being the only prisoner on the floor in cuffs and shackles didn't bode well for his situation. His eyes stared a gray stare. He had no idea why he was there. Was it the teacher who had turned him in? If it was, what did the teacher know? What did he suspect? Peck closed his eyes long before he fell asleep.

Beams of a morning sun cut bright lines slanting down through shadows of adjoining cells. Dust particles floated like stars illuminated by the beams and disappeared again into the shadows. Peck had urinated in his jeans as he couldn't maneuver with his hands cuffed behind his back, even though a stainless-steel toilet bowl with no lid was a foot from his head next to his cot. Peck heard a bolt key in the cell door, and it slid open. He turned and sat up.

"Aww shit," the first officer said.

"What Sarge? The second officer asked.

"Didn't anyone ask him if he had to piss?" the first officer asked.

There was no answer.

"Goddammit," the first officer said. "You got pants in the bag, nature boy?"

Peck nodded his head.

The first officer looked at the two officers standing behind him.

"Get his pants. Get those off him and roll them up in a paper towel and put them in a plastic bag or something—but get him cleaned up and take him down to Interrogation Room A," the first officer said.

He stepped back and behind the second and third officers.

"See he eats before you bring him down," he said. "Have him there by ten, no later."

"Yes, Sarge," the second officer said.

"And look," the first officer whined, pointing to the toilet. "There's no shit paper. Get the man some paper. Where's the fucking toilet paper? Who prepped this cell, anyway?"

"Sorry, Sarge," the second officer said.

"This is county, guys. Let's show some class." The first officer stepped out and walked the dark corridor, looking at his watch.

Two officers unshackled Peck, removed his cuffs, and went to find his duffel bag in the property room. One returned and tossed in clean jeans and underwear, a half roll of paper towels and stepped back and checked the locked door. Peck distanced his eyes and his awareness, as though he were alone in a bayou. He took care of his personal needs and flushed the toilet. He splashed himself at the sink and used paper towels to dry his face and body before he pulled fresh underwear and his new jeans on. The two watching him and the cellmate's eyes down the hall were nothing more than eyes in a swamp, bog or tidal flow. They meant nothing to Peck. A cart was pushed down the corridor and to his cell. Another uniformed officer lifted a pie tin and a spoon from it and handed it to the second officer.

"When you're done, leave it on the floor over here," the food cart pusher told Peck. He pointed at a spot near a door to his cell.

The second officer handed Peck a tin of macaroni and meat sauce, a spoon and a plastic bottle of water, stepped out of the cell, and slid the door closed.

"It's nine thirty-seven," the first officer said. "We'll be back in twenty minutes to get you."

Peck watched them walk the corridor and out the door, letting it slam behind them. He looked at his wrists. It was the first time he could see them since last night. He turned his hand and looked at the scars from the fishhooks. He held the pie tin with one hand and twisted his other wrist. Then he shifted the pie tin to the other hand and twisted the other wrist about. It was as if he were appreciating what little freedom he had, even though he was caged like an animal. He picked up his spoon, looked at it in his hand, and shoveled food into his mouth until the pie tin was empty. He set the tin and spoon on the floor where the food cart man had said and stepped back and sat on a portion of his cot not dampened by his urinating in the night.

He waited. Steeped in thought, he turned and studied the scratching of letters and sketches of faces on the brick wall behind him. He stood, walked over and picked up the spoon, walked back and touched the wall with the spoon handle, seeing that the girth of the spoon handle fit most of the wall carvings. He stepped back and dropped the spoon into the pie tin, walked to the bunk and sat down.

When they came, there was no talking. They cuffed him in front this time, left the shackles on the bunk for some other time, and walked him the length of the corridor into an eye-squinting, brightly lit county police station area and to a door out of a Philip Marlow detective movie with a frosted glass pane on the top half and the letter A painted in black on its center. They pushed the door open, walked Peck to a table where a middle-aged detective in a suit and a detective woman in her thirties in a black pantsuit sat and waited with indifferent looks on their faces. The officers sat Peck across from the two and pushed his chair in.

"Thank you, officers," the lady detective said. "We won't need the cuffs. You can take them off."

The second officer obliged, removing Peck's cuffs and carrying them out with him.

"We could use some coffee," the male detective said.

He looked first at the lady detective who nodded yes and then over at Peck. "How do you like your coffee?"

Peck pursed his lips as though he would trust them one time. "Black," he mumbled. "Sugar."

There was no talking while they waited. Three Styrofoam cups were brought in and set on the table. The male detective handed Peck his cup, black with sugar.

"Do you know why we're here, Mr. Finch?" the female detective asked, breaking the quiet.

"We're not thinking about what happened to the money yet," the male detective interrupted.

The female detective rested back and sipped her coffee.

"Tell us what you did with the body," the male detective said.

Peck's head bolted up.

"You know the bayous and the swamps," the female detective said.

Peck watched her eyes.

"Where'd you hide the body?" she asked.

Peck sat with a cold blank stare at the tabletop.

"I bet it easy getting rid of a body if you know swamps," the female detective said.

"Okay, so let's start with the money," the male detective said.

Peck looked up.

"Three grand's a lot of money," the male detective said.

"Where did you spend it?" the lady detective asked.

"You only have a few hundred on you now," the male detective said.

Peck stared at the tabletop.

"A casino, right?" the lady detective asked. "You lost it at tables or was it in the slots?"

"My money says it was the tit bars," the male detective said.

"Now, be nice, Lieutenant," the female detective said.

"Did you drop three thousand dollars on lap dances? Easy to do," the male detective said.

There was a knock on the door and the first officer stepped in.

"Detectives?" the first officer asked.

"We're busy," the male detective said.

"There's a call," the first officer said.

"No interruptions," the lady detective said.

"Tell them we'll call back," the male officer said.

"The prisoner has a phone call on line three, sir."

"Officer, we're in an interrogation, here," the male detective said.

"But it's his call, Detective," the lead officer said.

"What are you saying?" the male detective asked.

"He's allowed a call. It's his call," the first officer said.

"Are you telling us he hasn't had his call?" the lady detective asked.

"No, Detective," first officer said. "I mean, yes that's what I'm telling you. Not yet. This will be it."

"God damn it," the male detective barked. "He's been here all night. Why hasn't he been permitted to make his call?"

The first officer had a look on his face that any answer he gave would be a wrong answer. He stood there.

"Did anyone even read him his Miranda rights?" the lady detective asked.

"Oh, yes, Detective. We recorded that," the first officer said.

The two detectives looked at each other and shook their heads.

"Line three," the first officer said.

The male detective slid a phone over the table to Peck. He and the lady detective stood and left the room.

"We'll be outside," the lady detective said. "Finish your call."

When the door closed behind them Peck looked at the flashing light on the phone. He picked up the handset and put it to his ear.

"Hello?" he asked. There was no sound at the other end. Peck saw a light still blinking, and he chanced pressing on its button.

"Hello?" he asked.

"Peck, is that you?"

"This is Peck, who dat?"

"Sasha," she said. "This is Sasha, Peck. You okay?"

"Oh cher, what I did?" Peck pleaded. "They talkin' crazy talk about dead body and money. What'd I did?"

"Peck, I don't know anything so I can't tell you anything," Sasha said. "Hold on, and I'll put Lily Cup on the phone. She's a lawyer. She'll help you."

"What I did?" Peck asked.

"Hello, Peck?"

"Yeah," Peck said. "What'd I did, cher? They lock me up."

"Peck, listen," Lily Cup said. "Until you're back here in Louisiana it's maybe safer if we don't talk, so please don't ask me anything, but trust me, I'll help you get out of this mess."

"Tell Peck something anyhow," Peck said.

"A private detective is coming to get you out of jail. He's going to fly you to Baton Rouge or New Orleans, and he'll drive you to Carencro. I'll meet you there."

"Carencro?" Peck asked. "What body they talkin' about? They talking a dead body, cher."

"Peck...Peck...did you understand me?" Lily Cup said. "A detective is coming and he'll fly you to Baton Rouge or New Orleans and then he'll drive you to Carencro. Do you understand?"

"What dead body?" Peck asked.

"Tell me you understand," Lily Cup said. "Do you understand?"

"*Oui,*" Peck said. "*Je comprends.*"

"Good," Lily Cup said. "Now promise me you won't say a word to anybody unless I'm with you."

"Yes'm," Peck said.

"Say you promise," Lily Cup said.

"What about the body?"

"They're fishing, Peck. Don't think about a body."

"But—"

"Peck, this is important. Tell me you understand and you promise."

"I promise, shore t'ing," Peck said.

"Good, they're just fishing, so get what they said about a body out of your head."

"Hokay, cher."

"Here's Sasha," Lily Cup said.

"Peck, are you okay?" Sasha asked.

"I'm scared like Bayou Chene," Peck said.

"You mean that girl—the girl you go see?" Sasha asked.

"Nah, nah, like gator man, I—"

"Don't be frightened, honey. Do what Lily Cup tells you. She knows what she's doing."

"Peck, we don't have long to talk and they could be listening. Tell it to me when you get here."

"I feel like Bayou Chene all over again," Peck said.

There was silence on the phone as Sasha thought of his despair. She clasped her mouth with a palm muffling sobs. She handed the phone to Lily Cup.

"Peck," Lily Cup said. "Everything is going to be all right, and no talking. Promise?"

"Promise," Peck said.

The call ended.

Peck watched shadows of people milling about through the frosted glass—outside the interrogation room. It was twenty minutes of Peck sitting there looking at the phone when the door opened and the third officer came in and without talking, cuffed him and walked him through the main station and down the dark corridor to his cell. This time he picked up the shackles, removed the handcuffs and left Peck alone in the cell.

The lunch cart came with a tin plate of food and a spoon. This time it was a knackwurst, beans and a plastic bottle of water. Three hours later a guard came to the cell and had Peck stick his hands between the bars; he cuffed him before opening the door and he led Peck to the station lobby. A heavy-set man with a balding head and twigs of hair stubble in his ears, a gravy stain on his shirt, and a tattered briefcase with worn leather straps, walked up to the guard. He looked Peck over and then in the eye.

"Here's the plan, Finch," the private detective said. "Name's Conway. You don't try anything funny, and we'll get along just fine."

He cuffed his left wrist to Peck's right wrist.

"You come along easy and we'll be best friends, Finch," the private detective said.

He turned around with his back to the station crowd, lifted brass knuckles from his pocket and held them up to Peck's nose and growled a whisper.

"Fuck with me or try to run, I'll bust your face open, rip your arm off and stick it up your ass. We pretty much understand each other?"

Peck nodded.

"Well good," the private detective said. "We're off to a good start."

The private detective put the brass knuckles in his pocket and looked over at a guard. "Where do I sign for him, and can I get a ride to the airport?"

"Over there," the guard said, pointing to a desk. "You want Trenton-Mercer?"

"What in the hell is a Trenton-Mercer?" Conway asked.

"It's a local airport," the guard said.

"Hell no," the private detective said. "I want Newark. I don't want no Mickey Mouse scramble through some bush-hop airport with a prisoner in tow."

"I'll call you a van," the guard said.

Peck caught the private detective's eye.

"Mr. Conway?" Peck asked quietly.

"What?" the private detective grunted.

"I can't fly," Peck said. I got no ID for true."

The private detective gave a wily smile. "You do now, Finch. I've got your social security card in my bag and the warrant."

"Oh," Peck said.

"You ever even been on a plane, Finch?"

"Nah, nah," Peck said.

"Be a good fella and just enjoy the ride," Conway said. "It's free, and we'll have us a good lunch at the airport before we board."

Peck somehow felt more secure. As secure as one could feel being handcuffed to a private detective. There was something with the private detective's candor he felt he could trust. He watched New Jersey go by as the van crossed through farm country, passing horse stables, pastures, and skimmed over historical industrial cities. The interstate in New Jersey was an overpass through manufacturing and warehouse buildings dating back to the Civil War, not like the great bayous it would pass over in Louisiana.

The Newark airport was a new experience for Peck. It was hard for a down bayou boy to imagine anything so large being so well organized. He accepted the humiliation of being handcuffed in public and stayed within tow, climbed steps in unison, clearing security and doing what he was told to do. They found a booth at a Chili's restaurant. Conway placed his jacket over their arms, which remained cuffed together.

"With only one arm, kid, we're better off ordering something we can eat with one hand," he said. "Order things I don't have to cut for you—and things that don't take two hands to hold."

Peck nodded as if he was open to suggestions.

"How about a bowl of chili, some potato salad, a couple of hot dogs and a Coke? Fries too."

Peck nodded his approval.

A plane was something Peck had only seen leaving a vapor trail high over the wetlands. He could not imagine what it would be like to sit in one, much less fly in one. The takeoff had Peck spellbound. His eyes gleamed at the experience, the feel of it, being pushed deep back into his seat. He looked out at a wing and at clouds rolling by, trying to imagine the mystery of what was happening to him, like wondering how a snake or gator can just float on top of the water. The exhilaration of the flying experience seemed to let him forget slugs in his stomach and wetting his pants for a spell. He'd keep them forever in his memory, though. Nature's way had no option for forgetting.

"Can I ax you, something, sir?" Peck asked.

"Ask," the private detective said.

"Back there, in jail, they was a smell," Peck said.

"It's a county lock up. They call it a holding tank. Folks usually don't shower before getting locked up," Conway said.

"Nah, nah, not inside but from outside," Peck said.

"Outside? Outside of the lockup?"

"*Oui.*"

"Did you say the smells?"

"*Oui.*"

"From outside?"

"*Oui.* What dat smell, you know?"

"Are you meaning the fishy smell, outside?"

"Dass it. What dat smell, sir?" Peck asked.

"Oh, that, and call me Conway."

"What it is, Conway?"

"Shad," Conway said.

"Shad?"

"Shad."

"You don't say. Shad like roe and river catch?" Peck asked.

"Same shad," Conway said.

"They net 'em?" Peck asked. "Smells like when tides out and nets are out of the water."

"They use a dart," Conway said.

"A dart?" Peck asked.

"A dart is a small tiny little thing—looks like a hook but there's no barb on it. Why it ain't no bigger than your little finger's nail. It's called a dart. Shad go upstream by the millions to spawn, just like salmon, but when they're on a spawning run, they don't feed along the way, you see, so they won't bite a hook."

Peck looked at the private detective intently, listening to his story.

"When they swim upstream and see one of these darts they'll snub it with their snout—pushing it out of the way."

"Why's dat?" Peck asked.

"Shad won't feed when they're going upstream to spawn. They'll snub it away with their snouts and it hooks into them— usually a gill and that's how they're caught. The dart sticks into their gill or their side, and you reel them in. Oh, they put up a fight—jump two, maybe three times."

Peck smiled as he so enjoyed the story of shad.

"I've seen them—big ones over 23 inches—jumping two, three feet out of the water."

"T'anks," Peck said.

"Mr. Finch," proclaimed the private detective as if it were a historic moment, "in County, you were on the shores of the Delaware River. You've heard about the famous Delaware River, haven't you?"

"No sir," Peck said.

"George Washington crossed the Delaware River right there where you were in Trenton."

"For true?" Peck asked.

"Right about where you were in the tank," Conway said.

"Ah," Peck said.

"They're having their annual shad festival now," Conway said. "All up and down the Delaware, from the jetty dam there in Trenton—why they're skinning them in yards, pulling row and cleaning them all around the courthouse where they're being judged."

"T'anks," Peck said. "Good story."

"The fish smell comes from the fryers," Conway said. "They'll stack 'em high just for the taking. It's all for charity or something."

Peck tipped his head back, looked out at the clouds floating by. There was no moon in sight this night and he fell asleep.

CHAPTER 18

IT WAS AN EARLY MORNING CAB RIDE from the airport and Peck sat alone, handcuffed to a park bench behind the hospice. A morning moon was his only welcome back to Carencro. A silhouette of a cypress branch was tattooed on the moon's surface and he watched it as if the moon was a lost mamma he didn't remember and imagined her looking back at him, with a sense he needed her.

A lady stepped from the parking area onto the lawn, pulling white driving gloves as she approached. Peck knew her. He studied her walk. Her black skirt had a designer slit baring a milky thigh. She wore a matching, tailored double-breasted jacket with an oversized diamond-clustered brooch awkwardly pinned to its lapel; white Nike walking shoes. She walked directly to his bench, removing Chanel sunglasses, grasping them in her hand with the gloves, and sat down without asking. She extended a hand as though they had never met, in the likelihood of prying eyes.

"Remember me?"

"Ah *oui*, I remember you, cher."

"I'm Lily Cup," she said in case he had forgotten her name.

Peck was grateful for her coming, but he gave her a look as if he was embarrassed by her seeing him in handcuffs after that night at Charlie's Blue Note. He slouched as though body language might best express his anger and he watched a turtle on the cypress root smiling up at the sun. He studied its carapace as if estimating its weight for soup.

"Sasha called me," Lily Cup said.

"When?" Peck asked.

"As soon as she knew which airport your flight was landing in. She called me so I could be here to meet with you. I drove over earlier."

"What they chargin' me on?" Peck asked.

Lily Cup didn't speak. She folded each glove, placed them and her sunglasses in her bag, and set it between them on the bench.

"Dey was talking murder in New Jersey, cher."

"Who was talking murder?"

"The detective, axin' me stuff."

"I don't know about New Jersey but nobody here has charged you with anything."

"So, why'd they arrest me first place?"

"They wanted you in for questioning," Lily Cup said.

"Makes no sense, cher."

"I'm here to protect your rights—I'll see you don't get trapped saying the wrong things and incriminate yourself."

"Just to get grilled I got to be handcuffed to a bench?"

Peck's head darted around; he cupped his free hand and pushed his arm as quickly as an attacking eel, snatching a brown beetle bug flying near him. He sat back and held it delicately between his finger and thumb, as if he were considering it as fish bait.

"Did'ja talk to my boss, Miss Lavender?" Peck asked.

"We met at Starbucks on my drive in."

"Crab say anythin'?"

"She's thinking with you being twenty-four and maybe can learn from all this, she'll drop the warrant and give you your lawn-mowing job back if Lafayette Parish gets the answers they need and drop it," Lily Cup said.

"Twenty-four, is that what I am, cher?"

"Yes. Sasha had me search records to find your birth certificate, so she could get you on a plane. Turns out Miss Lavender found it first and gave it to that detective."

"You find it, for true?"

"You were twenty-four one month and three days ago."

"Well, I'll be—"

"Handcuffs were the detective's idea. He convinced Miss Lavender."

"But for why?"

"I'm guessing so you don't run— he probably figured he wouldn't get paid if you ran and she doesn't want to be embarrassed, you gone again and having to explain it to her board."

"She knows I ain't no murderer, dass for true."

"Oh she knows now it's got nothing to do with anything like that."

"What, then?"

"When you two disappeared, she told the sheriff a patient was missing and that someone saw you with him and the sheriff put a warrant out for you—suspicion of kidnapping."

"A patient?"

"I know, it sounds ridiculous."

"It ain't like the patient don't have no name, cher. His name is Gabe, call him Gabe."

"I know Gabe. I'm not disrespecting him. But to the sheriff he's just a missing patient."

"Sorry."

"You're being detained for questioning. Well, it's that and the other thing the sheriff added—suspicion of taking someone across state lines against their will," Lily Cup said. "Whatever he could pile on so they could arrest you and get you here, he stacked it."

Peck thrust the beetle high so it would have time to spread its wings and take flight.

"*S'envoler gratuitement, bebette,*" Peck said. ("Fly free, bug.")

He looked for another bug.

"Any suspicion when they coming, cher?" Peck asked sarcastically.

"Soon."

Lily Cup looked at the clock on her cellphone. She lifted a mirror from her purse and checked her lipstick and eye shadow.

"Any minute, actually."

She opened her hand palm down and studied the veins and polished nails in the morning sun.

"Parish sheriff's driving from Lafayette. My guess is he'll pick up the district attorney on his way through. I suppose they'll come together," Lily Cup said.

"Seems funny," Peck said.

"I don't see life in prison as funny, Peck. Kidnaping is federal and it carries—"

"Nah nah, not dat."

"What could possibly seem funny about this mess you're in?"

"Bein' handcuffed to the same bench where I met Gabe firs' place."

"You met him here?"

"*Oui.*"

"Not in N'Orleans?"

"Here, cher. This bench."

"On this same bench?"

"*Oui.*"

"That is ironic," Lily Cup said.

"Ironic. You know, dass xactly the right word, cher."

He raised his head and let it roll articulately from his tongue.

"Ironic. Sasha teached me dat one—she used it a lot."

"She does, doesn't she?" Lily Cup asked.

"I'm going to New Orl-ee-anhs to learn to read, if I can get out of this mess. I didn't kidnap nobody."

"I know it—Sasha knows it. You have to convince a grand jury."

"I couldn't figure what would make a old army captain like him want to run from a place like dis, anyhow."

Peck pointed at the three-story antebellum on the crest of a lawn behind them.

"Back there was a roof over his head I gaurontee, three meals a day and a view from this here bench along Bayou Carencro," Peck said. "I know it ain't much to look at for a dying man, dass for true, snakes and all; it's purdy much dead already. Look at it, cher, all lined with quiet. Cypress trees dripping with moss flowing in breezes looking like they floatin' out there in lily pad flat still water; gators minding they own business; ducks; acres of sweet green lawn smelling a fresh cut most times; fat ole magnolia trees, willows sopping up swamp and over there yonder a way, dat shiny red and yeller sign looking for a breeze so it can flop and reflect morning sun, warning about gators."

Peck stretched his free arm and yawned.

Lily Cup turned her eyes from the bayou, watched him raise an arm and flex, his muscles rippling. Her mind seemed to wander behind a glazed stare, but she came to with a slight shake of her head.

"Sasha is Cajun French," Lily Cup said.

"I know."

"She speaks French when we go to Charlie's Blue Note," Lily Cup said.

"I'm Cajun French, cher. I know French purdy good—she say I know a lot more than I let on, but she was trying to teach me a new somethin' ever' day."

Lily Cup cast a glance at his thighs.

"I can only imagine," she mumbled.

"Gabe liked her a lot," Peck said. "Think she was his boo, cher?"

"Oh, she loves Gabe—but I don't think she loves him like that. She thinks he's magical," Lily Cup said. "I never saw her have such deep feelings for a man so fast—him so old and her with a boyfriend in Baton Rouge."

"It was the dancin', cher."

"She told me that and the way he'd say things to her."

"I t'ink it was the dancin'—only dat."

"They sure could dance."

"Ah, Peck could watch 'em dance all night, dass for true. Even did."

Lily Cup smiled, nodding her head.

"Creole man, they dance good, dass for true."

"She was melancholy because it was after he told her he was dying."

"Ah, oui."

"Did you know he ran away from the VA hospital in Pineville?"

"No, I didn't."

"He refused more treatments for his stomach cancer."

"Is dat what he's got, for true?"

"You didn't know?"

"I knowed he was sick bad off, but I didn't know it was cancer, cher."

"He told Sasha somewhere along the way."

"I suspected he told her, but I didn't know all dat about the cancer and the treatments he run from," Peck said.

"She never knew any of it until after you were on the road."

"Memphis must be when he tole her," Peck said. "That's about when she got weepy-eyed."

The fog lifted and Lily Cup studied the morning moon between the Cypress trees—the living monuments of Acadiana.

"Look at the moon, Peck. It's beautiful."

"*Oui.*"

"I remember a full moon in the Quarter. Sasha told me she had a feeling there was something *gris gris*—dark and cursed—a hospice being in Carencro," Lily Cup said.

"Dass for true."

"Sasha is observant like that—she has been ever since grade school. She told me there was no irony in it."

"There's that word again, cher."

"She said it was mystical, Gabe being dropped here by a stranger."

"I don' know dat."

"A man found him fallen on a road outside of Opelousas, picked him up, didn't know where to take him and didn't want to take him to the law. He brought him here to a doctor he knew. Gabe was out of his pain medicine, cramped and passed out. The doctor saw his plastic wristband ID and called the VA hospital. The VA told him Gabe qualified for hospice; he had months to live and was refusing treatment. The doctor told him he could get his pain medicine and stay if he wanted."

"He ran from here too," Peck said.

"That's just it," Lily Cup said. "Why from here? That's what riled everyone."

"For music, he say, but—"

"Heaven only knows," Lily Cup said.

"To him, sitting was dying, cher. He warn't ready—"

"Maybe it was this place."

"What'cha mean?"

"Listen to it, Peck."

"I hear it."

"Maybe screeching birds from the bayou spooked him."

"Maybe smelling death," Peck said.

"You could be right."

"Dass what this place is, cher."

"I believe people know when they start to die," Lily Cup said.

"Yes'm, I know dat for true," Peck said.

"And the alligators," Lily Cup said.

"People's jus' like animals—a critter's blank eyes says he knows when he's dying—being kilt or natural, it don't matter, he knows."

"This is where the terminally ill wait to die," Lily Cup said.

"Dass for true."

"Sasha believes Gabe was dropped off here just so he could meet you, Peck."

"For true?"

"It was destiny so you could bring him to her, and they could dance."

"Sasha was good for Gabe—she woke his blank eyes," Peck said.

Peck and Lily Cup watched a rippling in the swamp water. A large heron flew overhead.

"Carencro is a Cajun French word," Lily Cup said.

"Ah, oui."

"It means carrion crow."

"Oui."

"Flesh eaters—"

"Oui."

"—dead flesh eaters. Vultures," Lily Cup said.

"I know buzzards—give me willies."

"Roost high in cypresses, feast on fish die-offs," Lily Cup said.

"Ever' time," Peck said.

"It's rite of passage in nature, and I wouldn't say this too loud, but they haunt this bayou, waiting on death for supper with terminal patients sitting on benches watching."

"Buzzards prolly watching them back," Peck said. "Ils ont une façon de sentir la mort." ("They have a way of smelling death.")

"Where in N'Orleans did you two bump into each other that night?" Lily Cup asked.

"Nah, nah," Peck said.

"It wasn't N'Orleans?"

"Nah, nah, cher."

"So how'd you both wind up on Frenchman Street?" Lily Cup asked.

"Gabe, aw he'd been here four, maybe t'ree weeks. He liked watching me 'cause I near spent a full hour at sunup throwing my trotline into the bayou and tying it off down there on dat willow root what sticks out at the water edge. He'd set and watch my floater corks to see if a mashwarohn or snapper took it under and see what else my rig might catch while I was tending lawn chores."

Lily Cup sat back and gazed through the moss of the swampy bayou.

"I love morning moons," Lily Cup said.

"I watch em most times."

"You too?"

"*Oui.*"

"What do you see when you watch a morning moon, Peck?"

"Crepe."

"You see a crepe?"

"*Oui*, sometimes."

"What would you know about crepes, Peck?"

"I know'd crepes."

"To you the moon is a crepe?"

"Morning moon like dat one is, cher. *Oui.* Look at it."

"Interesting. Yes, I can see it."

"A big crepe."

"There's a red and orange sky," Lily Cup said. "Like marmalade."

"I see it."

"Red sky in morning, sailor take warning," Lily Cup said, saluting the horizon.

"Ah *oui.*"

"To me a morning moon is a reminder," Lily Cup said.

"Reminder?"

"It reminds me I'm alive. It reminds me to remember that my heart beats and that I breathe."

Peck rested back.

"I see mamma," Peck said.

"You see your momma in the moon?"

"*Oui.*"

"That's so sweet."

Peck lowered his head.

"Is it sad, Peck, seeing your momma?"

"Nah, nah, I'm good," Peck said.

"What's that word you use, Peck—mashwarohn?"

"Catfish."

"Just like little boys, you and Gabe."

"We never talked for longest time," Peck said. "We'd catch an eye or two back and forth—you know how strangers did?"

"I know what you mean."

"I knew Gabe wasn't up to his own self, spirit-wise."

"You could tell?"

"A man can tell dat sort of t'ing looking into a man's eyes no matter what color a man is. A black man's eyes, like Gabe's, are best at showing hopeless in daylight. He'd set here unhappy—*mal pris.* I'd watch his eyes out of a corner of my eye mostly, my arm blocking my face. One day it come to me. Why it give me chills untangling trotlines knowing a man as healthy looking as me in this godforsaken place jus' setting on a bench with nothing to did but watch me throw my trotline while he was seeing his death tunnel. It was 'nuff to depress any fool."

"Well, I'll be, Peck."

"Hanh?"

"You, my friend, are a poet."

"A grow'd ole man with no family don' have nothing but himself to remember knowing."

"Aging can be so sad."

"Most he knowed is dead or long gone or out of his head."

"How old do you think he was?" Lily Cup asked.

"Is he dead, cher?"

"I don't know."

"He never said," Peck said. "I never ax."

"Weren't you curious?"

"I don' 'spect a body give age thought when he's dying. He told me he thought about wadin' the bayou and let gators take care of business."

"He said that?"

"He say gators would like black meat and thought he'd be good bait."

"How lonely it must be to grow old and not have anybody."

"*Beaucoup de viande sur les os,*" Peck added. ("Plenty of meat on the bones.")

They watched the stillness of the reeds sticking up from the swamp. A turtle plopped from the cypress root into the bayou.

"It was July fourth week, cher. I know, I had to mow Sunday before visitors come and T'ursday regular time. It was T'ursday when I was fixing to throw my trotline. I was puttin' cut bait on fishhooks of dis here one snood and I stuck hooks deep between my thumb and my palm and thought, looking over here at Gabe, hurtin' as it was, it was a sign."

"You saw a sign?"

"I snipped the snood both sides of the hooks with my weed clipper, grabbed my wire snips and walked over to this here bench to get the hook out and get something off my chest same time. I just plain come right out and ax Gabe if he wanted to get out of here."

"Is that true?" Lily Cup asked.

"*Oui.*"

"As simple as that?"

"What you mean, cher?"

"You stuck your hand with fishhooks, thought it was a sign, walked over here and asked him that?"

"True as I'm born, cher, simple as me."

"What'd Gabe say?"

"He say, 'Oh hell yes.'"

"He just came out and said, 'Oh hell yes'?"

"Didn't blink an eye," Peck said.

"What'd you say?"

"I say why don't ya just leave. You're free to go and where would ya go anyway, if you did get out and my name's Peck, what's yours?"

"I'll be damned," Lily Cup said.

"He shook my good hand and say, 'Pleased to meet you, Peck, my brother.'"

"That's how you two began?"

"He started calling me his brother first off—he say, 'name's Gabriel—you can call me Gabe, son.' He told me if he left he thought they would maybe take his pill bottle away and dat would kill him sure."

"He wanted to live," Lily Cup said.

"When I got the hooks out I ax him again where he'd go and he ax me if I liked jazz and I told him I liked music good and dass when he say it."

"What'd he say?" Lily Cup asked.

"I gived him my wire clipper to snip barbs off the hooks in my hand after I pushed them through."

"Ewwww," Lily Cup said. "Ow."

Peck held his hand up.

"You can see the scars. I bled a lot."

"What did he say?"

"He ax me could I see he gets to Newport so's he and me could drink scotch and listen to jazz at some fair or festival or carnival."

"The Newport Jazz Festival?"

"I know it was a jazz festival now, cher, but I didn't knowed what he was talking about back then. It's an important one, dat jazz festival."

"So you left together from here?"

"*Oui.*"

"His pills were an opioid, Peck. How'd you get him out of here with his pills through the nurses and security?"

"I looked him in the eye to see if he was worth trouble and decided quick, like Sasha did, I liked the kindly ole black man who ain't never harmed a flea."

"I remember liking him when I met him, Peck."

"I wanted it to be on a good foot starting out, so I flat out fessed to him I weren't all dat bright, but I had a knack for cunning, as my foster nanna used to tell me, and I might could get him out of here with his pills if he'd put some work clothes on, drop his duffel out his bedroom window and pretend he worked for me and we walked through the worker's fence gate."

"Did he have to think about it?"

"Gabe looked out over this bayou here, in a stare, and told me flat out his hospice room weren't nothing but a casket wit air-conditioning and a flat-screen TV," Peck said.

"So sad," Lily Cup said.

"Being black and in army so long is what made him talk straight out 'n direct like dat—least dass what he'd say."

"He's one in a million," Lily Cup said.

"Sides, they weren't time to think. He say you'd did dat for me? I told him I weren't about to keep throwing my trotline here day after day while watching a old man die where he don't want to."

"Awww."

"A tear come down from his eye. He shook his pill bottle, making sure it was full up. I told him it'd be best if we kept looking natural, so if we didn't want to get caught and ax a lot of questions and maybe lose his pills, we had to up and did it right then and there—no t'inking about it. Told him I'd run in for a bandage, let them see my blood so they wouldn't suspect not hearing me mow for a while and I'd look to see if my pay envelope was in my slot. I'd go around and pick up his duffel and meet him by the mower on side by the fence."

"Was your money there?"

"No, but I seed a atlas map sticking out from a shopping bag, grabbed it and put it under my T-shirt.."

"It was the blood," Lily Peck said.

"Hanh?"

"The blood on your hands and then you both disappear like that. I bet that's it. I bet that's why they put out a warrant. Him gone without telling anyone and you with bloody hands and gone too."

Peck lifted his hand and looked at the scar.

"And you both just walked out, no one asking why?"

"God's my judge."

"I'll be goddamned," Lily Cup said.

"This here's Lewisana, cher."

"What's that got to do with anything?"

"A lawn boy with a bandaged-up hand walking out toting a army duffel next to a overweight black man in work clothes ain't going to draw no attention in Carencro."

"You have a point."

Lily Cup looked about for cars driving in. There were none.

"It won't be long," Lily Cup said. "Sometime tomorrow after the bigwigs have their coffee and cinnamon buns in the judge's chamber there'll be a hearing before a grand jury. The judge isn't allowed in a grand jury room. He's around in case there's an indictment, and he needs to set bail. It'll be pretty much routine, if I haven't missed something."

"I'm in trouble, dass for true."

"That depends," Lily Cup said.

"Hanh?"

"If Gabe's alive I most likely can get you off unless the DA starts getting some television coverage on it and a bug up his butt and decides to make it a reality show, with him running for office again. Everything about this whole mess is circumstantial, and he knows it."

Lily Cup turned to catch Peck's eye. She touched his shoulder with her finger to get his attention.

"Just remember one thing, Peck."

"Hanh?"

"Sasha says you don't mean to be, but sometimes you're your own worst enemy, so try to keep your mouth shut and let me do the talking when they come."

Lily Cup turned forward, crossing her legs, widening the slit in the skirt on her thigh. Peck gave it pause. He looked at her white Nikes with no socks and the large diamond brooch that had come undone just as she caught it and fumbled to refasten it. She pinned it, patted it with her fingers as if saying hello to her gramma who gave it to her. They sat there in the still of the morning.

"Lily Cup, how's a ravishing woman—ya know, dat stuff Gabe say about Sasha—like your own self come to be a lawyer?"

"What do you mean?"

"Ain' it a man's world, lawyering?"

"Excuse me?"

"Daddy close with people at the capital, is he?"

She turned her face within inches of Peck's nose. He had hit a nerve. "Peck, now I'm warning you and please listen. People could be watching us right now. Today's not a day to be getting ideas like pretending we're close and familiar out here where people can see us. It's not funny, and it's dangerous, so cut it out."

"Cher, I wasn't—"

"What you and I did at Charlie's Blue Note is staying in the past, and it gives you no cause. And I was drinking."

"But I—"

"This is serious business."

"It was good for me at Charlies, cher."

"It was good for me too but—"

Peck smiled.

"But if you bring suspicion of those sorts of things, even in a joking way you do with your patois, they could open an ethics thing and throw me off the case. Where would you be then?"

"I swear, Lily Cup, I won' say a word to none of them."

"And that goes for Sasha too."

"Hanh?"

"She'll be in the courthouse tomorrow."

"Why?"

"In case the grand jury wants to put her on the stand. They're calling in all witnesses. I'm warning you. If you want to get out of this mess and ever see New Orleans again, don't so much as look at her."

"Kin I call her phone to ax if Gabe's alive?"

"No."

"Why, cher?"

"Not until this thing is over. That is, if you don't want me thrown off the case and the FBI taking it over. Kidnapping is a federal offense, Peck—it could carry life."

"For true? But I didn't—"

"Don't go messing it up now. Keep your business in your pants and your mouth shut."

"I won't even look at her."

"I can't make you but if you're smart, you'll give me your phone," Lily Cup said. "I don't want you tempted."

"I won't, cher, I promise."

Lily Cup held out her hand.

"I can't call her, cher—I don't know how to work it."

"It's for your own good," Lily Cup said.

Peck handed Lily Cup his phone, still in its packaging.

"So, women can't be lawyers, Peck?"

Peck didn't respond.

"Is it how you really think?" Lily Cup asked.

Peck looked at her shoes and brooch...her thigh through the slit.

"No...but you...well, you're beautiful clear enough, and plenty smart, dass for true, but it's just sometimes how you dress in clothes looking like you're a—"

"I thought traveling with Gabe would have taught you manners and how to hold your tongue, peckerwood."

"Name ain't Peckerwood," Peck said.

"I know your name. You hurt me."

"But peckerwood—"

"Don't worry, your real name is in all the papers."

"Where'd you get a name like Lily Cup, anyways?" Peck asked.

"It's my name, Lily Cup."

"For true, cher?"

"Born and raised in New Orleans and before you make some wise-ass comment, it's my real name. Lily Cup Lorelai Tarleton and I graduated law, at Harvard, and I practice criminal law in and around New Orleans, trying to keep fools like you out of prison, or from ending up in Angola, getting the needle."

"But Lily Cup?" Peck asked.

"Conceived on a picnic blanket in Chalmette, if you must know—1981, it was. As the story went, while Daddy was introducing me into my momma, so to speak, right next to a wooden bowl of potato-salad, Momma rolled in passion, her butt cheeks crushing a tube of Lily Tulip paper cups they brought for their mint juleps, and a julep wasn't a drink you can drink from a bottle. Nine months to the day Momma wouldn't let Daddy name me Tulip because of the crushed Lily Tulip cups—and made him promise her no *Tulip*. He gave her his word and then wrote Lily Cup on my birthing papers out in the hall without her knowing."

"I'll be," Peck said.

"You asked," Lily Cup said.

"T'ink of it, cher...me getting Peckerwood for being a smart ass and there you go earning Lily Cup cause your momma was getting—ya know—plowed at a picnic."

"I never have liked potato salad," Lily Cup said to herself.

"Now dass a story, I guarontee."

"Whole world hears it every Thanksgiving," Lily Cup said.

"Your daddy is something else."

"He's gone now, but he surely was."

"He didn't mean no harm wit naming you dat, cher."

"Harvard accepted me, so it couldn't have been all bad."

Lily Cup sat up at hearing a distant car's sound, turned and looked over at the entrance driveway.

"They're here, Peck."

"Where?"

"That's them parking. I'm going over to meet them."

She grabbed Peck's free hand and gave it a squeeze.

"Let's hope he's alive," Lily Cup said.

"Ain't dat for true," Peck said.

"Remember, please shut up and when they take you in, do what they tell you. They'll know to only question you outside of a grand jury room with me present. Let me do the talking."

"Yes'm," Peck said.

"Sit up straight, Peck."

"Hanh?"

"Show them you amount to something."

Peck sat up and watched a turtle crawl to the end of the cypress root and drop into the water. He rested back with a blank stare, looking at the morning moon.

CHAPTER 19

TWO UNIFORMED POLICE OFFICERS stood guard in the echoes of the historic marbled entry hall of the Carencro City courthouse. On a distant bench on the north side of the hall sat Sasha. Sasha was wearing a tailored, conservative gray pantsuit and jacket, a black satin blouse buttoned to her neck, and conservative heels. Purposely ignoring Peck and Lily Cup directly across the lobby corridor, she thumbed an iPhone, reading and answering emails. There was a Starbucks cup on the bench next to her bag. Sitting a few feet over from Sasha on the same bench was Miss Lavender, director of the hospice in Carencro. Miss Lavender was reading a book. Several feet from Miss Lavender, private detective Conway was sitting with a wrinkled, empty sandwich wrap in one hand, holding two donuts and a large Styrofoam coffee cup in the other. Several napkins lay on the bench seat beside him. Every time someone would enter or leave the courthouse, the tall brass doors would sound a deep clunk together, like shrimp trawlers bumping a dock coming into port. The whispering of people in the hall echoed like they would inside a basilica.

"You look nice, Peck," Lily Cup said. "Is that a new shirt?"

"Sasha, up bayou in Memphis give it," Peck said.

"Peck, the detectives or the district attorney may try to hassle you and call you Boudreaux Clemont Finch. Just don't let them fluster you," she said.

"Dass my name, cher," Peck said. "I good with it."

"And what's going on here isn't a trial. They're asking a lot of people a lot of questions, trying to find out what happened to Gabe."

"Did Gabe die, did he? You can tell me, cher."

Lily Cup either didn't hear Peck or ignored the question.

"Attorneys aren't allowed in a grand jury room," Lily Cup said. "Remember, they want to learn what you know, not what you don't know. Don't be offering things for them to think about. It could only dig a hole deeper. Don't tell them things they don't ask for."

"I know bait good and trotlines," Peck said. "I be hokay."

What Peck wasn't sharing with Lily Cup was how his treatment in that New Jersey lockup jarred him, and how it reopened memories of times when he was four, five and six, forced to carry bait buckets for the drunkard gator man until his hands bled or his back burned from the sun a tar red so raw he would try to sleep at night sitting up leaning on his shoulder. He has nightmares of a rope tied around him under his armpits being dragged behind a flat boat as bait on alligator hunts—rifle shots over his head—praying someone would pull him in the boat in time. He wasn't sharing how he learned patience by waiting hours on end hiding from gator man in cypress trees watching alligators float like logs without moving a muscle until the time was right. He wasn't sharing how gators must know everything, being they were a million years old and man was fish bait at maybe seventy, eighty.

The grand jury room door opened. A man stepping out let it close behind him. He walked in quick pace the length of the hall toward the judge's chambers at the east end.

"Morning, Counselor Tarleton," the man said, tipping two fingers on his forehead as a friendly salute, greeting counsel as he passed.

"Good morning, your honor," Lily Cup said.

"Welcome to Carencro," he said.

She watched him walk the hall and into his chambers. "He's the local judge," Lily Cup said. "He was in there telling them he'd be around in case they make a decision on indicting you, if he's needed to set bail."

"Decision?" Peck asked.

"This is a grand jury, Peck. It's not like a jury trial. Behind those doors they can't say you're guilty or innocent. All they can do is say they don't think you should be charged with a crime or they could say they think you should be charged," Lily Cup said.

Peck clenched his fists, as though in fear.

"Just be yourself and tell the truth," Lily Cup said.

"Will you be in there with me?" Peck asked.

"I can't go in with you, but I'll be with you all the way," she said.

One of the uniformed officers answered his cellphone. As he talked he walked over to private detective Conway and paused, waiting to finish the call. He leaned and spoke with Conway. Conway stood, and they both walked over to Lily Cup and Peck.

"Miss Tarleton?" the uniformed officer asked.

"Yes, officer?" Lily Cup asked.

"The grand jury has begun, and I'm to stay here with you and your client while they call everyone in one at a time. Your client will be the last one called."

"That'll be fine. I'll go get some coffee. My treat, would you like a cup officer?" Lily Cup asked.

She stood and picked up her valise and shoulder bag.

"That'd be nice, counselor," the uniformed officer said. "An iced black is fine. Thank you, ma'am."

"Peck," Lily Cup said. "I'll be right back. Like the officer said, if they call you, it will be after everyone else."

"Do they call you?" Peck asked.

"Honey, listen to me," Lily Cup said. "Attorneys aren't allowed in a grand jury room. There's no need to be frightened, just tell the truth."

"Peck," Private Detective Conway said. "I know it's all pretty secret stuff. I think they try to make it scary. They can't even take notes or minutes in there."

"I'll have to cuff him to a bench, counselor," the uniformed officer said. "Regulations, ma'am, in case I get called away."

"That'd be fine," Lily Cup said.

Lily Cup gave a look at Peck as if to try to explain the handcuffs. He simply raised his wrist, offering it for cuffing.

"Private Detective Conway," the uniformed officer said. "You may go in now."

Lily Cup gave Peck a deserving smile of thanks for helping with the handcuffs, turned and headed out the front door to a Starbucks.

Private Detective Conway was the first witness called into the room. The bailiff held a Bible before him and asked him to place his hand on it and swear to truthful testimony.

"Private Detective Conway," the district attorney said. "Do you know why we're here today before a grand jury of Lafayette Parish?"

"No sir," Conway said. "I was fulfilling a portage assignment and asked to appear, but other than what I read on the warrant, I don't know details."

"Private Detective Conway, what if I were to tell you suspicions before this grand jury are those of kidnapping, grand theft, and possibly murder?" the district attorney asked. "Might you see where the observations and opinions of a professionally trained and experienced eye like yourself might be of help in determining a person of interest's likelihood for committing the crimes we've outlined?"

"Yes, sir," Conway said. "I can see that."

"Private Detective Conway, how many years have you been a private detective or in a similar capacity?"

"I tried twice but I did not pass the law boards after I graduated LSU in 1994, so I apprenticed with a bounty hunter and got my license as a private detective in Shreveport. I found the work rewarding and I bought him out last year in May, when he retired."

"Are you active as a bounty hunter?" the district attorney asked.

"I mainly do out-of-state portages—" Conway started.

"They seem to run from Louisiana, don't they, Private Detective Conway?" the district attorney mused.

"—transferring in prisoners, like young Peck, who's sitting out there, thanks to me."

"Young Peck?"

"My portage," Conway said.

"You're of course referring to a Mr. Boudreaux Clemont Finch, is that correct Detective Conway?"

"Yes. His name is Finch, but he preferred I call him Peck."

"Do you always do what a prisoner prefers?" the district attorney asked.

"I try to get along with them, best I'm able," Conway said. "We'll get along if he knows the rules, and if I know his requests are within my power—and it's an easy portage. A thousand miles is quite a spell being handcuffed to a man—bathrooms, restaurants, things like that. Best we get along."

"Private Detective Conway, with your experienced observation could Mr. Finch, or Peck, as you call him, murder a man?" the district attorney asked.

Detective Conway started, thinking.

"In your opinion, of course, detective Conway."

"I don't think so," Conway said.

"You're saying you don't think this man could murder someone."

"Doesn't seem the sort."

"Private detective Conway, could this Peck you brought here from a jail cell in Trenton, New Jersey—could he kidnap someone—anyone, in your opinion?"

"If you mean kidnap, like for ransom or for money?" Conway asked.

"Is there any other kind, Detective Conway?"

"I don't think he would do a thing like that. No sir, I don't."

"Private detective Conway, if I were to tell you there is a matter of a missing four thousand dollars belonging to the victim that was in this party of interest's care, would that maybe cause you to rethink your position?"

"You mean about Peck?" Conway asked.

"Your position about Peck, yes," the district attorney said.

Conway scratched his jaw. He reached up to his bald forehead and scratched. He lowered his eyelids and grimaced with determination.

"No sir, I don't," he said. "I don't think any of that would change my opinion of him one whit."

"Most curious," the district attorney said.

"Well, you asked," Conway said.

"I'm not questioning your veracity, private detective Conway, not in any manner...but would you please share with this grand jury just what insights you might have that enable you to think of our party of interest as not capable or as unlikely of such crimes?"

"The shad," Conway said.

"Excuse me?" the district attorney asked sarcastically.

Conway sat and waited.

"Did you say, the shad?"

"It was the shad," Conway repeated.

The district attorney swept his arm around as though he was presenting the private detective on a center stage.

"Kindly illuminate the men and women of this grand jury, private detective Conway," the district attorney said.

Sensing a trap but showing in his eyes he was sincere and certainly wanting justice served for the boy in the hall, Conway sat up in his seat.

"It was on the plane when the young man out there—"

"The man you call Peck, Detective Conway?"

"Yes sir, the man I call Peck asked me about the fish smells around the courthouse in Trenton."

"Let me get this straight. Did you say fish smells?"

"Trenton and other places were having their annual shad festival going all around the Delaware River," Conway said. "It's a very popular festival, I've heard. We were buckled in on the plane waiting for takeoff when he asked me. This Peck. He turned in his seat and looked me right in the eye, and he asked me—I remember he asked— 'back there, Mr. Conway, he said, what was that fish smell?'—that's sure enough what he asked me."

"Private detective Conway, a prisoner asks about a shad festival—"

"Oh, he didn't know about the festival."

"—a prisoner asks about the smell of fish and you can assume he's incapable of committing a crime?"

"He didn't ask about fish, he asked about the smell."

"On the plane, this Peck out of the blue asked you about the smell."

"He could smell it from his cell," Conway said.

"Ladies and gentlemen," the district attorney said. "This is beginning to sound a bit fishy to me."

"It's the way he did it," Conway said.

"Oh, enlighten us, please continue, private detective Conway," the district attorney said. "We're all ears."

"He did more than ask," Conway said.

The district attorney didn't bother talking; he waited.

"I know he couldn't have done those things because of the way he listened to me," Conway said.

"Things, Detective Conway?"

"Kidnap and murder," Conway said.

"Because of the way he listened to you?"

"I've been doing this for close to thirty years. I've seen it all pretty much. In my line of work, I see up close the kidnappers, murderers, and thieves, see—and one thing I know is they don't want to learn."

"You're saying that murderers and thieves don't—"

"They know it all. Least that's my look on things, anyway. I remember sitting on that plane near half an hour—could a been forty minutes—describing to this Peck fellow what it was like catching a shad—how they had to hit your dart just right; how they'd jump two, maybe three times when they did. I'm telling you as God is my witness, this boy didn't once take his eyes off me while hearing my story, not for one second. I don't think he's your man."

With his back to the detective, the district attorney watched the eyes of the jurors.

"Could money be a motive?" the district attorney asked.

"He had money on him," Conway said.

"Four thousand dollars is unaccounted for, detective Conway."

"He didn't have much, but he had enough to get by on. He had a Greyhound travel pass on him."

"I assume travel passes are pricey, detective Conway."

"I don't know, but I would imagine they are."

"A travel pass would take money, Detective Conway."

"A thief doesn't carry a Greyhound travel pass on him."

"And just what does a thief carry?" the district attorney sniped.

"He sure doesn't carry a bus pass," Conway said.

"And your theory is, Detective Conway?"

"He'd steal a car. A thief would steal a car."

"Thank you, private detective Conway. You may step down. Thank you for your insightful testimony."

"Can I say one more thing?" Conway asked.

"You're still under oath," the district attorney said, waving his hand and inviting Conway to speak.

"The boy was as feared and as frozen as a jack rabbit," Conway said.

"What's your point detective Conway?"

"If he was a thief or a killer, he'd have nerves of steel, have tattoos, gold watches, something fancy—a ring, maybe. But he wouldn't listen to a story about catching shad like he was a schoolboy. He has a duffel bag with one pair of jeans, two shirts, a spool of fishing line and some underwear in it. On his person he had pocket money, a bus pass, some handwritten notes and papers."

"Noted, private detective Conway," the district attorney said. "You may step down."

Conway stepped down and walked out through the large door. He held it as Sasha walked in. The district attorney gestured for her to take the stand and she obliged.

The bailiff held the Bible and swore her in.

"Miss Lissette," the district attorney said. "Can you state your name and where you live?"

"My name is Michelle Lissette. I've lived in New Orleans all my life. I attended Tulane. I have a real estate business and primarily deal with Garden District residential sales, rentals or historical restoration."

"Thank you, Miss Lissette," the district attorney said. "Do you know the nature of a grand jury, ma'am?"

"Not really. I think you indict people?"

"A grand jury listens," the district attorney said. "They listen to all known witnesses or parties of interest, and then they decide the viability of a case against someone moving forward. As the district attorney, it would be my decision, after hearing their feedback, as to whether to move a case forward or any other disposition."

"Now I understand," Sasha said. "Thank you."

"Miss Lissette, our purpose is to learn anything you might know that would be relevant to the party of interest we have before us in the name of one Boudreaux Clemont Finch and his relationship with one Gabriel Jordan," the district attorney said. "Miss Lissette, are either of these names familiar to you?"

"I know them both, Peck and Gabe," Sasha said.

"Please enlighten the grand jury as to your relationship with these men, Miss Lissette."

"I met them at Charlie's Blue Note. It's a small neighborhood jazz bar off Frenchman Street near the Quarter. My girlfriend and I sometimes go there to dance. It's safe because Charlie always walks us home. Peck and Gabe came in one night. They had red beans and rice, and a couple of drinks. Gabe drank Chivas—that's a scotch and Peck drank beer."

"Was there anything suspicious about their behavior?" the district attorney asked.

"No," Sasha said.

"Were you able to observe them throughout their time at Charlie's?"

"I danced with Gabe. He's a very good dancer."

"Would you say you were able to observe his demeanor by dancing with him?"

"In fact, I think we danced until almost midnight."

"Miss Lissette," the district attorney said, "the grand jury is here to listen to evidence given by parties who have had contact with the party of interest. It is in their purview to determine whether in their opinion after listening to your testimony there may or may not be a case going forward against that party."

"A case with those two? A case like what?" Sasha asked. "I can't imagine one."

"Miss Lissette," the district attorney said. "It'd serve our interest if you would let me ask the questions."

"Fine with me," Sasha said. "But I think I know those two pretty well, and I can't imagine either of them as bad guys."

"Miss Lissette," the district attorney said, "one of the charges pending on the outcome of this grand jury is that of transporting a person against their will across a state line. Are you aware of any conversations you overheard that would lead you to believe Mr. Jordan was being forced to leave Louisiana against his will, particularly by Mr. Finch?"

"I can do better than that," Sasha said.

"By all means, Miss Lissette. Please illuminate us."

"Peck wasn't even with us when Gabe told me he was going to the Newport Jazz festival in Newport, Rhode Island," Sasha said. "He and Peck were headed there because Gabe wanted to go, not because Peck wanted to go."

"Miss Lissette," the district attorney said, "all well in good, but did you personally witness Mr. Jordan leaving this Charlie's with Mr. Finch?"

"No," Sasha said.

"So, all of this conjecture is supposition on your part, might that be fair to say, Miss Lissette?"

"No," Sasha said.

"Miss Lissette, you're trying the grand jury's patience," the district attorney said. "Would you care to explain?"

"I said I didn't see them leaving Charlie's," Sasha said. "But I did see them come out of Charlie's."

"Games with us can be costly and punishable with a contempt of court, Miss Lissette," the district attorney said. "Kindly be warned."

"When Gabe told me he was heading to the Newport Jazz festival, he said they were hitchhiking. I offered to drive them as far as Memphis is all," Sasha said. "I went home and got my car and came back. That's when I saw them coming out of Charlie's."

"So, it was you who drove Gabriel Jordan and Mr. Finch out of state, Miss Lissette?" the district attorney asked.

"Well not that, either," Sasha said. "Gabe liked my Bentley and asked if he could drive. He had a valid license, so I let him. So, you see, Gabe drove himself out of the state of Louisiana in my Bentley—and with Peck asleep in the back seat. If he was taking someone across a state line against their will he was not doing a good job of it. He was sound asleep most of the way."

The district attorney dropped his papers on the table on top of his briefcase. He turned in a circle, thinking. He turned again.

"Ladies and gentlemen of the grand jury," he began. "Let's say we're able to corroborate the veracity of this witness. After all, she would appear to have a substantial equity in her local community interest and not be inclined to play with risks. If what she says is the case, and we are to believe her, and also the testimony prior to Miss Lissette, what we might have is a local kidnapping."

"Peck didn't kidnap anyone," Sasha said.

"Young lady, if Peck so much as walked that dying old man out through the gates of the hospice," the district attorney said. "A case for kidnapping might bear listening to."

"I don't know any of that," Sasha said. "All I know is Gabe wanted to go to Newport. He would have tried even without Peck."

The district attorney raised his index finger in the air as if with a thought. "And if this man, one Gabriel Jordan, has deceased," the district attorney said. "This could be involuntary manslaughter. Removing a man from a facility who needs close and constant medical attention. This could be the case, if the man has passed."

Sasha was too upset and angry to cry at the thought of Gabe dying.

"It's not like that," Sasha said wringing her hands.

"Miss Lissette, to your knowledge, is Gabriel Jordan alive or dead?" the district attorney asked.

"I spoke to him two nights ago," Sasha said. "He was alive."

"I ask again, Miss Lissette, is Gabriel Jordan, a man allegedly taken from the safety of hospice care alive or dead?" the district attorney asked.

This time Sasha lifted a tissue from her bag and dabbed her eyes.

"I don't know," she said.

"How long would it take you to determine if Mr. Gabriel Jordan is alive or dead with absolute provable verification from credible witness testimony?"

"Maybe an hour or so," Sasha said.

"Grand jury members," the district attorney said. "I propose we walk to an enjoyable lunch. The county is treating today. We'll give Miss Lissette her hour or so and reconvene back here at one thirty. In the meantime, Miss Lissette, you are under a full gag order not to divulge anything about this line of questioning with any other awaiting witnesses. We'll see you back here at one thirty."

Sasha stepped down from the witness stand and walked out.

CHAPTER 20

SASHA MADE HER WAY into the hall, letting the grand jury room door close freely behind her. Miss Lavender was still seated on the far wall bench with an open book in hand; Lily Cup, Peck, and one uniformed officer on the bench closest to the grand jury room door. Sasha dashed across the hall, heels spiking on the cold marble to the far bench, where she sat and proceeded to text Lily Cup without looking across the lobby at her.

"Not allowed to talk with anyone about the grand jury," she texted.

"You can if they've released you."

"They haven't."

"Explain."

"In deep shit. I have to prove Gabe is alive."

"So? Call and see if he answers," Lily Cup texted. "If he does, he's alive. Duh!"

"Not that easy," Sasha texted.

"He's in a hotel, right?"

"Yes."

"Well, if he doesn't answer, ask the front desk if they have seen him this morning," Lily Cup texted.

"I have to have a credible witness," Sasha texted.

"I'll be your witness," Lily Cup texted.

"Can't. Gag order, I can't talk to any witnesses or their attorneys," Sasha texted.

"You have a f#!?ing gag order like that and you don't bother to tell the lead defense attorney about it in your first text?!!!!" Lily Cup texted.

"PULEEZE no drama. Save it for a trial if I fuck this up," Sasha texted. "You know your way around courts. Who can I get on short notice as a credible witness?"

"Now? Today?"

"I have an hour and a half to put it together or else the kid could be in big trouble maybe."

Lily Cup set her phone on the bench, opened her valise and shuffled papers. Then, almost as if it were a stroke of brilliance, she snapped her finger, picked up her phone and started texting again.

"Judge Thibodaux," she texted.

"What's a Judge Thibodaux?" Sasha texted.

"See the door marked 'Chambers'?"

"Where?"

"Down at the end of the hall?"

Sasha looked down the length of the marble hall.

"Not that end, the other end of the hall," Lily Cup texted.

Sasha saw the door and gave a cartoon smile.

"That's Judge Thibodaux's office," Lily Cup texted. "He's in there. I saw him."

Sasha stood, straightened her suit coat, saw to it her pants creases were aligned and blouse tucked. She was reaching and tightening the velvet ribbon knot tying her hair back as her phone signaled. She picked it up.

"Word is he's an old fart— likes tits," Lily Cup texted. "Watch y'self."

Sasha stood erect, at first as if she was rising to accept the challenge, then let her shoulders droop in thought, knowing what was at stake. Fueled with resolve, she began walking in quick, short steps while unbuttoning a blouse button, then the next button down, then the next, her heels echoing through the grand marble foyer. With her back to Lily Cup and Peck she looked down quickly, assessing whatever cleavage she was able to liberate on short notice, and raised an arm, giving a thumbs-up signal as she pushed the door with the gold leaf lettering marked *Chamber*. The reception area was pecan wood paneled, empty and deep, and rolling films of cigar smoke billowed from an office two doors back. Holding her phone in one hand, her carryall in the other, she made her way down the short hallway and peered in the doorway where the smoke emanated.

"Excuse me?" Sasha queried.

Behind the desk a silver-haired man in a leather wingback crushed his newspaper down with both hands, his eyes bugged, nearly dropping the cigar from his mouth.

"Excuse me?" Sasha repeated.

"Ma'am?"

"I'm looking for Judge Thibodaux. Are you Judge Thibodaux, by any chance?"

The man took the cigar from his mouth. "Why, yes, I am...I'm Judge Thibodaux, but the lady out front will be more than obliging, I'm certain..."

Sasha took charge and stepped in the office, making her way to the front of the judge's desk. She strategically leaned over and down from a standing position, setting her carryall bag on the floor.

"How may I be of service, young lady?" the judge asked, taking his cigar from one hand and placing it in the ashtray. "Please, take a seat. I'm at your service."

Sasha sat down, leaning forward in the chair.

"Judge Thibodaux, there's no one out front and I know this is short notice—a man as important and as busy as you—but I need a credible witness because if I don't have a credible witness and proof that a certain man is alive by one thirty today there's going to be all kinds of trouble."

"Young lady, does this by chance have to do with any case before me now?" Judge Thibodaux asked anxiously.

Sasha looked at her phone and began thumbing through local restaurant menu pages, answering the judge remotely.

"On? Case? Before you? Oh, no sir, how could it?" Sasha asked.

Sasha stood again and leaned down, offering her hand to the judge. The judge accepted the offer, lingered as he gently shook her hand.

"My name is Michelle Lissette, and I'm in real estate. I've come from New Orleans to get papers in order for a project and to the best of my knowledge you wouldn't be trying any cases down in New Orleans, since it's a different parish and district.

Did you know there were 64 parishes in Louisiana, Judge? I just have to prove a man's alive and I could do it myself, but you know how they are. They want me to have a credible third-party witness give a statement, so I need a credible witness to help me, and do you like calamari, Judge?"

Sasha sat down with a bounce.

The judge's head limped forward in anticipation. Then he caught it and paused as his mind caught up.

Oh, I do love calamari—I'm partial to a Béchamel red sauce with just a touch of butter." he said.

As the judge folded his newspaper and spoke on about how much cream should be in the sauce, Sasha touched her phone keys and held it to her ear.

"Drago's Seafood."

"Hello? I'd like two orders of calamari, please."

"Is this a pick up?"

"Can you add a Béchamel sauce with butter and...hold on, please," Sasha said, looking over at Judge Thibodaux.

"How many oysters, Judge?" Sasha asked.

The judge fanned both of his hands open as if he were surrendering in the battle of New Orleans.

"We don't have Béchamel, ma'am, we have a private recipe red sauce for the calamari."

"Send that sauce and send two dozen fresh oysters on shaved ice, horseradish, cocktail sauce—but do not mix them. We'll do it here," Sasha said.

"Two calamari, red sauce on the side, two dozen oysters, anything else?"

"Can you send it over to Judge Thibodaux's chambers, please?"

There was a pause.

"Yes ma'am, we'll bring it right over."

Sasha raised her brow.

"You know where that is?" she asked.

"We know."

"Good, see you soon. Oh, and there's no one out front, so just bring it back here, okay?"

"We'll bring it soon."

Sasha ended the call and held her finger up as if to hold the moment and dialed one more restaurant.

"Antoni's, how may I help you?"

"Hello. You have Italian, right?" Sasha asked.

"Only the best."

"Good, do you have a Béchamel sauce?"

"Of course, we have Béchamel—the best."

"Can you send a pint of your Béchamel sauce right away?"

"What entree?"

"No entree, just a pint of Béchamel."

"Of course."

"You can? Send it to Judge Thibodaux's office."

"Twenty minutes."

"You know where?"

"We know the judge."

"Just walk on back. There's no one up front."

Sasha set her phone on the table next to her chair.

"You are one popular guy, Judge."

"Are all realtors from New Orleans as scrappy?" the judge asked.

"We have to move quick down there, Judge. We could all be under water at any minute."

"How may I help you?"

"Judge, does your phone do conference?"

"It does."

Sasha stood, leaned over his desk and picked up his phone receiver.

"Nine?" Sasha asked.

"Yes, ma'am. Dial nine for an outside line."

Sasha dialed the Courtyard Marriott in Providence and as it started ringing, she set the receiver down and pushed the conference speaker button.

"Courtyard by Marriott, how may we direct your call," the operator queried.

"Hello. I'm trying to reach a Mr. Gabriel Jordan," Sasha said. "He's a guest there."

"One moment, I'll ring Mr. Jordan's room," the operator said.

Eight rings with no answer and the phone went into voicemail. Sasha hung up, picked up the receiver and dialed again.

"Hold on, Judge," she said.

"Nothing on my docket today, take your time."

"Courtyard by Marriott, how may we direct your call," the operator queried.

"Hello, I just called for a Mr. Gabriel Jordan, and he didn't answer in his room," Sasha said.

"Would you like me to try again?" the operator asked.

"No, no. Could you ask people at the desk if they'd seen him around this morning—maybe getting coffee or catching an Uber? Please? It's important."

Sasha tapped two fingernails impatiently on the desktop, leaning down on one arm, waiting for answers from the conference speaker.

"No one remembers seeing Mr. Jordan this morning," the operator said. "But we have busy mornings with checkout and our continental breakfast. Very busy indeed."

"Thank you," Sasha said. She pushed the button to hang up and sat down.

"Might I ask where you were calling?" Judge Thibodaux asked.

The judge's question was interrupted by the first deliveryman from a restaurant. Sasha handed him her credit card to swipe and pointed at a side conference table for the man to place the bags. She invited the judge over with a welcoming smile. She signed the tab and thanked the deliveryman. As he exited, he was interrupted by the delivery of the Béchamel sauce. Sasha lifted a twenty from her bag and held it up.

"Will this take care of it?" she asked.

"Oh yes, ma'am," he answered. "Hi, Judge," he threw in, snapping the twenty from her hand and leaving.

With calamari and a Béchamel dip and fresh raw oysters on shaved ice, any gathering becomes family in kind. In southern Louisiana, it's almost a religious experience—as sacred as morning beignets with chicory coffee and cinnamon.

"Were you reared in the Big Easy, child?" Judge Thibodaux asked.

"Judge, I was born in a ladies' toilet in Vieux Carré," Sasha said. "Momma lived in Faubourg Lafayette, and she found making it home an inconvenience when her water broke while she was standing in line to get a praline at the oyster bar."

"Oh my," Judge Thibodaux said. "You certainly were christened Mardi Gras early. It's no wonder you have fire in your blood. I can tell you're a woman who controls her own destiny."

"*Jeanne d'Arc était stupide,*" Sasha said.

"Young lady, I do understand enough of the French to know without ample reason, my momma, a devoted follower of the church might have suggested you've blasphemed against a holy saint who was publicly burned at the stake, with such sentiment," Judge Thibodaux said.

Sasha smiled, shaking her head a definite no.

"So, tell me, for the record, and in your humble opinion, of course, why was Joan of Arc stupid?" the judge asked.

"She should have peed on the matches," Sasha said.

While it sank in, the judge choked and snorted cocktail sauce into his nose, causing him to stand coughing, laughing, guffawing, gulping water, trying to get in control. Sasha's giggle turned into a nervous tremble as she watched his contortions, hoping he didn't have a heart attack. By the time he got in full control and sat down again all they both could do at first was inhale and then give a loud exhale.

Composure gained with a vocal sigh, the judge picked up a ring of calamari, and asked again, "Just where are you trying to call?"

"Providence, Rhode Island, Judge. My friend is up there going to the Newport Jazz Festival every day all week."

"Those are great fun," Judge Thibodaux said.

"You've been there?"

"The Newport Jazz Festival?" the judge asked."

"Yes."

"Oh, my yes. More than once."

"More than once?" Sasha asked.

"We stayed in Newport the times we went," Judge Thibodaux said.

"We couldn't get him reservations in Newport, Judge. That's why he's in Providence."

"We'd sail the intercostal all the way up. We actually moored in the center of Newport, and we'd jitney to shore daily during the festival. We saw Mel Torme and George Shearing together one night, and so many others. It was a marvelous time. Your friend is fortunate."

"Did you dance?" Sasha asked.

"Oh, my yes, we danced," he said, gazing at a ring of calamari in a memory trance. "My Barbara hated the smell of cigar on my dinner jacket, but how she loved to dance."

"He's there now, Judge, at the festival...the man I have to prove is alive...he probably left the hotel early this morning in Uber," Sasha said. "Oh well—we just missed him."

"He couldn't have," Judge Thibodaux said, looking at his tall floor clock, which was about to chime on the half hour.

"Excuse me?"

"He couldn't have left yet."

"What do you mean, Judge? Did you say he couldn't have?"

The judge held up two last oysters, one in either hand, offering one to Sasha, holding his up like a glass of fine wine.

"Let's toast," he said. "A toast to the Newport Jazz Festival and to the music that binds this ruptured nation together and sees that it'll always remember Southern Louisiana."

"Here's to Louisiana," Sasha said.

"Here's to Louis Armstrong," Judge Thibodaux said.

They tipped back, swallowing their horseradish-cocktail oysters whole. Sasha set the shell down and licked her fingers.

"What'd you mean, Judge—you said he couldn't have—like he couldn't have left yet is how you put it? What did you mean?"

"This is a weekday, darlin'."

"So?"

"So, any performances before the festival on three weekdays are in concert halls and private venues, but mostly at night. These are what you might say added attractions, but not the actual Newport Jazz Festival itself—which is presented after regional fans get off from work for the weekend. The weekend is festival time for the all-daytime and late nighttime sitting out under a summer sky or in the tent. The festival is three days away."

"Judge, you are amazing, you blessed, blessed man." Sasha hopped up, stepped around the table, bent down before him and kissed the judge on the middle of his forehead, leaving a Lancôme red lipstick mark ablaze.

"Oh my," Judge Thibodaux said.

Sasha stepped behind the desk, lifted the receiver and called the Providence information operator.

"Providence?" Sasha asked. "Connect me with the main downtown police station for Providence, please."

There was a pause.

The judge looked over, a bit puzzled, but his docket was clear. He went back to work on the calamari.

"Hello, I'm calling from the district courthouse in Carencro, Louisiana," Sasha said.

"Yes," Sasha said. "Yes, Louisiana. I need one of your officers to go to the Point Street Bridge. We have reason to believe an elderly gentleman is lost. Can you please send someone there to look for him? He may even be under the bridge."

The answering officer took down Sasha's name (Michelle Lissette), the name of the target, one Gabriel Jordan, and finally the private, unpublished phone number for Judge Thibodaux's desk line that Sasha read off the phone itself. Sasha shared in whispers to the judge that Officer Brandon Kelsey was being assigned to go over to the bridge, and Officer Kelsey would indeed be calling back with a full report. With that Sasha stepped around the desk.

"Officer Brandon Kelsey," Sasha said. "Thank you so much. We'll be here waiting."

Sasha set the phone receiver down.

"I need a drink, Judge Thibodaux, can I buy you a drink?"

Judge Thibodaux stood, dabbing his fingers with a napkin. "I have some sherry or a fine port, or perhaps a smooth bourbon," he said.

"Whatever you're having I'll have," Sasha said. "And go ahead and get a fresh cigar, Judge. I like your cigar smoke."

"Such a delight you are," Judge Thibodaux said.

Sasha looked at the clock on her phone and tapped it with her fingernails. She had thirty-five minutes before her time ran out.

As they waited, they mused and talked about family history and the state of the economy, and if they'd ever get the lumber barons to stop supplying big box store chains with Cypress chips for mulch. How tens of thousands of acres of Louisiana cypress trees were being cut and ground into mulch each year while southern Louisiana was sliding into the gulf, causing the annual flooding in New Orleans.

The phone rang. Sasha jumped up and grabbed it on the second ring.

"Judge Thibodaux's office," Sasha said. "Oh, yes, hold on."

Sasha hit the conference button.

"Officer Brandon Kelsey?" Sasha asked. "Is that you?"

"It is me, Miss Lissette," Officer Brandon Kelsey said. "We have found and identified—picture ID and Social Security card—your man, one Gabriel Jordan, alive and well."

Sasha reached for a tissue.

"Was he under the bridge?" Sasha asked.

"Under the bridge, Miss Lissette, just as you suggested he would be," Officer Brandon Kelsey said.

The judge leaned toward the desk.

"Officer, this is Judge Thibodaux, Carencro, Louisiana District Court. Officer Kelsey, what is your station's ID and may we ask your badge number, for our records?"

"Providence Central, Judge," Officer Brandon Kelsey said. "My badge number is 4S014, and I'm a sergeant, your honor."

"Thank you, Officer Kelsey," Judge Thibodaux said. "And for the record again, did you make a positive ID on this person?"

"Yes, your honor," Officer Brandon Kelsey said. "Physical, picture ID and Social Security."

"And do you find him in visibly good health?" Judge Thibodaux asked.

"I do, Judge," Officer Brandon Kelsey said. "He was sitting under the bridge with others, listening to one of the locals play his saxophone."

"Thank you, Officer Kelsey. Will you kindly fax me a report of this when you get back to your station?"

"I will, your honor."

The judge gave him the fax number.

"Your honor, Mr. Jordan would like to use my phone to speak," the officer said. "Would that be permissible, sir?"

"Of course," Judge Thibodaux said. "Put him on."

"Sasha?" Gabe shouted.

"He calls me that sometimes," Sasha whispered with a grin.

"Hi honey," Sasha said. "How's the festival?"

"When's he coming?" Gabe asked.

"Soon," Sasha said. "Maybe tomorrow."

"Sasha, I've been thinking a lot, and I want you to do something for me," Gabe said. "You're going to need a witness. Can you get a witness, darlin'? You can call me at the hotel later, when you have one."

The judge winked at Sasha.

"I've got one here and now. What's up?"

"You have a witness there with you on the phone?" Gabe asked.

"Sitting here with me," Sasha said. "A good one."

"This is as good a time as any, let me get something out of my pocket I wrote down," Gabe said. "Okay, here goes."

Gabe cleared his throat on the speaker and began to read.

"I, Gabriel Jordan, being of sound mind do bequeath all my worldly possessions, holdings, pensions, and financial accounts to Boudreaux Clemont Finch, currently residing in Carencro, Louisiana..."

Sasha broke into tears.

"And I want it all in a trust for him effective immediately and I name one Michelle Lissette as the sole trustee to see he has a real home and he gets his GED, into college and a degree, at which time there should be more than enough to get him started with a shrimp boat or a small farm. I am Captain Gabriel Jordan, retired, and Officer Brandon Kelsey here is my witness on this end."

There was silence.

"Well?" Gabe asked.

"I don't have the words," Sasha said.

"Well, is it legal?" Gabe asked.

"I'll have it typed up, he'll have to sign it and it'll be good to go," Judge Thibodaux said.

The judge then gave her a thumbs-up.

"It'll be legal," Sasha said. "I'll fax it to your hotel, you sign it."

Gabe may have pumped a victory fist in the air, knowing it was legal, as the saxophone wailed in the background "When Sunny Gets Blue" in celebration. It flowed from the conference speaker, and tears rolled down Sasha's cheeks.

"Sasha?" Gabe asked.

"Yes?"

"Go find that peckerwood and tell him to sign me out of that coffin and come up and listen to some jazz and drink some wine."

"I promise," Sasha sobbed into the phone. "I love you, Gabe."

"Baby, you should have heard the harmonica trio last night," Gabe said. "They played Scott Joplin for two hours. Oh, my god—do you remember the old Harmonicats, or are you too young?"

"I'll call you tonight," Sasha said. "It'll be late. Love you."

She hung up.

Sasha walked over to the judge, in tears. She motioned him with a repeated swirling turn of her hand to stand up. He stood and she gave him a look and a long, warm hug. She took her tissue and rubbed the lipstick from his forehead and cheek and kissed him on the neck.

"You are the best, Judge Thibodaux. You are a wonderful man."

"Thank you for a delightful morning," Judge Thibodaux said. "My recorder picked up everything and once that officer's fax comes through, I will have all the papers drawn up, the will and everything. I'll see you get it in New Orleans. You see it gets signed before a Notary."

"I don't know how to thank you," Sasha said.

"You might save a dance for me when I come down for my monthly Brennan's breakfast sabbatical."

"I promise that dance. There's a place off Frenchman Street."

"I look forward to it and will wait with bated breath."

"Judge, I need one last little favor. I have to get something signed by you saying you know Gabe is alive."

The judged looked over at Sasha, contemplated and smiled.

"I'll do better, little lady," Judge Thibodaux said. "Walk with me over to that grand jury, and I'll tell them personally." Judge Thibodaux took his robe from a coat hanger, swirled it around behind him and put it on.

"You knew about the...you know...me and the grand jury?"

"Not at first, young lady, but when certain names were bantered about over calamari and oysters, it all started to become more familiar," the judge said.

"Why the robe, Judge?" Sasha said. "It's not a court, is it?"

"Batman to the rescue," he said.

Sasha closed her eyes and rested her head down on the judge's shoulder. She gave him a squeeze.

"I thought judges and attorneys weren't allowed in a grand jury room, Judge."

"We aren't—as spectators—no law against interruption. Now we'd best start walking that long hall, Michelle," Judge Thibodaux pointing to his clock. You barely have seven minutes left."

CHAPTER 21

HELLO?" Gabe asked.

"Did I wake you, sweetie?" Sasha asked.

"What time is it?"

"Eleven thirty here, so it's after midnight for you."

"I was reading a book," Gabe said. "A northern white boy in 1953 sees a young black girl in trouble in Little Rock, and he works up the nerve to ask Ernest Hemingway to help him help her."

"I'm reading too...mail," Sasha said. "Street's lousy with drunks."

"Did you tell him?" Gabe asked.

"I think you should be the one to tell him," Sasha said. "He'll be there with you tomorrow."

"Is that when his bus gets in?"

Sasha sat straight up, hand over her mouth.

"Oh, my God, you don't know," Sasha said.

"Know what, baby?" Gabe asked.

"The hospice had a warrant out for Peck, telling the sheriff he kidnapped you. The district attorney had him arrested and pulled off his bus up in New Jersey. It was awful, Gabe."

"Are you pulling one on me, darlin'?"

"You can make this stuff up. That's what yesterday was all about. I had to prove to a grand jury that you were still alive. They were trying to pin kidnapping and murder charges on him. It's why the judge was in the room with me as a witness when I got you on the phone."

"What?" Gabe asked.

"I completely forgot to tell you. I wasn't allowed to talk to anyone about it or I would be held in contempt of court."

"This is like a bad dream," Gabe said.

"Tell me about it," Sasha said. "More like a nightmare from hell."

"All this happened yesterday?"

"Today, here, we're an hour behind you," Sasha said. "They were talking involuntary homicide for Peck if I couldn't prove you were alive. It's been a nightmare for the past two days. Lily Cup represented him. She was good."

"So, how's Peck?" Gabe asked. "Is he cleared now?"

"Thanks to you, you sweet, sweet man," Sasha said. "And to a judge I owe a dance to."

"My baby," Gabe said. "What would we do without you?"

Sasha pulled tissues and dabbed her eyes. "I miss you, Gabe."

"You never told me—is he back on a bus?" Gabe asked.

"No. We have an ID for him now, so I'm putting him on a plane in Lafayette early. He'll be there tomorrow."

"Is he with you?" Gabe asked.

"Lily Cup drove him to Carencro after the grand jury today," Sasha said. "He wanted to mow their lawn and pick up the place. I'll get him from his saw blade shanty in the morning and take him to the airport."

"Sombitch wanted his trotline," Gabe mused.

"That too, I'm sure."

"You must be exhausted."

"I could use a martini."

"How about a dance, darlin'?" Gabe asked.

There was a long, quiet pause. Sasha's knuckles were rolled on her lips. She thought of her dying friend, alone in the night and so far away as tears streamed down her cheeks.

"You need to bond with Peck," Sasha said. "This will be a good time for you two to talk."

"You're one unselfish woman," Gabe said. "I'm blessed you're in my life, and God knows I love my butterfly—but you fill my soul, friend."

Her mind lost in a moment—Sasha wept into the phone.

Gabe placed a marker in his book and set it down. With the receiver to his ear he leaned over and poured a cold cup of coffee. He was stalling for time as he thought. What would Captain Jordan do?

"Okay, okay," Gabe said, as though he just called a meeting to order.

"What?" Sasha asked.

"Here's the plan."

Sasha perked, eyes widened as if she had been awakened.

"Yes?"

"The festival is in three days. The big finale is under the tent."

Sasha wrenched her eyes with Gabe's use of the word *finale*.

"And?"

"Easy. I want you up here for the big finale," Gabe said.

"Gabe, I don't think I..."

"I don't want any arguments."

"You're up to something, I can tell," Sasha said.

"I need you here to watch after Peck while I see a doc."

"Are you worse?" Sasha asked.

"No," Gabe said. "I've met two doctor partners who want to put me through the ropes at their clinic. Thought maybe I'd check it out."

"Where did you meet them?" Sasha asked.

"One plays a good sax, and I met him sitting next to him in one exhibition concert. His partner had surgery during the concert, so I met him at another time, during the Scott Joplin celebration."

"Who are they again?"

"They're specialists," Gabe said. "I was telling them how I was on borrowed time and they told me no one was ever on borrowed time, and they'd like to have a look."

"You ran away from doctors here, Gabe."

"I think I trust these two, darlin'."

"Oh, my God," Sasha said.

"Woman, get on a plane and come dance with old Gabe."

There was a long pause.

"Okay."

"My baby."

"Make me room reservations. I'll see you in two days. Meantime I have to go talk to some people, change a few things around."

"Go, darlin', I'll wait here for Peck all day tomorrow if I have to."

They hung up.

Sasha made it over to Charlie's Blue Note just after midnight. Lily Cup was sitting at the bar with a cigar and a glass of port.

"No rye tonight?"

"Sipping a port. No court tomorrow, I'm on vacation."

"Would you put that stinky thing out?" Sasha asked, climbing on to a barstool.

"It's not lit," Lily Cup said.

"Charlie, a martini please, darling?" Sasha said.

"Where've you been?" Lily Cup said. "Why're you looking so...like that?"

"I've been at the office. I wanted to tell you you've been great. I'm so proud of you and Gabe says thanks for helping Peck. Wants to know how much he owes. It's pro bono and everything, right? That's what I told him."

"Oh, you'll pay for it," Lily Cup said.

"I'm sure I will."

"I need to borrow your Caddy SUV to go to an Ole Miss game."

"This summer?" Sasha asked.

"No, this fall when they start up playing. Bunch of friends have been talking about going."

"The keys are in my desk anytime you need it."

"What'd you do in there today?"

"Where?"

"With Judge Thibodaux. How'd you pull it off—get him to virtually cause a shutdown of a grand jury?"

"Oh, I don't know."

"That's bullshit."

"He listened to reason, I guess, and came to our rescue."

"You mean he wasn't a dirty old man?"

"He was a perfect gentleman."

"Old tit man, a gentleman? Give me a break."

"Oh, the judge enjoyed a casual glance at my girls, but other than that, not a lewd word or unwelcomed gesture."

"Imagine that—the word on the street is—"

"He was a perfect gentleman."

Lily Cup lighted her cigar.

"We enjoyed a lovely brunch and some sherry."

"He didn't even come on to you?" Lily Cup asked.

"We talked about saving the cypress trees. We talked about the best seasonings for a good Béchamel. We even talked about how he and his wife loved to dance before she died."

"You just can't listen to some people," Lily Cup said. "They just talk. They like gossip. Here I thought he was an old rake."

"Everybody sees things differently," Sasha said. "I learned it in real estate."

"How's that?"

"A husband will want a house because it's close to his work and the trees are mature; the wife will want it because of the schools, and she smelled a chocolate cake in the oven; a kid will want it because it has a lock on his bedroom door."

"It's all pretty simple," Lily Cup said. "People talk gets involved and fucks everything up."

"Pretty much," Sasha said.

The two sat at the bar sipping drinks for another half hour. They didn't speak a word. They would offer gestures if someone walked in or the music changed. They would watch people dancing in the reflection of the mirror on the wall. They'd known each other since—Sasha says since six; Lily Cup says she exaggerates and that they were five. They'd been through school together; they'd been through boyfriends and breakups together, heartaches and lost relatives. They knew what they had done for Peck and for Gabe. They knew they had done it because it was who they were.

"What's next for Peck, ya think?" Lily Cup asked.

"Gabe's leaving him everything," Sasha said.

"Everything?"

"I didn't see you to tell you."

"Does he even have anything?"

"He's been collecting Social Security and Army pension for a lot of years. He's a saver."

"That makes good karma," Lily Cup said.

"It was in the stars," Sasha said.

"They really love each other."

"Yep," Sasha said.

"You could see it," Lily Cup said.

"Peck worships the man. Gabe's the father he never had."

"Is Gabe just going to, like, turn it over? Just give it to him?"

"I'm the executor," Sasha said. "It'll be in a trust. We'll get him in school and maybe college or trade school."

"Think Peck will want to do all that?"

"He says he does."

"That's good, then."

"Yep."

Sasha took a sip of her martini. "You know what this means, don't ya?"

"No, what does it mean?"

"Just means now he's family, you can't fuck him."

"What?"

"He's family now. You can't fuck him."

"Why, I never—!"

"Now, now, now, girlfriend," Sasha said. "Don't be bullshitting a bull-shitter."

"You don't know what you're talking about," Lily Cup growled.

"You seem to forget, girlfriend, I saw him nailing your ass right back there in that bathroom—you were three sheets to the wind, screaming for Jesus."

"You did? I was? I didn't think anybody..."

"You might have pulled it off in the men's room, but to walk into the ladies' room and see his pants down around his knees and that fine ass of his pumping between your turkey legs—"

"Shut up. No way."

"—his head bumping the Tampon dispenser..."

"Okay, okay—enough!" Lily Cup said.

They stared at each other, a reflection in the mirror behind the bar.

"If I can't fuck him again, you surely can't, that's for damn sure."

"I've never—" Sasha started.

"Yeah, right— I still have the pic you texted me from Memphis of his schlong."

"Oh, that," Sasha said.

"I'm not saying you did or didn't, but you can't fuck him now."

"That's right," Sasha said, in a proper, responsible tone of voice. "We can't fuck Peck—I suggest you write it on your wrist so when you drink your rye you won't forget."

"I can be a lady," Lily Cup said.

Sasha furrowed her brow looking at the cigar in Lily Cup's hand. Lily Cup huffed a scowl in return.

"I'll have you remember, Michelle Lissette, that I got a certificate of achievement at Mrs. Winston's finishing school that summer and you didn't."

"That was well over thirty years ago."

"It's framed and on my bedroom wall if you ever want to see it."

"Are you going to keep bringing that up forever?"

"What? Me bring up Mrs. Winston walking in on you holding your panty band out, showing yourself to Hank and Kenneth Buchanan?" Lily Cup asked.

"I lost a bet."

"You lost a bet? Oh, that's rich."

"I bet that Hank couldn't get Mariah Randall to kiss him," Sasha said.

"Bad bet," Lily Cup said. "They married each other after college."

"At least I pay my bets."

"At least I have the good sense to know propriety and social mores," Lily Cup said. "I shan't think of fucking Peck ever, ever again. It hasn't so much as entered my mind."

"That's what you said about Kenneth Buchanan," Sasha said.

The two looked into the mirror for several sips, savoring their memories, listening to the music, perhaps letting the events of the day unwind in their minds while Charlie emptied a bottle in Lily Cup's glass.

"So, would a blowjob be out of the question?" Lily Cup asked.

Sasha spit her olive, snorted four short gravelly snorts, pounding one fist on the bar, the other hand shaking her full martini glass loose from her fingertips up, over and behind the bar, shattering it on the back wall below the mirror. Her forehead now on the bar, her nostrils writhing in snorts and gasps of laughter.

Lily Cup reached into Sasha's handbag and "borrowed" her credit card, holding it in the air.

"Charlie?" Lily Cup asked. "Check please?"

CHAPTER 22

GABE WAS LIGHTLY SNOOZING when there was rapping on the door.

"Just a minute," he said.

The old man got to his feet, stepped over to the door in his socks, and pulled it open. Young Peck stood in the hall with a grin. The fish out of water was learning the trotlines and snoods of a completely new world barely a week old to him. A world outside the bayous he always called home. He was learning of a world filled with fears and surprises. At this moment, however, he was enjoying that he had taken his first ever flight alone and managed to get to the hotel from the airport in a strange city.

He was delighted to see his friend once again.

"How y'all are, Gabe?"

Gabe grabbed his arm and pulled him for a hug.

"My brother," Gabe said. "My brother."

"What I'm gonna did is take care of you now," Peck said.

They stepped into the room and Peck dropped his duffel.

Gabe was an old soldier. He wanted to hear how Peck caught the pill robber and knife stabber, but he knew army debriefings, and he knew the story would come in its own time. Right now, he just wanted to greet his friend.

"Gabe, I flied a whole ten states. Nothing to it, kind of. Lewisana is how you call the Pelican state all the way to this here Providencial, Rhode Island," Peck said.

"That's right," Gabe said. "That's right. Ten states."

"Whoo!" Peck said.

"Peck, where'd you pick up those names? And it's Providence, not Providencial."

"Providence, Rhode Island," Peck said.

"Did you figure it out yourself?"

"Nah, nah. A lady told me, dass for true," Peck said. "I told her lots of land down there under the plane, and she say ten states we fly over and she say I'm going to told you about them."

"A lady taught you all that in that short amount of time?" Gabe asked.

Peck grinned.

"And you remembered it just like that?" Gabe asked.

"Dass for true, Gabe. I like to did dat, learning like dat."

Gabe stepped to the coffee urn and poured two cups. He handed one to Peck.

"*La dame parlait français,*" Peck said

"The lady spoke French?" Gabe asked.

"*Oui,*" Peck said.

"Peck, I couldn't love you more if you were my own son."

"Makes Peck proud, dass for true," Peck said.

"I'm going to ask you something, son, but it'll have to be in English, I'm not up on my French as I should be."

"Ax," Peck said.

"Now it doesn't matter one way or another, but can you count...you know...do you know your numbers, son?" Gabe asked.

Peck's eyes looked as if he knew it was a test he was willing to take because he respected Gabe too much to mislead him. He wanted to demonstrate his number skill limitations in his own way.

"Sometimes," he said.

He handed Gabe his coffee cup and reached in a pocket, pulled out an assortment of bills, selected four and stuffed the balance back in his pocket. He held them up one at a time.

"One dollar," Peck said. "Five dollar, ten dollar, twenny dollar."

"That's good," Gabe said. "That's real good, my brother."

Peck grinned.

Gabe held up three fingers. "How many is this, Peck?"

Peck didn't respond.

Gabe held up seven fingers. "Do you know how many this is?"

Peck didn't respond.

"You can't add or count, can you Peck?"

Peck didn't respond.

"You've grown up in a world where you've traded for rent and bartered for food and books and arithmetic never came up."

"It never had too," Peck said.

"You don't have a television, do you Peck."

"Nah, nah."

"You live in a world of trading. Interesting."

"I'm sorry, ole man."

"No problem," Gabe said. "Let's try something. Hold your hands in the air," Gabe said.

"Hanh?"

"Hold your hands up," Gabe said. "You've got the bills down pat, now I'm going to show you how easy counting is."

Peck raised both hands.

"Spread your fingers," Gabe said.

Peck spread the fingers of both hands.

"Hold them steady."

Gabe touched each finger and thumb in turn and counted.

"One, two, three, four, five, six, seven, eight, nine, ten," Gabe said.

Peck grinned, kept his hands up, encouraging Gabe to do it again.

"One, two, three, four, five, six, seven, eight, nine, ten," Gabe said.

Peck shook his fingers in the air as though he could feel knowledge entering his brain.

"*Encore*," Peck said.

"One," Gabe said.

"One," Peck repeated.

"Two," Gabe said.

"Two," Peck repeated.

"Three," Gabe said.

"Three," Peck repeated.

"Four," Gabe said.

"Four," Peck repeated.

Two grown men standing in the middle of the hotel room and counting together from one to ten eleven different times. By the eleventh time Peck could recite the numbers one to ten on his own and in order. He was beside himself. He was like a boy with an ice cream treat. The look on his face was as if it was his first flight in a plane alone, challenging him not ever to be afraid again, to demand more from his mind, to explore the worlds that had been shut out for him in the past from ignorance. He kept repeating one through ten, and the more he repeated them, the faster he could say the numbers.

"Wait, Gabe, look what I'm going to did."

Peck pulled bills from his pocket and sorted out a small pile of singles. One at a time he dropped them on the bed as he counted.

"One, two, three, four, five, six, seven," Peck said.

Gabe demonstrated simple addition by having Peck count a stack of four one-dollar bills in one pile and a stack of three one-dollar bills in another to see what four plus three was when he counted them all. Peck was beside himself.

Gabe reached to shake Peck's hand. It was an eye-to-eye handshake, like a proud poppa and son would never forget.

"Okay, that's the lesson for today," Gabe said. "I'm proud."

"I like dat," Peck said. "I like to did dat."

"Put your money away," Gabe said. "I had time on my hands yesterday, so I bought you a few things. Pull the shades so we can see them in the daylight."

Peck moved his duffel to the footstool. Gabe pulled the top bureau drawer under the television, lifted out three plastic shopping bags and handed them to Peck.

"Here's a couple of Polo shirts, cargo shorts, a belt, and some leather boat-deck moccasins. I got twelves, Peck. What size foot do you have, son?" Gabe asked.

Peck shrugged his shoulder, leaned and pulled a sneaker off. He held it up and pointed to the numeral 12 on the inside of the shoe.

"Oh, I get it," Gabe said. "You can't read. It's twelve."

Gabe took the shoe from Peck's hand, looked at the number and contemplated how he might teach Peck how to read it. He handed the shoe back.

"Another lesson for another day," Gabe said. "I'll be down in the lobby, getting some air. You try on anything you'd like and meet me there, and we'll go to lunch, and then we'll head over to Newport for the festival," Gabe said. "Take your time."

"I be down," Peck said.

"Peck," Gabe said, "I'm taking you to a diner two blocks from here. Only seats maybe twenty people. They have the best chicken pot pie and steamed corn on the cob with a block of butter to rub it on. Son, I'm telling you, it'll melt in your mouth."

Gabe arranged for Uber to be at the hotel at three for their ride to Newport. As they walked to the diner, Gabe pointed out landmarks and downtown attractions, especially the river. As they entered the diner, the owner welcomed Gabe with a "good morning, Captain," and Gabe found his favorite booth empty and gave Peck his pick of the seats.

"I can only eat half of their chicken pot pie. I'm good for two ears of corn, but if you're getting pot pie, I'm going to ask them to put half of mine on top of yours."

Peck was open to any proposition when it came to food. He was celebrating having made it through an ordeal with the law he still didn't fully comprehend, but now he was with his friend.

Gabe placed an order for the food and coffee.

"I want to tell you something," Gabe said. "In that hotel room you learned in ten minutes what it might take a youngn' a week to learn in school."

"For true?" Peck asked.

"Ten minutes," Gabe said. "Now why do you suppose nobody's taken the time to teach you basics like counting? It boils my grits, it does—selfish bastards."

"Maybe nobody ain't had the ten minutes, Gabe, dass for true," Peck said.

"Try the corn," Gabe said. "Rub it in butter, get some pepper on it."

The two busied themselves.

"That's all ending here and now, my friend," Gabe said.

"What you mean?" Peck asked.

"Sasha knows," Gabe said.

"Knows?" Peck asked.

"She wanted me to be the one to tell you," Gabe said. "I've gone and adopted you."

"Hanh?"

"I'm going to put you in school, help you get a driver's license. Hell, maybe you can even start a crabbing or shrimping business someday."

"Dass for true, Gabe?"

"It starts here and now, my brother. You good with that?"

"I don't want to forgot nothing, Gabe," Peck said. "Can you told me dat again?"

"It's not a legal adoption, Peck, but you're twenty-four, and I'm an old man and I reckon a handshake is all we need to tell the world we're family—that is, if you're good with me being family, son."

"I'm good with dat," Peck said.

"From now on, you're going to a tutor and get your high school diploma," Gabe said. "You'll learn how to read and write and how to drive, and you're not going to stop learning until you want to, and from the looks of it what you learned flying a whole ten states up here, you've only just begun."

"T'anks, Gabe. T'anks."

"Eat your pie before it gets cold."

Peck's eyes were a wondrous gaze, staring at Gabe's that had nothing but truth in them. Peck stuffed a forkful of chicken and carrot in his mouth. Not taking his eyes off Gabe, he chewed, swallowed, and sipped of coffee in thought.

"What about lawn mowin'?" Peck asked.

"Witch can mow her own goddam—" Gabe started. He caught himself. He had to set an example for his new student.

"They'll do fine without you," he said. "Sasha will call them and see they pay you what they owe you."

"Is school hard to did? Do you for real t'ink...?"

"Peck," Gabe said. "Slide me four sugar packets, son."

Without thinking, Peck lifted the sugar packets from the silver bowl, counted out four and slid them over the table, mouthing in turn a one, two, three, four, as he pushed each. As soon as Gabe stopped them with his palm they both looked up at each other and smiled.

"See how easy learning is, son?" Gabe asked. "We'll get your coon-ass gibberish as good as your French— why hell, you could be governor or something someday."

Peck beamed.

"Those two ears are yours, my brother," Gabe said. "Get butter."

Gabe sipped his coffee.

The Uber ride to Newport was, for Peck, a chance to take in every detail and nuance of a world new to him. For the first time he was in a land where it snowed regularly in the winter; where they ate a northern cod caught in nets more than they did bayou southern catfish caught on poles or trotlines.

Gabe reached a folded twenty-dollar bill over the seat to the driver and asked him to take the extra time to show them the historic city, the rambling palatial mansions, the ocean-front, the grass tennis courts, and churches dating back to the pilgrims. Peck took it all in, this time not as a hunter or predator he had to be growing up in marshland wilds and surviving in the bayou, but this time as the student awakened in him.

CHAPTER 23

GABE RESERVED A CAR AND DRIVER for the afternoon. He had been in New England during his early army days and enjoyed sharing his memories of it with Peck, the sights of Newport. Peck watched from the moving car's window, would point a finger and count things—up to ten of them—as they'd drive by: stop signs, boats in a bay, people strolling on sidewalks. They heard music, had the car stop and wait as they sat on the stoop of an open door listening to a jazz piano competition in a filled studio hall. After hearing three players, Gabe looked at his watch and they headed back to Providence. It was on the way when Gabe thought he could make use of the drive time and help Peck tackle *th* sounds. He was inspired by Peck's ability to pronounce properly the word *three* when he counted out loud. As they drove into Warwick, he attempted to back into a pronunciation topic.

"Peck," Gabe asked. "Why is it you say *three*, and not *t'ree?*"

"Hanh?" Peck asked.

"You say three—like when you count, you say one, two, three," Gabe said. "Why is it you don't say one, two, t'ree? Just curious."

Peck squirmed like a child who had to go to the bathroom. "Ain' *three* right, Gabe?"

"Count to ten for me," Gabe said.

"Hanh?"

"Go ahead, count it out. I'll show you what I mean."

Peck looked warily from the corner of his eye, as if he were about to walk into the barbed hooks of a trotline. "One, two, three, four, five, six, seven, eight, nine, ten," Peck said. "Are you funnin' at me, Gabe?"

"Say *three*, Peck," Gabe said.

"Three," Peck said.

"Perfect. Now see, when you say *three,* you don't say *t'ree,*" Gabe said. "Now say it again: *three.*"

"Three," Peck said.

"Okay, now say this: 'Look at that truck over there.'"

"What?" Peck asked.

"Go on, say it. Say, 'Look at that truck over there.'"

"Look at dat truck over dare," Peck said.

The driver stared at them in the rearview mirror.

"You mind watching the road, Robert?" Gabe asked.

Gabe turned to Peck. "Peck, this time try saying this one. Say, 'Look at *three* trucks over *three* miles.'"

"Hanh?" Peck asked.

"Just try it. Say, 'Look at *three* trucks over *three* miles,'" Gabe said.

"Look at *three* trucks over *three* miles," Peck said.

"See, you can do it. You can do the *th* sounds. Once more: 'Look at three trucks over three miles.'"

With an accomplished grin on his face, Peck repeated, "Look at *three* trucks over *three* miles."

"So, if *three* isn't *t'ree,* then doesn't it make sense that *that* isn't *dat,* and *they* isn't *dey*?" Gabe asked.

Peck looked as if he might be open to listening to the question again for clarification. Not certain he'd broken through, Gabe scratched his head, searching for another approach. Peck watched the agony Gabe seemed to be in, smiled sympathetically at his friend's good intentions and opted to put him out of his misery.

"You dance, old man," Peck said. "Let Peck do the t'inkin'."

Gabe smiled and pointed at the front window.

"Look yonder, Peck," Gabe said. "Look who's here."

Sasha was strolling in front of the hotel, her cellphone to her ear. She had no bag visible.

"Looks like she's checked in or can't stay," Gabe said.

The Uber car circled toward an unloading space.

"Pull over there, Robert," Gabe said. "We'll get out."

Sasha saw Peck stepping out of the car and smiled, holding up a finger for more time to finish her phone call. Gabe told his driver they'd be calling him tomorrow.

Sasha clicked her phone off, gave Peck a hug around his neck and then Gabe. She held Gabe tightly, motionless, without a word said between them. When they let go, she became all business.

"I want the number for those doctor guys," she said, holding her hand out.

"Hello to you too," Gabe said, with a frown.

"Give it," Sasha said. "I want their names and numbers."

Gabe dug into his pocket.

"Can I show you something we learned today?" Gabe asked.

"Sure," Sasha said. "But no stalling. Give me their numbers."

"Peck, show Sasha how you can count to ten."

Gabe handed a business card to Sasha. Sasha looked at the card then impatiently up at Peck.

"One, two, three, four, five, six, seven, eight, nine, ten," Peck said.

"And?" Sasha asked.

"Peck can count," Gabe said. "He counts from one to ten. Want to see it again? Watch."

"One, two, three, four, five, six, seven, eight, nine, ten," Peck said.

Sasha looked at the card in her hand then up at Peck.

"Does he make you 'arf' like a seal and throw you a fish every time you do it?" Sasha asked.

Peck snorted a goofy, guttural guffaw. Gabe smirked in defeat.

"You two get lost," Sasha said. "I have a call to make."

"Are we doing dinner tonight?" Gabe asked.

"Will the sax man be under the bridge tonight?" Sasha asked.

"He'll be there," Gabe said.

"Then we're doing takeout," Sasha said. "Anything you want, but we're eating under Point Street Bridge."

"He knows you'll be in town," Gabe said.

"Good," Sasha said.

Sasha held her opened hand pointing toward the hotel doors and waited for Gabe and Peck to go through them.

"I'll be up in a minute."

She walked to a park bench pressing numbers on her phone.

"Fineman Docherty Clinic," a voice answered.

"Hello, my name is Michelle Lissette, and I'm looking for a Doctor Michael Docherty."

"Doctor Docherty is not in."

"Do you know when he'll be back?"

"Doctor Docherty has gone for the day."

"Do you know if Doctor Larry Feinman is in?"

"He is."

"He is?" Sasha asked. "May I speak with him, please?"

"This is Doctor Feinman."

"You're Dr. Feinman?" Sasha asked. "Hello Dr. Feinman, my name is Michelle Lissette, and a friend, Gabe Jordan, told me about meeting you and your partner and I'm in town and wanted to see if you were serious about wanting to check him out like he said you told him you were. Were you serious?"

"We're both quite fond of Gabe, and yes we're serious."

"Good," Sasha said. "How soon can you do it?"

"We'll look at the schedule in the morning; it might be a few weeks out."

"Weeks?" Sasha asked.

"Typically, we book up several weeks in advance. I'll look in the morning and see what's available."

"Can't you do it any sooner? I mean it was a wonderful gesture on your part, but can't it be done sooner?"

"By sooner, just what did you have in mind? Our schedules are full."

"How about tonight?" Sasha asked.

Dr. Feinman snickered into the phone.

"Could you do it tonight?" Sasha asked.

"You were serious?"

"Yes."

"Tonight?"

"What's wrong with tonight?"

"We have long days here at the clinic. Today was another long day."

"You already said your days are all booked up," Sasha said.

"And they are, but—"

"So, what's wrong with doing it at night?"

"I'm not certain—"

"Doctor Feinman," Sasha said, "if you got told you only had days to live would you actually care whether your last day on earth was during daylight or dark?"

Sasha looked at the clock on her cellphone.

"Would he have to fast before the tests?" she queried.

"Eight hours. Only water."

"Eight hours? He can do that."

"Have him here at one in the morning."

"Thank you, Doctor Feinman. We'll be at your lab at one."

"See you at one. Now I'd better go get some rest," Dr. Feinman said.

"God bless you and God bless everyone in your lab, Dr. Feinman," Sasha said. "Goodbye."

Sasha's hotel room was on a different floor. She stopped at Gabe's room. Peck let her in.

"Here's the deal, guys," she announced. "Gabe, your doctor friends are opening their lab tonight just for you, and they're going to put you through every test."

"What?" Gabe asked.

"I want no arguments."

"Tonight?"

"Well, at one a.m. in the morning, actually. We have to be there then, but you have to fast for eight hours first, so go to bed and only drink water. Peck and I will leave you alone and come get you when it's time."

"It'll just be another big waste of time."

"Be a good boy, Gabe. Tomorrow we'll see sax man."

"A lot of poking and prodding."

Sasha grabbed a towel from a bureau and threw it at Gabe.

"Shut up!" she snapped.

"Well, it's true," Gabe said.

"Gabe, when's the last time anyone told you that you might be able to live? Answer me that."

"A big zero," Gabe said.

"These two guys are brilliant," Sasha said. "You said it yourself."

"Are they saying I might be able to live?"

"No."

"Well, there you go."

"But they're not saying you're going to die, either."

"And your point is?"

"They're saying they don't know. When's the last time anyone has said they don't know?"

"What time?" Gabe asked.

"Go to bed," Sasha said. "We'll wake you. You'll need your strength."

Gabe relented and moved to his bed and sat on it.

"Peck, come with me. Let him sleep," Sasha said.

They pulled the drapes and left Gabe alone. Peck and Sasha went to the front of the hotel and watched the setting sunset. Sasha led Peck to a park bench overlooking the river. A small boat was floating from one iron basket to another, lighting the fire logs. They cast a warm glow.

"Peck," Sasha asked. "Has Gabe talked to you about school?"

"He teached me how to count, dass for true," Peck said.

"And that's a good thing," Sasha said. "But has he talked about your going back to school full time?"

"You mean with kids?" Peck asked.

"No kids," Sasha said. "With a tutor, but after you get your high school GED, maybe then college or a trade school. Would you like that?"

"He teached me to count."

"A tutor will teach you all that—counting, reading, writing. What do you think?"

"Could I t'row my trotline and mow lawns and do dat?" Peck asked.

"We were thinking we'd get you an apartment in New Orleans. You could earn money cleaning my real-estate office and Lily Cup's law offices at night. You could go to your tutor most of the day."

"For true?" Peck asked.

"Wouldn't you like to learn all you can and start your business and have a place of your own?" Sasha asked.

"Peck know who he's going to marry, cher."

"Marry?"

"*Oui.*"

"Who?"

Peck didn't answer.

"I know, you're thinking that Elizabeth girl down in Anse La Butte, right? The one you diddle while her boyfriend is offshore?"

Peck sheepishly looked about as if he were hoping no one heard Sasha announce his indiscretions to the world.

"Millie," Peck said.

"Who?"

"I'm gonna marry Millie."

Sasha sat up. "Millie? The girl who called me?"

"I love Millie," Peck said.

"Does she love you?"

"I t'ink so, maybe," Peck said.

Sasha saw contentment in Peck's smile.

"Peck, if you could make wishes come true, and you only had one wish, what would you wish for? What would your life be like?"

"Gabe don' die," Peck said.

Sasha looked at Peck's eyes, smiled gently, pursed her lips and held back a cry while witnessing Gabe's friend—as unconditionally devoted to him as a son would be.

"You still want a pirogue?" Sasha asked. "To pull traps?"

"If I be smart, like you say," Peck said. "I'd want me a farm with one, two, maybe three acres for planting, like melons and zucchini, like dat. And then one, two, three, four, five acres' marsh bottom for burying my own crawdad traps."

"Not blue crab?" Sasha asked.

"Blue crab for sure, but mo money in crawfish," Peck said.

"That sounds nice, Peck. A nice dream. Think city girl Millie would go for the farming and crawfish beds? It's pretty hard work."

Peck didn't answer. He stood and walked Sasha to Gabe's favorite Providence diner, stepped in and waved hello to its owner. He talked Sasha through his and Gabe's favorites—corn on the cob with fresh creamery butter, sliced whole tomatoes with salt and pepper, and chicken pot pie. Sasha took her business jacket off, hung it on a hook and let Peck order the entire meal. She watched his eyes as he confidently told the lady server what they wanted. He was particularly proud to say, "We gonna cahoot together and can we start with two ears between us, if dat be fine? Dat be two for the lady and two for me...and we gonna did shicken pot pies too. Two of them too— but only one each."

The waitress knew Peck from his visits with Gabe. She made him comfortable with a simple, "Yes sir, will that be all?"

Peck held up two fingers. "Two beers," he said.

Sasha studied Peck's eyes, recognizing what Gabe had said earlier— that Peck had counted on his fingers the three acres of planting land for farming he wanted and the five acres of low, wet marshland he wanted for crawfish traps—and his being able to count those acres was light-years from twenty-five years of a mentally muted silence, as he scratched a life in the bayous, not having to know how to count, just having to know how to avoid snakes and alligators and how to catch a dinner he'd eat alone and how to mow and sharpen axe blades to pay for a small cot in the back of the boat-builder's blade-sharpening shed.

"Millie would be lucky to get you," Sasha said.

CHAPTER 24

MICHELLE, YOU TWO ARE WELCOME TO WAIT in the waiting room, or go and come back," Dr. Feinman said.

"If you'll give me a cell number, I can text you when we're finished."

"How long do you think?" Sasha asked.

"Several hours. Maybe four."

"We'll find an all-night place," Sasha said. "The diner or something else."

"Suit yourselves," Dr. Feinman said.

"Will you call me, Doctor?" Sasha asked. "At any time, please?"

"One of us will call you, I promise."

Sasha took Gabe's hand.

"Bye, sweety," Sasha said. "Play nice."

Sasha and Peck watched Gabe and several nurses in smocks pass through double doors and out of sight. Sasha ordered an Uber.

"We wait for Gabe?" Peck asked.

"I've got an idea," Sasha said. "Come with me."

Sasha asked the driver to take them to a Dunkin' Donuts and wait for them in the car. Sasha stepped over to the menu board to read it.

"Peck, tell the nice lady which donuts you want," Sasha said, pointing to a donut assortment case. "Pick ten you like."

"You want a dozen?" the waitress asked.

"He'll pick ten," Sasha said. Go ahead, Peck."

"They come in dozens, lady," a manager in the kitchen said.

"He can't count to twelve," Sasha said. "Peck, go ahead and pick ten."

The manager came to the front, ready for battle.

"Our donuts come in singles or they come in dozens, ma'am. We would have to charge you for singles if you only get ten, but we'd charge you the dozen rate if you select a dozen. It would be much cheaper if your friend got twelve."

"So, let him pick ten—give him two free ones, and charge him for a dozen," Sasha said.

"Carole," the manager growled. "Just handle it."

He left in a miff.

When he was out of earshot.

"Who starched his undies, Carole?" Sasha asked.

"He gets like that sometimes," Carole said.

"Lucky you," Sasha mumbled.

"He shouldn't work nights," Carole said.

"Peck," Sasha said. "Pick ten, then pick two more, does that work?"

"That's clever," Carole said.

"Dat be good, cher," Peck said.

"While he's thinking what can I get you, hon?"

"Is there like a big thing, maybe a large thermos you sell we can get with five or six cups of coffee in it?" Sasha asked. "I'll buy the thermos."

"We have the Box O' Joe," Carole said.

"The box of what?" Sasha asked.

"It holds ten, ten-ounce cups."

"A box would be good, ten cups would be good, but is there a thermos or something to hold coffee, keep it warm?" Sasha asked.

"It's our Box O' Joe. Let me show you one, hon."

Waitress Carole brought an empty Box O' Joe container from under the counter and handed it to Sasha.

"See this here?" she asked. "It'll hold ten cups and keeps it warm and everything."

"Imagine that, a cardboard coffee container," Sasha said.

"It's popular," Carole said.

"Well okie-dokie, then. You've sold me, Carole. We'll take a Box O' Joe."

"Where you from, hon?" Carole asked.

"N'Orleans."

"I figured you weren't from around here."

"It's a long way away," Sasha said.

"Don't have Box O' Joe down there, I don't suppose," Carole said.

"We don't get out much in the Quarter. We have Café du Monde," Sasha said. "There we get it in china cups if we sit in, with a couple of beignets typically. Tourists get disposable cups."

"Bet them Café du Monde folks don't give you a hard time like our manager, huh?" Carole asked.

"We just flash our tits and they give us beads with our beignets and coffee."

Carole grinned.

Sasha winked at Carole.

"Don't believe everything you see about New Orleans on YouTube, honey—night Carole, and thanks."

Peck carried the package to the car and put it in the trunk.

"Take us to the Point Street Bridge," Sasha said.

Sasha told the driver he was welcome to join them for coffee and donuts or leave and she'd call him as soon as she heard from the doctor. The driver opted to go home and sleep. Peck carried the donuts and coffee down the slope and in under the bridge.

"He's gone," Sasha said.

"Who's gone, cher?" Peck asked.

"Donald," Sasha said. "He plays sax here."

Peck poured two coffees and handed one to Sasha. He lifted the lid of the donut box, took a glazed and sat on the lawn and watched the river flow by.

"Is it true you don't know your mom or dad, Peck?" Sasha asked.

"Dass for true, cher," Peck said.

"You don't have to talk about it if you don't want to," Sasha said.

"S'hokay."

"I'm happy you and Gabe found each other."

"I knowed Gabe was good straight off," Peck said. "He got honest eyes."

"He does, I agree," Sasha said.

They sipped their coffees. Sasha picked a powdered donut, broke it in half with her fingers and let half stay in the box.

"Was your foster nanna lady nice?" Sasha asked. "Do you ever see her?"

"*Elle me laisser utiliser l'homme gator*," Peck said. ("She let gator man use me.")

"*Comment ça?*"

"He maked me carry bait shrimp buckets to his boat," Peck said. "If I drop one he whack me with a strap."

"How old were you?"

"Couldn't swim."

"Can you swim now?"

"Yes'm."

"How old?"

Peck looked at her as if he had told her already.

"When you say you couldn't swim, are you saying you were really young?" Sasha asked.

"*Oui.*"

"Like maybe you were young, like three, four or five? Is that what you're saying?"

"*Oui?*"

"And that man would beat you?"

Peck didn't answer.

Sasha picked up the other half of the powdered donut.

"Where was your foster nanna all this time?"

"Bayou Chene, I t'ink cher, by Choctaw."

"I don't mean where did she live. I meant why wasn't she protecting you from this man?"

"I run off after he maked me gator bait."

"Gator bait?" Sasha asked.

"*Oui.*"

"Explain that to me."

"Gator man taked me long way into bayou in boat."

"I know, a pirogue."

"Nah, nah, not a pirogue, in a boat with motor. He make me jump in the water with rope tied on me. He start the motor and pull me off back a long ways, looking for gators to come get me. If he seed one he'd pull me up and shoot it."

"This sounds like a bad dream, Peck," Sasha said. "Are you imagining all this or did he really do that to you?"

Peck didn't answer.

"What's his name?"

"Gator man."

"Where does he live?"

"Bayou Chene, 'tween Bayou Sorrel and Choctaw, with foster nanny, dass for true."

Sasha lifted her phone and started a text to herself.

"What's her name?"

"Prudhomme," Peck said. "Alayna Prudhomme, 'tween Bayou Sorrel and Choctaw."

"When he did that— pulled you— did you ever see alligators?"

"Nah, nah, I died," Peck said.

"You died?"

"I died."

"What do you mean, you died?"

"Gator man throwed me in off the boat and I turned my whole self dead with no eyes or no air—just dead is all."

A tear rolled down Sasha's cheek and glistened in reflection of the full moon.

"How many times did gator man make you die, Peck?"

"Don't know."

"Did he do this a lot?"

"Couldn't count den, cher."

Sasha held her coffee cup to her cheek and looked off into the river. "Did you tell your foster nanna?"

"*Oui.*"

"What'd she say?"

"*Tu devrais être reconnaissant qu'il t'enseigne.*" Peck said. ("You should be grateful he's teaching you.")

"How did you get away?"

"I climb a bald cypress and hided in the hollow up over the limb. I stay hid there." Peck held up four fingers. "This many day, cher."

Then he remembered he could count now.

"Four days," Peck said. "I hided in the cypress hollow four days then run off and didn't stop until Carencro. I lied about how old I was and got me a job killing calf at the slaughter barn."

Sasha keyed in the towns into her phone.

"That's sixty-five miles," she said.

"I run, cher. Hided myself in the back of a truck."

"How old were you when you ran away?"

"I cud swim."

"You say slaughter barn."

"*Oui*."

"You mean you swept up, carried feed?"

"I bonk 'em dead."

Sasha winced.

"Got good at it. Dey drop with one bonk on head between eyes. Foreman string 'em up after dat."

Sasha looked as though she were in a bad dream. She'd heard stories like this, but hard to believe they really happened.

"Dey seen I was too young and a lady fired me."

"What did you do then?" Sasha asked. "Where did you go?"

"I heard the sawing down by the track and ax the boat builder man if'n he need a worker. He say I could sharpen axe blades for sleeping on the cot in his saw blade shed. I told him I do it if I could earn out the lawn mower he had setting there doing nothin'. He say yes and gived me a trotline too."

Sasha's phone sounded. She read the name on the screen.

"Hello, Doctor Feinman?"

"It is."

"Everything okay?"

"He's resting."

"Is he okay?"

"All his signs are good."

"When will he wake up?"

"In several hours."

"Did you find anything out?" Sasha asked.

"We'll be reviewing lab results soon."

"When can you talk about it?" Sasha asked.

"We'll meet this morning, sometime. We could see you at one."

"Doctor Feinman, you have no idea what this means to us," Sasha said. "You people are kind, and God will thank you for this."

"Are you staying in the city?"

"Yes. I'm checked in at the Courtyard."

"That's where Gabe is staying, if I'm not mistaken."

"That's right," Sasha said. "So, we come get Gabe around nine, and meet you for the results at one?"

"Yes."

"He'll be starving," Sasha said. "Tell him we'll eat in the morning with him."

"I will."

"Thank you, Doctor," Sasha said. "Gabe loves his morning coffee."

"I'll see he gets some."

Sasha ended the call.

"He's asleep. We'll go get him in the morning."

"I heard," Peck said.

"Let's walk to the hotel. I'll set an alarm and wake in the morning if you want to go with me. We'll take him to the diner," Sasha said.

"*Oui.*"

He stood, gathering the Box O' Joe and remaining donuts.

Sasha stepped over and put her hand on his cheek. She gave him a gentle kiss on the other cheek.

"Listen to what I have to say, Mr. Boudreaux Clemont Finch."

Peck stood motionless.

"I mean this from the bottom of my heart."

"You died back there all those years ago. I can't begin to imagine what it was like for you—your dying like that every time that gator man did that to you."

Peck closed his eyes.

"Look at me, Peck."

Peck opened his eyes.

"I want you to know God cared because He saw to it you couldn't count all those deaths you had to go through."

Peck lowered his head. Sasha put her hand under his chin and raised his head up.

"Now you have Gabe, Peck. It's all different now. You have a daddy who loves you and wants to care for you."

A tear bubbled in Peck's eye.

"You'll never have to die again, Peck. Never, ever."

Peck leaned his head down on the top of Sasha's head, a tear dropping onto her forehead.

"Peck, Gabe is your resurrection. You'll never have to die again."

Peck and Sasha held hands climbing the knoll and walking back to the hotel.

CHAPTER 25

MORNING, SUNSHINE," Sasha said. "Did you get a good night's sleep?"

"I could eat a horse," Gabe said. "Where's Peck?"

"I let him sleep in. We'll go to the hotel, you change your clothes and we can either go to the diner, or we've found a Dunkin' Donuts."

The car was waiting. Sasha held Gabe's door while he climbed in and went around and got in beside him.

"Saxman Don wasn't there when we got to the bridge last night," Sasha said.

"You didn't get to hear him?"

"It was fine, Peck and I sat there and talked."

"Sorry. I think he stays until one. My guess is the earlier crowd likes to listen, and they're bigger tippers. Later crowd the drunks and noise makers."

"Peck and I had a long talk," Sasha said.

Sasha tapped Gabe on the thigh and gave him a sign she didn't want to talk about it in front of the driver.

"So which is it?" she asked.

"Which is what?"

"The diner or Dunkin' Donuts."

"The hotel has a breakfast set up in the lobby."

"I thought you'd want corn on the cob you keep going on about," Sasha said. "At the diner."

"I bet if I showed her how, Ruth could make corn fritters," Gabe said. "Corn fritters and scrambled eggs—oh, brother."

"Ruth?" Sasha asked with a tease.

"That's her name."

"Have you been messing around Providence on me, Gabe? Getting pretty personal, aren't we? She's Ruth, eh?"

"Ruth is the morning waitress at the diner," Gabe said.

"I'll just bet she is," Sasha winked.

"They like to be called servers nowadays, but she's the niece of the owner—his name is Doug—and her brother plays backup rhythm guitar around the area if anyone needs it."

"What?"

"I've been here awhile, darlin', I know some people."

"Do you like sleep over at the diner?" Sasha asked.

"I'm an inquisitive guy, what can I say?"

"Lily Cup and I've been going to Charlie's Blue Note for ten years

and you know more about this Ruth gal in three days than we know about Charlie."

"I'm a social animal, I guess," Gabe said. "There's more to life than dancing, you know."

Sasha smirked. "Yeah, sounds like it—there's corn on the cob."

"Holding those ears, watching the butter drip," Gabe said.

"I love it when you talk dirty," Sasha said.

The car pulled up to the hotel. They got out and watched it drive off.

"What time?" Gabe asked.

"We have to be there at one o'clock."

"Okay."

"If you don't want to go, I'll go alone," Sasha said.

Gabe didn't answer. Sasha put her arms around him.

"Get Peck," Sasha said.

"I'm starving," Gabe said.

"Go get dressed. We'll see what Ruth thinks about corn fritters."

"I'm certain Ruth could talk her uncle into making them," Gabe said.

"That's not what I'm worried about," Sasha mused.

"What?" Gabe asked.

"She'll want to smear corn fritters all over your body, you dirty old man."

Gabe shook his head, rolling his eyes, choking in an early morning grin. "Are you coming up?"

"I'll wait down here," Sasha said. "I'll check my emails."

Gabe stepped away and walked to the elevator. Sasha watched the door close, then went outside to a distant park bench on the lawn in front of the hotel. She pressed dial, then speaker.

"Hello?" Lily Cup asked in a weak, crackly morning voice.

"Did I wake you?" Sasha asked.

"What time is it?" Lily Cup asked.

"Oh shit," Sasha said. "I totally forgot the hour time difference."

"Don't worry about it," Lily Cup said. "I had to get up to answer the phone anyway."

"Very funny."

"Is Gabe all right?" Lily Cup asked.

"They gave him tests, ran him through their machines, I don't know what all, but we won't know until one this afternoon."

"So, what's the real reason you called? What'cha' need?"

"You are so rude," Sasha said.

"Me?"

"Why would you assume I only called because I needed something. How rude."

"I know you," Lily Cup said.

"Girlfriend you only think—"

"I know when you wake me up you need something."

"You fresh thing."

"It's not just to talk."

"Why I never. I can't ever remember calling you this early—ever."

"LSU homecoming, 2011—"

"What?"

"You called me at four-seventeen in the morning to tell me some basketball dude had just given you three orgasms."

"I would so never call you to tell you that," Sasha said.

"No, you're right," Lily Cup said.

"I know I am, I would so never—"

"You called to tell me you wanted to marry him, but you were at the ice machine in the hall filling an ice bucket and you couldn't remember his name or his hotel room number."

"Honey, what do you know about swamps or marshes in the Bayou Chene area, between Bayou Sorrel and Choctaw?"

"Doesn't ring a bell," Lily Cup said.

"Damn."

"Why?"

"As a kid, Peck was abused by a pig he called gator man," Sasha said.

"Gator man?"

"Peck calls him gator man."

"That's deep bayou spooky talk, girlfriend— gator man."

"Like from the time he was four. You wouldn't believe what he went through."

"Oh yeah, I would. I'm up at Angola prison at least once a month. I saw a man in chains who was caught feeding wise-guy-killed bodies to feral hogs he kept half-starved in concrete pens. I've seen—"

"Enough," Sasha said.

"I'm sorry," Lily Cup said.

"Enough...too early in the morning."

"Now you know why I can't sleep half the time."

"I love you," Sasha said.

"I love you too, baby cakes. I'll light a candle for Gabe at Saint Louis Cathedral."

"Would you do that?"

"Just be with your friends—some quality time. You deserve it."

"Thank you," Sasha said.

"Michelle?"

"Yeah?"

"Get me some names, without being too obvious."

"I'll work on it."

"People and places, get me what you can."

These women had a pact since the sixth grade that they won't ever say goodbye to each other. Sasha clicked her phone off and walked back to the lobby to wait for Gabe and Peck to come down.

The wait at the diner was no more than fifteen minutes. Most of the work crowd was already at work.

"Ruth, I'd like you to meet our friend, Michelle. She's up from New Orleans," Gabe said.

Waitress Ruth poured three cups of coffee, smiling at Sasha while listening to Gabe.

"Good morning," Ruth said. "Good to meet you. What can I get everybody?"

"Ruth, I've been meaning to talk to you about your fabulous corn on the cob," Gabe said.

"We pick the best," she said. "Well we don't actually pick it. We go to the farmer's market and pick out the best, is a better way of putting it."

"You're missing a golden opportunity, Ruth," Gabe said.

"Oh? And how's that, Gabe?"

"There's so many other things you can do with corn," Gabe said. "Especially as good as the corn you serve."

"You mean things like corn chowder, corn fritters, cornbread, corn waffles, and corn pancakes?"

Gabe's mouth dropped open. Waitress Ruth turned the menu in his hand over to nearly half a page of corn items.

"Only August and September, though. Best months for fresh corn, Gabe," waitress Ruth said. "Now what can I get everybody?"

Following breakfast, it was too early for music. Sasha didn't want to stress Gabe out and purposely chose not to talk about what Peck had told her under the bridge. She opted for a nap and a meet-up in the lobby at twelve thirty for their one o'clock meeting.

The Uber driver was there on time, and both Dr. Feinman and Dr. Michael Docherty welcomed Sasha and Gabe at the door and walked them back to a conference room. Peck took a seat in the waiting area.

Gabe, Sasha, the two doctors settled in their seats as Dr. Feinman opened a file folder.

"How are you feeling, Gabe?" Dr. Feinman asked. "Were you able to get some rest?"

"I feel fine," Gabe said. "They've come a long way in the poking and prodding departments. I felt nothing. Slept like a baby."

"Good," Dr. Feinman said. "Gabe, you're a soldier. And as a soldier you know that when you plan the strategy for battle, you have to weigh the risk for every move you take."

"Like chess," Gabe said.

"Yes, like chess," Dr. Feinman said.

"The King can't really die in chess," Sasha interrupted. "You just tip him over, but he doesn't die."

"Point taken," Dr. Feinman said.

"How long I got?" Gabe asked.

"Gabe, we've confirmed you have stomach cancer," Dr. Feinman said. "Not long, unless something is done."

No one spoke.

"We've also confirmed that it hasn't metastasized."

"Meaning?" Gabe asked.

"Meaning it's just in your stomach."

"Am I missing something?" Gabe asked. "Or is there supposed to be some good news in here somewhere?"

"The good news is both Dr. Docherty and I think a total gastrectomy might be your solution. It would take all of the cancer out of your body."

"Take it all out?" Gabe asked. "How?"

"It's complex surgery," Dr. Docherty said. "We remove the entire stomach. That way we remove all the active cancer cells."

"Would it add anything to my life?"

"It could be years," Dr. Feinman said.

"Years?" Gabe asked.

Tears flowed from Sasha's eyes. She sat watching Gabe's eyes.

"Tell me how it works," Gabe said. "If I have no stomach."

"You'll receive a general anesthesia for sleep and pain control," Dr. Feinman said. "We make an incision from below your breastbone down to your navel. We surgically remove the stomach and the nearby lymph nodes. We may also need to remove your spleen and portions of your esophagus, pancreas, and intestines. After the cancer has been removed, we attach your esophagus to your small intestine to form an alternate stomach. This will enable you to continue to swallow, eat, and digest food. Because of the limited capacity of your new stomach, you'll need to eat smaller amounts of food on a more frequent basis."

"Corn kernels are tiny, honey," Sasha said, smiling through tears.

"How long does it take, doc?" Gabe asked.

"A total gastrectomy takes two to three hours to perform. If you undergo this procedure, you should plan on staying in the hospital for at least a week. You'll need three to six months for recovery."

"Doc, after the week, can I fly?" Gabe asked.

"I'd like to have you around for regular checkups for a month," Dr. Docherty said. "After that you can fly, sure."

"You said risk," Sasha said.

"Gabe's not a young man," Dr. Feinman said. "It could be a shock to his heart. He could have a heart attack."

"Dr. Feinman and Dr. Docherty," Sasha said. "With all due respect—our Gabriel here walked from Kenner, Louisiana all the way to the Quarter, and then we danced until midnight. Oh, I think his heart can take it."

"You a dancer, Gabe?" Dr. Docherty asked. "We knew your love for jazz, but you're a dancer. Great exercise."

"Why do you think I've followed him up here?" Sasha asked. "Do you know how hard it is to get a lug on the dance floor these days?"

"You do have a point," Dr. Feinman said.

"A girl finds a good dancer, we stalk them," Sasha said.

"And all this time I thought you've been following me around for my looks and that jungle fever experience I read about in the tabloids," Gabe mused.

"So what say you, Gabe?" Dr. Feinman asked.

"Years?" Gabe asked.

"Could be years," Dr. Feinman said.

"I'd rather lose you trying, than lose you because you didn't take a chance of giving you years," Sasha whispered.

"Will my veteran's insurance pay for it?" Gabe asked.

"Every cent, and if it didn't, it'd be on us, dancer man," Dr. Docherty said.

Sasha reached and pinched Gabe's ear. "Say it," she said.

"Ow," Gabe said.

"Say it!" Sasha said.

"Yes."

"Louder."

"All right, all right, yes! Let's do it. Now, woman, let go of my ear."

"Tuesday, then," Dr. Feinman said. "Gabe, fast from midnight, drink only water. I'd eat light today and tomorrow."

"Anything else?" Sasha asked.

"I'll text you the name of an agent for temporary housing in the area if you'll need a place for the month or so," Dr. Docherty said.

"I think the Courtyard will be better for him. Breakfasts already there, housekeeping," Sasha said. "The diner's close by."

"That makes sense," Dr. Docherty said.

"Well then," Dr. Feinman said. "We'll see you Tuesday."

"Gabe, will you be at the finale today?" Dr. Docherty asked. "It's a piano tribute to George Shearing."

"We wouldn't miss it," Gabe said. "Did you know Shearing started playing at three—in England—and he played the accordion as well?"

Gabe's voice was energized, like that of a schoolboy. He felt an honest confidence there could be a quality future of many more dances and saxophone wails in years to come.

"I didn't know about the accordion," Dr. Docherty said.

"Oh yeah. As a boy, young Shearing would listen endlessly to all the jazz and blues greats on 78 records, and he got so he could mimic them. That's how he became so versatile. An all-time great."

"You certainly know your jazz," Dr. Docherty said.

"Tell you what, let's all go to the festival together next year," Gabe said. "My treat."

"Gabe, if you make me cry..." Sasha started.

"Okay, sorry, see you gentleman on Tuesday," Gabe said as he led Sasha to the door.

He paused and turned.

"Thank you both."

CHAPTER 26

DO WE HAVE SEATS for the performance in Newport?"
Sasha asked.

"Some of the festival is under an open tent," Gabe said. "We sit on the lawn. It's right in front of a bay where yachts are moored."

"Then we'll do a picnic lunch," Sasha said. "We can listen to Shearing and talk about what we have to do to get ready for a crazy week ahead."

"My baby," Gabe said. "You've done enough, and I love you for every minute of it. You don't have to hang around. I know you have a business to look after and your days are valuable. I'll be all right."

"*Oh, tu vieil homme têtu!*" Sasha cried. ("Oh, you stubborn old man!")

Sasha leaned forward.

"Driver? What's your name?" Sasha asked.

"Robert," the driver said.

"Please don't listen, Robert," Sasha said, turning toward Gabe.

"Why you self-centered old fool of a man," she said. "When will you stop pretending you're Sir Lancelot and start knowing who your friends are?"

"Darlin' I didn't mean..." Gabe started.

"Mean, schmean. You don't have the slightest clue how women think if you thought I would up and leave you to go through this alone."

"I don' t'ink ole Gabe meant he..." Peck started.

"You shut up, peckerwood. You're no better. Just the same as your twin, here. You don't know the first thing about women, either."

"What you mean?" Peck asked.

"Millie."

"What about Millie?"

"Didn't you tell me under the bridge you were going to marry her?" Sasha asked.

"Millie?" Peck asked.

"Yes, Einstein, I just said it—Millie," Sasha said. "Who was she to you—you said it under the bridge—the girl you're going to marry?" Sasha asked.

"I stay at her house there," Peck said.

"Did you kiss her?" Sasha asked.

"Hanh?"

"I'll know if you're lying. Did you kiss her?"

"Hokay," Peck said.

"For two days you were in Carencro at the grand jury and not until under the bridge last night did you ever talk about her."

Peck sat speechless.

"Have you kissed her?"

"Ah, *oui*."

"I knew it. Look at him, Gabe, he's a mess."

Gabe smiled. "Is she all you can think about, son?"

"Yes," Peck said.

"Day and night?"

"Purdy much."

"You're in love with her, Peck," Sasha said.

"Yes'm."

"Does she know it?"

"I dunno," Peck said.

"You talk about marrying her—you're up here eating donuts under a bridge, and she doesn't have a clue?" Sasha asked.

Peck stared out the window.

"Either a man tells a girl he loves her so much he can't sleep or eat or think straight, or he doesn't. Which is it?"

"I love Millie dat much."

Sasha pointed at Gabe.

"You really want to help this man get well?"

"Yes'm, I sure..." Peck started.

"Then get your head straight and start living your life like it means something," Sasha said.

"Hanh?"

"Only you can make it mean something, Peck. Nobody else can do it for you. Do it for Gabe—but especially do it for yourself. You can't make excuses for not taking chances and wasting your life."

"I understand," Peck said.

"You haven't told her, have you?" Sasha asked.

"Dat I love her?" Peck asked.

"That's what we're talking about. Have you?" Sasha asked.

"Nah, nah," Peck said.

"You're another piece of work," Sasha said.

She turned and looked out the window.

"You and Gabe belong together."

Sasha pulled herself forward by the back of the front seat.

"Robert, drop these bums at the hotel and let me out at that bench."

"Yes, ma'am," the driver said.

"We have three hours before it starts, but it'll be crowded if we want to sit close to the bandstand," Gabe said. "We should try to get there early."

"I have to make some calls," Sasha said. "Meet in an hour."

"What will we do about food and a blanket to sit on?" Gabe asked.

"I'll ask around, maybe find a cooler or a picnic basket somewhere," Sasha said. "The deli will have salads and sandwiches. You two wait in the hotel. I'll go see, after I make my calls."

"How about a bucket?" Gabe asked.

"A bucket?"

"Kentucky Fried Chicken—a bucket."

"Oh, my lord."

"A big bucket, potato salad, and biscuits," Gabe said.

"Peck?" Sasha asked.

"I like shicken, cher," Peck said.

"I should have known. I'm traveling with Chef Paul and James Beard," Sasha said. "I'm picking the wine. We'll get it on the way to Newport. Robert, drop me and wait here while we get organized. Then we'll go to Newport."

"No problem," the driver said.

When Sasha sat on the bench, she gave a sigh of relief. There was hope for Gabe. He might be able to live out the rest of his life getting to the things he now only has a keener awareness of. She touched *Lily Cup* on her phone and looked around to be certain she was alone and touched *speaker*.

"So, where are you?" Lily Cup asked.

"Exhausted and still in Providence," Sasha said.

"Everything okay?"

"I need you to tell the ladies at my office I won't be in for a week at least," Sasha said. "They have to cover my open houses and closings. If they need me, we can Facetime."

"Is Gabe getting worse?" Lily Cup asked.

"That's just it," Sasha said. "These two internal specialists met Gabe at the festival. They have a high-tech oncology lab. They tested him through the night and they think they can operate and remove all the cancer."

"Oh, my God," Lily Cup said. "He must be ecstatic."

"They're operating on him Tuesday."

"It's a miracle."

"Somebody should be here with him."

"Of course," Lily Cup said.

"We're sending Peck back to New Orleans," Sasha said. "Can you pop over to my office and ask Amy if she can find him a reasonable studio or efficiency apartment?"

"How close in?" Lily Cup asked.

"The tutor is in the Garden District," Sasha said. "Close enough to walk or bike between that and our offices."

"He can have my dad's old bike," Lily Cup said.

"Come up with some kind of cleaning schedule for him. Tell Nettie she doesn't have to clean our offices anymore. No cut in pay but she'll still clean our homes. Figure out what to pay Peck."

"Our office will pay our share."

"Whatever you think is fair."

"Your James came by yesterday," Lily Cup said. "He's asking where you are, and if you've dumped him."

"I can't think about James now," Sasha said. "I'll call him tonight."

"At least leave him a message or something," Lily Cup said. "Put him out of his misery."

"Peck's in love," Sasha said.

"No."

"He's a goner."

"In this short time—what's it been, a few days?"

"Blind love."

"With who—not you, please tell me?"

"A girl named Millie he met on the bus."

"I'll be."

"I mean, the boy's unwired."

"On a bus?"

"He jumped off the bus at her stop, somewhere in Tennessee."

"Maybe you and I should take more bus rides," Lily Cup said.

"I'm thinking Peck stays through the operation Tuesday," Sasha said. "I'll put him on a bus to New Orleans on Wednesday."

"He can fly now, why not on a plane?" Lily Cup asked.

"He has business in Tennessee," Sasha said. "The lady he's cottoned to lives there."

"His love?"

"He's down for the count."

"Our Peck—cheating on us already, eh? Bet she's young and, well young."

"He hasn't said, only that he loves her," Sasha said.

"Did he meet her before he got arrested and was flown in for the grand jury?"

"Yes."

"He didn't mention her to me," Lily Cup said.

"Nothing?" Sasha asked. "You with him all day at the grand jury. He didn't say anything to you about her?"

"Not a word, but I'm sure he had prison on his mind."

"That's true."

"Speaking of Peck," Lily Cup said. "Did you get any names—you know?"

"I did. Hang on, let me look at my phone."

Sasha scrolled emails, looking for one she sent to herself. She remembered texts and looked for a text she might have sent.

"Here," she said, "his foster nanna was an Alayna Prudhomme. I have Bayou Chene...and this one says it's between Bayou Sorrell and Choctaw."

"This is good. And the guy?"

"All I have is Peck called him gator man," Sasha said.

"Got it," Lily Cup said.

"I think the guy has his own place—maybe boats."

"Got it."

"So, what can you do with all of that?"

"I can smell around."

"They're not good people."

"I've got it."

"Are you still in trial?"

"I lost," Lily Cup said.

"I'm sorry," Sasha said.

"Well, I actually lost, and won at the same time."

"Oh?"

"I got Andre off the murder charge."

"You got him off murder? That's a big win, sweetie."

"Too circumstantial, but—and this is a big but—he got two years in Angola for selling firearms without a license...and basically from the trunk of his Lincoln, actually. The circumstantial was that the murder weapon had serial numbers on it. To win the murder rap I had to rat him out and prove all the guns in his trunk had their serial numbers removed, so he couldn't have done it—the murder."

"And so they busted him for weapon sales," Sasha said.

"At least he doesn't get the needle for murder."

"You're a genius, girlfriend."

"Andre thinks so."

"Do you still get paid?"

"Oh yeah. He paid plenty."

"That sounded pretty smart, what you did."

"I'm driving up to Angola tomorrow—see that he behaves himself. Maybe I can get him out in six months with good behavior."

"Are you ever afraid of going to Angola alone?" Sasha asked. "I heard it's nasty."

"Honey, Angola is safer for me than the streets of New Orleans after midnight," Lily Cup said. "Andre will protect me."

"Really?" Sasha asked.

"Andre has his fingers in everything. He knows everyone he needs to know. It's like he's an octopus with arms all throughout Louisiana."

"Amazing," Sasha said. "Harvard would shit."

"Andre wouldn't let anything happen to his star attorney," Lily Cup said.

"You are a star," Sasha said. "And thank you for making sense out of that whole kidnapping thing Peck was in."

"You made it happen," Lily Cup said. "You and Judge Thibodaux, you vamp."

"Okay, sweetie. Love you," Sasha said.

"Let me know when Peck will be here," Lily Cup said.

"I will. Give Charlie and the band hugs for me."

The ride to Newport, Rhode Island was pleasant, a reflective ride. Sasha sat in the middle of the back seat with her head rested back, holding each of her boy's hands, like a mother.

Peck appeared contented that the dark moment that started in New Jersey was behind him, and he was now with a man who thought of him as a son.

Gabe's smile out the window made it appear as if a great weight had been lifted from his shoulders; as he felt for the first time in months there wasn't the finality of a giant brick wall facing him, but perhaps an open tunnel to a hopeful reality.

Sasha, exhausted and weary, was content to put her emails aside for the drive through historic Rhode Island. The past week or so changed her life, between that of impetuously following a shooting star from a dance floor in a jazz joint just off Frenchman Street to Beale Street in Memphis and now to feeling more family warmth than she had known most of her adult life. Other than her childhood friend, Lily Cup, she had never been more attached to such sincere, interesting characters. She's become connected, as if she has known them for years.

The tent crowd was quiet and respectful; plastic cups kept the noise of tinkling ice cubes down. Two entertainers from local groups took turns playing their own Shearing impressions. They played "Lullaby of Birdland," "Misty," "How High the Moon," and "Let there be Love." They played the entire *Guys and Dolls* score as performed by the velvet fog, Mel Torme and accompanied by jazz pianist George Shearing in concert at a Newport Jazz Festival a long time ago.

"This wine is mellow, smooth, buttery," Gabe said.

"Listen to you," Sasha said.

"What is it?"

"I can't believe we have a bucket of fried chicken with two ninety-dollar bottles of Arnot-Roberts Chardonnay, Trout Gulch 2014," Sasha said.

"It reminds me," Gabe said.

"Why would that not surprise me?" Sasha asked.

"Back when I was active in the army, I remember a time when I was being self-conscious."

"You? Self-conscious?" Sasha asked.

"About being black. After we got back from 'Nam I'd go out of my way to avoid all the black clichés, like chicken and grits and greens."

"Are you talking soul food?"

"That too, but everything changed in Paris."

"Paris will do that," Sasha said.

"Another captain and I were enjoying the sights and fountains. We started up to Sacre Coeur basilica, approaching the Montmartre steps."

"I've been there," Sasha said.

"Well now, if you've been to Paris you know this is almost a religious experience."

"It is."

"The fact that this marvel lasted through two wars that decimated most of Europe was a miracle in its own right."

"And?"

"And coming down the long steps of this holy experience were two brothers—black dudes talking with each other about what a groovy visit Paris was, each holding a bucket of Kentucky Fried chicken in one hand and a bottle of French wine in the other."

"Ha!" Sasha bellowed.

"Can you imagine? Two buckets of Kentucky Fried coming down the Montmartre steps in Paris—with French wine."

Sasha picked up a leg of chicken, held it and looked at it.

"Well, excuse *moi*, boys," Sasha said. "Bon appetite."

That evening they sat in Gabe and Peck's room with coffee, cognac, and conversation.

"Tell us how, Peck. Tell us what happened," Gabe said. "You caught the under the bridge knife guy...tell us how it all went down."

Peck told the story of his meeting Millie on the bus. He told of her doll, of the braces on her teeth, of her Bible, and of the twinkle in her eyes. He told of how he remembered the image of the Kingston sign as the place they got off the bus, and that was where Millie told him to get off if he ever came back. He told of how Millie knew her way around a library as well as he knows his way around a bayou. He told of how they tracked and found the knife man, how he had to kill the dog, and how he tied him up like a gator with his two-hundred-pound test line that would only tighten if the knife man fought it or tried to get loose.

"You mean the spool of fishing line you got free for buying that bag in Memphis?" Sasha asked.

"Yes'm," Peck said.

The story gave Sasha and Gabe great pause. Peck came from another world than theirs, but in his world good was just as good and evil was just as universal. They shared their amazement at how the college girl and Peck worked together as a formidable team, looking back only after the police were notified and an arrest was made. They understood the life-threatening dangers both walked into—facing a man who had already stabbed a man in the chest and face and wouldn't be selective about his victims. The more they listened, the more Sasha and Gabe felt that Millie was the perfect foundation Peck needed—and they both needed each other. Sasha hinted that she'd have a talk with Peck about schooling and outline a plan for him to think about. She left the two to go to her room and get a night's sleep.

"Don't sit up and talk all night," Sasha said.

Back in her room, Sasha touched *Lily Cup* on her phone.

"Hi," Lily Cup said.

"Did I ever tell you about the hailstorm and the bridge and Gabe getting hit?" Sasha asked.

"You drinking?" Lily Cup asked.

"No."

"Tell me again. I like that story."

Sasha proceeded to tell Lily Cup about their road trip to Memphis and how Peck and this girl Millie he met on the bus figured out where the knife man was and how they went and caught him.

"Holy shit," Lily Cup said.

"What?" Sasha asked.

"I don't know that part. Peck and the girl Millie did all that?"

"When they arrested him in New Jersey and were asking him about bodies and money, he thought he'd killed the knife man. Until they took him to you in Louisiana, he thought he'd murdered the guy."

"If he thought he could have killed him he must have hurt him pretty badly," Lily Cup said.

"That's just it," Sasha said. "He tied the guy up with two-hundred-pound test fishing line. He bought a bag, you know like a duffle or workout bag in a sporting store in Memphis, and they gave him a spool of two-hundred-pound test fishing line. He tied the dude up with his fishing line. He said he's seen gators tied like that."

"You couldn't book this act," Lily Cup said.

"The girl called the troopers and told them he was tied up in his trailer and anchored to the refrigerator," Sasha said.

"Millie called the police?" Lily Cup asked.

"Yes, Millie," Sasha said.

"Fishing line?" Lily Cup asked.

"Two-hundred-pound fishing line."

"I lit a candle for Gabe."

"Love you," Sasha said.
"Love you," Lily Cup said.
They ended the call.

CHAPTER 27

LILY CUP CHECKED HER HANDBAG with a guard and pulled a chair around to sit down opposite Andre. She looked about, scanning the placement of the inmate's visitors, leaned forward and lowered her voice.

"Andre, do you know any good cops down in Bayou Chene, near Choctaw or maybe Bayou Sorrell?" she whispered.

"Andre knows good cops everywhere," Andre said. "Some he knows, how you say, better than others is all. Why you ask?"

"This kid I know was in a jam there."

"Talk to Andre."

"Well, he's not a kid—he's twenty-four now. This happened when he was a young kid. Someone, I can't tell you who, asked me to help him so I helped him," Lily Cup whispered. "It was nothing he really did—no crime or anything like that—it was all circumstantial and a grand jury was just asking if he was main witness to something. Anyway, I got him off, but while doing all that I learned he grew up there, you know, in that Choctaw area—like back in the swamps, bayous, and marshlands. A hard life growing up, he was made to do bad things for a man they called *gator man*."

"Swamp people have their ways," Andre said.

"The kid can't read or write, so we're helping him, a friend and me—we're getting him into school. You know, like we're giving him a break, a second chance."

"You talking or dancing with Andre, *mon ami?*"

"I'm serious, Andre."

"You talking a hard life—a gator man—or are you talking a break and a second chance?" Andre asked. "You're dancing with Andre."

Lily Cup leaned in, her elbow on the table, her knuckles covering the sides of her mouth.

"Andre this kid was dumped when he was just a baby somewhere back in that marshland or bayou around there, in '90—maybe '91," she whispered. "Alayna Prudhomme is one of the names, somewhere between Bayou Sorrel and Choctaw, I think. Least that's what I hear."

"This Prudhomme," Andre said. "She knows this gator man?"

"They must have been fucking, that's what I'm thinking," Lily Cup said. "The bitch probably collecting state money for keeping the kid. It's been fifteen years. Who knows now? They both could be dead. All I know is this *gator man* is nasty."

"Man cannot stoop so low as to not get love from a woman or a dog," Andre said.

"When the kid could walk, she'd let this guy, *gator man*, chain him with a dog collar under a porch. Enslaved him for hard labor in daylight when he was like six, carrying bait shrimp buckets to his boat, used him as gator bait at night. The kid got his mouth taped so he couldn't scream, and he'd get pulled in dark bayous behind a boat far enough back he would attract the bigger gators. He was just a helpless kid."

"This gator man is not a nice person," Andre said.

"Ya think?"

"Not what you would call the fatherly type."

Lily Cup looked into Andre's eyes as if she knew she connected.

"He's a good boy, this boy?"

"He's a good boy, Andre. A decent kid."

Using no names Lily Cup went on to tell Andre how she and Sasha met Peck and how Peck was helping Gabe make a dream come true living out the last days of his life by going to Newport to listen to jazz. She told how Gabe was beaten and robbed of his cancer pain medicine under a bridge in Hazelton, Mississippi, and how the robber stabbed another man in the face and how Peck and a girl tracked him down three states away and caught him, and how Peck tied him with two hundred-pound fishing line and left him bound to the refrigerator leg while they called the troopers and told them where the robber was tied up.

"Three states?" Andre asked.

"Can you imagine?" Lily Cup asked.

"That's a long way from a bayou."

"The kid and this girl he likes tracked him."

"The kid's a good tracker."

"He's a good kid, Andre."

"He sounds like a good boy."

"Just needs a break."

"Two hundred-pound line, you don't say?" Andre asked.

"He saw gator man tie alligator snouts with it," Lily Cup said.

"How did he get away? This friend you can't talk about—how'd he get away from this gator man? His kind is hard to get away from, especially for good gator-bait boys, anyway."

"He told my friend he climbed a bald cypress and hid in its trunk hollow, standing barefoot in the dark on broken buzzard eggs and live ants for four days until he heard the gator man throwing empty whiskey bottles against a rock all pissed off that he couldn't find the kid and driving off with another bottle probably to see the Prudhomme skank. I think the kid was like eight or nine. He ran seventy miles before stopping with his feet bloody. He's been alone ever since, mowing lawns, fishing for food. He lives in a saw shed. He sharpens blades for a mill or boat builder or something in barter for a sleeping cot, hot plate and a trotline."

"What you want a good cop for?"

"I want—"

"For a bad man?"

"He's a bastard," Lily Cup said.

Andre looked into Lily Cups eyes with a cold stare.

"I want a good cop to find the bastard, Andre."

"I need good coffee," Andre said. "I need Scotch."

Lily Cup knew from experience, that in the world she worked in if someone changes a subject, best she change it too. She also knew Andre knew she couldn't get him Scotch.

"Anything I can get you?" Lily Cup asked.

Lily Cup made mental notes of requests Andre had for simple things like writing paper, magazines, and cans of peaches. They made light conversation until a guard signaled it was time for him to return to his cell and for her to leave.

"You behaving yourself, Andre? Are you being a good boy so I can get you out of here early?"

Andre leaned into Lily Cup.

"Leave it to Andre."

"I don't want him hurt, Andre."

Andre stood.

"Just find the bastard."

Andre waited for a guard to come over and walk him to his cell.

It was 11:45 a.m. in Providence when both Dr. Feinman and Dr. Docherty came to a waiting area in scrub smocks and invited Sasha and Peck into a conference room, closing the door behind them.

"Gabe has a wonderful constitution," Dr. Feinman said.

"You should see him dance," Sasha said.

"He came through with flying colors," Dr. Feinman said.

Sasha held the palms of her hand to her mouth in prayerful thanks.

"His heart rate hardly fluctuated," Dr. Docherty said. "Usually we see a change in heart rate with the stress of a major surgery like this."

"Gabe's a black man," Peck said. "He seen worse, bein' black."

There wasn't a person at the table who didn't understand what the man who grew up in the wilds of a Louisiana bayou meant. They reflected on the thought, like it was a poetic riff from a jazz instrument.

"Is he awake?" Sasha asked.

"It'll be an hour or so," Dr. Feinman said.

"Can we see him then?"

"He'll be groggy at first, but it'll be good for him to see you."

"We'll grab lunch and come back," Sasha said. "Is there anything special we need to know? Any rules?"

"We'd like to see a couple hundred feet before we let him out of here," Dr. Docherty said.

"You want centipedes, Doc?" Sasha quipped nervously.

"We need him to get out of bed and walk as soon as he can. Each day he needs to walk a little further. The goal is to get him up to two hundred or more feet in one stretch. Let's say a week—seven days in a row he does two hundred feet. Then he can move to the hotel."

"Perfect," Sasha said. "When the man isn't dancing, he's walking."

"It may take several days, could take a week. Let him pace himself. Just encourage him," Dr. Docherty said.

"He's got an incredible constitution," Dr. Feinman said.

"He's a regular Forrest Gump," Sasha said.

"He's a lucky man."

"We'll see you after lunch, gentlemen. Thank you for everything."

Before they walked to the diner, Sasha sat with Peck on the park bench and gave him a tutorial on how to use his new cellphone.

"You can count to ten, Peck, so this should be easy for you," Sasha said.

Just as Gabe repeated the one to ten count eleven times, Sasha pointed at each number in order and counted them aloud again and again. Eventually Peck took the cell from her hand and pointed to each number and said its name.

"One, two, three, four, five, six, seven, eight, nine," Peck said. "And dis one here is zero."

Sasha showed him how to dial, how to make a call, and how to hang up. She taught him how to answer a call.

"Who's the most important person in your life, Peck?" Sasha asked.

"Hanh?"

"The most important person in your life."

"Gabe."

"That won't work. Gabe doesn't have a phone."

"They's one in his room at the hotel," Peck said.

Sasha grinned at Peck's simple awareness, seeing all things.

"So there is," Sasha said. "Okay, so Gabe is the most important, so he'll be number one. I'll put a one before his name, and if you want to call him you just touch the name here that has a one in front of it. When the hotel answers, you ask for him. Got it?"

"I t'ink so," Peck said.

"I have Millie's number in my cell from the time she called," Sasha said.

One at a time Sasha filled his phone contact directory with the important names with a leading number in front, so he could identify who he'd be calling. 1 was Gabe; 2 was Millie; 3 was Sasha. A good start.

"Let's go eat," Sasha said.

On the way to the diner Peck asked what the text slots were and she explained they didn't matter as he couldn't read them until after he learned to read.

"This here one is Millie," Peck said, pointing to the number 2 on his directory."

"That's Millie all right," Sasha said. "Don't press it yet. We have to see bus schedules and all that first. Do you still have your Discover America pass?"

"Yes'm," Peck said.

Sasha and Peck celebrated lunch discussing the miracle that Gabe had made it through an operation that could add years to his life.

"Isn't it good to know Gabe might be around to see you get your schooling, Peck?" Sasha asked.

"You t'ink I can did dat?"

"Only if you try. If you like it, will you go all the way?"

"Hanh?"

"Like to college?" Sasha asked.

"Yes'm," Peck said.

"Want to talk about Millie?"

"Hokay."

"You really love her?"

"Oh, *oui*, cher."

"So, if you love her, and let's say she loves you, you should give her time to finish her school, and she should help you finish yours," Sasha said.

"So we get married?" Peck asked.

"After she finishes school," Sasha said.

"Ahh, *oui*."

"We'll give you the biggest wedding the Quarter has seen—well Frenchman Street anyway, in Charlie's Blue Note."

"*Hoot*!" Peck said.

"After you finish school you can buy that farm, or crawfish bog or be president or anything you want."

"And Gabe live with us, hanh?"

"He would love it."

Sasha scrolled her phone, found Greyhound bus lines and booked an evening seat for Peck on a bus that went through Knoxville.

"You're set, Peck," Sasha said. "Call Millie, see if she wants to see you, and if she'll pick you up tomorrow at eleven forty-five at the Kingston stop."

Peck took a gulp of coffee. He picked up his phone and touched the name with the number two in front of it and held it to his ear. Soon a big grin came over his face.

"Hello?"

"Hello, cher, this is Peck."

"Peck? I dreamed about you last night."

"How you are, cher?"

"I miss you so bad."

"Can you pick me up in Kingston at eleven forty-five?"

"You're here? I'll be right over."

"Tomorrow, cher."

"Yes! Yes! I'll be there waiting—eleven forty-five."

"You wanna see me, cher?"

"More than anything in the world."

"I wanna see you too, dass for true."

"I love you, Mr. Boudreaux Clemont Finch. Eleven forty-five. I'll be there."

"Bye, cher," Peck said.

Peck ended his first call with a grin that plastered his face.

"Feels good, doesn't it?" Sasha asked. "Love."

"Oh, *oui*," Peck said. "So good."

Gabe was awake. There were tubes down his nostrils and wires on his chest and wrists. He was weak in voice, but his eyes twinkled at the sight of Sasha and Peck walking into the room.

"Not too long," the nurse said. "Tomorrow will be better. He's been through a lot."

"Hi honey," Sasha said, sitting on a chair next to the bed and holding Gabe's hand.

Gabe squeezed her hand.

Peck held his hand up as a waved hello for Gabe. Gabe smiled at Peck and raised his thumb.

"Honey, Peck is going to catch a bus to New Orleans. Lily Cup will set him up in a small apartment, and he starts schooling with a tutor on Monday, in the Garden District."

Gabe nodded agreement.

"He's going to see his Millie on his way down," Sasha said. "And it's okay because he agrees if they do anything they're going to wait until she's out of school."

Gabe nodded and smiled.

"And when Peck buys his crawfish farm, he's going to need you for swimming around distracting the alligators so he can pick up his traps," Sasha said.

Gabe started to laugh, then grimaced, and motioned to Sasha that it was pulling at his sutures.

"Oops. Sorry," Sasha said.

Gabe squeezed her hand, telling her thank you for another chance. A tear formed in her eye as she stood to leave. He held her hand and pulled her close to him and whispered in her ear.

"Go see Don," Gabe whispered. "Have him play 'When Sunny Gets Blue.'"

His hand loosened, and he fell asleep.

CHAPTER 28

LATE THAT EVENING, sitting in the Greyhound depot waiting area, Sasha pulled a debit card from her bag and handed it to Peck.

"Can you remember this combination: four, three, two, one?"

"Yes'm," Peck said. "Four, three, two, one."

"Good. Remember those four numbers in that order and keep them secret. This card will get you anything you'll need on your trip. It'll get you school supplies when you get to New Orleans. Hand it to the clerk at checkout, and if they ask you to enter your pin number, remember that code—four, three, two, one—and touch those numbers in that order."

Peck pointed to the name on the card.

"What this say, cher?"

"That's you, Peck. It says Boudreaux C. Finch. They couldn't fit Clemont on it. But that's you, Mr. Finch."

Peck smiled and held the card for a closer look. The embossed name matched the name on his new ID card. He turned it over and there was a signature on the back.

"I signed your name on it," Sasha said. "That's how you will sign your name when you can write. I just did it for you."

"T'anks."

Sasha held out a sealed envelope.

"This has some cash for the road. Use the card when you see things you need, though," Sasha said. "Don't lose it."

At the depot exit they found his bus. Sasha held Peck for a long goodbye. He was family now. Knowing Gabe was going to have a chance at more time was a game-changer for everyone somehow. It made this moment real, more permanent. She almost felt maternal.

"You go slow with Millie," Sasha said.

Peck listened, nodding his head.

"Don't overwhelm her. Give her plenty of time to know if she really loves you enough to be with you forever—"

"I will, I promise."

"—and that you're not just a rebound love for her."

"Rebound?" Peck asked.

Sasha stepped back looking Peck in the eyes.

"Peck," Sasha said. "You ever have a big fish on one hook and a smaller fish on another hook at the same time—?"

"*Oui.*"

"—and you can't pull the big one in through the briar barbs under water, only the small one?"

"*Oui,*"

"You take the small one home and eat it, right?"

"*Oui,*"

"But wouldn't you have rather had the big one?"

"Ah, *oui*," Peck said, understanding the metaphor.

"Get it?" Sasha asked.

"*Oui,*" Peck said. "Be sure Peck is big fish, not little fish, cher."

Sasha walked him to the bus, handed him a sack of bottled water and sandwiches, and kissed him on the cheek.

"What do I tell her momma and daddy?" Peck asked.

Sasha reflected but didn't answer.

"I'll see you in New Orleans, honey," Sasha said. "Maybe you and I can fly up here on weekends to see Gabe and take him to the diner until he can come home."

"Corn," Peck said.

"You know?" Sasha asked. "I think corn would be perfect for him. You're right."

"Bye, cher," Peck said. "I love you for what you are, dass for true."

"Parents like the truth, Peck," Sasha said. "Just be yourself."

Sasha watched the bus pulling around the back of the station, bouncing a tilt from the driveway to the street and then on down to the highway, its roof washed with the gold of the streetlights as it passed under them on its eventual journey south.

Knowing her life had changed since an evening of dancing at Charlie's Blue Note, Michelle Lissette walked alone the many blocks through downtown Providence to the river and then to Point Street Bridge. As she neared it, she could hear the wail of the sax.

In the still of a cloud covered and seemingly moonless night she became Sasha again, making her way down the grassy slope and under the bridge, waving a gentle hand toward Don. He riffed from his slow blues wail into "When Sunny Gets Blue" without pause.

Sasha sat in tears. The torment of what Peck had been through and of almost losing Gabe stirred on her face like the shadows of a lonely get well card. The moment of change closing in, and it may have been dawning on her how lucky she was to have these two new friends, and how rewarding it was to be able to be there for them.

She sat and listened to gentle saxophone sounds until the others and lovers dwindled and moved on with a threat of rain, and Don began folding his tent from another early morning of jazz and mellow blues. He raised a plastic bottle of water and swallowed it all without stopping for breath. He stepped around the ledge, picking up cups and pieces of paper his listeners had left behind. He removed the mouthpiece and packed his instrument in the royal blue velvet lining, closed and locked the leather case.

He held his hand outstretched and offered Sasha a hand up the grassy knoll to the sidewalk. The two walked together, slowly, without talking for three blocks. Sasha folded a hundred-dollar bill, held it up for him to see and slipped it in his pocket.

"Gabe thanks you for being here for him," Sasha said.

Don smiled, and they split with a fist pump, Don going straight for three more blocks to his apartment to smoke cigarettes and drink vodka alone in the dark with his memories, and Sasha going left a block to the hotel to be alone maybe with thoughts of getting some rest.

Peck learned how easy it was to sleep through the night on an all-nighter bus. It wasn't until the bus departed the bedlam of that New York City stop and the bustle of the Newark New Jersey terminal. He couldn't help noticing how much activity there was at city stations, alive with people moving about, while only one or two boarded buses. It was as if big city terminals were clubs of warmth and welcomed noises for the homeless or for people who couldn't sleep alone. Soon the bus made its way up into the Pennsylvania mountains under a rich, full moon. Could it be, Peck wondered to himself, that Gabe or Sasha were looking at the same moon and thinking of him? He remembered watching the moon as a child with a dog collar padlocked around his neck, chained under gator man's side porch. He'd grasp the wooden lattice with his little fingers and look up at the full moon as if to wonder if his real mother and real father ever looked at the moon while he did, and if they ever thought about him. He would pray to the moon to tell them he was certain they would like him now, because he wasn't a crying baby anymore, and now he could carry buckets of bait shrimp and not spill them and he could earn his keep. He would ask the moon to tell them if he saw them.

Under the glow of the moon and gentle swaying motion of the bus Peck dozed off about the same time Gabe opened his eyes.

"Lord," Gabe said under his breath. "Lord, I've been meaning to thank you. Actually, before the operation I thought I'd be thanking you in person, but since I made it through I've wanted the right moment and the right words and it's going to take me some time to get through this, and I don't have so much breath, so just bear with me as I'll need some time, and my catheter friend is taken care of my business, so there won't be any interruptions. Lord, I'm not good with words, you already know that, but you've bestowed on me so many other blessings, and I feel like I'm almost reborn today, just waking up after this operation, and I've been brought up to show appreciation, to always say thank you, and I'm going to do it properly if it takes all night.

"When I lost my boy in Iraq, and then I lost my butterfly, Lord, I thought you were truly telling me it was quitting time. I apologize for my doubt and questioning you. Please forgive the words I might have used those days. And when I found the cancer I figured it was your plan all along that we three go together and be done with it, but then you go and put that turn in my road, in Carencro, Louisiana it was, and I would never besmirch the Almighty with a presumption that this tattered old soul was the least bit worthy of a miracle, but Lord you put me on that dance floor off that Frenchman Street alley and one night of red beans and rice and Joe Williams, and it was a rebirth in me that could only be heaven-sent.

"I don't know what you have in store for me now—whether I'll live out a good life or get hit and run over by a truck when I walk out of here, but I want to thank you from the bottom of my heart—which is just about all that's left in there. Thank you for the time I had with my butterfly, and thank you for my son, and thank you for my new family—Michelle and Boudreaux. Oh, my Lord and God, you couldn't have aligned the stars any better than how you blessed us all the ways you have. Boudreaux is a good boy, you already knew that. He's the reason I'm here praying tonight and not days closer to pushing up dandelions. I feel like you put him here for me to look after, and you made me whole again to do it. And our Sasha friend doesn't have a bad bone in her body, and she'll watch after the boy long after I'm gone. So, thank you, Lord, I'll get some rest now. Thank you for listening. Amen."

Gabe closed his eyes and slept.

Peck's bus pulled into the Knoxville station for a thirty-minute food break. The next unscheduled stop would be Kingston Pike, where Millie would be waiting for him. Peck grabbed his duffel and stepped off the bus to stretch his legs. He figured there would be vittles when he arrived in Kingston, so he chose to just walk around, exploring outside the terminal. Across the street was a used bookstore. Peck couldn't read the sign, but his eyes brightened when he saw the posters of books in the window. He crossed the street and cautiously stepped in. After a small conversation, the clerk seemed to know to be patient with Peck, and he was helpful.

"I'm going to learn to read and write," Peck said. "You have a book with all the words maybe?"

The clerk went to the second row and picked three new books from a shelf and brought them forward.

"Here is a dictionary. It's one of the best there is," the clerk said. "These two come in a pair—a dictionary and a thesaurus."

Peck pointed at the one book. "All the words?"

"Yep," the clerk said.

"How much?" Peck asked.

"Twenty-four ninety-five, plus tax."

Peck knew his range went only to ten on the counting scale, so he opted to reach in his pocket and pull out his debit card. Within seconds he counted to himself, four, three, two, one— and within minutes he was crossing the street to the bus station with the wrapped dictionary he was looking forward to learning from. Carrying it gave him an emboldened sense of confidence. As he crossed the street, in the distance he could see his bus driver consoling a woman, her head down, who seemed as if she was crying.

"Lady," the bus driver said. "I'm really sorry, I just don't think your friend was on my run. He could be on the one that comes through at two thirty. If he's not on the bus, and you didn't see him in the terminal, I sure can't help you, lady. Anybody you can call?"

Peck stepped around, his bag with his new dictionary in one hand, his duffel in the other. He saw that the girl covering her eyes with a tissue and sobbing was his Millie.

He paused, stood there, shifted both bags to one hand with a grin on his face and tapped her on the shoulder. Millie looked up as if he was annoying her, but after seeing him her brows shot up, her eyes burst open, and then came a toothy grin as she leaped with one hop up on him. He caught her, her arms over his shoulders, hanging on, as he held her waist. She kissed him again and again.

"Lady, it appears you have found your man," the bus driver said.

Millie's arm reached out and waved.

"We're loading, buddy," the bus driver said. "If you're going."

"I'm with her," Peck said. As she continued to kiss his chin and cheeks and nose, he freed his one arm and pointed a finger to the back of her head.

"I'm going with this one," Peck said.

The driver smiled coyly, crawled into his seat, and closed the door, giving Peck a thumbs up.

They loosened their clinch and grabbed a booth in the café where Millie spoke a mile a minute, explaining that when she knew the bus number she could find out all the stops and she decided she wanted to come to Knoxville and get him here, so they could talk before she took him home, and when he wasn't on the bus and not in the terminal her heart sank, and she couldn't stop crying. She ordered two orders of French fries and two BLT sandwiches and water and threw a glance at Peck to see if he was okay with a BLT.

"That poor man," Millie said of the bus driver.

"Oh, I bet he's seed some t'ings," Peck said.

"Daddy and Momma are so happy you're coming. Daddy's cooking brisket just for you, and he wants to take you out on his boat. Momma is making you bread pudding."

Peck smiled.

"There's just one little thing, Peck," Millie said.

"Hanh?"

"Nothing we can't get around, mind you."

"Like what?"

"I thought I should tell you before we get there, and you find out that way."

"Tell me, cher," Peck said.

"I love it when you call me cher."

Millie reached over the table and placed her hand over Peck's and was completely distracted.

"Oh, did you hear about our stab-in-the-face friend?" Millie asked.

"Nah, nah," Peck said. "The Brock guy or the bad guy?"

"The bad guy, of course, silly," Millie said.

"Tell me, cher," Peck said.

"So the state troopers went to his trailer and found him just as we left him. He couldn't move a muscle the way you tied him. It was in the newspaper. They even had to shoo a raccoon that had wandered in and was in the creep's garbage can—and they found a bag filled with all sorts of stolen pharmaceutical pills and capsules. A garbage bag full. The paper said it was a legal discovery as they had probable cause to search his place. The reporter even said the dog was probably killed in self-defense."

"This all good?" Peck asked.

"There's more," Millie said.

"*Bon*," Peck said.

"*Le bâtard* pleaded guilty to stabbing Brock if they didn't press charges on the pills," Millie said. "Daddy says he'll get ten years as he's done this before—robbed people on the highway, usually at truck stops. They have him on videos, but he would always leave the state where he robbed people."

Peck held Millie's hand and remembered Sasha's advice to go slow.

"Is that what you were tellin' me cher?"

"Okay," Millie said. "So the deal is the vermin showed up, and he's going to be having dinner with us, and I don't blame you if you get mad, but he just dropped in, and nobody invited him, and he's been apologizing and all that stuff, and are you mad at me?"

"Vermin?" Peck asked.

"The snake," Millie said.

"Snake?"

"The old boyfriend," Millie sang melodically. "Stephen."

"Ah," Peck said. "Stephen, the snake."

"He's more like an ingrown toenail."

"He knows 'bout Peck, this Stephen Toenail?"

"He will in forty minutes," Millie sang again.

"Won't your momma alretty did tole 'em?" Peck asked.

"Oh, no way," Millie said. "Daddy said why spoil the fun by telling him and miss out on all the fireworks."

"Do your daddy and momma know, like dat we...?" Peck started.

"No," Millie said, lifting her nose. "Nobody's business and nothing to tell anyway."

"So, what he mean 'bout fireworks, cher?"

"Oh, that," Millie said. "Stephen is so jealous he can't stand boys around me ever. He still thinks he owns me."

Peck looked at the smile of satisfaction in her eyes.

"You like the farm, for true, cher?" Peck asked.

"Chickens and tomatoes?" Millie asked, leaning forward.

"*Oui.*"

"More than anything."

"So, what you do when you seed a snake, hanh?" Peck asked.

"Simple," Millie said. "If it's little, I'd shoo it away. If it's big, I run get you to catch it for bait."

Peck's mouth dropped. Millie put her hand over her braces, grinned and raised her brows.

"Did I say that right?"

Pecked took his phone from his pocket, opened it and touched the number two button in front of Millie's name. Her cell rang within seconds, and she looked at it curiously and put it to her ear.

"Hello?" she asked.

Phone to his ear, Peck leaned forward, looking into her eyes while talking into his phone.

"I need to brought myself with a beau'tinous lady to some brisket and puddin', cher, can you did dat for me, farm girl?" Peck asked. He watched her eyes sparkle and tear up. He closed his phone and held her hand.

"If we sit here all day, they'll be no brisket or bread pudding left," Millie said.

"Snakes don't eat much," Peck said.

For the entire trip from Knoxville to the Kingston exit the two held hands when it was safe, and the only thing said between them was Peck asking Millie how much longer she had in school, and Millie telling him three semesters, but she was taking French as well, and not to ever mention to her folks what they did last time he was there when they caught the knife man.

"*C'est bon,*" Peck said, holding up three fingers for three semesters.

"I know that's good," Millie said.

"*Oui,*" Peck said.

They pulled onto the drive, and Peck lifted his package and duffel from the floor.

Late the same afternoon, Sasha, with the help of two nurses, got Gabe out of bed, and he walked in slow, short steps ten feet, to the other side of the hall and ten feet back to the bed.

"Only one hundred eighty to go," Sasha said.

CHAPTER 29

AT THE HOUSE, PECK OFFERED CORDIAL HUGS to the momma and the reverend. They were warm and gracious and asked how long he could stay—the special young man who would stop a bus just to make a person happy. The momma's interest was inspired in spreading the gospel with the example he set, the daddy's was to get some fishing in. While they made their pleasantries, the Ingrown Toenail was in the bathroom skulking. Peck took the opportunity of his absence to inquire about the fishing tackle in the garage. Reverend offered it and asked if he could join him on the dock while waiting on the brisket and potatoes in the smoker.

"Peck," the reverend said, "I have a package of frozen shrimp we can try as bait. I hear they use frozen shrimp offshore in Galveston. I'd like to try it here. Would that do us?"

"Shrimp *bon* in saltwater," Peck said. "Les' try it in fresh water."

Millie's expression was pleased that her two favorite men would be down on the dock and out of harm's way from an inevitable Ingrown Toenail drama.

"You two be back in an hour," the momma said. "Millie and I will have salads and deviled eggs done about then, and we'll be ready for the brisket and potatoes."

At the dock, the reverend gave Peck two rods and kept two for himself. He used frozen shrimp on one and a lure on the other that he stood and cast. Peck took some time and prepared frozen shrimp on both rods. He tied eight shrimp just above three pronged hooks and lowered them to the bottom, letting the bait rest on the bottom with floating bobbers to watch. He sat on the dock with his legs hanging over.

"Have you always lived in Louisiana, son?" the reverend asked.

"Oui," Peck said. "I growed some at Bayou Chene, near Petit Anse Bayou 'tween Bayou Sorrel and Choctaw, but then I go to Carencro."

"Do you have family there?" the reverend asked. "In Carencro?"

"Je ne connais pas mes parents, Révérend. Jamais fait," Peck said. ("I don't know my parents, Reverend. Never did.")

"I never..." Peck started.

"I understand what you said, son," the reverend said. "And I'll be proud to tell you you've done one outstanding job of knowing life's values and of being a good and merciful Christian."

"When I growed I'd talk to the moon and pretend my mamma was the moon telling me how to behave, Reverend," Peck said. "The moon told me good, dass for true."

"You were your own parent," Reverend said.

"I don' know what that meaned," Peck said.

"Such a heartfelt story. You're a special person, Peck."

"T'anks," Peck said.

"It's none of my business, son," Reverend said. "But can you read and write?"

Peck lifted the debit card from his pocket and held it up.

"I'm going to New Or–lee–anhs and learn me to read, Reverend," Peck said. "I starting right away, then school and university."

"Can you manage that on your own? May we help?"

"Nah, nah, t'ank ya," Peck said. "Captain Gabe Jordan adopted Peck and he put me in learning all everything."

"What a nice man he must be," Reverend said. "This Captain Gabe fellow."

"Oui," Peck said. "God gived me Gabe to save his life from hospice, and He gived Gabe me to save mine and put me in school."

"Praise the Lord," the reverend said.

The reverend reeled in a bass, unhooked it and dropped it in the ice chest. He cast the lure out again.

"So how have you supported yourself all this time?"

"I mow and rake lawn at hospice on Bayou Carencro, and I throwed my trotline and catch things I sell— snappers, mashwarohn, like dat."

Reverend reeled in another largemouth bass, unhooked it and placed it in the ice chest.

"Mashwarohn?" the reverend asked just as he got another strike. "What's that?"

He reeled in a bass.

"Catfish," Peck said. "Mashwarohn is Cajun for catfish."

"Where do you live?" the reverend asked.

"I catch the crawfish snakes and cut them for bait for my trotline and I got a cot and hot plate in a boat builder's blade shed in back of the wood mill, barter it for sharpenin' they saw blades."

As reverend reeled in another bass he said, "I need to go turn the brisket one last time and take out the potatoes. You stay here a few more minutes, son. See if you can have some luck."

"Okay," Peck said.

"Bring the ice chest when you come up, will you?" the reverend asked.

"*Oui*," Peck said.

As the reverend walked up the hill, Peck watched until he was out of sight. He got on his knees and hand over hand pulled one of his fishing lines until he surfaced what was a ten-pound mashwarohn. He smiled and snipped the line, letting it swim away. He tugged on his other line. It was empty, so he reeled it in and discarded the shrimp that was on that line, throwing it in the lake.

They each had a plate in their hand and lined up near the smoker for the reverend to slice portions of brisket and fork over a potato.

"So how do you know Millie?" Ingrown Toenail asked.

Peck learned long ago that brevity always worked to an advantage in a negotiation with an alligator, or an arm-wrestle with a drunk.

"Bus," Peck said.

"What do you mean, bus? You live around here?"

"Nah, Nah," Peck said.

"So, you just got off here?"

"*Oui.*"

"Talk English."

"Yes, I got off here."

"What are you, a stalker?"

"I'm a fish'r."

"A fisherman?" Ingrown Toenail asked.

"*Oui.*"

"Oh, that's rich. As if Millie would actually be the least bit interested in a Frenchie frog fisherman."

"Nah, nah," Peck said.

"Like you would know what Millie likes."

Reverend placed portions on Peck's and then on Ingrown Toenail's plates, and they turned toward the house. Peck leaned toward Ingrown Toenail.

"I know what Millie don't like, cher," Peck said.

Ingrown Toenail looked at him in disgust.

"She don't like you," Peck said.

He stepped in the doorway and walked over to get an iced tea. He waited for the momma to come in and seat everyone. She was at the head of the table. Peck was to her left and Millie was to her right.

Ingrown Toenail sat with a pout to the right of Millie. He'd throw snarly looks over at Peck, but Peck has seen worse on snapping turtles staring him down.

Reverend said the blessing and thanked the Lord for all gathered at the table. He asked for a blessing of the food and of the lives of each there. He said they were blessed for having met Peck and prayed for every success for Peck in his school days ahead.

"School?" Millie asked, interrupting the reverend. "Sorry, Daddy."

"*Oui,*" Peck said.

"When?" Millie asked.

"When I get to New Or–lee–anhs," Peck said. "Right away, I start."

"Ask me, he's going to need a lot more than school," Ingrown Toenail said. "Can't make a pig out of a sow's ear— right, Reverend?"

"Stephen, behave," the momma said. "That's not polite. Be Christian, son."

"And it's a purse," Millie said. "Can't make a purse..."

"Even if you did have school, what could you do with it?" Ingrown Toenail asked.

Millie looked at Stephen as if she were tired of his rudeness.

"Why look at me? He's too old to be good anywhere, Millie."

Peck set his fork down and waited, as if he challenged Ingrown Toenail to dare give him the floor.

Ingrown Toenail accepted the challenge with a sneer.

"How would you know what to do with an education anyway? You'd still be a redneck."

"I'd ax Millie to marry me," Peck said.

Everyone's fork hit their plates. Millie's mouth dropped open—her eyes teared up. She sat frozen with her hand over a grinning mouth.

Reverend looked down at the momma and then he looked at Peck with a curious squint in his eye.

"Just what are your intentions, young man?" he asked.

Peck stood and stepped over to the computer table near the back door and picked up his shopping bag. He walked back, sat down and lifted out the package and unwrapped the dictionary and held it up.

"Reverend, sir?" Peck asked, then looking over at Millie's momma. "Momma?"

Once he had their undivided attention he began.

"I know I ain't intelligent, and I know'd they is smarter, but there won't ever be nobody who will love Millie more'n me ever, and dass for true. Now Millie has herself three (he held up three fingers) semesters more in university and I got all dat time and more after dat to get it did right, but I promise with all my heart, cher, if your daddy, the reverend say yes and your mommy say yes and you say yes, in three semesters I will know ever' word in this here book, and I spend every day of our life telling you one or two and what they mean."

"This is such a crock," Ingrown Toenail said.

"Hush, "Millie said. "The man is talking."

"Reverend, sir?" Peck asked. "If'n Millie will have me after we both get our school, can I marry her?"

The reverend didn't think twice. He simply looked over at Millie.

"Millie?" the reverend asked.

"Oh please, Daddy," Millie said.

The reverend looked down at a smiling momma.

"Young man needs his education, Momma," the reverend said. "He can't fish."

"Is that a yes, Daddy?" Millie asked.

"And you'll wait until after school for both of you?" the reverend asked.

"Yessir," Peck said. "My word."

"Then the yes would have to come from our dumplin', it would seem. Millie?"

Millie looked at Peck, her eyes streaming in tears. "Yes, yes, I will marry you."

"This is such a crock..." Ingrown Toenail said.

Millie pushed her seat back, stood and ran to her room. On her return she carried her baby doll, Charlie. She walked over and handed it to Peck to cradle it in his arm. He did so and picked up his fork with his other hand and stabbed a piece of brisket. Millie stepped around to her side of the table.

"Stephen," Millie said. "Either stay and be a gentleman or you may leave."

It was nine o'clock in Providence while Sasha was walking with Gabe through the hospital hall.

"You did a hundred feet two times today, honey," Sasha said.

"I'm ready for the Boston Marathon," Gabe said.

"If you keep this up, you'll be in your hotel by next week and able to travel in September."

"When can we dance?"

"Whenever you ask, pookie."

Sasha pushed the door to his room, and he made his way in. Just before he got to the bed Sasha took him by the arm to steer him around by the window.

"Come over here," Sasha said. "I have a surprise for you."

"What the...?" Gabe started.

Sasha opened the window and stuck her head out.

"Over here," Sasha shouted. "He's here in this one."

She pulled her head back in and smiled at Gabe just as a saxophone on the lawn below began playing "When Sunny Gets Blue."

"My baby," Gabe said.

VaaaaaVeeVeeVaaVoooooOVaaaVaaaVaVaVaVeeeeeVa...

"You are something else."

Its wails echoed off hospital walls, and people gathered on the lawn.

"Wanna dance?" Sasha asked.

Gabe moved his walker aside and embraced her. He swayed once, twice. Sasha kissed him on the neck just as she looked down and saw flashing police lights on a patrol car below.

"Uh oh, there's trouble," Sasha said.

Gabe looked out. "Will they arrest him or just ticket him?"

"I'll go down," Sasha said. "Watch my bag."

Most of the staff enjoyed the antics of the sax. The head nurse was the one who had called the police. No one had to tell Sasha that. She could tell by the scowl on her face.

"Officer, officer," Sasha shouted as she ran toward the scene. "It's all my fault, officer. I'm to blame."

"Don was disturbing the peace, lady," the officer said. "We leave him alone if he stays under the bridge, but the hospital called and reported the nuisance."

"Nurse Cratchet up there is a bitch, officer," Sasha said. "Everybody else loved it. He was playing for an old man up there just out of an operation."

"If you want to defend him, ma'am, you'll have to go tell it to the judge," the officer said.

"Say that again, officer," Sasha said.

"Excuse me?" the officer asked.

"Say what you just said," Sasha said. "About the judge."

"I said you'll have to tell that to the judge, lady."

"You're Officer Kelsey, aren't you?" Sasha asked.

"Lady, do we know each other?"

"Officer Brandon Kelsey," Sasha said.

"I am."

"I knew it. I'm good with names and voices. I'm in real estate."

"But—"

"I was the one with Judge Thibodaux in his chamber in the Carencro Louisiana courthouse when you found and were witness to a man being alive and then witnessing his living will."

"Now I remember. That's right," the officer said. "I did do that. So, you're the—"

"I'm her," Sasha said, extending her hand for a shake.

"Well, I'll be," the officer said. "Don, you got lucky tonight. I'm letting you go without a ticket."

"You remember the man?" Sasha asked. "The man you witnessed for?"

"I do," the officer said.

Sasha pointed up to Gabe, looking out the window three flights up.

"That's him," Sasha said. "That's the one and only Gabriel Jordan."

The officer looked up at Gabe and waved.

"He was operated on and is going to live."

The officer stepped around and looked at Don. "So, what are you waiting for, Don?"

"I'm going, I'm going," Don said. "I'm out of here."

"The hell you are," the officer said.

"What?"

"What were you playing for our friend up there?"

"'When Sunny Gets Blue,' officer," Don said.

The officer looked at Sasha.

"Nobody but Nurse Cratchet complained?"

"Not a soul," Sasha said.

"Finish it," the officer said.

"What?" Don asked.

"Finish it," the officer said. "Or I'll run you in."

Don started a new riff of "When Sunny Gets Blue." The officer told everyone to disperse, and he told Don to go back to the bridge after he was finished. Sasha kissed the officer on the cheek, thanked him, and went back inside.

Sasha stepped off the elevator with Nurse Cratchet standing there, as if stalking her, arms folded, and scowl matching her personality. She wasn't about to give Sasha the benefit of acknowledging how Sasha managed the softer side of the law, allowing the lovely music to entertain patients.

"Visiting hours are over."

Sasha walked toward Gabe's room.

"You'll have to go," Nurse Cratchet said.

"In a little bit," Sasha said, brushing by her.

"Now," Nurse Cratchet said. "Or I'll call security."

Sasha turned on a dime. "Look, here, wicked witch of the north. I don't know what got your panties in a wad, but if that man doesn't do his walks he won't get out of here, and I'm his official walker, so you call security, and I call my lawyer, and this time next week you'll work for me, as I'll own the hospital."

Nurse Cratchet harrumphed and walked away.

In the room, Gabe was in bed with a broad smile.

"My baby," Gabe said. "That was something. Please tell Don thanks for me. Tell him that was special."

"You know who that cop was?" Sasha asked.

"I do," Gabe said. "From under the bridge."

"Isn't it a small world?"

"Your phone has been making all kinds of sounds," Gabe said.

Sasha picked it from her purse.

"A text," Sasha said. "Listen to this. *'Hi Michelle, this is Millie. Peck asked my folks if he could marry me after we're out of school, and they said yes and I said yes and I love him so much, and he wanted me to tell you and his dad, Gabe, and he is going to stay here again tomorrow, and then he will be on the bus to New Orleans and start school. XOXOXO Millie.'"*

"We picked a winner in that boy," Gabe said.

"You picked him," Sasha said. "I was a hooker, remember?"

"Oh my," Gabe giggled. "That's right."

"But he is a winner," Sasha said. "She sounds like a winner too."

"She does," Gabe said.

"So where are you going to live when you get out of here?" Sasha asked.

"How much do I have put away?"

"Enough to be comfortable."

"I'm a dad again," Gabe said. "You're a realtor. Do I have enough to get a small three-bedroom in the Garden District?"

"So, we don't get Peck an apartment?"

"He'll live at home," Gabe said. "Least until he's out of school."

"One floor," Sasha said. "So you can save your knees for dancing. I'll look at some shotgun houses. There're some deals."

"See you tomorrow, baby?" Gabe asked.

"Yeppers," Sasha said. "Hundred fifty feet tomorrow."

Sasha kissed Gabe on the neck and went back to the hotel.

In her room she soaked in a hot tub bath, lifted her phone and answered Millie's text. *"Thanksgiving or Christmas, pick one. But you and your family come to New Orleans, and we celebrate you and Peck. XOXO Michelle."*

CHAPTER 30

BY MID OCTOBER GABE AND PECK WERE SETTLED in a modest three-bedroom shotgun cottage in the Garden District. Peck could count change, had mastered the alphabet and was reading at a fourth-grade level. He was taking French, as the thinking was learning conjugations and sentence structure in English might be easier for him if he learned it in a language that he already knew quite well. The tutor found his animal science aptitude to be particularly strong and was pushing him into working on projects and visiting museums around the city.

Peck was becoming an avid reader. He'd look up a word he wasn't certain of in his dictionary. He memorized the pronunciation of vowels and consonants, and he would master one child's book, reading it aloud several times by memory, and go on to the next. Daily he would dictate to his tutor messages that he wanted texted to his Millie, and she would help him read Millie's responses.

On Thanksgiving Millie's family joined her and visited New Orleans for the holiday weekend. The reverend and the momma stayed at Sasha's, and Millie stayed in the third bedroom with Gabe and Peck. They took to Gabe right off, admiring his kindness and generosity toward others. They were most impressed when Peck greeted them at the airport with a "Welcome to New Orleans and Happy Thanksgiving," without a hint of patois. Oh, he could turn it on when he wanted to, but with his new knowledge of diction he so enjoyed feeling a part of society. He and Millie held hands and were inseparable, walking through the Garden District and on daylight tours in the Quarter. They would talk of children and of gardens and crawfish beds and catfish farms, and Peck would read a book to Millie, and Millie would sit there in tears and know that every word he read was him saying *I love you* to her. She would ask him what would grow best in the soil they would have, and he said tomatoes and onions, maybe zucchini and melons.

"Lots of shickens," he would say. "But you have to put them in at night to keep them safe from the critters."

Gabe cooked turkey and stuffing; the momma made her bread pudding, and Sasha brought a green bean casserole and rolls and salad. Millie made the sweet potatoes with marshmallows; and with his reading and counting skills and with some help, Peck was able to master the recipe and oven temperatures for pecan pie with Karo syrup, and he made three. He also used his debit card to buy a pot of turtle soup for those curious enough to try.

Each morning Peck and Millie would catch a streetcar and then walk the distance to the Café du Monde for coffee and beignets and look into each other's eyes as Gabe would say coffee and chicory and a beignet in New Orleans was not a luxury but a morning prayer.

The reverend and the momma joined Sasha and Gabe at Charlie's Blue Note one evening, and although they drank iced tea, they did enjoy the red beans and rice and slow dancing to authentic New Orleans jazz. While they were away, Millie and Peck made haste, expressing their passion for each other being alone at home.

"We could cut quite a rug, in college," the reverend would say.

It was at the Blue Note when they decided, and Sasha as well, that everyone should come for Christmas in Tennessee. They could get to see Knoxville decorated and have a grand time, and it was certain Santa would come to the house on the Kingston Road exit. Weather permitting, they could also get some fishing in.

To get them off on their Christmas trip, Lily Cup drove Gabe, Sasha, and Peck to the airport and pulled up to the curbside attendant, leaving the car running. Peck and Gabe wished Lily Cup a Merry Christmas and got out to grab the bags.

"What are you doing for Christmas, sweetie?" Sasha asked.

"Mom needs the company," Lily Cup said. "With Dad gone she's happiest if we just go out somewhere. We'll think of something."

"We'll be back on Sunday," Sasha said.

"Let me know," Lily Cup said. "I'll pick you up."

"You look nice," Sasha said. "You going to a party?"

"Christmas party at Angola," Lily Cup said. "Going to see some of my clients, take them a little something."

"Are you allowed to give them gifts?" Sasha asked.

"They open them up and rewrap them, but yes," Lily Cup said. "And the inmates can give visitors gifts. Things they have or made while in there. It helps them feel part of the human race. At Christmas, they even let the prisoners who are in for nonviolent crimes visit their guests in lounge chairs in the main sitting area. So I'll see Andre out there today. He was a good boy—only busted for gun-running."

"Love you," Sasha said.

"Love you back," Lily Cup said, and they air-kissed goodbye.

Lily Cup drove into Angola, parked and took a shopping bag filled with gifts out of her trunk. Most were simple trinkets or souvenir keepsakes she had wrapped, just so a prisoner would be able to unwrap a gift. Andre's gift was a jigsaw puzzle.

"You look lovely," Andre said. "So festive."

"Why thank you, Andre," Lily Cup said. "You look nice. You've shaved, a nice shirt and everything. Are you being a good boy?"

"I deliver mail on my cell block. Know most everybody. Being good so you can get me out," Andre said.

"Well, you can be good to be good too," Lily Cup said.

"So I heard a story, Lily Cup," Andre said.

"Is it a Christmas story, Andre?"

"It's kind of like a Christmas story."

"Open your present first, Andre."

Lily Cup pulled the package from the shopping bag. Andre opened it to find a jigsaw puzzle.

"A paddlewheel," Andre said.

"It's the Mississippi Queen," Lily Cup said. "500 pieces."

"A Mississippi River steamboat," Andre said.

Andre studied the box as a child would on Christmas morning. The colors, the steamboat, the pelicans along the shore.

"Look at the pelicans watching it go by, it's coming into N'Orleans—headed to Bourbon Street," Andre said.

"Some people frame their puzzles after they put them together, Andre. They can look nice all framed pretty in like a TV room or den or someplace."

"Thank you, my friend," Andre said.

Andre reached to the floor and picked up a small box wrapped with paper and ribbon. He didn't hand it to Lily Cup but set it on the table before him.

"You want to hear a Christmas story?" he asked.

"I love Christmas stories, Andre," Lily Cup said.

"Now I don't know where I heard this one, Lily Cup. Important you know that," Andre said. "Could have been on television or something like that."

Lily Cup looked as if she sensed Andre was sending a message with the buildup.

"Okay," Lily Cup said, with a bit of hesitation.

"This rich guy, see, could have been from England or somewhere like that—yeah, England," Andre said. "He wants to get him an alligator. Oh, he wants a big one, that's for sure— like to have it stuffed and put over a bar or in his den somewhere, maybe his club."

Lily Cup listened.

"So, somebody—I don't know who, maybe a park ranger. You know, those guys with the hats," Andre said. "Well maybe this park ranger tells this English guy he needs to go to Choctaw and ask for gator man, you know, like the one with old lady Prudhomme somewhere down there, like she's his old lady, he tells the guy. So, they find the gator man and the English guy tells him he wants a big gator, maybe over seventeen feet and he'll pay five thousand to shoot one. Well that gator man says for five thousand he would take him out personally, but it had to be at sunset, when gators and crocs wake up, and they'd have to be in two boats. Gator man always goes alone in his pirogue because he has to stand all the way, and stand and pole row, and he don't want more people who might tip it so he falls in. And the other boat had to stay thirty feet away, and there was a fancy video camera with the infra-red lenses that would shoot in the night on that boat to make sure it didn't get too close and maybe bump the other boat."

Lily Cup listened.

"So, Lily Cup, they go out in two boats, just like the gator man says, and they're back in the bayou just where the swamp begins. The pirogue got on the deep side of some big old bald cypress, and this near twenty-foot gator comes up from behind like a fast log and gator man signals back to English in the other boat to get ready to shoot, and wouldn't you know, his pirogue went and jerked, and gator man lost his balance, dropped his pole, and he fell out?"

"Did he get right back in his boat?" Lily Cup asked.

"Oh no," Andre said.

"What happened?"

"A young gator he don't waste no time and took his head clean off with one snap and a quick twist, and the big ole one, the near twenty-footer? Why that gator took him under to bury until he rots and seasons good to eat later. That gator man didn't feel a thing, or so the English guy who was telling the story told somebody."

"Did he call the police?"

"I'm glad you asked that, *mon ami*. You see, the Englishman he come to shore. He sees these two what you call vagrant trappers. They not doing so good with their traps, don't you know, cause one of them asks English for money to buy cigarettes, see, so he tells the trappers what happened and what should he do? They looked at his anchor rope and saw that it was dry, so he couldn't have used the anchor rope to pull and jerk gator man's pirogue, and then they watched the video recorder and saw that the boats weren't close to each other, but sure enough they saw gator man's boat jerk good and him falling in the bayou."

"And?"

"One of them said he must have hit a root. They couldn't see nothing jerking the boat, one said," Andre said. "The other wondered should they call the sheriff."

"Did they call?" Lily Cup asked.

"The storyteller, he never finished the story. I don't know," Andre said.

"If those two took the time to check the anchor rope and watch the video, seems they would have called the sheriff," Lily Cup said.

"As the story goes, *mon ami*, English gave them—the vagrants who asked him for cigarette money—why he gave them two thousand dollars each and told them to be sure to go look up the Prudhomme lady and give it all to her. He counted it out in their hands, two thousand dollars each. Then he left. I guess for England or France or somewhere those rich guys travel. Nobody ever said what happened after that."

Lily Cup sat back. She didn't say a word. She knew better than to talk or ask questions. She knew everything Andre had told her he presented to her as third-party hearsay. It was worthless as evidence anywhere.

Andre handed the small box to Lily Cup.

"Merry Christmas, my friend," Andre said. "Open this later."

"Thank you, Andre. Merry Christmas."

"Maybe you can, how they say, re-gift it to someone."

Lily Cup stood, holding the package, looking Andre in the eye.

"Andre don't mind, *mon ami*."

When Lily Cup got to her car, she unwrapped the box and opened it. It was a large spool of black, two-hundred-pound test fishing line. The spool was empty.

She texted Sasha.

"Hey," she texted.

"Hey," Sasha texted.

"You in Knoxville?"

"Nearby, yes."

"He's gone."

"Who's gone?"

"Gator man."

"Where?"

"You don't want to know."
"You're right. I don't want to know."
"You never will."
"Love you," Sasha texted.
"Love you," Lily Cup texted.

Lest I forget...

Thank you, New Orleans.

Thanks to your Orleans Criminal District Court especially to Counselor Lindsay Jay Jeffrey for patience in putting order in my court.

A heartfelt thank you to the esteemed Leah Chase, matriarch of the historic Dooky Chase Restaurant and the iconic leading lady of New Orleans for the best part of a century. I'm humbled and flattered by the hours given myself and my researcher by Leah Chase. What you taught me about life, the hope you always saw for America, the roads you have traveled inspired my painting an accurate mural of my Acadian heritage and of New Orleans in my story.

Thanks Marty and Corneilius, my research assistants; Eddie (Ned) Reid for my Gabe—and the Big Easy and its legendary Pontchartrain Hotel and The Columns Hotel.

Special thanks to the one who made it possible - Judge Laurie A. White for encouraging members of the courts of New Orleans to help the arts, and this storyteller in attempting to present an accurate picture of events in the city of flavors she loves so much...and thank you Judge Laurie A. White for turning a blind eye on a bit of my 'misspelling' the letter of the law here and there for my spin of a tale.

...and thank you Pamela.

JMA